THE FUTURE I

There have been all kinds of notions and guesses as to how it would end. All sorts of notions except the single fact that we are what we are—and that point is proved beyond a shadow of a doubt by THE LARGE ANT.

You can insure almost anything—a cat, a diamond ring, a pitching arm or pair of dancing feet, a house—but how do you insure the future? PROTOTAPH.

You can't be in two places at the same time, can you? And if you could be, you might well find yourself running THE RED QUEEN'S RACE.

Fawcett Crest Books
edited by Isaac Asimov, Martin Harry Greenberg,
and Joseph D. Olander:

SPACE MAIL 24312 $2.50

THE FUTURE I

edited by
Isaac Asimov,
Martin Harry Greenberg and
Joseph D. Olander

FAWCETT CREST • NEW YORK

THE FUTURE I

Published by Fawcett Crest Books, a unit of CBS Publications, the Consumer Publishing Division of CBS Inc.

Copyright © 1980 Isaac Asimov, Martin Harry Greenberg and Joseph D. Olander.
All Rights Reserved

ISBN: 0-449-24366-4

Printed in the United States of America

First Fawcett Crest printing: January 1981

10 9 8 7 6 5 4 3 2 1

INTRODUCTION: FIRST PERSON

by ISAAC ASIMOV

TECHNICALLY speaking, there are several different ways of writing a story.

You may, for instance, have a number of characters and refer to each of them by name and by the pronouns "he" or "she" or, possibly, "it." You are then telling the story in the "third person."

You may, if you wish, play no favorites, treating each character with equal impersonality, repeating what they say and describing what they do, indicating their facial expressions and tones of voice, but never directly indicating their thoughts. A particular character may *say* what he or she is thinking, but in that case that character must take full responsibility for the truth of the statement. It may be a lie and the writer need not directly indicate whether it is a lie or not.

Such impersonal third-person stories, dealing only with words and actions, are particularly adapted to adventure stories, or to cerebral stories such as the classic mystery. Knowing the thoughts might very well be irrelevant in the first case and might spoil the suspense in the second.

Total impersonality is uncommon, of course, because there is a certain aridity about it. Usually, there is a protagonist, some one person who is the center of the action and who is on scene most or all of the time, and with whom the sympathy (or, at least, interest) of the reader lies.

The visual media—stage, motion picture, television—are just about exclusively this sort of impersonal third person, though usually with some protagonist.

In the visual media, the viewer may, of course, be allowed to deduce the thoughts of the characters. Direct information, such as the Shakespearean soliloquy, or the asides of Eugene O'Neill's *Strange Interlude,* are now either passé or are considered stagy and artificial. However, a skillful writer, without ever giving his characters' thoughts directly, can make them unmistakable in the course of the speech and action.

Those who deal in the written word have more leeway. In books and stories it is permissible, even common, to describe the thinking processes of the characters directly, where that is deemed desirable.

On occasion, a writer may delve into the thoughts of all the characters indiscriminately in a kind of omniscient and godlike third person. This is not only very difficult to do, demanding enormous skill if the thoughts are to be distinguished from each other, but is very apt to confuse the reader, since in real life, you know the thoughts of only one character, yourself.

It is much more common, then, for a writer to delve into the thoughts of only one character at a time. The story may be broken up into separate scenes, each containing a number of characters, and in each you may view events through the eyes of only one character and are made aware of the thoughts of only that one character. This mimics life and is easily acceptable.

It is possible to shift from one character to another, seeing different scenes through different eyes. In a long novel, numerous characters may have their turn as protagonists without confusing the reader (given skillful writing).

It is also possible to remain with one character; to tell a long story, involving many characters and many scenes, yet keeping the readers' viewpoint fixed on one protagonist, seeing through only his eyes, thinking only his thoughts, throughout the entire story.

Such a one-viewpoint third-person tale is comfortable for the reader, for again this is how he experiences life, for he sees only through his own eyes and thinks only his own thoughts.

Naturally a skillful writer can make it plain what other characters are thinking through indirect information, but then, in real life, you can sometimes tell what other people are thinking (or you think you can).

The more you delve into the thoughts of your characters, and the more you confine your delving to one character per scene or even one character per story, the greater the tendency to shift from events to emotion, from doing to thinking, from action to reaction.

A one-viewpoint third-person story tends to be slower, more thoughtful, more emotional, than an impersonal third-person story. Each variety (or anything in between) can suit a particular story and not suit another. Each can suit a particular reader and not suit another. There is no "right" or "wrong" involved, or even any "better" or "worse."

A one-viewpoint third-person story is so like the

personal experience of an individual in real life that there is a sharp temptation to pretend that the story *does* represent an individual in real life; that an individual *is* telling a story that *really* happened to him.

In that case, there is an "I" in the story, and it is told in the "first person."

There has to be a suspension of disbelief, of course. We know, when we think about it, that unless the story is strict autobiography, it is just as fictional as a third-person story, that the narrator is not really telling a true story, and actually does not exist.

Nevertheless, if the writer is at all skillful we don't bother thinking that. We read it *as though* it were a true story being told by someone who lived through it.

It is possible to take a one-viewpoint third-person story and change the name and pronouns of the protagonist to "I," "me," "my," and so on. It might not then be necessary to change any other word of the story in order to convert it from third person to first person.

In that case, what's the difference between a one-viewpoint third-person story and a first-person story?

There *is* a difference. In a one-viewpoint third-person story, the protagonist, however permanently on scene and however constantly exposing his thoughts, need not expose those thoughts at crucial moments. Those thoughts are under the control of the author. The reader realizes that and accepts the fact that it may be important to conceal thought.

In a first-person story, however, the protagonist is taken as having control over his own thoughts and for him to conceal those thoughts seems to the reader to be unnatural. Thus, "private-eye detective" stories are often told in first person with, however, the narrator's thoughts frequently concealed for the sake of suspense. That is what gives these stories a kind of unnatural hardness that some readers like and some don't.

The particular intimacy of first-person narration, the permanently lowered guard where thoughts are concerned, makes it more nearly possible to tell a story almost entirely in thoughts, in emotion, in reaction; distinctly more so than in any kind of third-person narration. First person offers the writer a particular opportunity to be more experimental, more harrowing, more powerful.

It is with that thought in mind that we have prepared an anthology of first-person science fiction, choosing for the most part (but not entirely) just those stories that enable the writer to look inward with all the power and turmoil that that entails.

And because I myself almost never write first-person, so that my views may be suspect, we have asked Barry Malzberg (who almost always writes first-person) to give his views on the subject in the afterword.

LOVE IS THE PLAN
THE PLAN IS DEATH

by JAMES TIPTREE, JR.

James Tiptree, Jr., is the pen name used by Dr. Alice Sheldon, a retired psychologist. Her true identity was one of the best-kept secrets in the science fiction world for almost ten years. Since her first appearance in the sf magazines in 1968 she has acquired a major reputation and four major awards: a Hugo Award in 1974 for "The Girl Who Was Plugged In"; the Hugo and the Nebula for the magnificent "Houston, Houston, Do You Read?"; and a Hugo for the story you are about to read and love.

Her shorter sf is available in three collections—*Ten Thousand Light Years from Home* (1973); *Warm Worlds and Otherwise* (1975); and *Star Songs of an Old Primate* (1978).

Just like the title says, this one is a love story.

REMEMBERING—

Do you hear, my little red? Hold me softly. The cold grows.

I remember.

—I am hugely black and hopeful, I bounce on six legs along the mountains in the new warm! ... *Sing the changer, Sing the stranger! Will the changes change forever?* ... All my hums have words now. Another change!

Eagerly I bound on sunward following the tiny thrill in the air. The forests have been shrinking again.

15

Then I see. It is me! Me-Myself, MOGGADEET—I have grown bigger more in the winter cold! I astonish myself, Moggadeet-the-small!

Excitement, enticement shrilling from the sun-side of the world. I come! ... The sun is changing again, too. *Sun is walking in the night! Sun is walking back to Summer in the warming of the light!* ... Warm is MeMoggadeet Myself. Forget the bad-time winter.

Memory quakes me.

The Old One.

I stop, pluck up a tree. So much I wanted to ask the Old One. No time. Cold. Tree goes end over end downcliff, I watch the fatclimbers tumble out. Not hungry.

The Old One warned me of the cold—I didn't believe him. I move on, grieving ... *Old One told you, The cold, the cold will hold you. Chill cold! Kill cold. In the cold I killed you.*

But it's warm now, all different. I'm Moggadeet again.

I bound over a hill and see my brother Frim.

At first I don't know him. A big black old one! I think. And in the warm, we can speak!

I surge toward him bashing trees. The big black is crouched over a ravine, peering down. Black back has shiny ripples like—It IS Frim! Frim-I-hunted-for, Frim-run-away! But he's so big now! Giant Frim! *A stranger, a changer—*

"Frim!"

He doesn't hear me; all his eye-turrets are under the trees. His end is sticking up oddlike, all atremble. What's he hunting?

"Frim! It's me, Moggadeet!"

But he only quivers his legs; I see his spurs pushing out. What a fool, Frim! I remind myself how timid he is, I try to move gently. When I get closer I'm astonished again. I'm bigger than he is now! *Changes!* I can see right over his shoulder into the ravine.

Hot yellow-green in there. A little glade all lit with

sun. I bend my eyes to see what Frim is after and all astonishments blow up the world.

I see you.

I saw you.

I will always see you. Dancing in the green fire, my tiny red star! So bright! So small! So perfect! So fierce! I knew you—Oh yes I knew you in that first instant, my dawnberry, my scarlet minikin. *Red!* A tiny baby red one, smaller than my smallest eye. And so brave!

The Old One said it. Red is the color of love.

I see you swat at a hopper twice your size, my eyes bulge as you leap after it and go rolling, shrilling *Lililee! Lilileee-ee!* in baby wrath. Oh my mighty hunter, you don't know someone is looking right into your tender little love-fur! Oh yes! Palest pink it is, just brushed with rose. My jaws spurt, the world flashes and reels.

And then Frim, poor fool, feels me behind him and rears up.

But what a Frim! His throat-sacs are ballooning purple-black, his plates are engorged like the Mother of the storm-clouds! Glittering, rattling his spurs! His tail booms! "It's mine!" he bellows—I can hardly understand him. He jumps straight at me!

"Stop, Frim, stop!" I cry, dodging away bewildered. It's warm—how can Frim be wild, kill-wild?

"Brother Frim!" I call gently, soothingly. But something is badly wrong! My voice is bellowing too! Yes, in the warm and I want only to calm him, I am full of love—but the kill-roar is rushing through me, I too am swelling, rattling, booming! Invincible! To crush—to rend—

Oh, I am shamed.

I came to myself in the wreckage of Frim, Frim-pieces everywhere, myself is sodden with Frim. But I did not eat him! I did not! Should I take joy in that? Did I defy the Plan? But my throat was closed. Not because it was Frim but because of darling you. *You!* Where are you? The glade is empty! Oh fearful fear, I

have frightened you, you are run away! I forget Frim.
I forget everything but you my heartmeat, my precious tiny red.

I smash trees, I uproot rocks, I tear the ravine open!
Oh, where are you hiding? Suddenly I have a new
fear: Has my wild search harmed you? I force myself
calm. I begin questing, circling, ever wider over the
trees, moving cloud-silent, thrusting my eyes and ears
down into every glade. A new humming fills my throat.
Oooo, Oo-oo, Rum-a-looly-loo, I moan. Hunting, hunting for you.

Once I glimpse a black bigness far away and I am
suddenly up at my full height, roaring. Attack the
black! Was it another brother? I would slay him, but
the stranger is already vanishing. I roar again. No—*it
roars me,* the new power of black. Yet deep inside,
Myself-Moggadeet is watching, fearing. Attack the
black—even in the warm? Is there no safety, are we
truly like the fatclimbers? But at the same time it
feels—Oh, right! Oh, good! Sweet is the Plan. I give
myself up to seeking you, my new song longing *Oo-loo*
and *Looly rum-a-loo-oo-loo.*

And you answered! You!

So tiny you, hidden under a leaf! Shrilling *Li! Li!
Lililee!* Trilling, thrilling—half-mocking, already im-
perious. Oh, how I whirl, crash, try to look under all
my feet, stop frozen in horror of squashing the *Lilili!
Lee!* Rocking, longing, moaning Moggadeet.

And you came out, you did.

My adorable firemite, threatening ME!

When I see your littlest hunting claws upraised my
whole gut melts, it floods me. I am all tender jelly.
Tender! Oh, tender-fierce like a Mother, I think! Isn't
that how a Mother feels? My jaws are sluicing juice
that isn't hunger-juice—I am choking, with fear of
frighting you or bruising your tininess—I ache to grip
and knead you, to eat you in one gulp, in a thousand
nibbles—

Oh the power of *red*—the Old One said it! Now I feel

my special hands, my tender hands I always carry hidden—now they come swelling out, come pushing toward my head! What? What?

My secret hands begin to knead and roll the stuff that's dripping from my jaws.

Ah, that arouses, you, too, my redling, doesn't it?

Yes, yes, I feel—torment—I feel your shy excitement! How your body remembers even now our love-dawn, our very first moments of Moggadeet-Leely. Before I knew You-Yourself, before you knew Me. It began then, my heartlet, our love-knowing began in that very first instant when your Moggadeet stared down at you like a monster bursting. I saw how new you were, how helpless!

Yes, even while I loomed over you marvelling—even while my secret hands drew and spun fate—even then it came to me to pity that long ago, last year when I was a child, I saw other little red ones among my brothers, before our Mother drove them away. I was only a foolish baby then; I didn't understand. I thought they'd grown strange and silly in their redness and Mother did well to turn them out. Oh stupid Moggadeet!

But now I saw *you*, my flamelet—I understood! You were only that day cast out by your Mother. Never had you felt the terrors of a night alone in the world; you couldn't imagine that such a monster as Frim was hunting you. Oh my ruby nestling, my baby red! Never, I vowed it, never would I leave you—and have I not kept that vow? Never! I, Moggadeet, *I would be your Mother.*

Great is the Plan, but I was greater!

All I learned of hunting in my lonely year, to drift like the air, to leap, to grip so delicately—all these learnings became for you! Not to bruise the smallest portion of your bright body. Oh, yes! I captured you whole in all your tiny perfection, though you sizzled and spat and fought me like the sunspark you are. And then—

And then—

I began to—Oh, terror! Delight-shame! How can I speak such a beautiful secret?—the Plan took me as a Mother guides her child and with my special hands I began to—

I began to bind you up!

Oh yes! Oh yes! My special hands that had no use, now all unfurled and engorged and alive, never stopping the working in the strong juice of my jaws—they began to *bind* you, passing over and around and beneath you, every moment piercing me with fear and joy. I wound among your darling little limbs, into your inmost delicate recesses, gently swathing and soothing you, winding and binding until you became a shining jewel. Mine!

—But you responded. I know that now. We know! Oh yes, in your fierce struggles, shyly you helped me, always at the end each strand fell sweetly into place . . . *Winding you, binding you, loving Leelyloo!* . . . How our bodies moved in our first weaving song! I feel it even now, I melt with excitement! How I wove the silk about you, tying each tiny limb, making you perfectly helpless. How fearlessly you gazed up at me, your terrifying captor! You! You were never frightened, as I'm not frightened now. Isn't it strange, my loveling? This sweetness that floods our bodies when we yield to the Plan. Great is the Plan! Fear it, fight it—but hold the sweetness yet.

Sweetly began our lovetime, when first I became your new true Mother, never to cast you out. How I fed you and caressed and tended and fondled you! What a responsibility it is to be a Mother. Anxiously I carried you furled in my secret arms, savagely I drove off all intruders, even the harmless banlings in the grass, in fear every moment that you were stifled or crushed!

And all the warm nights long, how I cared for your helpless little body, carefully releasing each infant limb, flexing and stretching it, cleaning every scarlet

morsel of you with my giant tongue, nibbling your
baby claws with my terrible teeth, reveling in your
baby hum, pretending to devour you while you shrieked
with glee, *Li! Lilili! Love-lili, Leelylee!* But the greatest
joy of all—

We spoke!

We spoke together, we two! We communed, we
shared, we poured ourselves one into the other. Love,
how we stammered and stumbled at the first, you in
your strange Mother-tongue and I in mine! How we
blended our singing wordlessly and then with words,
until more and more we came to see with each other's
eyes, to hear, to taste, to feel the world of each other,
until I became Leelyloo and you became Moggadeet,
until finally we became together a new thing, Moggadeet-Leely, Lilliloo-Mogga, Lili-Moggalooly-deet!

Oh love, we are the first? Have others loved with
their whole selves? Oh sad thinking, that lovers before us have left no trace. Remember us! Will you
remember, my adored, though Moggadeet has spoiled
everything and the cold grows? If only I could hear
you speak once more, my red, my innocent one. You
are remembering, your body tells me you remember
even now. Softly, hold me softly yet. Hear your
Moggadeet!

You told me how it was being you, yourself, tiny-
redling-Lilliloo. Of your Mother, your dreams, your
baby joys and fears. And I told you mine, and all my
learnings in the world since the day when my own
Mother—

Hear me, my heartmate! Time runs away.

—On the last day of my childhood my Mother called
us all under her.

"Sons! S-son-n-nss!" Why did her dear voice creak
so?

My brothers came in slowly, fearfully from the summer green. But I, small Moggadeet, I climb eagerly up
under the great arch of her body, seeking the golden
Mother-fur. Right into her warm cave I come, where

her Mother-eyes are glowing, the cave that sheltered us so strongly all our lives, as I shelter you, my dawn-flower.

I long to touch her, to hear her speak and sing to us again. Her Mother-fur troubles me, it is tattered and drab. Shyly I press against one of her huge food-glands. It feels dry, but a glow sparks deep in her Mother-eye.

"Mother," I whisper. "It's me, Moggadeet!"

"SONNNNNS!" Her voice rumbles through her armor. My big brothers huddle by her legs, peering back at the sunlight. They look so funny, shedding, half gold, half black.

"I'm afraid!" whimpers my brother Frim nearby. Like me Frim still has his gold baby fur. Mother is speaking again but her voice booms so I can hardly understand.

"WINNN-TER! WINTER, I SAY! AFTER THE WARM COMES THE COLD WINTER. THE COLD WINTER BEFORE THE WARM COMES AGAIN, COMES . . ."

Frim whimpers louder, I cuff him. What's wrong, why is her loving voice so hoarse and strange now? She always hummed us so tenderly, we nestled in her warm Mother-fur sucking the lovely Mother-juices, rocking to her steady walking-song. *Ee-mooly-mooly, Ee-mooly-mooly,* while far below the earth rolled by. Oh, yes, and how we held our breaths and squealed when she began her mighty hunting-hum! *Tann! Tann! Dir! Dir! Dir Hataan! HATONN!* How we clung in the thrilling climax when she plunged upon her prey and we heard the crunching, the tearing, the gurgling in her body that meant soon her food-glands would be richly full.

Suddenly I see a black streak down below—a big brother is running away! Mother's booming voice breaks off. Her great body tenses, her plates clash. Mother roars!

Running, screaming down below! I burrow up into her fur, am flung about as she leaps.

"OUT! GO OUT!" she bellows. Her terrible hunting-limbs crash down, she roars without words, shuddering, jolting. When I dare to peek out I see the others all have fled. All except one!

A black body is lying under Mother's claws. It's my brother Sesso—yes! But mother is tearing him, is eating him! I watch in horror—Sesso she cared for so proudly, so tenderly! I sob, bury my head in her fur. But the beautiful fur is coming loose in my hands, her golden Mother-fur is dying! I cling desperately, trying not to hear the crunches, the gulps and gurgling. The world is ending, all is terrible, terrible.

And yet, my fireberry, even then I almost understood. Great is the Plan!

Presently Mother stops feeding and begins to move. The rocky ground jolts by far below. Her stride is not smooth but jerks me, even her deep hum is strange. *On! On! Alone! Ever alone. And on!* The rumbling ceases. Silence. Mother is resting.

"Mother!" I whisper. "Mother, it's Moggadeet. I'm here!"

Her stomach plates contract, a belch reverberates in her vaults.

"Go," she groans. "Go. Too late. Mother no more."

"I don't want to leave you. Why must I go? Mother!" I wail, "Speak to me!" I keen my baby hum, *Deet! Deet! Tikki-takka! Deet!* hoping Mother will answer, crooning deep, *Brum! Brrumm! Brumaloo-brum!* Now I see one huge Mother-eye glow faintly but she only makes a grating sound.

"Too late. No more . . . The winter, I say. I did speak . . . Before the winter, go. Go."

"Tell me about Outside, Mother," I plead.

Another groan or cough nearly shakes me from my perch. But when she speaks again her voice sounds gentler.

"Talk?" she grumbles, "Talk, talk, talk. You are a strange son. Talk, like your Father."

"What's that, Mother? What's a Father?"

She belches again. "Always talk. The winters grow, he said. Oh, yes. Tell them the winters grow. So I did. Late. Winter, I spoke you. Cold!" Her voice booms. "No more! Too late." Outside I hear her armor rattle and clank.

"Mother, speak to me!"

"Go. Go-o-o!"

Her belly-plates clash around me. I jump for another nest of fur but it comes loose in my grip. Wailing, I save myself by hanging to one of her great walking limbs. It is rigid, thrumming like rock.

"GO!" She roars.

Her Mother-eyes are shriveling, dead! I panic, scramble down, everything is vibrating, resonating around me. Mother is holding back a storm of rage!

I leap for the ground, I rush diving into a crevice, I wiggle and burrow under the fearful bellowing and clanging that rains on me from above. Into the rocks I go with the hunting claws of Mother crashing behind me.

Oh my redling, my little tenderling! Never have you known such a night. Those dreadful hours hiding from the monster that had been my loving Mother!

I saw her once more, yes. When dawn came I clambered up a ledge and peered through the mist. It was warm then, the mists were warm. I knew what Mothers looked like; we had glimpses of hugh horned dark shapes before our own Mother hooted us under her. Oh yes, and then would come Mother's earth-shaking challenge and the strange Mother's answering roar, and we'd cling tight, feeling her surge of kill-fury, buffeted, deafened, battered while our Mother charged and struck. And once while our Mother fed I peeped out and saw a strange baby squealing in the remnants on the ground below.

But now it was my own dear Mother I saw lurching

away through the mists, that great rusty-grey hulk so horned and bossed that only her hunting-eyes showed above her armor, swiveling mindlessly, questing for anything that moved. She crashed her way across the mountains and as she went she thrummed a new harsh song. *Cold! Cold! Ice and Lone. Ice! And cold! And end.* I never saw her again.

When the sun rose I saw that the gold fur was peeling from my shiny black. All by itself my hunting-limb flashed out and knocked a hopper right into my jaws.

You see, my berry, how much larger and stronger I was than you when Mother sent us away? That also is the Plan. For you were not yet born! I had to live on while the warm turned to cold and while the winter passed to warm again before you would be waiting. I had to grow and learn. To *learn,* my Lilliloo! That is important. Only we black ones have a time to learn— the Old One said it.

Such small learnings at first! To drink the flat water-stuff without choking, to catch the shiny flying things that bite and to watch the storm-clouds and the moving of the sun. And the nights, and the soft things that moved on the trees. And the bushes that kept shrinking, shrinking—only it was me, Moggadeet, growing larger! Oh yes! And the day when I could knock down a fatclimber from its vine!

But all these learnings were easy—the Plan in my body guided me. It guides me now, Lililoo, even now it would give me peace and joy if I yielded to it. But I will not! I will remember to the end, I will speak to the end!

I will speak the big learnings. How I saw—though I was so busy catching and eating more, more, always more—I saw all things were changing, changing. *Changers!* The bushes changed their buds to berries, the fatclimbers changed their colors, even the sun changed, and the hills. And I saw all things were together with others of their kind but only me, Moggadeet. I was alone. Oh, so alone!

I went marching through the valleys in my shiny new black, humming my new song *Turra-tarra! Tarra Tan!* Once I glimpsed my brother Frim and I called him, but he ran like the wind. Away, alone! And when I went to the next valley I found the trees all mashed down. And in the distance I saw a black one like me—only many times as big! Huge! Almost as big as a Mother, sleek and glossy-new. I would have called but he reared up and saw me and roared so terribly that I too fled like the wind to empty mountains. Alone.

And so I learned, my redling, how we are alone even though my heart was full of love. And I wandered, puzzling and eating ever more and more. I saw the Trails; they meant nothing to me then. But I began to learn the important thing.

The cold.

You know it, my little red. How in the warm days I am me, Myself-Moggadeet. Ever-growing, ever-learning. In the warm we think, we speak. We love! We make our own Plan, Oh, did we not, my lovemate?

But in the cold, in the night—for the nights were growing colder—in the cold night I was—what?—Not Moggadeet. Not Moggadeet-thinking. Not Me-Myself. Only Something-that-lives, acts without thought. Helpless-Moggadeet. In the cold is only the Plan. I almost thought it.

And then one day the night-chill lingered and lingered and the sun was hidden in the mists. And I found myself going up the Trails.

The Trails are a part of the Plan too, my redling.

The Trails are of winter. There we must go all of us, we blacks. When the cold grows stronger the Plan calls us upward, upward, we begin to drift up the Trails, up along the ridges to the cold, the night-side of the mountains. Up beyond the forests where the trees grow scant and turn to stony deadwood.

So the Plan drew me and I followed, only half-aware. Sometimes I came into warmer sunlight where I could stop and feed and try to think, but the cold fogs rose again and I went on, on and up. I began to catch sight of others like me far along the mountain-flank, moving steadily up. They didn't rear or roar when they saw me. I didn't call to them. Each one alone we climbed on toward the Caves, unthinking, blind. And so I would have gone too.

But then the great thing happened.

—Oh no, my Lililoo! Not the *greatest*. The greatest of all is you, will always be you. My precious sunmite, my red lovebaby! Don't be angry, no, no, my sharing one. Hold me softly. I must say our big learning. Hear your Moggadeet, hear and remember!

In the sun's last warm I found him, the Old One. A terrible sight! So maimed and damaged, parts rotting and gone. I stared, thinking him dead. Suddenly his head rolled feebly and a croak came out.

"Young . . . one?" An eye opened in his festering head, a flyer pecked at it. "Young one . . . wait!"

And I understood him! Oh, with love—

No, no, my redling! Gently! Gently hear your Moggadeet. We *spoke,* the Old One and I! Old to young, we shared. I think it cannot happen.

"No old ones," he creaked. "Never to speak . . . we blacks. Never. It is not . . . the Plan. Only me . . . I wait . . ."

"Plan," I ask, half-knowing. "What is the Plan?"

"A beauty," he whispers. "In the warm, a beauty in the air . . . I followed . . . but another black one saw me and we fought . . . and I was damaged, but still the Plan made me follow until I was crushed and torn and dead . . . But I lived! And the Plan let me go and I crawled here . . . to wait . . . to share . . . but—"

His head sags. Quickly I snatch a flyer from the air and push it to his torn jaws.

"Old One! What is the Plan?"

He swallows painfully, his one eye holding mine.

"In us," he says thickly, stronger now. "In us, mov-

ing us in all things necessary for the life. You have
seen. When the baby is golden the Mother cherishes it
all winter long. But when it turns red or black she
drives it away. Was it not so?"

"Yes, but—"

"That's the Plan! Always the Plan. Gold is the color
of Mother-care but black is the color of rage. Attack
the black! Black is to kill. Even a mother, even her
own baby, she cannot defy the Plan. Hear me, young
one!"

"I hear. I have seen," I answer. "But what is red?"

"Red!" He groans. "Red is the color of love."

"No!" I say, stupid Moggadeet! "I know love. Love
is gold."

The Old One's eyes turns from me. "Love," he sighs.
"When the beauty comes in the air, you will see . . ."
He falls silent. I fear he's dying. What can I do? We
stay silent there together in the last misty sunwarm.
Dimly the slopes I can see other black ones like myself drifting steadily upward on their own Trails among
the stone-tree heaps, into the icy mists.

"Old One! Where do we go?"

"You go to the Caves of Winter. That is the Plan."

"Winter, yes. The cold. Mother told us. And after
the cold winter comes the warm. I remember. The
winter will pass, won't it? Why did she say, the winters grow? Teach me, Old One. What is a Father?"

"Fa-ther? A word I don't know. But wait—" His
mangled head turns to me. *"The winters grow?* Your
mother said this? Oh cold! Oh, lonely," he groans. "A
big learning she gave you. This learning I fear to
think."

His eye rolls, glaring. I am frightened inside.

"Look around, young one. These stony deadwoods.
Dead shells of trees that grow in the warm valleys.
Why are they here? The cold has killed them. No
living tree grows here now. Think, young one!"

I look, and true! It is a warm forest killed to stone.

"Once it was warm here. Once it was like the valleys. But the cold has grown stronger. The winter grows. Do you see? *And the warm grows less and less.*"

"But the warm is life! The warm is Me-Myself!"

"Yes. In the warm we think, we learn. In the cold is only the Plan. In the cold we are blind ... Waiting here, I thought, was there a time when it was warm here once? Did we come here, we blacks, in the warm to speak, to share? Oh young one, a fearful thinking. Does our time of learning grow shorter, shorter? Where will it end? Will the winters grow until we can learn nothing but only live blindly in the Plan, like the silly fatclimbers who sing but do not speak?"

His words fill me with cold fear. Such a terrible learning! I feel anger.

"No! We will not! We must—we must hold the warm!"

"Hold the warm?" He twists painfully to stare at me. "Hold the warm ... A great thinking. Yes. But how? How? Soon it will be too cold to think, even here!"

"The warm will come again," I tell him. "Then we must learn a way to hold it, you and I!"

His head lolls.

"No ... When the warm comes I will not be here ... and you will be too busy for thinking, young one."

"I will help you! I will carry you to the Caves!"

"In the Caves," he gasps, "In each Cave there are two black ones like yourself. One is living, waiting mindless for the winter to pass ... And while he waits, he eats. He eats the other, that is how he lives. That is the Plan. As you will eat me, my youngling."

"No!" I cry in horror. "I will never harm you!"

"When the cold comes you will see," he whispers. "Great is the Plan!"

"No! You are wrong! I will break the Plan," I shout. A cold wind is blowing from the summit; the sun dies.

"Never will I harm you," I bellow. "You are wrong to say so!"

My scaleplates are rising, my tail begins to pound. Through the mists I hear his gasps.

I recall dragging a heavy black thing to my Cave. *Chill cold, kill cold . . . In the cold I killed you.* Leelyloo. He did not resist.

Great is the Plan. He accepted all, perhaps he even felt a strange joy, as I feel it now. In the Plan is joy. But if the Plan is wrong? *The winters grow.* Do the fatclimbers have their Plan too?

Oh, a hard thinking! How we tried, my redling, my joy. All the long warm days I explained it to you, over and over. How the winter would come and change us if we did not hold the warm. You understood! You share, you understand me now, my precious flame— though you can't speak I feel your sharing love. Softly . . .

Oh, yes, we made our preparations, our own Plan. Even in the highest heat we made our Plan against the cold. Have other lovers done so? How I searched, carrying you my cherry bud, I crossed whole mountain ranges, following the sun until we found this warmest of warm valleys on the sunward side. Surely the cold would be weak here, I thought. How could they reach us here, the cold fogs, the icy winds that froze my inner Me and drew me up the Trails into the dead Caves of Winter?

This time I would defy!

This time I have *you.*

"Don't take me there, my Moggadeet!" You begged, fearful of the strangeness. "Don't take me to the cold!"

"Never, my Leeliloo! Never, I vow it. Am I not your Mother, little redness?"

"But you will change! The cold will make you forget. Is it not the Plan?"

"We will break the Plan, Lili. See you are growing larger, heavier, my fireberry—and always more beautiful! Soon I will not be able to carry you easily, I could never carry you to the cold Trails. And I will never leave you!"

"But you are so big, Moggadeet! When the change comes you will forget and drag me to the cold."

"Never! Your Moggadeet has a deeper Plan! When the mists start I will take you to the farthest, warmest cranny of this cave, and there I will spin a wall so you can never be pulled out. And I will never never leave you. Even the Plan cannot draw Moggadeet from Leelyloo!"

"But you will have to go hunting for food and the cold will take you then! You will forget me and follow the cold love of winter and leave me there to die! Perhaps that is the Plan!"

"Oh, no, my precious, my redling! Don't grieve, don't cry! Hear your Moggadeet's Plan! From now on I'll hunt twice as hard. I'll fill this cave to the top, my fat little blushbud, I will fill it with food now so I can stay by you all the winter through!"

And so I did, didn't I my Lilli? Silly Moggadeet, how I hunted, how I brought lizards, hoppers, fatclimbers and banlings by the score. What a fool! For of course they rotted, there in the heat, and the heaps turned green and slimy—but still tasting good, eh, my berry? —so that we had to eat them then, gorging ourselves like babies. And how you grew!

Oh, beautiful you became, my jewel of redness! So bursting fat and shiny-full, but still my tiny one, my sunspark. Each night after I fed you I would part the silk, fondling your head, your eyes, your tender ears, trembling with excitement for the delicious moment when I would release your first scarlet limb to caress and exercise it and press it to my pulsing throat-sacs. Sometimes I would unbind two together for the sheer joy of seeing you move. And each night it took longer, each morning I had to make more silk to bind you up. How proud I was, my Leely, Lillilo!

That was when my greatest thinking came.

As I was weaving you so tenderly into your shining cocoon, my joyberry, I thought, why not bind up living

fatclimbers? Pen them alive so their flesh will stay
sweet and they will serve us through the winter!

That was a great thinking, Lilliloo, and I did this,
and it was good. Fatclimbers in plenty I walled in a
little tunnel, and many, many other things as well,
while the sun walked back towards winter and the
shadows grew and grew. Fatclimbers and banlings
and all tasty creatures and even—Oh, clever Moggadeet!—all manner of leaves and bark and stuffs for
them to eat! Oh, we had broken the Plan for sure now!

"We have broken the Plan for sure, my Lilli-red.
The fatclimbers are eating the twigs and bark, the
banlings are eating juice from the wood, the great
runners are munching grass, and we will eat them
all!"

"Oh, Moggadeet, you are brave! Do you think we
can really break the Plan? I am frightened! Give me a
banling, I think it grows cold."

"You have eaten fifteen banlings, my minikin!" I
teased you. "How fat you grow! Let me look at you
again, yes, you must let your Moggadeet caress you
while you eat. Ah, how adorable you are!"

And of course—Oh, you remember how it began
then, our deepest love. For when I uncovered you one
night with the first hint of cold in the air, I saw that
you had changed.

Shall I say it? Your secret fur. Your *Mother-fur.*

Always I had cleaned you there tenderly, but without difficulty to restrain myself. But on this night
when I parted the silk strands with my huge hunting
claws, what new delights met my eyes! No longer pink
and pale but fiery red! *Red!* Scarlet blaze like the
reddest sunrise, gold-tipped! And swollen, curling,
dewy—Oh! Commanding me to expose you, all of you.
Oh, how your tender eyes melted me and your breath
musky-sweet and your limbs warm and heavy in my
grasp!

Wildly I ripped away the last strands, dazed with
bliss as you slowly stretched your whole blazing red-

ness before my eyes. I knew then—*we* knew!—that
the love we felt before was only a beginning. My
hunting-limbs fell at my sides and my special hands,
my weaving hands grew, filled with new, almost painful life. I could not speak, my throat-sacs filling, filling! And my love-hands rose up by themselves, pressing
ecstatically, while my eyes bent closer, closer to your
glorious *red!*

But suddenly the Me-Myself, Moggadeet awoke! I
jumped back!

"Lilli! What's happening to us?"

"Oh, Moggadeet, I love you! Don't go away!"

"What is it, Leelyloo? Is it the Plan?"

"I don't care! Moggadeet, don't you love me?"

"I fear! I fear to harm you! You are so tiny. I am
your Mother."

"No Moggadeet, look! I am as big as you are. Don't
be afraid."

I drew back—Oh, hard, hard!—and tried to look
calmly.

"True, my redling, you have grown. But your limbs
are so new, so tender. Oh, I can't look!"

Averting my eyes I began to spin a screen of silk, to
shut away your maddening redness.

"We must wait, Lillilloo. We must go on as before. I
don't know what this strange urging means; I fear it
will bring you harm."

"Yes, Moggadeet. We will wait."

Add so we waited. Oh yes. Each night it grew more
hard. We tried to be as before, to be happy, Leely-
Moggadeet. Each night as I caressed your glowing
limbs that seemed to offer themselves to me as I
swathed and unswathed them in turn, the urge rose
in me hotter, more strong. To unveil you wholly! To
look again upon your whole body!

Oh yes, my darling, I feel—unbearable—how you
remember with me those last few days of our simple
love.

Colder . . . colder. Mornings when I went to harvest

the fatclimbers there was a whiteness on their fur and
the banlings ceased to move. The sun sank ever lower,
paler, and the cold mists hung above us, reaching
down. Soon I dared not leave the cave. I stayed all day
by your silken wall, humming Motherlike, *Brum-a-
loo, Mooly-mooly, Lilliloo, Love Leely*. Strong Moggadeet!

"We'll wait, fireling. We will not yield to the Plan!
Aren't we happier than all others, here with our love
in our warm cave?"

"Oh, yes, Moggadeet."

"I'm Myself now. I am strong. I'll make my own
Plan. I will not look at you until . . . until the warm,
until the Sun comes back."

"Yes, Moggadeet . . . Moggadeet? My limbs are
cramped."

"Oh, my precious, wait—see, I am opening the silk
very carefully, I will not look—I won't—"

"Moggadeet, don't you love me?"

"Leelyloo! Oh, my glorious one! I fear, I fear—"

"Look, Moggadeet! See how big I am, how strong!"

"Oh, redling, my hands—my hands—what are they
doing to you?"

For with my special hands I was pressing, pressing
the hot juices from my throat-sacs and tenderly,
tenderly parting your sweet Mother-fur and *placing
my gift within your secret places*. And as I did this our
eyes entwined and our limbs made a wreath.

"My darling, do I hurt you?"

"Oh, no, Moggadeet! Oh, no!"

Oh, my adored one, those last days of our love!

Outside the world grew colder yet, and the fatclimbers ceased to eat and the banlings lay still and
began to stink. But still we held the warmth deep in
our cave and still I fed my beloved on the last of our
food. And every night our new ritual of love became
more free, richer, though I compelled myself to hide
all but a portion of your sweet body. But each dawn it

grew hard and harder for me to replace the silken bonds around your limbs.

"Moggadeet! Why do you not bind me! I am afraid!"

"A moment, Lilli, a moment. I must caress you just once more."

"I'm afraid, Moggadeet! Cease now and bind me!"

"But why, my lovekin? Why must I hide you? Is this not some foolish part of the Plan?"

"I don't know, I feel so strange. Moggadeet, I—I'm changing."

"You grow more glorious every moment, my Lilli, my own. Let me look at you! It is wrong to bind you away!"

"No, Moggadeet! No!"

But I would not listen, would I? Oh foolish Moggadeet-who-thought-to-be-your-Mother. Great is the Plan!

I did not listen, I did not bind you up. No! I ripped them away, the strong silk strands. Mad with love I slashed them all at once, rushing from each limb to the next until all your glorious body lay exposed. At last—I saw you whole!

Oh, Lilliloo, greatest of Mothers.

It was not I who was your Mother. You were mine. Shining and bossed you lay, your armor newly grown, your mighty hunting limbs thicker than my head! What I had created. You! A Supermother, a Mother such as none have ever seen!

Stupefied with delight, I gazed.

And your huge hunting limb came out and seized me.

Great is the Plan. I felt only joy as your jaws took me.

As I feel it now.

And so we end, my Lilliloo, my redling, for your babies are swelling through your Mother-fur and your Moggadeet can speak no longer. I am nearly devoured. The cold grows, it grows, and your Mother-eyes are growing, glowing. Soon you will be alone with our children and the warm will come again.

Will you remember, my heartmate? Will you remember and tell them?

Tell them of the cold, Leelyloo. Tell them of our love.

Tell them . . . *the winters grow.*

CLOSED SICILIAN

by BARRY N. MALZBERG

As of this writing, Barry N. Malzberg has published some twenty-five novels and more than two hundred shorter stories in the science fiction/fantasy field, the majority of them important, almost always powerful works that have won him critical acclaim. Few writers have understood the opportunities and limitations of commercial fiction as well as Malzberg, or have fought as hard to bring recognition to those who he feels have been unfairly neglected or abused.

"Closed Sicilian" is one of a small group of superior science fiction stories with a chess background. It provided the basis for his excellent and underappreciated novel *Tactics of Conquest* (1973).

1. P-K4

HE *would* open with his standard King's Pawn, looking to transpose into the Ruy Lopez at the earliest opportunity, and I have known this in dreams as in study for most of my life, yet I cannot transcend the thrill of mingled terror and anticipation with which, nevertheless, I react to his first move. Sitting across from me in perfect repose, his suddenly alien eyebrows curl into the faintest and most tremulous posture of inquiry as his eyes flick beyond me and with

37

studied disinterest to the audience of nine hundred
million around and below us. Due to the high ethics of
the match and the scrupulous efforts that I have
conducted throughout to force the spectators to con-
form to the code of play, they do not react to his gaze,
nor do they murmur. Seated with my back to them,
facing the bleak panels of this high-walled room in
which we play, I am able to bring my utmost concentration to the board and thus my line of sight de-
scends and my opponent, at this moment, no longer
exists.

We are playing for the fate of the Universe. Previ-
ously we have played for the fate of the world, the
worlds, the Solar System, the Milky Way, the Galaxy
and the known Cosmos, but due to an apparent series
of close defeats I have suffered due to the clever ma-
nipulations of the Overlords, the stakes have been
progressively raised from one match to the next, and
from this final confrontation there can be no appeal. I
am not concerned. My game is in perfect order; I have
spent eight months with my miniature chessboard
and the Blue Book of my opponent's games preparing
myself for this last great test. Several times I have
forced postponents due to feigned illness or displea-
sure with the match conditions in order that I might
have every opportunity to bring my studies to fruition.
Pausing only for food and sleep, a couple of errant
comminglings with terrestrial females who I have had
sent to my quarters, I have dedicated myself utterly to
the comprehension of my opponent's weaknesses and
the development of strategic lines of attack that involve
much original thought. I cannot fail the Universe in
this last and most conclusive of all our tests, and now
I know that essential control has passed into me. I feel
small surges of power radiating through my bearded
and distinguished frame; I feel a little tremor of my
opponent's weakness intersect my own synapses and
pass through them quickly. He has been greedy and

should have cashed in on the Galaxy. But now he will pay by losing all.

I sit in perfect serenity, and when I have used up the time I have allotted myself on the clock, I make my response:

1. P-K4

Originally, my opponent and I did not seem fated for such great and meaningful confrontation. We were born within months of one another, spent our early years being raised in the same complex, discovered chess together and passed many pleasant years solving the mysteries of the game. As youths, we did not otherwise neglect more routine pastimes; we went out with the same girls, progressed with them sexually at about the same rate, shared classes and areas of subject interest—chemistry and textiles, as I recall, although it is hard to remember this far back; since I became involved in this, my early life has become so dim—and in fact became chess professionals on the same day, meeting all of the qualifications of the League and receiving our initial assignments. Only then, in fact, did our paths diverge; my opponent went to Brooklyn to become a promising newcomer on a team that needed shoring up badly, whereas I went to Bismarck, North Dakota, Ganymede, where I led the team in my first season to a tie for third place in the satellite division. Who was to have known when we were innocent lads growing up together in the towers that it would be he because of his fatal weakness to fall into the hands of the malevolent X'Thi, scourge and enemy of all humanity, whereas I, no xenophobe but loyal to my heritage from the beginning, would become the last bulwark of defense against occupation of the Universe by these terrible aliens? Who would have known? . . . But as my opponent himself said in one of the authorized interviews before the match (I have cooperated in these myself to build up the gate), *the ways of life are strange* and now I have succeeded in blockading the King's Pawn and cramping his position as early as his second move. What now, then? I look at him with a careful, triumphant smile and stand, take myself hurriedly backstage where refreshing snacks and fruit juices are available to us at all times by the courtesy of the Earth Federation and the X'Thi Congress, one of the few areas in which these deadly enemies have shown cooperation. Soon enough, there will be no need for further concessions:

2. Q-B3

When I return, having had a cruller and a small nourishing handful of Jovian lice, the aspect of the stage has subtly altered; the lighting has changed; my opponent is leaning backward, hands on knees, with a contented expression on his face; and small darting tadpoles of light draw me irresistibly to fixate upon the board. He has pushed his Queen peremptorily, a characteristic that he has evinced in several previous games, but it is one of those critical weaknesses upon which I have concentrated in my studies, and I am prepared now to punish him terribly for it.

My opponent has always had this tendency to develop his major pieces too rapidly. On Nulla, in the Solar Championships of 2256, who can forget that famous game in which he prematurely wedged open his Rook file with an unsound sacrifice and then, doubling his Rooks through additional sacrifices on the twelfth move, proceeded to dismember the hapless Wojewscking in the finals? Yet, all along, as the Blue Book reveals, Wojewscking could have averted the disaster through playing his Queen's Bishop to the seventh rank (now undefended because of the sacrifices) and castling. Well, there is no way of explaining such things; Wojewscking was playing in the uncongenial gravity of Uranus, whereas my opponent had prepared himself for the Championship by residing on that un-

happy planet for three Earth weeks prior to the opening. It does not matter; Wojewscking's disaster only
made my opponent more attractive to the vicious and
malevolent X'Thi when they came into known space
in 2271 and sought a proper turncoat who would help
them to enact their dreadful schemes. Under the illu-
sion that they had possession of the best chess player
in the Federation, they allowed my opponent to play
for progressively higher stakes, and now they will lose
the Universe.

Looking at him in the strange lighting, I see that he
is both smaller and older than I remembered him to
be, and I feel a flare of pity instantly canceled by cold
resolve. I am a man of some personal limitations and
minor neurotic traits, but when I play chess, as it has
been noted, I become steel, and there will be no re-
morse for my opponent, that traitor now, simply because he is aging and destroyed by pressure:

2. QN-QB3

The aim is to develop my minor pieces quickly while
he falls into the lure of launching an early, unsound
attack. "Just imagine," I remember saying to him in
the projects of our youth, oh, so many years ago when
we were playing yet another of our casual games,
"what would it be like if we could play chess for the
fate of the Universe? Wouldn't it make more sense
than fighting wars or things? We could be the two
best players in the world and countries could choose
up sides, and that way one game or a series could
settle everything."

"But if we were playing for the fate of the Universe,
it would be more than just the world and countries
and people then, wouldn't it?" my opponent said, dem-
onstrating even then, at the age of twelve or thirteen,
that treacherous cunning with which, years later, he
would leap into the hands of the ugly and tormenting
X'Thi when they offered to resolve all differences by

playing off the worlds. "But of course I don't think chess could ever be that important," he added, pushing his Knight's Pawn to the seventh rank and forcing a checkmate, which I could have easily avoided if I had not felt pity for his youth, his abandonment, his unhappy upbringing in the Projects and had wanted to give him a gift in the form of a small crushing defeat.

It is a long way from that to this, but I am entrapped by so such feelings of pity or mystery today. Let it be said and be done: I deliberately threw the matches for the world, the worlds, the Solar System, the Milky Way, the known Galaxy in order to force this final confrontation. I knew that, spurred on by their greed and thoughts of an easy victory, the X'Thi would accept our proposals for continued games, upping the stakes, and I have been merely waiting for this great opportunity to toy with them and crush them:

3. B-B4

Continuing his unsound attack by posting the King's Bishop at an unsafe square. The normal continuation in the Ruy Lopez would be *B-B5,* but he has a weakness for variations of this sort and now will pay for them dearly.

The X'Thi are corrupt, deadly, vicious and evil, and are prefigured in detail by *The Revelations of St. John the Divine,* which talk about that great Snake that in the last days will appear to battle Mankind at Apocalypse. Actually, the X'Thi do not look like snakes; they are, in fact, rather pleasantly humanoid in appearance, but no matter of that; the tempter and the Final War would have to come in the guise of the familiar. (Note the Book of Job.) I have a minor interest in Bible lore, which is one of my few areas of relaxation outside of my lifelong dedication to the art and lore of Caissa. Clearly, what my opponent and I are now contending is the last and great battle between the forces of light and darkness that will usher in the divine era of the Second Coming, but this enormous obligation does not cause me to tighten with pressure (I feed upon it), but instead makes me relaxed and easeful. Not only are my skills superior to his despite the apparent record of successive defeats; my cause is essentially righteous, whereas his, of course, is that of Satan. It is always unwise to open a Queen prematurely when fighting for the cause of Satan.

The murmurs of the spectators, evenly divided by fiat between humanity and X'Thi, the combined political leaders of all the separate worlds, that is, admitted by invitation only, rise slightly and billow toward me as I prepare my first and devastating combination:

3. QN-R4

Threatening the Bishop and unleashing a devastating attack upon the Queen side. My opponent seems to pale and puts a hand indelicately to his mouth as he leans forward, the implications of the move and his terrible error with the Bishop already clear to him. For an instant, just an instant, I want to reach across the board and take his hand, take it as I might have in the old days and say, "Listen, it's all right, don't be unhappy, don't take it personally, it really doesn't matter that much at all, and it's no reflection on you as a person if you lose a game of chess," but this would be preposterous since everything depends upon this game of chess, and if he loses (as now he must), the X'Thi would surely draw and quarter him before winking out of our Universe forever. "It's pointless, it has nothing to do with the situation, relax, take comfort," I want to say to him, but this is surely insane since the situation is climactic and irrevocable.

What has happened to me simply enough is that I am being assaulted by feelings of sentiment on the precipice of my immortal victory. I would not put it beyond the cunning and tormenting X'Thi to have contrived this themselves by manipulation of certain devices within the chair, the hall, the lighting, which can change my brain waves and interfere with normal psychic functioning. It was for this reason that I insisted that security in the hall be so tight and that the fruit juices and snacks be prepared and tasted by my own staff before their emplacement backstage, but I always knew that, given the final test, my will would be stronger than theirs and that none of their terrible devices could affect me.

They do not affect me now. I lean back in my chair, feeling a slight, cramping pressure within the bowels diminish, feeling all sentiment depart, and look out toward the audience for the first time; blue haze in the darkness, wisps of smoke, the soft purring of the atmospheric reservoirs that maintain the segregated sections of the hall at the proper balance for the two races. "Well," I say to him, then turning back, his face like an egg caught between two lights, his features crazed and crayoned, weaving insubstantially against that bleak shell, "what are you going to do now, eh? What are you going to do now, you traitorous son-of-a-bitch?" And then I take from my inside pocket one of the foul cigars I have brought for just this occasion and, extracting matches, light it deliberately in front of him, pouring out smoke, extinguishing the match, making him gasp as plumes of gray waft toward the great dome. Lasker was famous for tactics of this sort in 1924, but it is not 1924; it is more than three centuries later and here I am yet, and now humanity, the seed of Abraham, will overtake the Universe and I am glad, glad, for I know my name will be legion.

"My friend," my opponent gasps, "my old friend, this is too terrible," and incredibly, leaves his chair to reach toward me in a mad embrace and I dodge it only at the last instant (I abhor physical contact of any sort now) and with a shudder, revolve my chair, leap out of it. "My old friend," he says again, "this cannot be," but he subsides; the features seemed washed and muddled by some fluid; he returns to his chair and ponders the board silently, chin in his hand.

Suddenly it is all too much for me—the signals must have become displaced, and it is he, not I, who is undone by sentiment—and I hurry backstage again, seeking the soothing fruit juices and the knowledge that when I return he will have made the evasive move with the Bishop, losing a full tempo, to demonstrate his irrevocable loss:

4. QxP Mate

When I do return I see his before I see the board, and he is weeping. For a moment I want to embrace him then, if only in a kind of comfort, but the years of discipline and denial are too ingrained, the task too enormous, to allow me such failure, and so I take my chair and look at the board then to consider the best way in which I can continue to crush him.

TRANSIT OF EARTH

by ARTHUR C. CLARKE

Arthur C. Clarke has been one of the titanic figures in science fiction since the appearance of *Childhood's End* in 1953. Although he has a reputation as an author of technological science fiction, some of his most memorable work has had strong transcendental effects, especially *The City and the Stars* (1956), *2001: A Space Odessey* (1968), and *Rendezvous with Rama* (1973). His most recent novel (which he claims is his last) is The Hugo Award winning *The Fountains of Paradise* (1979).

"Transit of Earth" first appeared in *Playboy* in 1971.

NOTE: *All the astronomical events described in this story take place at the times stated.*

TESTING, one, two, three, four, five. . . .

Evans speaking. I will continue to record as long as possible. This is a two-hour capsule, but I doubt if I'll fill it.

That photograph has haunted me all my life; now, too late, I know why. (But would it have made any difference if I *had* known? That's one of those meaningless and unanswerable questions the mind keeps returning to endlessly, like the tongue exploring a broken tooth.)

I've not seen it for years, but I've only to close my eyes and I'm back in a landscape almost as hostile—and as beautiful—as this one. Fifty million miles Sunward and 72 years in the past, five men face the camera amid the Antarctic snows. Not even the bulky furs can hide the exhaustion and defeat that mark every line of their bodies, and their faces are already touched by death.

There were five of them. There were five of us and, of course, we also took a group photograph. But everything else was different. We were smiling—cheerful, confident. And our picture was on all the screens of Earth within ten minutes. It was months before *their* camera was found and brought back to civilization.

And we die in comfort, with all modern conveniences—including many that Robert Falcon Scott could never have imagined when he stood at the South Pole in 1912.

Two hours later, I'll start giving exact times when it becomes important.

All the facts are on the log, and by now the whole world knows them. So I guess I'm doing this largely to settle my mind—to talk myself into facing the inevitable. The trouble is, I'm not sure what subjects to avoid and which to tackle head on. Well, there's only one way to find out.

The first item: In 24 hours, at the very most, all the oxygen will be gone. That leaves me with the three classical choices. I can let the CO_2 build up until I become unconscious. I can step outside and crack the suit, leaving Mars to do the job in about two minutes. Or I can use one of the tablets in the med kit.

CO_2 buildup: Everyone says that's quite easy—just like going to sleep. I've no doubt that's true; unfortunately, in my case it's associated with nightmare number one.

I wish I'd never come across that damn book—*True Stories of World War Two,* or whatever it was called.

There was one chapter about a German submarine, found and salvaged after the war. The crew was still inside it—*two* men per bunk. And between each pair of skeletons, the single respirator set they'd been sharing.

Well, at least that won't happen here. But I know, with a deadly certainty, that as soon as I find it hard to breathe, I'll be back in that doomed U-boat.

So what about the quicker way? When you're exposed to a vacuum, you're unconscious in ten or fifteen seconds, and people who've been through it say it's not painful—just peculiar. But trying to breathe something that isn't there brings me altogether too neatly to nightmare number two.

This time, it's a personal experience. As a kid, I used to do a lot of skin diving when my family went to the Caribbean for vacations. There was an old freighter that had sunk 20 years before, out on a reef with its deck only a couple of yards below the surface. Most of the hatches were open; so it was easy to get inside to look for souvenirs and hunt the big fish that like to shelter in such places.

Of course it was dangerous—if you did it without scuba gear. So what boy could resist the challenge?

My favorite route involved diving into a hatch on the foredeck, swimming about 50 feet along a passageway dimly lit by portholes a few yards apart, then angling up a short flight of stairs and emerging through a door in the battered superstructure. The whole trip took less than a minute—an easy dive for anyone in good condition. There was even time to do some sightseeing or to play with a few fish along the route. And sometimes, for a change, I'd switch directions, going in the door and coming out again through the hatch.

That was the way I did it the last time. I hadn't dived for a week—there had been a big storm and the sea was too rough—so I was impatient to get going. I deep-breathed on the surface for about two minutes, until I felt the tingling in my fingertips that told me it was time to stop. Then I jackknifed and slid gently down toward the black rectangle of the open doorway.

It always looked ominous and menacing—that was part of the thrill. And for the first few yards, I was almost completely blind; the contrast between the tropical glare above water and the gloom between decks was so great that it took quite a while for my eyes to adjust. Usually, I was halfway along the corridor before I could see anything clearly; then the illumination would steadily increase as I approached the open hatch, where a shaft of sunlight would paint a dazzling rectangle on the rusty, barnacled metal floor.

I'd almost made it when I realized that this time the light wasn't getting better. There was no slanting column of sunlight ahead of me, leading up to the world of air and life. I had a second of baffled confusion, wondering if I'd lost my way. Then I realized what had happened—and confusion turned into sheer panic. Sometime during the storm, the hatch must have slammed shut. It weighed at least a quarter of a ton.

I don't remember making a U-turn; the next thing I recall is swimming quite slowly back along the passage and telling myself, "Don't hurry—your air will last longer if you take it easy." I could see very well now, because my eyes had had plenty of time to become dark-adapted. There were lots of details I'd never noticed before—such as the red squirrelfish lurking in the shadows, the green fronds and algae growing in the little patches of light around the portholes, and even a single rubber boot, apparently in excellent condition, lying where someone must have kicked it off. And once, out of a side corridor, I noticed a big grouper staring at me with bulbous eyes, his thick lips half-parted, as if he were astonished at my intrusion.

The band around my chest was getting tighter and tighter; it was impossible to hold my breath any longer—yet the stairway still seemed an infinite distance ahead. I let some bubbles of air dribble out of my mouth; that improved matters for a moment, but, once I had exhaled, the ache in my lungs became even more unendurable.

Now there was no point in conserving strength by flippering along with that steady, unhurried stroke. I snatched the ultimate few cubic inches of air from my face mask—feeling it flatten against my nose as I did so—and swallowed it down into my starving lungs. At the same time, I shifted gear and drove forward with every last atom of strength.

And that's all I remember until I found myself spluttering and coughing in the daylight, clinging to the broken stub of the mast. The water around me was stained with blood and I wondered why. Then, to my great surprise, I noticed a deep gash in my right calf; I must have banged into some sharp obstruction, but I'd never noticed it and even now felt no pain.

That was the end of my skin diving until I started astronaut training ten years later and went into the underwater zero-g stimulator. Then it was different, because I was using scuba gear, but I had some nasty moments that I was afraid the psychologists would notice and I always made sure that I got nowhere near emptying my tank. Having nearly suffocated once, I'd no intention of risking it again.

I know exactly what it will feel like to breathe the freezing wisp of near vacuum that passes for atmosphere on Mars. No, thank you.

So what's wrong with poison? Nothing, I suppose. The stuff we've got takes only 15 seconds, they told us. But all my instincts are against it, even when there's no sensible alternative.

Did Scott have poison with him? I doubt it. And if he did, I'm sure he never used it.

I'm not going to replay this. I hope it's been some use, but I can't be sure.

* * *

The radio has just printed out a message from Earth, reminding me that transit starts in two hours. As if I'm likely to forget—when four men have already died so that I can be the first human being to see it. And the only one for exactly 100 years. It isn't often that Sun, Earth and Mars line up neatly like this; the last time was in 1905, when poor old Lowell was still writing his beautiful nonsense about the canals and the great dying civilization that had built them. Too bad it was all delusion.

I'd better check the telescope and the timing equipment.

The Sun is quiet today—as it should be, anyway, near the middle of the cycle. Just a few small spots and some minor areas of disturbance around them. The solar weather is set calm for months to come. That's one thing the others won't have to worry about on their way home.

I think that was the worst moment, watching *Olympus* lift off Phobos and head back to Earth. Even though we'd known for weeks that nothing could be done, that was the final closing of the door. It was night and we could see everything perfectly. Phobus had come leaping up out of the west a few hours earlier and was doing its mad backward rush across the sky, growing from a tiny crescent to a half-moon; before it reached the zenith, it would disappear as it plunged into the shadow of Mars and became eclipsed.

We'd been listening to the countdown, of course, trying to go about our normal work. It wasn't easy, accepting at last the fact that 15 of us had come to Mars and only ten would return. Even then, I suppose there were millions back on Earth who still could not understand; they must have found it impossible to believe that *Olympus* couldn't descend a mere 4000 miles to pick us up. The Space Administration has been bombarded with crazy rescue schemes; heaven knows, we'd thought of enough ourselves. But when the permafrost under landing pad three finally gave way and *Pegasus* toppled, that was that. It still seems a miracle that the ship didn't blow up when the propellant tank ruptured.

I'm wandering again. Back to Phobos and the countdown. On the telescope monitor, we could clearly see the fissured plateau where *Olympus* had touched down after we'd separated and begun our own descent. Though our friends would never land on Mars, at least they'd had a little world of their own to explore; even for a satellite as small as Phobos, it worked out at 30 square miles per man. A lot of territory to search for strange minerals and debris from space—or to carve your name so that future ages would know that you were the first of all men to come this way.

The ship was clearly visible as a stubby, bright cylinder against the dull gray rocks; from time to time, some flat surface would catch the light of the swiftly moving Sun and would flash with mirror brilliance. But about five minutes before lift-off, the picture became suddenly pink, then crimson—then vanished completely as Phobos rushed into eclipse.

The countdown was still at ten seconds when we were startled by a blast of light. For a moment, we wondered if *Olympus* had also met with catastrophe; then we realized that someone was filming the takeoff and the external floodlights had been switched on.

During those last few seconds, I think we all forgot our own predicament; we were up there aboard *Olympus,* willing the thrust to build up smoothly and lift the ship out of the tiny gravitational field of Phobos—and then away from Mars for the long fall Sunward. We heard Commander Richmond say, "Ignition," there was a brief burst of interference, and the patch of light began to move in the field of the telescope.

That was all. There was no blazing column of fire, because, of course, there's really no ignition when a nuclear rocket lights up. "Lights up" indeed! That's another hangover from the old chemical technology.

But a hot hydrogen blast is completely invisible; it seems a pity that we'll never again see anything so spectacular as a Saturn or a Korolov blastoff.

Just before the end of the burn, *Olympus* left the shadow of Mars and burst out into sunlight again, reappearing almost instantly as a brilliant, swiftly moving star. The blaze of light must have startled them aboard the ship, because we heard someone call out, "Cover that window!" Then, a few seconds later, Richmond announced, "Engine cutoff." Whatever happened, *Olympus* was now irrevocably headed back to Earth.

A voice I didn't recognize—though it must have been the commander's—said, "Good-bye, *Pegasus*," and the radio transmission switched off. There was, of course, no point in saying, "Good luck." *That* had all been settled weeks ago.

I've just played this back. Talking of luck, there's been one compensation, though not for us. With a crew of only ten, *Olympus* has been able to dump a third of her expendables and lighten herself by several tons. So now she'll get home a month ahead of schedule.

Plenty of things could have gone wrong in that month; we may yet have saved the expedition. Of course, we'll never know—but it's a nice thought.

I've been playing a lot of music—full blast, now that there's no one else to be disturbed. Even if there were any Martians, I don't suppose this ghost of an atmosphere could carry the sound more than a few yards.

We have a fine collection, but I have to choose carefully. Nothing downbeat and nothing that demands too much concentration. Above all, nothing with human voices. So I restrict myself to the lighter orchestral classics; the *New World Symphony* and Grieg's piano concerto fill the bill perfectly. At the moment, I'm listening to Rachmaninoff's *Paganini Variations,* but now I must switch off and get down to work.

There are only five minutes to go; all the equipment is in perfect condition. The telescope is tracking the Sun, the video recorder is standing by, the precision timer is running.

These observations will be as accurate as I can make them. I owe it to my lost comrades, whom I'll soon be joining. They gave me their oxygen so that I can still be alive at this moment. I hope you remember that, 100 or 1000 years from now, whenever you crank these figures into the computers.

Only a minute to go; getting down to business. For the record, year 1984, month May, day 11, coming up to four hours, 30 minutes, Ephemeris Time . . . *now.*

Half a minute to contact; switching recorder and timer to high speed. Just rechecked position angle to make sure I'm looking at the right spot on the Sun's limb. Using power of 500—image perfectly steady even at this low elevation.

Four thirty-two. Any moment, now. . . .

There it is . . . there it is! I can hardly believe it! A tiny black dent in the edge of the Sun, growing, growing, growing. . . .

Hello, Earth. Look up at me—the brightest star in your sky, straight overhead at midnight.

Recorder back to slow.

Four thirty-five. It's as if a thumb were pushing into the Sun's edge, deeper and deeper—fascinating to watch.

Four forty-one. Exactly halfway. The Earth's a perfect black semicircle—a clean bit out of the Sun—as if some disease were eating it away.

Four forty-eight. Ingress three-quarters complete.

Four hours, 49 minutes, 30 seconds. Recorder on high speed again.

The line of contact with the Sun's edge is shrinking fast. Now it's a barely visible black thread. In a few seconds, the whole Earth will be superimposed on the Sun.

Now I can see the effects of the atmosphere. There's a thin halo of light surrounding that black hole in the Sun. Strange to think that I'm seeing the glow of all the sunsets—and all the sunrises—that are taking place around the whole Earth at this very moment.

Ingress complete—four hours, 50 minutes, five seconds. The whole world has moved onto the face of the Sun, a perfectly circular black disk silhouetted against that inferno, 90 million miles below. It looks bigger than I expected; one could easily mistake it for a fair-sized sunspot.

Nothing more to see now for six hours, when the Moon appears, trailing Earth by half the Sun's width. I'll beam the recorded data back to Lunacom, then try to get some sleep.

My very last sleep. Wonder if I'll need drugs. It seems a pity to waste these last few hours, but I want to conserve my strength—and my oxygen. I think it was Dr. Johnson who said that nothing settles a man's mind so wonderfully as the knowledge that he'll be hanged in the morning. How the hell did *he* know?

Ten hours, 30 minutes, Ephemeris Time. Dr. Johnson was right. I had only one pill and don't remember any dreams.

The condemned man also ate a hearty breakfast. Cut that out.

Back at telescope. Now the Earth's halfway across the disk, passing well north of center. In ten minutes, I should see the Moon.

I've just switched to the highest power of the telescope—2000. The image is slightly fuzzy but still fairly good, atmospheric halo very distinct. I'm hoping to see the cities on the dark side of Earth.

No luck. Probably too many clouds. A pity—it's theoretically possible, but we never succeeded. I wish. . . . Never mind.

*   *   *

Ten hours, 40 minutes. Recorder on slow speed. Hope I'm looking at the right spot.

Fifteen seconds to go. Recorder fast.

Damn—missed it. Doesn't matter—the recorder will have caught the exact moment. There's a little black notch already in the side of the Sun. First contact must have been about ten hours, 41 minutes, 20 seconds, E.T.

What a long way it is between Earth and Moon—there's half the width of the Sun between them. You wouldn't think the two bodies had anything to do with each other. Makes you realize just how big the Sun really is.

Ten hours, 44 minutes. The Moon's exactly halfway over the edge. A very small, very clear-cut semicircular bite out of the edge of the Sun.

Ten hours, 47 minutes, five seconds. Internal contact. The Moon's clear of the edge, entirely inside the Sun. Don't suppose I can see anything on the night side, but I'll increase the power.

That's funny.

Well, well. Someone must be trying to talk to me. There's a tiny light pulsing away there on the darkened face of the Moon. Probably the laser of Imbrium Base."

Sorry, everyone. I've said all my goodbyes and don't want to go through that again. Nothing can be important now.

Still, it's almost hypnotic—that flickering point of light, coming out of the face of the Sun itself. Hard to believe that even after it's traveled all this distance, the beam in only 100 miles wide. Lunacom's going to all this trouble to aim it exactly at me and I suppose I should feel guilty at ignoring it. But I don't. I've nearly finished my work and the things of Earth are no longer any concern of mine.

Ten hours, 50 minutes. Recorder off. That's it—until the end of Earth transit, two hours from now.

*   *   *

I've had a snack and am taking my last look at the view from the observation bubble. The Sun's still high; so there's not much contrast, but the light brings out all the colors vividly—the countless varieties of red and pink and crimson, so startling against the deep blue of the sky. How different from the Moon—though that, too, has its own beauty.

It's strange how surprising the obvious can be. Everyone knew that Mars was red. But we didn't really expect the red of rust—the red of blood. Like the Painted Desert of Arizona; after a while, the eye longs for green.

To the north, there is one welcome change of color; the cap of carbon-dioxide snow on Mt. Burroughs is a dazzling white pyramid. That's another surprise. Burroughs is 25,000 feet above Mean Datum; when I was a boy, there weren't supposed to be any mountains on Mars.

The nearest sand dune is a quarter of a mile away and it, too, has patches of frost on its shaded slope. During the last storm, we thought it moved a few feet, but we couldn't be sure. Certainly, the dunes *are* moving, like those on Earth. One day, I suppose, this base will be covered—only to reappear again in 1000 years. Or 10,000.

That strange group of rocks—the Elephant, the Capitol, the Bishop—still holds its secrets and teases me with the memory of our first big disappointment. We could have sworn that they were sedimentary; how eagerly we rushed out to look for fossils! Even now, we don't know what formed that outcropping; the geology of Mars is still a mass of contradictions and enigmas.

We have passed on enough problems to the future and those who come after us will find many more. But there's one mystery we never reported to Earth nor even entered in the log. The first night after we landed, we took turns keeping watch. Brennan was on duty and woke me up soon after midnight. I was annoyed—it was ahead of time—and then he told me that he'd seen a light moving around the base of the Capitol. We watched for at least an hour, until it was my turn to take over. But we saw nothing; whatever that light was, it never reappeared.

Now, Brennan was as level-headed and unimaginative as they come; if he said he saw a light, then he saw one. Maybe it was some kind of electric discharge or the reflection of Phobos on a piece of sand-polished rock. Anyway, we decided not to mention it to Lunacom unless we saw it again.

Since I've been alone, I've often awaked in the night and looked out toward the rocks. In the feeble illumination of Phobos and Deimos, they remind me of the skyline of a darkened city. And it has always remained darkened. No lights have ever appeared for me.

Twelve hours, 49 minutes, Ephemeris Time. The last act's about to begin. Earth has nearly reached the edge of the Sun. The two narrow horns of light that still embrace it are barely touching.

Recorder on fast.

Contact! Twelve hours, 50 minutes, 16 seconds. The crescents of light no longer meet. A tiny black spot has appeared at the edge of the Sun, as the Earth begins to cross it. It's growing longer, longer. . . .

Recorder on slow. Eighteen minutes to wait before Earth finally clears the face of the Sun.

The Moon still has more than halfway to go; it's not yet reached the midpoint of its transit. It looks like a little round blob of ink, only a quarter the size of Earth. And there's no light flickering there anymore. Lunacom must have given up.

Well, I have just a quarter hour left here in my last home. Time seems to be accelerating the way it does in the final minutes before a liftoff. No matter, I have everything worked out now. I can even relax.

Already, I feel part of history. I am one with Captain Cook, back in Tahiti in 1769, watching the transit of Venus. Except for that image of the Moon trailing along behind, it must have looked just like this.

What would Cook have thought, 200 years ago, if he'd known that one day a man would observe the whole Earth in transit from an outer world? I'm sure he would have been astonished—and then delighted.

But I feel a closer identity with a man not yet born. I hope you hear these words, whoever you may be. Perhaps you will be standing on this very spot, 100 years from now, when the next transit occurs.

Greetings to 2084, November 10! I wish you better luck than we had. I suppose you will have come here on a luxury liner—or you may have been born on Mars and be a stranger to Earth. You will know things that I cannot imagine; yet somehow I don't envy you. I would not even change places with you if I could.

For you will remember my name and know that I was the first of all mankind ever to see a transit of Earth. And no one will see another for 100 years.

Twelve hours, 59 minutes. Exactly halfway through egress. The Earth is a perfect semicircle—a black shadow on the face of the Sun. I still can't escape from the impression that something has taken a big bite out of that golden disk. In nine minutes, it will be gone and the Sun will be whole again.

Thirteen hours, seven minutes. Recorder on fast.

Earth has almost gone. There's just a shallow black dimple at the edge of the Sun. You could easily mistake it for a small spot, going over the limb.

Thirteen hours, eight.

Goodbye, beautiful Earth.

Going, going, going, goodbye, good—

I'm OK again now. The timings have all been sent home on the beam. In five minutes, they'll join the accumulated wisdom of mankind. And Lunacom will know that I stuck to my post.

But I'm not sending this. I'm going to leave it here for the next expedition—whenever that may be. It could be ten or twenty years before anyone comes here again; no point in going back to an old site when there's a whole world waiting to be explored.

So this capsule will stay here, as Scott's diary remained in his tent, until the next visitors find it. But they won't find me.

Strange how hard it is to get away from Scott. I think he gave me the idea. For his body will not lie frozen forever in the Antarctic, isolated from the great cycle of life and death. Long ago, that lonely tent began its march to the sea. Within a few years, it was buried by the falling snow and had become part of the glacier that crawls eternally away from the pole. In a few brief centuries, the sailor will have returned to the sea. He will merge once more into the pattern of living things—the plankton, the seals, the penguins, the whales, all the multitudinous fauna of the Antarctic Ocean.

There are no oceans here on Mars, nor have there been for at least five billion years. But there is life of some kind, down there in the badlands of Chaos II, that we never had time to explore. Those moving patches on the orbital photographs. The evidence that whole areas of Mars have been swept clear of craters by forces other than erosion. The long-chain, optically active carbon molecules picked up by the atmospheric samplers.

And, of course, the mystery of Viking 6. Even now, no one has been able to make any sense of those last instrument readings before something large and heavy crushed the probe in the still, cold depths of the Martian night.

And don't talk to me about *primitive* life forms in a place like this! Anything that's survived here will be so sophisticated that we may look as clumsy as dinosaurs.

There's still enough propellant in the ship's tanks to

drive the Marscar clear around the planet. I have three hours of daylight left—plenty of time to get down into the valleys and well out into Chaos. After sunset, I'll still be able to make good speed with the head lamps. It will be romantic, driving at night under the moons of Mars.

One thing I must fix before I leave. I don't like the way Sam's lying out there. He was always so poised, so graceful. It doesn't seem right that he should look so awkward now. I must do something about it.

I wonder if *I* could have covered 300 feet without a suit, walking slowly, steadily—the way he did to the very end.

I must try not to look at his face.

That's it. Everything shipshape and ready to go.

The therapy has worked. I feel perfectly at ease— even contented, now that I know exactly what I'm going to do. The old nightmares have lost their power.

It is true, we all die alone. It makes no difference at the end, being 50 million miles from home.

I'm going to enjoy the drive through that lovely painted landscape. I'll be thinking of all those who dreamed about Mars—Wells and Lowell and Burroughs and Weinbaum and Bradbury. They all guessed wrong —but the reality is just as strange, just as beautiful as they imagined.

I don't know what's waiting for me out there and I'll probably never see it. But on this starveling world, it must be desperate for carbon, phosphorus, oxygen, calcium. It can use me.

And when my oxygen alarm gives its final ping, somewhere down there in the haunted wilderness, I'm going to finish in style. As soon as I have difficulty in breathing, I'll get off the Marscar and start walking— with a playback unit plugged into my helmet and going full blast.

For sheer, triumphant power and glory, there's nothing in the whole of music to match the *Toccata and Fugue in D Minor*. I won't have time to hear all of it; that doesn't matter.

Johann Sebastian, here I come.

BERNIE THE FAUST

by WILLIAM TENN

William Tenn (Professor Philip Klass of Penn State
University) was one of the funny, talented writers
who made *Galaxy Science Fiction* so wonderful in
the 1950s. His satirical stories left few institutions
and social movements of the time untouched, and it
is a shame that his professorial duties have restricted
his writing activity in recent years. The great bulk of
the sixty or so stories he has produced are available
in six collections, including *The Human Angle* (1956)
and *The Square Root of Man* (1968).

"Sting" operations are big news as this headnote
is being written, but we are reasonably certain that
there has never been a con game to equal the one in
"Bernie the Faust."

BERNIE the Faust. That's what Ricardo calls me. I
don't know what I am.

Here I am, I'm sitting in my little nine-by-six office.
I'm reading notices of government-surplus sales. I'm
trying to decide where lies a possible buck and where
lies nothing but more headaches.

So the office door opens. This little guy with a dirty
face, wearing a very dirty, very wrinkled Palm Beach
suit, he walks into my office, and he coughs a bit and
he says:

65

"Would you be interested in buying a twenty for a five?"

That was it. I mean, that's all I had to go on.

I looked him over and I said, *"Wha-at?"*

He shuffled his feet and coughed some more. "A twenty," he mumbled. "A twenty for a five."

I made him drop his eyes and stare at his shoes. They were lousy, cracked shoes, lousy and dirty like the rest of him. Every once in a while, his left shoulder hitched up in a kind of tic. "I give you twenty," he explained to his shoes, "and I buy a five from you with it. I wind up with five, you wind up with twenty."

"How did you get into the building?"

"I just came in," he said, a little mixed up.

"You just *came* in." I put a nasty, mimicking note in my voice. "Now you just go right back downstairs and come the hell out. There's a sign in the lobby—NO BEGGARS ALLOWED."

"I'm not begging." He tugged at the bottom of his jacket. It was like a guy trying to straighten out his slept-in pajamas. "I want to sell you something. A twenty for a five. I give you—"

"You want me to call a cop?"

He looked very scared. "No. Why should you call a cop? I haven't done anything to make you call a cop!"

"I'll call a cop in just a second. I'm giving you fair warning. I just phone down to the lobby and they'll have a cop up here fast. They don't want beggars in this building. This is a building for business."

He rubbed his hand against his face, taking a little dirt off, then he rubbed the hand against the lapel of his jacket and left the dirt there. "No deal?" he asked. "A twenty for a five? You buy and sell things. What's the matter with my deal?"

I picked up the phone.

"All right," he said, holding up the streaky palm of his hand. "I'll go. I'll go."

"You better. And shut the door behind you."

"Just in case you change your mind." He reached

into his dirty, wrinkled pants pocket and pulled out a card. "You can get in touch with me here. Almost any time during the day."

"Blow," I told him.

He reached over, dropped the card on my desk, on top of all the surplus notices, coughed once or twice, looked at me to see if maybe I was biting. No? No. He trudged out.

I picked the card up between the nails of my thumb and forefinger and started to drop it into the wastebasket.

Then I stopped. A card. It was just so damned out of the ordinary—a slob like that with a card. A card, yet.

For that matter, the whole play was out of the ordinary. I began to be a little sorry I hadn't let him run through the whole thing. After all, what was he trying to do but give me an offbeat sales pitch? I can always use an offbeat sales pitch. I work out of a small office, I buy and sell, but half my stock is good ideas. I'll use ideas, even from a bum.

The card was clean and white, except where the smudge from his fingers made a brown blot. Written across it in a kind of ornate handwriting were the words *Mr. Ogo Eksar*. Under that was the name and the telephone number of a hotel in the Times Square area, not far from my office. I knew that hotel: not expensive, but not a fleabag either—somewhere just under the middle line.

There was a room number in one corner of the card. I stared at it and I felt kind of funny. I really didn't know.

Although, come to think of it, why couldn't a panhandler be registered at a hotel? "Don't be a snob, Bernie," I told myself.

Twenty for five. What kind of panhandling pitch would follow it? I couldn't get it out of my mind!

There was only one thing to do. Ask somebody about it. Ricardo? A big college professor, after all. One of my best contacts.

He'd thrown a lot my way—a tip on the college building program that was worth a painless fifteen hundred, an office-equipment disposal from the United Nations, stuff like that. And any time I had any questions that needed a college education, he was on tap. All for the couple, three hundred, he got out of me in commissions.

I looked at my watch. Ricardo would be in his office now, marking papers or whatever it is he does there. I dialed his number.

"Ogo Eksar?" he repeated after me. "Sounds like a Finnish name. Or maybe Estonian. From the eastern Baltic, I'd say."

"Forget that part," I said. "This is all I care about." And I told him about the twenty-for-five offer.

He laughed. "That thing again!"

"Some old hustle that the Greeks pulled on the Egyptians?"

"No. Something the Americans pulled. And not a con game. During the Depression, a New York newspaper sent a reporter around the city with a twenty-dollar bill which he offered to sell for exactly one dollar. There were no takers. The point being that even with people out of work and on the verge of starvation, they were so intent on not being suckers that they turned down an easy profit of nineteen hundred percent."

"Twenty for one? This was twenty for five."

"Oh, well, you know, Bernie, inflation," he said, laughing again. "And these days it's more likely to be a television show."

"Television? You should have seen the way the guy was dressed!"

"Just an extra, logical touch to make people refuse to take the offer seriously. University research people operate much the same way. A few years back, a group of sociologists began an investigation of the public's reaction to sidewalk solicitors in charity drives. You know, those people who jingle little boxes on

street corners: HELP THE TWO-HEADED CHILDREN, RE-
LIEF FOR FLOOD-RAVAGED ATLANTIS? Well, they
dressed up some of their students—"

"You think he was on the level, then, this guy?"

"I think there is a good chance that he was. I don't
see why he would have left his card with you, though."

"That I can figure—now. If it's a TV stunt, there
must be a lot of other angles wrapped up in it. A
giveaway show with cars, refrigerators, a castle in
Scotland, all kinds of loot."

"A giveaway show? Well, yes—it could be."

I hung up, took a deep breath, and called Eksar's
hotel. He was registered there all right. And he'd just
come in.

I went downstairs fast and took a cab. Who knew
what other connections he'd made by now?

Going up in the elevator, I kept wondering. How did
I go from the twenty-dollar bill to the real big stuff,
the TV giveaway stuff, without letting Eksar know
that I was on to what it was all about? Well, maybe
I'd be lucky. Maybe he'd give me an opening.

I knocked on the door. When he said "Come in," I
went in. But for a second or two I couldn't see a thing.

It was a little room, like all the rooms in that hotel,
little and smelly and stuffy. But he didn't have the
lights on, any electric lights. The window shade was
pulled all the way down.

When my eyes got used to the dark, I was able to
pick out this Ogo Eksar character. He was sitting on
the bed, on the side nearest me. He was still wearing
that crazy rumpled Palm Beach suit.

And you know what? He was watching a program
on a funny little portable TV set that he had on the
bureau. Color TV. Only it wasn't working right. There
were no faces, no pictures, nothing but colors chasing
around. A big blob of red, a big blob of orange and a
wiggly border of blue and green and black. A voice
was talking from it, but all the words were fouled up:
"Wah-wah, de-wah, de-wah."

Just as I went in, he turned it off. "Times Square is a bad neighborhood for TV," I told him. "Too much interference."

"Yes," he said. "Too much interference." He closed up the set and put it away. I wished I'd seen it when it was working right.

Funny thing, you know? I would have expected a smell of liquor in the room. I would have expected to see a couple of empties in the tin trash basket near the bureau. Not a sign.

The only smell in the room was a smell I couldn't recognize. I guess it was the smell of Eksar himself, concentrated.

"Hi," I said, feeling a little uncomfortable because of the way I'd been with him back in the office. So rough I'd been.

He stayed on the bed. "I've got the twenty," he said. "You've got the five?"

"Oh, I guess I've got the five, all right," I said looking in my wallet hard and trying to be funny. He didn't say a word, didn't even invite me to sit down. I pulled out a bill. "OK?"

He leaned forward and stared, as if he could see—in all that dimness—what kind of a bill it was. "OK," he said. "But I'll want a receipt. A notarized receipt."

Well, what the hell, I thought, a notarized receipt. "Then we'll have to go down. There's a druggist on 45th."

"Let's go," he said, getting to his feet with several small coughs that came one, two, three, four, right after one another.

On the way to the druggist, I stopped in a stationery store and bought a book of blank receipts. I filled out most of one right there. New York, N.Y., and the date. *Received from Mr. Ogo Eksar the sum of twenty dollars for a five-dollar bill bearing the serial number.................* "That OK?" I asked him. "I'm putting in the serial number to make it look as if you want that particular bill, you know, what the lawyers call the value-received angle."

He screwed his head around and read the receipt. Then he checked the serial number of the bill I was holding. He nodded.

We had to wait for the druggist to get through with a couple of customers. When I signed the receipt, he read it to himself, shrugged and went ahead and stamped it with his seal.

I paid him the two bits; I was the one making the profit.

Eksar slid a crisp new twenty to me along the counter. He watched while I held it up to the light, first one side, then the other.

"Good bill?" he asked.

"Yes. You understand: I don't know you, I don't know your money."

"Sure. I'd do it myself with a stranger." He put the receipt and my five-dollar bill in his pocket and started to walk away.

"Hey," I said. "You in a hurry?"

"No." He stopped, looking puzzled. "No hurry. But you've got the twenty for a five. We made the deal. It's all over."

"All right, so we made the deal. How about a cup of coffee?"

He hesitated.

"It's on me," I told him. "I'll be a big shot for a dime. Come on, let's have a cup of coffee."

Now he looked worried. "You don't want to back out? I've got the receipt. It's all notarized. I gave you a twenty, you gave me a five. We made a deal."

"It's a deal, it's a deal," I said, shoving him into an empty booth. "It's a deal, it's all signed, sealed and delivered. Nobody's backing out. I just want to buy you a cup of coffee."

His face cleared up, all the way through that dirt. "No coffee. Soup. I'll have some mushroom soup."

"Fine, fine. Soup, coffee, I don't care. I'll have coffee."

I sat there and studied him. He hunched over the soup and dragged it into his mouth, spoonful after spoonful, the living picture of a bum who hadn't eaten all day. But pure essence of bum, triple-distilled, the label of a fine old firm.

A guy like this should be lying in a doorway trying to say no to a cop's night stick, he should be coughing his alcoholic guts out. He shouldn't be living in a real honest-to-God hotel, or giving me a twenty for a five, or eating anything as respectable as mushroom soup.

But it made sense. A TV giveaway show, they want to do this, they hire a damn good actor, the best money can buy, to toss their dough away. A guy who'll be so good a bum that people'll just laugh in his face when he tries to give them a deal with a profit.

"You don't want to buy anything else?" I asked him,

He held the spoon halfway to his mouth and stared at me suspiciously. "Like what?"

"Oh, I don't know. Like maybe you want to buy a ten for a fifty. Or a twenty for a hundred dollars?"

He thought about it, Eksar did. Then he went back to his soup, shoveling away. "That's no deal," he said contemptuously. "What kind of deal is that?"

"Excuse me for living. I just thought I'd ask. I wasn't trying to take advantage of you." I lit a cigarette and waited.

My friend with the dirty face finished the soup and reached for a paper napkin. He wiped his lips. I watched him: he didn't smudge a spot of the grime around his mouth. He just blotted up the drops of soup. He was dainty in his own special way.

"Nothing else you want to buy? I'm here, I've got time right now. Anything else on your mind, we might as well look into it."

He balled up the paper napkin and dropped it into the soup plate. It got wet. He'd eaten all the mushrooms and left the soup.

"The Golden Gate Bridge," he said all of a sudden.

I dropped the cigarette. "What?"

"The Golden Gate Bridge. The one in San Francisco. I'll buy that. I'll buy it for . . ." He lifted his eyes to the flourescent fixtures in the ceiling and thought for a couple of seconds. ". . . say a hundred and a quarter. A hundred and twenty-five dollars. Cash on the barrel."

"Why the Golden Gate Bridge?" I asked him like an idiot.

"That's the one I want. You asked me what else I wanted to buy—well, that's what else. The Golden Gate Bridge."

"What's the matter with the George Washington Bridge? It's right here in New York, it's across the Hudson River. Why buy something all the way out on the Coast?"

He grinned at me as if he admired my cleverness. "Oh, no," he said, twitching his left shoulder hard. Up, down, up, down. "I know what I want. The Golden Gate Bridge in San Francisco. A hundred and a quarter. Take it or leave it."

"I'll take it. If that's what you want, you're the doctor. But look—all I can sell you is my share of the Golden Gate Bridge, whatever equity in it I may happen to own."

He nodded. "I want a receipt. Put that down on the receipt."

I put it down on the receipt. And back we went. The druggist notarized the receipt, shoved the stamping outfit into the drawer under the counter and turned his back on us. Eksar counted out six twenties and one five from a big roll of bills, all of them starchy new. He put the roll back into his pants pocket and started away again.

"More coffee?" I asked, catching up. "A refill on the soup?"

He turned a very puzzled look at me and kind of twitched all over. "Why? What do you want to sell now?"

I shrugged. "What do you want to buy? You name it. Let's see what other deals we can work out."

This was all taking one hell of a lot of time, but I had no complaints. I'd made a hundred and forty dollars in fifteen minutes. Say a hundred and thirty-eight fifty, if you deducted expenses such as notary fees, coffee, soup—all legitimate expenses, all low. I had no complaints.

But I was waiting for the big one. There had to be a big one.

Of course, it could maybe wait until the TV program itself. They'd be asking me what was on my mind when I was selling Eksar all that crap, and I'd be explaining, and they'd start handing out refrigerators and gift certificates for Tiffany's and . . .

Eksar had said something while I was away in cloudland. Something damn unfamiliar. I asked him to say it again.

"The Sea of Azov," he told me. "In Russia. I'll give you three hundred and eighty dollars for it."

I'd never heard of the place. I pursed my lips and thought for a second. A funny amount—three hundred and eighty. And for a whole damn sea. I tried an angle.

"Make it four hundred and you've got a deal."

He began coughing his head off, and he looked mad. "What's the matter," he asked between coughs, "three hundred and eighty is a bad price? It's a small sea, one of the smallest. It's only fourteen thousand square miles. And do you know what the maximum depth is?"

I looked wise. "It's deep enough."

"Forty-nine feet," Eksar shouted. "That's all, forty-nine feet! Where are you going to do better than three hundred and eighty for a sea like that?"

"Take it easy," I said, patting his dirty shoulder. "Let's split the difference. You say three eighty, I want four hundred. How about leaving it at three ninety?" I didn't really care: ten bucks more, ten bucks less. But I wanted to see what would happen.

He calmed down. "Three hundred and ninety dollars for the Sea of Azov," he muttered to himself, a little sore at being a sucker, at being taken. "All I want is the sea itself; it's not as if I'm asking you to throw in the Kerch Strait, or maybe a port like Taganrog or Osipenko . . ."

"Tell you what." I held up my hands. "I don't want to be hard. Give me my three ninety and I'll throw in the Kerch Strait as a bonus. Now how about that?"

He studied the idea. He sniffled. He wiped his nose with the back of his hand. "All right," he said, finally. "It's a deal. Azov *and* the Kerch Strait for three hundred ninety."

Bang! went the druggist's stamp. The bangs were getting louder.

Eksar paid me with six fifties, four twenties and a ten, all new-looking bills from that thick roll in his pants pocket.

I thought about the fifties still on the roll, and I felt the spit start to ball up in my mouth.

"OK," I said. "Now what?"

"You still selling?"

"For the right price, sure. You name it."

"There's lots of stuff I could use," he sighed. "But do I need it right now? That's what I have to ask myself."

"Right now is when you've got a chance to buy it. Later—who knows? I may not be around, there may be other guys bidding against you, all kinds of things can happen." I waited awhile, but he just kept scowling and coughing. "How about Australia?" I suggested. "Could you use Australia for, say, five hundred bucks? Or Antarctica? I could give you a real nice deal on Antarctica."

He looked interested. "Antarctica? What would you want for it? No—I'm not getting anywhere. A little piece here, a little piece there. It all costs so much."

"You're getting damn favorable prices, buddy, and

you know it. You couldn't do better buying at wholesale."

"Then how about wholesale? How much for the whole thing?"

I shook my head. "I don't know what you're talking about. What whole thing?"

He looked impatient. "The whole thing. The world. Earth."

"Hey," I said. "That's a lot."

"Well, I'm tired of buying a piece at a time. Will you give me a wholesale price if I buy it all?"

I shook my head, kind of in and out, not yes, not no. Money was coming up, the big money. This was where I was supposed to laugh in his face and walk away. I didn't even crack a smile. "For the whole planet—sure, you're entitled to a wholesale price. But what is it, I mean, exactly *what* do you want to buy?"

"Earth," he said, moving close to me so that I could smell his stinking breath. "I want to buy Earth. Lock, stock and barrel."

"It's got to be a good price. I'll be selling out completely."

"I'll make it a good price. But this is the deal. I pay two thousand dollars, cash. I get Earth, the whole planet, and you have to throw in some stuff on the Moon. Fishing rights, mineral rights and rights to buried treasure. How about it?"

"It's a hell of a lot."

"I know it's a lot," he agreed. "But I'm paying a lot."

"Not for what you're asking. Let me think about it."

This was the big deal, the big giveaway. I didn't know how much money the TV people had given him to fool around with, but I was pretty sure two thousand was just a starting point. Only what was a sensible, businesslike price for the whole world?

I mustn't be made to look like a penny-ante chiseler on TV. There was a top figure Eksar had been given by the program director.

"You really want the whole thing," I said, turning back to him, "the Earth and the Moon?"

He held up a dirty hand. "Not all the Moon. Just those rights on it. The rest of the Moon you can keep."

"It's still a lot. You've got to go a hell of a lot higher than two thousand dollars for any hunk of real estate that big."

Eksar began wrinkling and twitching. "How—how much higher?"

"Well, let's not kid each other. This is the big time now! We're not talking about bridges or rivers or seas. This is a whole world and part of another that you're buying. It takes dough. You've got to be prepared to spend dough."

"How much?" He looked as if he were jumping up and down inside his dirty Palm Beach suit. People going in and out of the store kept staring at us. "How *much*?" he whispered.

"Fifty thousand. It's a damn low price. And you know it."

Eksar went limp all over. Even his weird eyes seemed to sag. "You're crazy," he said in a low, hopeless voice. "You're out of your head."

He turned and started for the revolving door, walking in a kind of used-up way that told me I'd really gone over the line. He didn't look back once. He just wanted to get far, far away.

I grabbed the bottom of his filthy jacket and held on tight.

"Look, Eksar," I said, fast, as he pulled. "I went over your budget, way over, I can see that. But you know you can do better than two thousand. I want as much as I can get. What the hell, I'm taking time out to bother with you. How many other guys would?"

That got him. He cocked his head, then began nodding. I let go of his jacket as he came around. We were connecting again!

"Good. You level with me, and I'll level with you.

Go up a little higher. What's your best price? What's the best you can do?"

He stared down the street, thinking, and his tongue came out and licked at the side of his dirty mouth. His tongue was dirty, too. I mean that! Some kind of black stuff, grease or grime, was all over his tongue.

"How about," he said, after a while, "how about twenty-five hundred? That's as high as I can go. I don't have another cent."

He was like me: he was a natural bargainer.

"You can go to three thousand," I urged. "How much is three thousand? Only another five hundred. Look what you get for it. Earth, the whole planet, and fishing and mineral rights and buried treasure, all that stuff on the Moon. How's about it?"

"I can't. I just can't. I wish I could." He shook his head as if to shake loose all those ties and twitches. "Maybe this way, I'll go as high as twenty-six hundred. For that, you will give me Earth and just fishing rights and buried-treasure rights on the Moon? You keep the mineral rights. I'll do without them."

"Make it twenty-eight hundred and you can have the mineral rights, too. You want them, I can tell you do. Treat yourself. Just two hundred bucks more, and you can have them."

"I can't have everything. Some things cost too much. How about twenty-six fifty, without the mineral rights and without the buried-treasure rights?"

We were both really swinging. I could feel it.

"This is my absolutely last offer," I told him. "I can't spend all day on this. I'll go down to twenty-seven hundred and fifty, and not a penny less. For that, I'll give you Earth and just fishing rights on the Moon. Or just buried-treasure rights. You pick whichever one you want."

"All right," he said. "You're a hard man; we'll do it your way."

"Twenty-seven fifty for the Earth and either fishing rights or buried-treasure rights on the Moon?"

"No, twenty-seven even, and no rights on the Moon. I'll forget about that. Twenty-seven even, and all I get is the Earth."

"Deal!" I sang out, and we struck hands. We shook on it.

Then, with my arm around his shoulders—what did I care about the dirt on his clothes when the guy was worth twenty-seven hundred dollars to me?—we marched back to the drugstore.

"I want a receipt," he reminded me.

"Right," I said. "But I put the same stuff on it: that I'm selling you whatever equity I own or have a right to sell. You're getting a lot for your money."

"You're getting a lot of money for what you're selling," he came right back. I liked him. Twitches and dirt or not, he was my kind of guy.

We got back to the druggist for notarization, and, honest, I've never seen a man look more disgusted in my life. "Business is good, huh?" he said. "You two are sure hotting it up."

"Listen, you," I told him. "You just notarize." I showed the receipt to Eksar. "This the way you want it?"

He studied it, coughing. "Whatever equity you own or have a right to sell. All right. And put in, you know, in your capacity as sales agent, your professional capacity."

I changed the receipt and signed it. The druggist notarized.

Eksar brought that lump of money out of his pants pocket. He counted out fifty-four crisp new fifties and laid them on the glass counter. Then he picked up the receipt, folded it and put it away. He started for the door.

I grabbed up the money and went with him. "Anything else?"

"Nothing else," he said. "It's all over. We made our deal."

"I know, but we might find something else, another item."

"There's nothing else to find. We made our deal."
And his voice told me he really meant it. It didn't
have a trace of the tell-me-more whine that you've got
to hear before there's business.

I came to a stop and watched him push out through
the revolving door. He went right out into the street
and turned left and kept moving, all fast, as if he was
in a hell of a hurry.

There was no more business. OK. I had thirty-two
hundred and thirty dollars in my wallet that I'd made
in one morning.

But how good had I really been? I mean, what was
the top figure in the show's budget? How close had I
come to it?

I had a contact who maybe could find out—Morris
Burlap.

Morris Burlap is in business like me, only he's a
theatrical agent, sharp, real sharp. Instead of selling
a load of used copper wire, say, or an option on a
corner lot in Brooklyn, he sells talent. He sells a
bunch of dancers to a hotel in the mountains, a piano
player to a bar, a disc jockey or a comic to late-night
radio. The reason he's called Morris Burlap is because
of these heavy Harris-tweed suits he wears winter
and summer, every day in the year. They reinforce
the image, he says.

I called him from a telephone booth near the entrance and filled him in on the giveaway show. "Now,
what I want to find out—"

"Nothing to find out," he cut in. "There's no such
show, Bernie."

"There sure as hell is, Morris. One you haven't
heard of."

"There's no such show. Not in the works, not being
rehearsed, not anywhere. Look: before a show gets to
where it's handing out this kind of dough, it's got to
have a slot, it's got to have air time all bought. And
before it even buys air time, a packager has prepared
a pilot. By then I'd have gotten a casting call—I'd

have heard about it a dozen different ways. Don't try
to tell me my business, Bernie; when I say there's no
such show, there's no such show."

So damn positive he was. I had a crazy idea all of a
sudden and turned it off. No. Not that. No.

"Then it's a newspaper or college research thing,
like Ricardo said?"

He thought it over. I was willing to sit in that stuffy
telephone booth and wait; Morris Burlap has a good
head. "Those damn documents, those receipts, newspapers and colleges doing research don't operate that
way. And nuts don't either. I think you're being taken,
Bernie. How you're being taken, I don't know, but
you're being taken."

That was enough for me. Morris Burlap can smell a
hustle through sixteen feet of rock-wool insulation.
He's never wrong. Never.

I hung up, sat, thought. The crazy idea came back
and exploded.

A bunch of characters from outer space, say they
want Earth. They want it for a colony, for a vacation
resort, who the hell knows what they want it for?
They got their reasons. They're strong enough and
advanced enough to come right down and take over.
But they don't want to do it cold. They need a legal
leg.

All right. These characters from outer space, maybe
all they had to have was a piece of paper from just one
genuine, accredited human being, signing the Earth
over to them. No, that couldn't be right. *Any* piece of
paper? Signed by *any* Joe Jerk?

I jammed a dime into the telephone and called
Ricardo's college. He wasn't in. I told the switchboard
girl it was very important: she said, all right, she'd
ring around and try to spot him.

All that stuff, I kept thinking, the Golden Gate
Bridge, the Sea of Azov—they were as much a part of
the hook as the twenty-for-a-five routine. There's one

sure test of what an operator is really after: when he
stops talking, closes up shop and goes away.

With Eksar, it had been the Earth. All that baloney
about extra rights on the Moon! They were put in to
cover up the real thing he was after, for extra bargaining power.

That's how Eksar had worked on me. It was like
he'd made a special study of how I operate. From me
alone, he had to buy.

But why me?

All that stuff on the receipt, about my equity, about
my professional capacity, what the hell did it mean? I
don't own Earth; I'm not in the planet-selling business. You have to own a planet before you can sell it.
That's law.

So what could I have sold Eksar? I don't own any
real estate. Are they going to take over my office,
claim the piece of sidewalk I walk on, attach the stool
in the diner where I have my coffee?

That brought me back to my first question. Who
was this "they"? Who the holy hell were "they"?

The switchboard girl finally dug up Ricardo. He was
irritated. "I'm in the middle of a faculty meeting,
Bernie. Call you back?"

"Just listen a second," I begged. "I'm in something,
I don't know whether I'm coming or going. I've got to
have some advice."

Talking fast—I could hear a lot of big-shot voices in
the background—I ran through the story from the
time I'd called him in the morning. What Eksar looked
like and smelled like, the funny portable color-TV he
had, the way he'd dropped all those Moon rights and
gone charging off once he'd been sure of the Earth.
What Morris Burlap had said, the suspicions I'd been
building up, everything. "Only thing is," I laughed a
little to show that maybe I wasn't really serious about
it, "who am I to make such a deal, huh?"

He seemed to be thinking hard for a while. "I don't

know, Bernie, it's possible. It does fit together. There's the UN aspect."

"UN aspect? Which UN aspect?"

"The UN aspect of the situation. The—uh—study of the UN on which we collaborated two years ago." He was using double talk because of the college people around him. But I got it. I got it.

Eksar must have known all along about the deal that Ricardo had thrown my way, getting rid of old, used-up office equipment for the United Nations here in New York. They'd given me what they called an authorizing document. In a file somewhere there was a piece of paper, United Nations stationery, saying that I was their authorized sales agent for surplus, secondhand equipment and installations.

Talk about a legal leg!

"You think it'll stand up?" I asked Ricardo. "I can see how the Earth is secondhand equipment and installations. But surplus?"

"International law is a tangled field, Bernie. And this might be even more complex. You'd be wise to do something about it."

"But what? What should I do, Ricardo?"

"Bernie," he said, sounding sore as hell, "I told you I'm in a faculty meeting, damn it! A *faculty* meeting!" And he hung up.

I ran out of the drugstore like a wild man and grabbed a cab back to Eksar's hotel.

What was I most afraid of? I didn't know: I was so hysterical. This thing was too big-time for a little guy like me, too damn dangerously big-time. It would put my name up in lights as the biggest sellout sucker in history. Who could ever trust me again to make a deal? I had the feeling like somebody had asked me to sell him a snapshot, and I'd said sure, and it turned out to be a picture of the Nike Zeus, you know, one of those top-secret atomic missiles. Like I'd sold out my country by mistake. Only this was worse: I'd sold out my whole goddamn world. I had to buy it back—I had to!

When I got to Eksar's room, I knew he was about ready to check out. He was shoving his funny portable TV in one of those cheap leather grips they sell in chain stores. I left the door open, for the light.

"We made our deal," he said. "It's over. No more deals."

I stood there, blocking his way. "Eksar," I told him, "listen to what I figured out. First, you're not human. Like me, I mean."

"I'm a hell of a lot more human than you, buddy boy."

"Maybe. But you're not from Earth—that's my point. Why you need Earth—"

"I *don't* need it. I'm an agent. I represent someone."

And there it was, straight out, you are right, Morris Burlap! I stared into his fish eyes, now practically pushing into my face. I wouldn't get out of the way. "You're an agent for someone," I repeated slowly. "Who? What do they want Earth for?"

"That's their business. I'm an agent. I just buy for them."

"You work on a commission?"

"I'm not in business for my health."

You sure as hell aren't in it for your health, I thought. *That cough, those tics and twitches*—Then I realized what they meant. This wasn't the kind of air he was used to. Like if I go up to Canada, right away I'm down with diarrhea. It's the water or something.

The dirt on his face was a kind of suntan oil! A protection against our sunlight. Blinds pulled down, face smeared over—and dirt all over his clothes so they'd fit in with his face.

Eksar was no bum. He was anything but. I was the bum. Think fast, Bernie, said to myself. This guy took you, and big!

"How much you work on—ten percent?" No answer: he leaned against me, and he breathed and he twitched.

"I'll top any deal you have, Eksar. You know what I'll give you? Fifteen percent! I hate to see a guy running back and forth for a lousy ten percent."

"What about ethics?" he said hoarsely. "I got a client."

"Look who's bringing up ethics! A guy goes out to buy the whole damn Earth for twenty-seven hundred! You call that ethics?"

Now he got sore. He set down the grip and punched his fist into his hand. "No, I call that business. A deal. I offer, you take. You go away happy, you feel you made out. All of a sudden, here you are back, crying you didn't mean it, you sold too much for the price. Too bad! I got ethics: I don't screw my client for a crybaby."

"I'm not a crybaby. I'm just a poor schnook trying to scratch out a living. Here, I'm up against a big-time operator from another world with all kinds of angles and gimmicks going for him."

"You had these angles, these gimmicks, you wouldn't use them?"

"Certain things I wouldn't do. Don't laugh, Eksar, I mean it. I wouldn't hustle a guy in an iron lung. I wouldn't hustle a poor schnook with a hole-in-the-wall office to sell out his entire planet."

"You really sold," he said. "That receipt will stand up anywhere. And we got the machinery to make it stand up. Once my client takes possession, the human race is finished, it's kaput, forget about it. And you're Mr. Patsy."

It was hot in that hotel-room doorway, and I was sweating like crazy. But I was feeling better. All of a sudden, I'd got the message that Eksar wanted to do business with me. I grinned at him.

He changed color a little under all that dirt. "What's your offer, anyway?" he asked, coughing. "Name a figure."

"*You* name one. You got the property, I got the dough."

"Aah!" he grunted impatiently, and pushed me out

of the way. He was *strong!* I ran after him to the elevator.

"How much you want, Eksar?" I asked him as we were going down.

A shrug. "I got a planet, and I got a buyer for it. You, you're in a jam. The one in a pickle is the one who's got to tickle."

The louse! For every one of my moves, he knew the countermove.

He checked out and I followed him into the street. Down Broadway we went, me offering him the thirty-two hundred and thirty he'd paid me, him saying he couldn't make a living out of shoving the same amount of money back and forth all day. "Thirty-four?" I offered. "I mean, you know, thirty-four fifty?" He just kept walking.

If I didn't get him to name a figure, any figure, I'd be dead.

I ran in front of him. "Eksar, let's stop hustling each other. If you didn't want to sell, you wouldn't be talking to me in the first place. You name a figure. Whatever it is, I'll pay it."

That got a reaction. "You mean it? You won't try to chisel?"

"How can I chisel? I'm over a barrel."

"OK, then. I'll give you a break and save myself a long trip back to my client. What's fair for you and fair for me and fair all around? Let's say eight thousand even?"

Eight thousand—it was almost exactly what I had in the bank. He knew my bank account cold, up to the last statement.

He knew my thoughts cold, too. "You're going to do business with a guy," he said, between coughs, "you check into him a little. You got eight thousand and change. It's not much for saving a guy's neck."

I was boiling. "Not much? Then let me set you straight, you Florence goddamn Nightingale! You're not getting it! A little skin I know maybe I have to give up. But not every cent I own, not for you, not for Earth, not for anybody!"

A cop came up close to see why I was yelling, and I had to calm down until he went away again. "Help! Police! Aliens invading us!" I almost screamed out. What would the street we were standing on look like in ten years if I didn't talk Eksar out of that receipt?

"Eksar, your client takes over Earth waving my receipt—I'll be hung high. But I've got only one life, and my life is buying and selling. I can't buy and sell without capital. Take my capital away, and it makes no difference to me who owns Earth and who doesn't."

"Who the hell do you think you're kidding?" he said.

"I'm not kidding anybody. Honest, it's the truth. Take my capital away, and it makes no difference if I'm alive or if I'm dead."

That last bit of hustle seemed to have reached him. Listen, there were practically tears in my eyes the way I was singing it. How much capital did I need, he wanted to know—five hundred? I told him I couldn't operate one single day with less than seven times that. He asked me if I was really seriously trying to buy my lousy little planet back—or was today my birthday and I was expecting a present from him? "Don't give your presents to me," I told him. "Give them to fat people. They're better than going on a diet."

And so we went. Both of us talking ourselves blue in the faces, swearing by everything, arguing and bargaining, wheeling and dealing. It was touch and go who was going to give up first.

But neither of us did. We both held out until we reached what I'd figured pretty early we were going to wind up with, maybe a little bit more.

Six thousand, one hundred and fifty dollars.

That was the price over and above what Eksar had given me. The final deal. Listen, it could have been worse.

Even so, we almost broke up when we began talking payment.

"Your bank's not far. We could get there before closing."

"Why walk myself into a heart attack? My check's good as gold."

"Who wants a piece of paper? I want cash. Cash is definite."

Finally, I managed to talk him into a check. I wrote it out; he took it and gave me the receipts, all of them. Every last receipt I'd signed. Then he picked up his little satchel and marched away.

Straight down Broadway, without even a goodbye. All business, Eksar was, nothing but business. He didn't look back once.

All business. I found out next morning he'd gone right to the bank and had my check certified before closing time. What do you thing of that? I couldn't do a damn thing: I was out six thousand, one hundred and fifty dollars. Just for talking to someone.

Ricardo said I was a Faust. I walked out of the bank, beating my head with my fist, and I called up him and Morris Burlap and asked them to have lunch with me. I went over the whole story with them in an expensive place that Ricardo picked out. "You're a Faust," he said.

"What Faust?" I asked him. "Who Faust? How Faust?"

So naturally he had to tell us all about Faust. Only I was a new kind of Faust, a 20th-Century American one. The other Fausts, they wanted to know everything. I wanted to own everything.

"But I didn't wind up owning," I pointed out. "I got taken. Six thousand, one hundred and fifty dollars' worth I got taken."

Ricardo chuckled and leaned back in his chair. "O my sweet gold," he said under his breath. "O my sweet gold."

"What?"

"A quotation, Bernie. From Marlowe's *The Tragical History of Dr. Faustus.* I forget the context, but it seems apt. '*O my sweet gold.*'"

I looked from him to Morris Burlap, but nobody can ever tell when Morris Burlap is puzzled. As a matter of fact, he looks more like a professor than Ricardo, him with those thick Harris tweeds and that heavy, thinking look. Ricardo is, you know, a bit too natty.

The two of them added up to all the brains and sharpness a guy could ask for. That's why I was paying out an arm and a leg for this lunch, on top of all my losses with Eksar.

"Morris, tell the truth. You understand him?"

"What's there to understand, Bernie? A quote about the sweet gold? It might be the answer, right there."

Now I looked at Ricardo. He was eating away at a creamy Italian pudding. Two bucks even, those puddings cost in that place.

"Let's say he was an alien," Morris Burlap said. "Let's say he came from somewhere in outer space. OK. Now what would an alien want with U.S. dollars? What's the rate of exchange out there?"

"You mean he needed it to buy some merchandise here on Earth?"

"That's exactly what I mean. But what *kind* of merchandise, that's the question. What could Earth have that he'd want?"

Ricardo finished the pudding and wiped his lips with a napkin. "I think you're on the right track, Morris," he said, and I swung my attention back to him. "We can postulate a civilization far in advance of our own. One that would feel we're not quite ready to know about them. One that has placed primitive little Earth strictly off limits—a restriction only desperate criminals dare ignore."

"From where come criminals, Ricardo, if they're so advanced?"

"Laws produce lawbreakers, Bernie, like hens produce eggs. Civilization has nothing to do with it. I'm beginning to see Eksar now. An unprincipled adventurer, a star-man version of those cutthroats who sailed the South Pacific a hundred years or more ago. Once in a while, a ship would smash upon the coral reefs, and a bloody opportunist out of Boston would be stranded for life among primitive, backward tribesmen. I'm sure you can fill in the rest."

"No, I can't. And if you don't mind, Ricardo—"

Morris Burlap said he'd like another brandy. I ordered it. He came close to smiling as Morris Burlap ever does and leaned toward me confidentially. "Ricardo's got it, Bernie. Put yourself in this guy Eksar's position. He wraps up his spaceship on a dirty little planet which it's against the law to be near in the first place. He can make some half-assed repairs with merchandise that's available here—but he has to buy the stuff. Any noise, any uproar, and he'll be grabbed for a Federal rap in outer space. Say you're Eksar, what do you do?"

I could see it now. "I'd peddle and I'd parlay. Copper bracelets, strings of beads, dollars—whatever I had to lay my hands on to buy the native merchandise, I'd peddle and I'd parlay in deal after deal. Maybe I'd start with a piece of equipment from the ship, then I'd find some novelty item that the natives would go for. But all this is *Earth* business know-how, *human* business know-how."

"Bernie," Ricardo told me, "Indians once traded pretty little shells for beaver pelts at the exact spot where the stock exchange now stands. Some kind of business goes on in Eksar's world, I assure you, but its simplest form would make one of our corporate mergers look like a game of potsy on the sidewalk."

Well, I'd wanted to figure it out. "So I was marked as his fish all the way. I was screwed and blued and tattooed," I mumbled, "by a hustler superman."

Ricardo nodded. "By a businessman's Mephistopheles fleeing the thunderbolts of heaven. He needed to double his money one more time and he'd have enough to repair his ship. He had at his disposal a fantastic sophistication in all the ways of commerce."

"What Ricardo's saying," came an almost soft voice from Morris Burlap, "is the guy who beat you up was a whole lot bigger than you."

My shoulders felt loose, like they were sliding down off my arms. "What the hell," I said. "You get stepped on by a horse or you get stepped on by an elephant. You're still stepped on."

I paid the check, got myself together and went away.

Then I began to wonder if maybe this was really the story after all. They both enjoyed seeing me up there as an interplanetary jerk. Ricardo's a brilliant guy, Morris Burlap's sharp as hell, but so what? Ideas, yes. Facts, no.

So here's a fact.

My bank statement came at the end of the month with that canceled check I'd given Eksar. It had been endorsed by a big store in the Cortlandt Street area. I know that store. I've dealt with them. I went down and asked them about it.

They handle mostly marked-down, surplus electronic equipment. That's what they said Eksar had bought. A walloping big order of transistors and transformers, resistors and printed circuits, electronic tubes, wiring, tools, gimmicks like that. All mixed up, they said, a lot of components that just didn't go together. He'd given the clerk the impression that he had an emergency job to do—and he'd take as close as he could get to the things he actually needed. He'd paid a lot of money for freight charges: delivery was to some backwoods town in northern Canada.

That's a fact, now; I have to admit it. But here's another one.

I've dealt with that store, like I said. Their prices are the lowest in the neighborhood. And why is it, do you think, they can sell so cheap? There's only one answer: because they buy so cheap. They buy at the lowest prices; they don't give a damn about quality:

all they want to know is, how much markup? I've personally sold them job lots of electronic junk that I couldn't unload anywhere else, condemned stuff, badly wired stuff, stuff that was almost dangerous—it's a place to sell to when you've given up on making a profit because you yourself have been stuck wih inferior merchandise in the first place.

You get the picture? It makes me feel rosy all over.

There is Eksar out in space, the way I see it. He's fixed up his ship, good enough to travel, and he's on his way to his next big deal. The motors are humming, the ship is running, and he's sitting there with a big smile on his dirty face: he's thinking how he took me, how easy it was.

He's laughing his head off.

All of a sudden, there's a screech and a smell of burning. That circuit that's running the front motor, a wire just got touched through the thin insulation, the circuit's tearing the hell out of itself. He gets scared. He turns on the auxilliaries. The auxilliaries don't go on—you know why? The vacuum tubes he's using have come to the end of their rope, they didn't have much juice to start with. *Blooie!* That's the rear motor developing a short circuit. *Ka-pow!* That's a defective transformer melting away in the middle of the ship.

And there he is, millions of miles from nowhere, empty space all around him, no more spare parts, tools that practically break in his hands—and not a single, living soul he can hustle.

And here am I, in my office, thinking about it, and *I'm* laughing my head off. Because it's just possible, it just could happen, that what goes wrong with his ship is one of the half-dozen or so job lots of really bad electronic equipment that I personally, me, Bernie the Faust, that I sold to that surplus store at one time or another.

That's all I'd ask. Just to have it happen that way.

Faust. He'd have Faust from me then. Right in the

face, Faust. On the head, splitting it open, Faust. Faust I'd give him!

The only trouble is I'll never know. All I know for sure is that I'm the only guy in history who sold the whole goddamn planet.

And bought it back.

ISHMAEL IN LOVE

by ROBERT SILVERBERG

The story of the transformation of Robert Silverberg from competent genre writer to an author of the first rank is now well known, and does not have to be repeated here. Suffice it to say that his last twenty works in this field have expanded its boundaries and at the same time proved that superior handling and execution can inject new life into the most mundane of sf's conventions. After a long retirement, he recently returned to science fiction with *Lord Valentine's Castle* (1980).

"Ishmael in Love" is one of the most unusual love stories you will ever read.

CALL me Ishmael. All human beings who know me do. My own kind does not make use of the unit-structural designation ("name") to distinguish individuals, but this is the name the humans gave to me, and it will do. I was named by Miss Lisabeth Calkins, for whom I feel protective-chivalrous-sexual emotions ("love"). Throughout my narrative it is understood that the designation "Ishmael" refers only to myself.

I am a member of an intelligent aquatic mammalian nonprimate nonhuman species, *Tursiops truncatus*, a bottle-nosed dolphin. I am eleven years old, which is to say that I am fully mature in all respects. My weight is 175 kg and my total length is 2.9 meters. I am employed at Gerard-Worzel Seawater Recovery Station, St. Croix, Virgin Islands, in a maintence capacity, having commenced there on your date of August 14, 1994. To my own species I am sexually desirable and also highly regarded for my mental development. I have a large vocabulary. I communicate well with members of *H. sapiens*. I have considerable mechanical ability, as you can see by my successs in switching on the electronic-acoustic device though which I am dictating this memoir.

I am a lonely mammalian organism who has commited acts of heroism on behalf of your species and wishes only the reward of a more intimate relationship ("love") with Miss Lisabeth Calkins. I beseech compassionate members of *H. sapiens* to speak favorably of me to her. I am loyal, trustworthy, reliable, devoted, and extremely intelligent. I would endeavor to give her stimulating companionship and emotional fulfillment ("happiness") in all respects within my power.

Permit me to explain the pertinent circumstances.

Category 1: My Employment.

Gerard-Worzel Seawater Recovery Station occupies a prominent position on the north shore of the island of St. Croix, in the West Indies. It operates on the atmospheric-condensation principle. All this I know from Miss Calkins ("Lisabeth"), who has described its workings to me in great detail. The purpose of our installation is to recover some of the fresh water, estimated at 200 million gallons per day, carried as vapor in the lower hundred meters of air sweeping over each kilometer of the windward side of the island.

A pipe .9 meter in diameter takes in cold seawater at depths of up to 900 meters and carries it approximately 2 kilometers to our station. The pipe delivers some 30 million gallons of water a day at a temperature of 5 degrees C. This is pumped toward our condenser, which intercepts approximately 1 billion cubic meters of warm tropical air each day. This air has a temperature of 25 degrees C. and a relative humidity of 70 to 80 percent. Upon exposure to the cold seawater in the condenser, the air cools to 10 degrees C. and reaches a humidity of 100 percent, permitting us to extract approximately 16 gallons of water per cubic meter of air. This salt-free ("fresh") water is delivered to the main water system of the island, for St. Croix is deficient in a natural supply of water suitable for consumption by human beings. It is frequently said by government officials who visit our installation on various ceremonial occasions that without our plant the great industrial expension of St. Croix would have been wholly impossible.

For reasons of economy we operate in conjunction with an aquicultural enterprise ("the fish farm") that puts our wastes to work. Once our seawater has been pumped through the condenser, it must be discarded; however, because it originates in a low-level ocean area, its content of dissolved phosphates and nitrates is 1500 percent greater than at the surface. This nutrient-rich water is pumped from our condenser into an adjoining circular lagoon of natural origin ("the coral corral") which is stocked with fish. In such an enhanced environment the fish are highly productive, and the yield of food is great enough to offset the costs of operating our pumps.

(Misguided human beings sometimes question the morality of using dolphins to help maintain fish farms. They believe it is degrading to compel us to produce fellow aquatic creatures to be eaten by man. May I simply point out, first, that none of us works here under compulsion, and second, that my species sees nothing immoral about feeding on aquatic creatures. We eat fish ourselves.)

My role in the functioning of the Gerard-Worzel Seawater Recovery Station is an important one. I

("Ishmael") serve as Foreman of the Intake Maintenance Squad. I lead nine members of my species. Our assignment is to monitor the intake valves of the main seawater pipe. These valves frequently become fouled through the presence on them of low-phylum organisms such as starfish or algae, hampering the efficiency of the installation. Our task is to descend at periodic intervals and clear the obstruction. Normally this can be achieved without the need for manipulative organs ("fingers") with which we are unfortunately not equipped.

(Certain individuals among you have objected that it is improper to make use of dolphins in the labor force when members of *H. sapiens* are out of work. The intelligent reply to this is that, first, we are designed by evolution to function superbly underwater without special breathing equipment, and second, that only a highly skilled human being could perform our function, and such human beings are themselves in short supply in the labor force.)

I have held my post for two years and four months. In that time there had been no significant interruption of intake capacity of the valves I maintain.

As compensation for my work ("salary") I receive an ample supply of food. One could hire a mere shark for such pay, of course, but above and beyond my daily pails of fish I also receive such intangibles as the companionship of human beings and the opportunity to develop my latent intelligence through access to reference spools, vocabulary expanders, and various training devices. As you can see, I have made the most of my opportunities.

Category 2: Miss Lisabeth Calkins.
Her dossier is on file here. I have had access to it though the spool-reader mounted at the edge of the dolphin exercise tank. By spoken instruction I can bring into view anything in the station files, although

I doubt that it was anticipated by anyone that a dolphin should want to read the personnel dossiers.

She is twenty-seven years old. Thus she is the same generation as my genetic predecessors ("parents"). However, I do not share the prevailing cultural taboo of many *H. sapiens* against emotional relationships with older women. Besides, after compensating for differences in species, it will be seen that Miss Lisabeth and I are of the same age. She reached sexual maturity approximately half her lifetime ago. So did I.

(I must admit that she is considered slightly past the optimum age at which human females take a permanent mate. I assume she does not engage in the practice of temporary mating, since her dossier shows no indication that she has reproduced. It is possible that humans do not necessarily produce offspring at each yearly mating, or even that matings take place at random, unpredictable times not related to the reproductive process at all. This seems strange and somehow perverse to me, yet I infer from some data I have seen that it may be the case. There is little information on human mating habits in the material accessible to me. I must learn more.)

Lisabeth, as I allow myself privately to call her, stands 1.8 meters tall (humans do not measure themselves by "length") and weighs 52 kg. Her hair is golden ("blond") and is worn long. Her skin, though darkened by exposure to the sun, is quite fair. The irises of her eyes are blue. From my conversations with humans I have learned that she is considered quite beautiful. From words I have overheard while at surface level I realize that most males at the station feel intense sexual desires toward her. I regard her as beautiful also, inasmuch as I am capable of responding to human beauty. (I think I am.) I am not sure if I feel actual sexual desire for Lisabeth; more likely what troubles me is a generalized longing for her presence and her closeness, which I translate into sexual terms simply as a means of making it comprehensible to me.

Beyond doubt she does not have the traits I normally seek in a mate (prominent beak, sleek fins). Any attempt at our making love in the anatomical sense would certainly result in pain or injury to her. That is not my wish. The physical traits that make her so desirable to the males of her species (highly developed milk glands, shining hair, delicate features, long hind limbs or "legs," and so forth) have no particular importance to me, and in some instances actually have a negative value. As in the case of the two milk glands in her pectoral region, which jut forward from her body in such a fashion that they must surely slow her when she swims. This is poor design, and I am incapable of finding poor design beautiful in any way. Evidently Lisabeth regrets the size and placement of those glands herself since she is careful to conceal them at all times by a narrow covering. The others at the station, who are all males and therefore have only rudimentary milk glands that in no way destroy the flow of lines of their bodies, leave them bare.

What, then, is the cause of my attraction for Lisabeth?

It arises out of the need I feel for her companionship. I believe that she understands me as no member of my own species does. Hence I will be happier in her company than away from her. This impression dates from our earliest meeting. Lisabeth, who is a specialist in human-cetacean relations, came to St. Croix four months ago, and I was requested to bring my maintenance group to the surface to be introduced to her. I leaped high for a good view and saw instantly that she was of a finer sort than the humans I already knew; her body was more delicate, looking at once fragile and powerful, and her gracefulness was a welcome change from the thick awkwardness of the human males I knew. Nor was she covered with the coarse body hair that my kind finds so distressing. (I did not at first know that Lisabeth's difference from the others at the station was the result of her being female. I had never seen a human female before. But I quickly learned.)

I came forward, made contact with the acoustic transmitter, and said, "I am the Forman of the Intake Maintenance Squad. I have the unit-structual designation TT-66"

"Don't you have a name?" she asked.

"Meaning of term, name?"

"Your—your unit-structural designation—but not just TT-66. I mean, that's no good at all. For example, my name's Lisabeth Calkins. And I—" She shook her head and looked at the plant supervisor. "Don't these workers have *names?*"

Their supervisor did not see why dolphins should have names. Lisabeth did—she was greatly concerned about it—and since she now was in charge of liaison with us, she gave us names on the spot. Thus I was dubbed Ishmael. It was, she told me, the name of a man who had gone to sea, had many wonderful experiences, and put them all down in a story-spool that every cultured person played. I have since had access to Ishmael's story—that *other* Ishmael—and I agree that it is remarkable. For a human being, he had unusual insight into the ways of whales, who are, however, stupid creatures for whom I have little respect. I am proud to carry Ishmael's name.

After she had named us, Lisabeth leaped into the sea and swam with us. I must tell you that most of us feel a sort of contempt for you humans because you are such poor swimmers. Perhaps it is a mark of my above-normal intelligence or greater compassion that I have no such scorn in me. I admire you for the zeal and energy you give to swimming, and you are quite good at it, considering all your handicaps. As I remind my people, you manage far more ably. in the water than we would on land. Anyway, Lisabeth swam well, by human standards, and we tolerantly adjusted our pace to hers. We frolicked in the water awhile. Then she seized my dorsal fin and said, "Take me for a ride, Ishmael!"

I tremble now to recollect the contact of her body with mine. She sat astride me, her legs gripping my body tightly, and off I sped at close to full velocity, soaring at surface level. Her laughter told of her delight as I launched myself again and again through the air. It was a physical display in which I made no use of my extraordinary mental capacity; I was, if you will, simply showing off my dolphinhood. Lisabeth's response was ecstatic. Even when I plunged, taking her so deep she might have feared harm from the pressure, she kept her grip and showed no alarm. When we breached the surface again, she cried out in joy.

Through sheer animality I had made my first impact on her. I knew human beings well enough to be able to interpret her flushed, exhilarated expression as I returned her to shore. My challenge now was to expose her to my higher traits—to show her that even among dolphins I was unusually swift to learn, unusually capable of comprehending the universe.

I was already then in love with her.

During the weeks that followed we had many conversations. I am not flattering myself when I tell you that she quickly realized how extraordinary I am. My vocabulary, which was already large when she came to the station, grew rapidly under the stimulus of Lisabeth's presence. I learned from her; she gave me access to spools no dolphin was thought likely to wish to play; I developed insights into my environment that astonished even myself. In short order I reached my present peak of attainment. I think you will agree that I can express myself more eloquently than most human beings. I trust that the computer doing the printout on this memoir will not betray me by inserting inappropriate punctuation or deviating from the proper spellings of the words whose sound I utter.

My love for Lisabeth deepened and grew more rich.

I learned the meaning of jealousy for the first time when I saw her running arm in arm along the beach with Dr. Madison, the power-plant man. I knew anger when I overheard the lewd and vulgar remarks of the human males as Lisabeth walked by. My fascination with her led me to explore many avenues of human experience; I did not dare talk of such things with her, but from other personnel at the base who sometimes talked with me, I learned certain aspects of the phenomenon humans call "love." I also obtained explanations of the vulgar words spoken by males here behind her back: most of them pertained to a wish to mate with Lisabeth (apparently on a temporary basis), but there were also highly favorable descriptions of her milk glands (why are humans so aggressively mammalian?) and even of the rounded area in back, just above the place where her body divides into the two hind limbs. I confess that that region fascinates me also. It seems so *alien* for one's body to split like that in the middle!

I never explicitly stated my feelings toward Lisabeth. I tried to lead her slowly toward an understanding that I loved her. Once she came overtly to that awareness, I thought, we might begin to plan some sort of future for ourselves together.

What a fool I was!

Category 3: The Conspiracy.

A male voice said, "How in hell are you going to bribe a dolphin?"

A different voice, more cultured, replied, "Leave it to me."

"What do you give him? Ten cans of sardines?"

"This one's special. Peculiar, even. He's scholarly. We can get to him."

They did not know that I could hear them. I was drifting near the surface in my rest tank, between shifts. Our hearing is acute, and I was well within auditory range. I sensed at once that something was amiss, but I kept my position, pretending I knew nothing.

"Ishmael!" one man called out. "Is that you, Ishmael?"

I rose to the surface and came to the edge of the tank. Three male humans stood there. One was a technician at the station; the other two I had never seen before, and they wore body covering from their feet to their throats, marking them at once as strangers here. The technician I despised, for he was one of the ones who had made vulgar remarks about Lisabeth's milk glands.

He said, "Look at him, gentlemen. Worn out in his prime! A victim of human exploitation!" To me he said, "Ishmael, these gentlemen come from the League for the Prevention of Cruelty to Intelligent Species. You know about that?"

"No," I said.

"They're trying to put an end to dolphin exploitation. The criminal use of our planet's only other truly intelligent species in slave labor. They want to help you."

"I am no slave. I receive compensation for my work."

"A few stinking fish!" said the fully dressed man to the left of the technician. "They exploit you, Ishmael! They give you dangerous, dirty work and don't pay you worth a damn!"

His companion said, "It has to stop. We want to serve notice to the world that the age of enslaved dolphins is over. Help us, Ishmael. Help us help you!"

I need not say that I was hostile to their purported purposes. A more literal-minded dolphin than I might well have said so at once, and spoiled their plot. But I shrewdly said, "What do you want me to do?"

"Foul the intakes," said the technician quickly.

Despite myself I snorted in anger and surprise. "Betray a sacred trust? How can I?"

"It's for your own sake, Ishmael. Here's how it works: you and your crew will plug up the intakes, and the water plant will stop working. The whole island will panic. Human maintenance crews will go down to see what's what, but as soon as they clear the valves, you go back and foul them again. Emergency water supplies will have to be rushed to St. Croix. It'll focus public attention on the fact that this island is dependent on dolphin labor—underpaid, overworked dolphin labor! During the crisis we'll step forward to tell the world your story. We'll get every human being to cry out in outrage against the way you're being treated."

I did not say that I felt no outrage myself. Instead I cleverly replied, "There could be dangers in this for me."

"Nonsense!"

"They will ask me why I have not cleared the valves. It is my responsibility. There will be trouble."

For a while we debated the point. Then the technician said, "Look, Ishmael, we know there are a few risks. But we're willing to offer extra payment if you'll handle the job."

"Such as?"

"Spools. Anything you'd like to hear, we'll get for you. I know you've got literary interests. Plays, poetry, novels, all that sort of stuff. After hours we'll feed literature to you by the bushel, if you'll help us."

I had to admire their slickness. They knew exactly how to motivate me.

"It's a deal," I said.

"Just tell us what you'd like."

"Anything about love."

"*Love?*"

"Love. Man and woman. Bring me love poems. Bring me stories of famous lovers. Bring me descriptions of sexual embrace. I must understand these things."

"He wants the *Kama Sutra*," said the one on the left.

"Then we bring him the *Kama Sutra*," said the one on the right.

*   *   *

Category 4: My Response to the Criminals.

They did not actually bring me the *Kama Sutra*. But they brought me a good many other things, including one spool that quoted at length from the *Kama Sutra*. For several weeks I devoted myself intensively to a study of human love literature. There were maddening gaps in the text, and I still lack real comprehension of much that goes on between man and woman. The joining of body to body does not puzzle me, but I am baffled by the dialectics of the chase, in which the male must be predatory and the woman must pretend to be out of season; I am mystified by the morality of temporary mating as distinct from permanent ("marriage"); I have no grasp of the intricate systems of taboos and prohibitions that humans have invented. This has been my one intellectual failure: at the end of my studies I knew little more of how to conduct myself with Lisabeth than I had before the conspirators had begun slipping me spools in secret.

Now they called on me to do my part.

Naturally I could not betray the station. I knew that these men were not the enlightened foes of dolphin exploitation that they claimed to be. For some private reason they wished the station shut down, that was all, and they had used their supposed sympathies with my species to win my cooperation. I do not feel exploited.

Was it improper of me to accept spools from them if I had no intention of aiding them? I doubt it. They wished to use me; instead I used them. Sometimes a superior species must exploit its inferiors to gain knowledge.

They came to me and asked me to foul the valves that evening. I said, "I am not certain what you actually wish me to do. Will you instruct me again?"

Cunningly I had switched on a recording device used by Lisabeth in her study sessions with the station dolphins. So they told me again how fouling the valves would throw the island into panic and cast a spotlight on dolphin abuse. I questioned them repeatedly, drawing out details and also giving each man a chance to place his voiceprints on record. When proper incrimination had been achieved, I said, "Very well. On my next shift I'll do as you say."

"And the rest of your maintenance squad?"

"I'll order them to leave the valves untended for the sake of our species."

They left the station, looking quite satisfied with themselves. When they were gone, I beaked the switch that summoned Lisabeth. She came from her living quarters rapidly. I showed her the spool in the recording machine.

"Play it," I said grandly. "And then notify the island police!"

Category 5: The Reward of Heroism.

The arrests were made. The three men had no concern with dolphin expolitation whatever. They were members of a disruptive group ("revolutionaries") attempting to delude a naïve dolphin into helping them cause chaos on the island. Through my loyalty, courage and intelligence I had thwarted them.

Afterward Lisabeth came to me at the rest tank and said, "You were wonderful, Ishmael. To play along with them like that, to make them record their own confession—marvelous! You're a wonder among dolphins, Ishmael."

I was in a transport of joy.

The moment had come. I blurted, "Lisabeth, I love you."

My words went booming around the walls of the tank as they burst from the speakers. Echoes amplified and modulated them into grotesque barking noises more worthy of some miserable moron of a seal. "Love you . . . love you . . . love you . . ."

"Why, Ishmael!"

"I can't tell you how much you mean to me. Come

live with me and be my love. Lisabeth, Lisabeth, Lisabeth!"

Torrents of poetry broke from me. Gales of passionate rhetoric escaped my beak. I begged her to come down into the tank and let me embrace her. She laughed and said she wasn't dressed for swimming. It was true: she had just come from town after the arrests. I implored. I begged. She yielded. We were alone; she removed her garments and entered the tank; for an instant I looked upon her beauty bare. The sight left me shaken—those ugly, swinging milk glands normally so wisely concealed, the strips of sickly white skin where the sun had been unable to reach, that unexpected patch of additional body hair—but once she was in the water I forgot my love's imperfections and rushed toward her. "Love!" I cried. "Blessed love!" I wrapped my fins about her in what I imagined was the human embrace. "Lisabeth! Lisabeth!" We slid below the surface. For the first time in my life I knew true passion, the kind of which the poets sing, that overwhelms even the coldest mind. I crushed her to me. I was aware of her forelimb-ends ("fists") beating against my pectoral zone, and I took it at first for a sign that my passion was being reciprocated; then it reached my love-hazed brain that she might be short of air. Hastily I surfaced. My darling Lisabeth, choking and gasping, sucked in breath and struggled to escape me. In shock I released her. She fled the tank and fell along its rim, exhausted, her pale body quivering. "Forgive me," I boomed. "I love you, Lisabeth! I saved the station out of love for you!" She managed to lift her lips as a sign that she did not feel anger for me (a "smile"). In a faint voice she said, "You almost drowned me, Ishmael!"

"I was carried away by my emotions. Come back into the tank. I'll be more gentle. I promise! To have you near me—"

"Oh, Ishmael! What are you saying?"

"I love you! I love you!"

I heard footsteps. The power-plant man, Dr. Madison, came running. Hastily Lisabeth cupped her hands over her milk glands and pulled her discarded garments over the lower half of her body. That pained me, for if she chose to hide such things from him, such ugly parts of herself, was that not an indication of her love for him?

"Are you all right, Liz?" he asked. "I heard yelling—"

"It's nothing, Jeff. Only Ishmael. He started hugging me in the tank. He's in love with me, Jeff, can you imagine? In *love* with me!"

They laughed together at the folly of the love-smitten dolphin.

Before dawn came I was far out to sea. I swam where dolphins swim, far from man and his things. Lisabeth's mocking laughter rang within me. She had not meant to be cruel. She who knows me better than anyone else had not been able to keep from laughing at my absurdity.

Nursing my wounds, I stayed at sea for several days, neglecting my duties at the station. Slowly, as the pain gave way to a dull ache, I headed back toward the island. In passing I met a female of my own kind. She was newly come into her season and offered herself to me, but I told her to follow me, and she did. Several times I was forced to warn off other males who wished to make use of her. I led her to the station, into the lagoon the dolphins use in their sport. A member of my crew came out to investigate— Mordred, it was—and I told him to summon Lisabeth and tell her I had returned.

Lisabeth appeared on the shore. She waved to me, smiled, called my name.

Before her eyes I frolicked with the female dolphin. We did the dance of mating; we broke the surface and lashed it with our flukes; we leaped, we soared, we bellowed.

Lisabeth watched us. And I prayed: *Let her become jealous.*

I seized my companion and drew her to the depths and violently took her, and set her free to bear my child in some other place. I found Mordred again. "Tell Lisabeth," I instructed him, "that I have found another love, but that someday I may forgive her."

Mordred gave me a glassy look and swam to shore.

My tactic failed. Lisabeth sent word that I was welcome to come back to work and that she was sorry if she had offended me, but there was no hint of jealousy in her message. My soul has turned to rotting seaweed within me. Once more I clear the intake valves, like the good beast I am, I, Ishmael, who has read Keats and Donne. Lisabeth! Lisabeth! Can you feel my pain?

Tonight by darkness I have spoken my story. You who hear this, whoever you may be, aid a lonely organism, mammalian and aquatic, who desires more intimate contact with a female of a different species. Speak kindly of me to Lisabeth. Praise my intelligence, my loyalty, and my devotion.

Tell her I give her one more chance. I offer a unique and exciting experience. I will wait for her, tomorrow night, by the edge of the reef. Let her swim to me. Let her embrace poor, lonely Ishmael. Let her speak the words of love.

From the depths of my soul . . . from the depths . . . Lisabeth, the foolish beast bids you good night, in grunting tones of deepest love.

THE SECRET PLACE

by RICHARD McKENNA

The late Richard McKenna (1913–1964) is best known
outside the science fiction genre as the author of
The Sand Pebbles (1962), a noteworthy novel that
was made into a very successful film vehicle for
Steve McQueen. Inside sf, McKenna will be remembered as the author of fewer than ten stories, all of
them memorable. Most can be found in *Casey
Agonistes and Other Science Fiction Fantasy Stories*
(1973).

"The Secret Place," which won a Nebula Award
in 1966, is a lovely story of mind travel, one that
exhibits the unique perspective that McKenna brought
to science fiction. We wish his stay had been a
longer one.

THIS morning my son asked me what I did in the
war. He's fifteen and I don't know why he never asked
me before. I don't know why I never anticipated the
question.

He was just leaving for camp, and I was able to put
him off by saying I did government work. He'll be two
weeks at camp. As long as the counselors keep pressure on him, he'll do well enough at group activities.
The moment they relax it, he'll be off studying an ant
colony or reading one of his books. He's on astronomy
now. The moment he comes home, he'll ask me again

just what I did in the war, and I'll have to tell him.

But I don't understand just what I did in the war. Sometimes I think my group fought a death fight with a local myth and only Colonel Lewis realized it. I don't know who won. All I know is that war demands of some men risks more obscure and ignoble than death in battle. I know it did of me.

It began in 1931, when a local boy was found dead in the desert near Barker, Oregon. He had with him a sack of gold ore and one thumb-sized crystal of uranium oxide. The crystal ended as a curiosity in a Salt Lake City assay office until, in 1942, it became of strangely great importance. Army agents traced its probable origin to a hundred-square-mile area near Barker. Dr. Lewis was called to duty as a reserve colonel and ordered to find the vein. But the whole area was overlain by thousands of feet of Miocene lava flows and of course it was geological insanity to look there for a pegmatite vein. The area had no drainage pattern and had never been glaciated. Dr. Lewis protested that the crystal could have gotten there only by prior human agency.

It did him no good. He was told his not to reason why. People very high up would not be placated until much money and scientific effort had been spent in a search. The army sent him young geology graduates, including me, and demanded progress reports. For the sake of morale, in a kind of frustrated desperation, Dr. Lewis decided to make the project a model textbook exercise in mapping the number and thickness of the basalt beds over the search area all the way down to the prevolcanic Miocene surface. That would at least be a useful addition to Columbia Plateau lithology. It would also be proof positive that no uranium ore existed there, so it was not really cheating.

That Oregon countryside was a dreary place. The search area was flat, featureless country with black lava outcropping everywhere through scanty gray soil in which sagebrush grew hardly knee high. It was hot and dry in summer and dismal with thin snow in winter. Winds howled across it at all seasons. Barker was about a hundred wooden houses on dusty streets, and some hay farms along a canal. All the young people were away at war or war jobs, and the old people seemed to resent us. There were twenty of us, apart from the contract drill crews who lived in their own trailer camps, and we were gown against town, in a way. We slept and ate at Colthorpe House, a block down the street from our headquarters. We had our own "gown" table there, and we might as well have been men from Mars.

I enjoyed it, just the same. Dr. Lewis treated us like students, with lectures and quizzes and assigned reading. He was a fine teacher and a brilliant scientist, and we loved him. He gave us all a turn at each phase of the work. I started on surface mapping and then worked with the drill crews, who were taking cores through the basalt and into the granite thousands of feet beneath. Then I worked on taking gravimetric and seismic readings. We had fine team spirit and we all knew we were getting priceless training in field geophysics. I decided privately that after the war I would take my doctorate in geophysics. Under Dr. Lewis, of course.

In early summer of 1944 the field phase ended. The contact drillers left. We packed tons of well logs and many boxes of gravimetric data sheets and seismic tapes for a move to Dr. Lewis's Midwestern university. There we would get more months of valuable training while we worked our data into a set of structure contour maps. We were all excited and talked a lot about being with girls again and going to parties. Then the army and part of the staff had to continue the field search. For technical compliance, Dr. Lewis decided to leave one man, and he chose me.

It hit me hard. It was like being flunked out unfairly. I thought he was heartlessly brusque about it.

"Take a jeep run through the area with a Geiger

once a day," he said. "Then sit in the office and answer the phone."

"What if the army calls when I'm away?" I asked
sullenly.

"Hire a secretary," he said. "You've an allowance
for that."

So off they went and left me, with the title of field
chief and only myself to boss. I felt betrayed to the
hostile town. I decided I hated Colonel Lewis and
wished I could get revenge. A few days later old Dave
Gentry told me how.

He was a lean, leathery old man with a white
mustache and I sat next to him in my new place at the
"town" table. Those were grim meals. I heard remarks
about healthy young men skulking out of uniform and
wasting tax money. One night I slammed my fork into
my half-emptied plate and stood up.

"The army sent me here and the army keeps me
here," I told the dozen old men and women at the
table. "I'd like to go overseas and cut Japanese throats
for you kind hearts and gentle people, I really would!
Why don't you all write to your Congressman?"

I stamped outside and stood at one end of the veranda, boiling. Old Dave followed me out.

"Hold your horses, son," he said. "They hate the
government, not you. But government's like the weather, and you're a man they can get aholt of."

"With their teeth," I said bitterly.

"They got reasons," Dave said. "Lost mines ain't
supposed to be found the way you people are going at
it. Besides that, the Crazy Kid mine belongs to us
here in Barker."

He was past seventy and he looked after horses in
the local feedyard. He wore a shabby, open vest over
faded suspenders and gray flannel shirts and nobody
would ever have looked for wisdom in that old man.
But it was there.

"This is big, new, lonesome country and it's hard on
people," he said. "Every town's got a story about a lost

mine or a lost gold cache. Only kids go looking for it.
It's enough for most folks just to know it's there. It
helps 'em to stand the country."

"I see," I said. Something stirred in the back of my
mind.

"Barker never got its lost mine until thirteen years
ago," Dave said. "Folks just naturally can't stand to
see you people find it this way, by main force and so
soon after."

"We know there isn't any mine," I said. "We're just
proving it isn't there."

"If you could prove that, it'd be worse yet," he said.
"Only you can't. We all saw and handled that ore. It
was quartz, just rotten with gold in wires and flakes.
The boy went on foot from his house to get it. The
lode's got to be right close by out there."

He waved toward our search area. The air above it
was luminous with twilight and I felt a curious surge
of interest. Colonel Lewis had always discouraged us
from speculating on that story. If one of us brought it
up, I was usually the one who led the hooting and we
all suggested he go over the search area with a dowsing
rod. It was an article of faith with us that the vein did
not exist. But now I was all alone and my own field
boss.

We each put up one foot on the veranda rail and
rested our arms on our knees. Dave bit off a chew of
tobacco and told me about Owen Price.

"He was always a crazy kid and I guess he read
every book in town," Dave said. "He had a curious
heart, that boy."

I'm no folklorist, but even I could see how myth
elements were already creeping into the story. For
one thing, Dave insisted the boy's shirt was torn off
and he had lacerations on his back.

"Like a cougar clawed him," Dave said. "Only they
ain't never been cougars in that desert. We backtracked
that boy till his trail crossed itself so many times it
was no use, but we never found one cougar track."

I could discount that stuff, of course, but still the story gripped me. Maybe it was Dave's slow, sure voice, perhaps the queer twilight, possibly my own wounded pride. I thought of how great lava upwellings sometimes tear loose and carry along huge masses of the country rock. Maybe such an erratic mass lay out there, perhaps only a few hundred feet across and so missed by our drill cores, but rotten with uranium. If I could find it, I would make a fool of Colonel Lewis. I would discredit the whole science of geology. I, Duard Campbell, the despised and rejected one, could do that. The front of my mind shouted that it was nonsense, but something far back in my mind began composing a devastating letter to Colonel Lewis and comfort flowed into me.

"There's some say the boy's youngest sister could tell where he found it, if she wanted," Dave said. "She used to go into that desert with him a lot. She took on pretty wild when it happened and then was struck dumb, but I hear she talks again now." He shook his head. "Poor little Helen. She promised to be a pretty girl."

"Where does she live?" I aked.

"With her mother in Salem," Dave said. "She went to business school and I hear she works for a lawyer there."

Mrs. Price was a flinty old woman who seemed to control her daughter absolutely. She agreed Helen would be my secretary as soon as I told her the salary. I got Helen's security clearance with one phone call; she had already been investigated as part of tracing that uranium crystal. Mrs. Price arranged for Helen to stay with a family she knew in Barker, to protect her reputation. It was in no danger. I meant to make love to her, if I had to, to charm her out of her secret, if she had one, but I would not harm her. I knew perfectly well that I was only playing a game called

"The Revenge of Duard Campbell." I knew I would not find any uranium.

Helen was a plain little girl and she was made of frightened ice. She wore low-heeled shoes and cotton stockings and plain dresses with white cuffs and collars. Her one good feature was her flawless fair skin against which her peaked, black Welsh eyebrows and smoky blue eyes gave her an elfin look at times. She liked to sit neatly tucked into herself, feet together, elbows in, eyes cast down, voice hardly audible, as smoothly self-contained as an egg. The desk I gave her faced mine and she sat like that across from me and did the busy work I gave her, and I could not get through to her at all.

I tried joking and I tried polite little gifts and attentions, and I tried being sad and needing sympathy. She listened and worked and stayed as far away as the moon. It was only after two weeks and by pure accident that I found the key to her.

I was trying the sympathy gambit. I said it was not so bad, being exiled from friends and family, but what I could not stand was the dreary sameness of that search area. Every spot was like every other spot and there was no single, recognizable *place* in the whole expanse. It sparked something in her and she roused up at me.

"It's full of just wonderful places," she said.

"Come out with me in the jeep and show me one," I challenged.

She was reluctant, but I hustled her along regardless. I guided the jeep between outcrops, jouncing and lurching. I had our map photographed on my mind and I knew where we were every minute, buy only by map coordinates. The desert had our marks on it: well sites, seismic blast holes, wooden stakes, cans, bottles and papers blowing in that everlasting wind, and it was all dismally the same anyway.

"Tell me when we pass a 'place' and I'll stop," I said.

"It's all places," she said. "Right here's a place."

I stopped the jeep and looked at her in surprise. Her voice was strong and throaty. She opened her eyes wide and smiled; I had never seen her look like that.

"What's special, that makes it a place?" I asked.

She did not answer. She got out and walked a few steps. Her whole posture was changed. She almost danced along. I followed and touched her shoulder.

"Tell me what's special," I said.

She faced around and stared right past me. She had a new grace and vitality and she was a very pretty girl.

"It's where all the dogs are," she said.

"Dogs?"

I looked around at the scrubby sagebrush and thin soil and ugly black rock and back at Helen. Something was wrong.

"Big, stupid dogs that go in herds and eat grass," she said. She kept turning and gazing. "Big cats chase the dogs and eat them. The dogs scream and scream. Can't you hear them?"

"That's crazy!" I said. "What's the matter with you?"

I might as well have slugged her. She crumpled instantly back into herself and I could hardly hear her answer.

"I'm sorry. My brother and I used to play out fairy tales here. All this was a kind of fairyland to us." Tears formed in her eyes. "I haven't been here since . . . I forgot myself. I'm sorry."

I had to swear I needed to dictate "field notes" to force Helen into that desert again. She sat stiffly with pad and pencil in the jeep while I put on my act with the Geiger and rattled off jargon. Her lips were pale and compressed and I could see her fighting against the spell the desert had for her, and I could see her slowly losing.

She finally broke down into that strange mood and I took good care not to break it. It was weird but wonderful, and I got a lot of data. I made her go out for "field notes" every morning and each time it was easier to break her down. Back in the office she always froze again and I marveled at how two such different persons could inhabit the same body. I called her two phases "Office Helen" and "Desert Helen."

I often talked with old Dave on the veranda after dinner. One night he cautioned me.

"Folks here think Helen ain't been right in the head since her brother died," he said. "They're worrying about you and her."

"I feel like a big brother to her," I said. "I'd never hurt her, Dave. If we find the lode, I'll stake the best claim for her."

He shook his head. I wished I could explain to him how it was only a harmless game I was playing and no one would ever find gold out there. Yet, as a game, it fascinated me.

Desert Helen charmed me when, helplessly, she had to uncover her secret life. She was a little girl in a woman's body. Her voice became strong and breathless with excitement and she touched me with the same wonder that turned her own face vivid and elfin. She ran laughing through the black rocks and scrubby sagebrush and momentarily she made them beautiful. She would pull me along by the hand and sometimes we ran as much as a mile away from the jeep. She treated me as if I were a blind or foolish child.

"No, no, Duard, that's a cliff!" she would say, pulling me back.

She would go first, so I could find the stepping stones across streams. I played up. She pointed out woods and streams and cliffs and castles. There were shaggy horses with claws, golden birds, camels, witches, elephants and many other creatures. I pretended to see them all, and it made her trust me. She talked and acted out the fairy tales she had once played with Owen. Sometimes he was enchanted and sometimes she, and the one had to dare the evil magic of a witch or giant to rescue the other. Sometimes I was Duard and other times I almost thought I was Owen.

Helen and I crept into sleeping castles, and we hid with pounding hearts while the giant grumbled in search of us and we fled, hand in hand, before his wrath.

Well, I had her now. I played Helen's game, but I never lost sight of my own. Every night I sketched in my map whatever I had learned that day of the fairyland topography. Its geomorphology was remarkably consistent.

When we played, I often hinted about the giant's treasure. Helen never denied it existed, but she seemed troubled and evasive about it. She would put her finger to her lips and look at me with solemn, round eyes.

"You only take things nobody cares about," she would say. "If you take the gold or jewels, it brings you terrible bad luck."

"I got a charm against bad luck and I'll let you have it too," I said once. "It's the biggest, strongest charm in the whole world."

"No. It all turns into trash. It turns into goat beans and dead snakes and things," she said crossly. "Owen told me. It's a rule, in fairyland."

Another time we talked about it as we sat in a gloomy ravine near a waterfall. We had to keep our voices low or we would wake up the giant. The waterfall was really the giant snoring and it was also the wind that blew forever across that desert.

"Doesn't Owen ever take anything?" I asked.

I had learned by then that I must always speak of Owen in the present tense.

"Sometimes he has to," she said. "Once right here the witch had me enchanted into an ugly toad. Owen put a flower on my head and that made me be Helen again."

"A really truly flower? That you could take home with you?"

"A red-and-yellow flower bigger than my two hands," she said. "I tried to take it home, but all the petals came off."

"Does Owen ever take anything home?"

"Rocks, sometimes," she said. "We keep them in a secret nest in the shed. We think they might be magic eggs."

I stood up. "Come and show me."

She shook her head vigorously and drew back. "I don't want to go home," she said. "Not ever."

She squirmed and pouted, but I pulled her to her feet.

"Please, Helen, for me," I said. "Just for one little minute."

I pulled her back to the jeep and we drove to the old Price place. I had never seen her look at it when we passed it and she did not look now. She was freezing fast back into Office Helen. But she led me around the sagging old house with its broken windows and into a tumbledown shed. She scratched away some straw in one corner, and there were the rocks. I did not realize how excited I was until disappointment hit me like a blow in the stomach.

They were worthless waterworn pebbles of quartz and rosy granite. The only thing special about them was they they could never have originated on that basalt desert.

After a few weeks we dropped the pretense of field notes and simply went into the desert to play. I had Helen's fairyland almost completely mapped. It seemed to be a recent fault block mountain with a river parallel to its base and a gently sloping plain across the river. The scarp face was wooded and cut by deep ravines and it had castles perched on its truncated spurs. I kept checking Helen on it and never found her inconsistent. Several times when she was in doubt I was able to tell her where she was, and that let me even more deeply into her secret life. One morning I discovered just how deeply.

She was sitting on a log in the forest and plaiting a little basket out of fern fronds. I stood beside her. She looked up at me and smiled.

"What shall we play today, Owen?" she asked.

I had not expected that, and I was proud of how quickly I rose to it. I capered and bounded away and then back to her and crouched at her feet. "Little sister, little sister, I'm enchanted," I said. "Only you in all the world can uncharm me."

"I'll uncharm you," she said, in that little girl voice. "What are you, brother?"

"A big, black dog," I said. "A wicked giant named Lewis Rawbones keeps me chained up behind his castle while he takes all the other dogs out hunting."

She smoothed her gray skirt over her knees. Her mouth drooped.

"You're lonesome and you howl all day and you howl all night," she said. "Poor doggie."

I threw back my head and howled.

"He's a terrible, wicked giant and he's got all kinds of terrible magic," I said. "You mustn't be afraid, little sister. As soon as you uncharm me I'll be a handsome prince and I'll cut off his head."

"I'm not afraid." Her eyes sparkled. "I'm not afraid of fire or snakes or pins or needles or anything."

"I'll take you away to my kingdom and we'll live happily ever afterward. You'll be the most beautiful queen in the world and everybody will love you."

I wagged my tail and laid my head on her knees. She stroked my silky head and pulled my long black ears.

"Everybody will love me." She was very serious now. "Will magic water uncharm you, poor old doggie?"

"You have to touch my forehead with a piece of the giant's treasure," I said. "That's the only onliest way to uncharm me."

I felt her shrink away from me. She stood up, her face suddenly crumpled with grief and anger.

"You're not Owen, you're just a man! Owen's enchanted and I'm enchanted too and nobody will ever uncharm us!"

She ran away from me and she was already Office Helen by the time she reached the jeep.

After that day she refused flatly to go into the desert with me. It looked as if my game was played out. But I gambled that Desert Helen could still hear me, underneath somewhere, and I tried a new strategy. The office was an upstairs room over the old dance hall and, I suppose, in frontier days skirmishing had gone on there between men and women. I doubt anything went on as strange as my new game with Helen.

I always paced and talked while Helen worked. Now I began mixing common-sense talk with fairyland talk and I kept coming back to the wicked giant, Lewis Rawbones. Office Helen tried not to pay attention, but now and then I caught Desert Helen peeping at me out of her eyes. I spoke of my blighted career as a geologist and how it would be restored to me if I found the lode. I mused on how I would live and work in exotic places and how I would need a wife to keep house for me and help with my paper work. It disturbed Office Helen. She made typing mistakes and dropped things. I kept it up for days, trying for just the right mixture of fact and fantasy, and it was hard on Office Helen.

One night old Dave warned me again.

"Helen's looking peaked, and there's talk around. Miz Fowler says Helen don't sleep and she cries at night and she won't tell Miz Fowler what's wrong. You don't happen to know what's bothering her, do you?"

"I only talk business stuff to her," I said. "Maybe she's homesick. I'll ask her if she wants a vacation." I did not like the way Dave looked at me. "I haven't hurt her. I don't mean her any harm, Dave," I said.

"People get killed for what they do, not for what they mean," he said. "Son, there's men in this town would kill you quick as a coyote, if you hurt Helen Price."

I worked on Helen all the next day and in the afternoon I hit just the right note and I broke her defenses. I was not prepared for the way it worked out. I had just said, "All life is a kind of playing. If you think about it right, everything we do is a game." She poised her pencil and looked straight at me, as she had never done in that office, and I felt my heart speed up.

"You taught me how to play, Helen. I was so serious that I didn't know how to play."

"Owen taught me to play. He had magic. My sisters couldn't play anything but dolls and rich husbands and I hated them."

Her eyes opened wide and her lips trembled and she was almost Desert Helen right there in the office.

"There's magic and enchantment in regular life, if you look at it right," I said. "Don't you think so, Helen?"

"I know it!" she said. She turned pale and dropped her pencil. "Owen was enchanted into having a wife and three daughters and he was just a boy. But he was the only man we had and all of them but me hated him because we were so poor." She began to tremble and her voice went flat. "He couldn't stand it. He took the treasure and it killed him." Tears ran down her cheeks. "I tried to think he was only enchanted into play-dead and if I didn't speak or laugh for seven years, I'd uncharm him."

She dropped her head on her hands. I was alarmed. I came over and put my hand on her shoulder.

"I did speak." Her shoulders heaved with sobs. "They made me speak, and now Owen won't ever come back."

I hardly knew what I was saying. I was afraid of

what I had done, and I wanted to comfort her. She jumped up and threw off my arm.

"I can't stand it! I'm going home!"

She ran out into the hall and down the stairs and from the window I saw her run down the street, still crying. All of a sudden my game seemed cruel and stupid to me and right that moment I stopped it. I tore up my map of fairyland and my letters to Colonel Lewis and I wondered how in the world I could ever have done all that.

After dinner that night old Dave motioned me out to one end of the veranda. His face looked carved out of wood.

"I don't know what happened in your office today, and for your sake I better not find out. But you send Helen back to her mother on the morning stage, you hear me?"

"All right, if she wants to go," I said. "I can't just fire her."

"I'm speaking for the boys. You better put her on that morning stage, or we'll be around to talk to you."

"All right, I will, Dave."

I wanted to tell him how the game was stopped now and how I wanted a chance to make things up with Helen, but I thought I had better not. Dave's voice was flat and savage with contempt and, old as he was, he frightened me.

Helen did not come to work in the morning. At nine o'clock I went out myself for the mail. I brought a large mailing tube and some letters back to the office. The first letter I opened was from Dr. Lewis, and almost like magic it solved all my problems.

On the basis of his preliminary structure contour maps Dr. Lewis had gotten permission to close out the field phase. Copies of the maps were in the mailing tube, for my information. I was to hold an inventory and be ready to turn everything over to an army quartermaster team coming in a few days. There was still a great mass of data to be worked up in refining the maps. I was to join the group again and I would have a chance at the lab work after all.

I felt pretty good. I paced and whistled and snapped my fingers. I wished Helen would come, to help on the inventory. Then I opened the tube and looked idly at the maps. There were a lot of them, featureless bed after bed of basalt, like layers of a cake ten miles across. But when I came to the bottom map, of the prevolcanic Miocene landscape, the hair on my neck stood up.

I had made that map myself. It was Helen's fairyland. The topography was point by point the same.

I clenched my fists and stopped breathing. Then it hit me a second time, and the skin crawled up my back.

The game was real. I couldn't end it. All the time the game had been playing me. It was still playing me.

I ran out and down the street and overtook old Dave hurrying toward the feedyard. He had a holstered gun on each hip.

"Dave, I've got to find Helen," I said.

"Somebody seen her hiking into the desert just at daylight," he said. "I'm on my way for a horse." He did not slow his stride. "You better get out there in your stink-wagon. If you don't find her before we do, you better just keep on going, son."

I ran back and got the jeep and roared it out across the scrubby sagebrush. I hit rocks and I do not know why I did not break something. I knew where to go and feared what I would find there. I knew I loved Helen Price more than my own life and I knew I had driven her to her death.

I saw her far off, running and dodging. I headed the jeep to intercept her and I shouted, but she neither saw me nor heard me. I stopped and jumped out and ran after her and the world darkened. Helen was all I could see, and I could not catch up with her.

"Wait for me, little sister!" I screamed after her. "I love you, Helen! Wait for me!"

She stopped and crouched and I almost ran over her. I knelt and put my arms around her and then it was on us.

They say in an earthquake, when the direction of up and down tilts and wobbles, people feel a fear that drives them mad if they cannot forget it afterward. This was worse. Up and down and here and there and now and then all rushed together. The wind roared through the rock beneath us and the air thickened crushingly above our heads. I know we clung to each other, and we were there for each other while nothing else was and that is all I know, until we were in the jeep and I was guiding it back toward town as headlong as I had come.

Then the world had shape again under a bright sun. I saw a knot of horsemen on the horizon. They were heading for where Owen had been found. That boy had run a long way, alone and hurt and burdened.

I got Helen up to the office. She sat at her desk with her head down on her hands and she quivered violently. I kept my arm around her.

"It was only a storm inside our two heads, Helen," I said, over and over. "Something black blew away out of us. The game is finished and we're free and I love you."

Over and over I said that, for my sake as well as hers. I meant and believed it. I said she was my wife and we would marry and go a thousand miles away from that desert to raise our children. She quieted to a trembling, but she would not speak. Then I heard hoofbeats and the creak of leather in the street below and then I heard slow footsteps on the stairs.

Old Dave stood in the doorway. His two guns looked as natural on him as hands and feet. He looked at Helen, bowed over the desk, and then at me, standing beside her.

"Come on down, son. The boys want to talk to you," he said.

I followed him into the hall and stopped.

"She isn't hurt," I said. "The lode is really out there, Dave, but nobody is ever going to find it."

"Tell that to the boys."

"We're closing out the project in a few more days," I said. "I'm going to marry Helen and take her away with me."

"Come down or we'll drag you down!" he said harshly. "We'll send Helen back to her mother."

I was afraid. I did not know what to do.

"No, you won't send me back to my mother!"

It was Helen beside me in the hall. She was Desert Helen, but grown up and wonderful. She was pale, pretty, aware and sure of herself.

"I'm going with Duard," she said. "Nobody in the world is ever going to send me around like a package again."

Dave rubbed his jaw and squinted his eyes at her.

"I love her, Dave. I'll take care of her all my life."

I put my left arm around her and she nestled against me. The tautness went out of old Dave and he smiled. He kept his eyes on Helen.

"Little Helen Price," he said, wonderingly. "Who ever would've thought it?" He reached out and shook us both gently. "Bless you youngsters," he said, and blinked his eyes. "I'll tell the boys it's all right."

He turned and went slowly down the stairs. Helen and I looked at each other, and I think she saw a new face too.

That was sixteen years ago. I am a professor myself now, graying a bit at the temples. I am as positivistic a scientist as you will find anywhere in the Mississippi drainage basin. When I tell a seminar student "The assertion is operationally meaningless," I can make it sound downright obscene. The students blush and hate me, but it is for their own good. Science is the only safe game, and it's safe only if it is kept pure.

I work hard at that. I have yet to meet the student I cannot handle.

My son is another matter. We named him Owen Lewis, and he has Helen's eyes and hair and complexion. He learned to read on the modern sane and sterile children's books. We haven't a fairy tale in the house—but I have a science library. And Owen makes fairy tales out of science. He is taking the measure of space and time now, with Jeans and Eddington. He cannot possibly understand a tenth of what he reads, in the way I understand it. But he understands all of it in some other way privately his own.

Not long ago he said to me, "You know, Dad, it isn't only space that's expanding. Time's expanding too, and that's what makes us keep getting farther away from when we used to be."

And I have to tell him just what I did in the war. I know I found manhood and a wife. The how and why of it I think and hope I am incapable of fully understanding. But Owen has, through Helen, that strangely curious heart. I'm afraid. I'm afraid he will understand.

THE LARGE ANT

by HOWARD FAST

A bestselling author for several decades as well as a
noted Hollywood screenwriter, Howard Fast has written more than thirty carefully crafted, socially conscious science fiction and fantasy stories. These were
collected as *The Edge of Tomorrow* (1961), *The
General Zapped an Angel* (1969; the title story is
one of the very best anti-Vietnam war stories in sf),
and *A Touch of Infinity* (1973). All of his sf work is
available in *Time and the Riddle* (1975).

"The Large Ant" may well be his finest story in
the science fiction field.

THERE have been all kinds of notions and guesses
as to how it would end. One held that sooner or later
there would be too many people; another that we
would do each other in, and the atom bomb made that
a very good likelihood. All sorts of notions, except the
simple fact that we were what we were. We could find
a way to feed any number of people and perhaps even
a way to avoid wiping each other out with the bomb;
those things we are very good at, but we have never
been any good at changing ourselves or the way we
behave.

I know. I am not a bad man or a cruel man; quite to the contrary, I am an ordinary, humane person and I love my wife and my children and I get along with my neighbors. I am like a great many other men, and I do the things they would do and just as thoughtlessly. There it is in a nutshell.

I am also a writer, and I told Lieberman, the curator, and Fitzgerald, the government man, that I would like to write down the story. They shrugged their shoulders. "Go ahead," they said, "because it won't make one bit of difference."

"You don't think it would alarm people?"

"How can it alarm anyone when nobody will believe it?"

"If I could have a photograph or two."

"Oh, no," they said then. "No photographs."

"What kind of sense does that make?" I asked them. "You are willing to let me write the story—why not the photographs so that people could believe me?"

"They still won't believe you. They will just say you faked the photographs, but no one will believe you. It will make for more confusion, and if we have a chance of getting out of this, confusion won't help."

"What will help?"

They weren't ready to say that, because they didn't know. So here is what happened to me, in a very straightforward and ordinary manner.

Every summer, sometime in August four good friends of mine and I go for a week's fishing on the St. Regis chain of lakes in the Adirondacks. We rent the same shack each summer; we drift around in canoes, and sometimes we catch a few bass. The fishing isn't very good, but we play cards well together, and we cook out and generally relax. This summer past, I had some things to do that couldn't be put off. I arrived three days late, and the weather was so warm and even and beguiling that I decided to stay on by myself for a day or two after the others left. There was a small flat lawn in front of the shack, and I made up my mind to spend at least three or four hours at short putts. That was how I happened to have the putting iron next to my bed.

The first day I was alone, I opened a can of beans and a can of beer for my supper. Then I lay down in my bed with *Life on the Mississippi,* a pack of cigarettes, and an eight-ounce chocolate bar. There was nothing I had to do, no telephone, no demands and no newspapers. At that moment, I was about as contented as any man can be in these nervous times.

It was still light outside, and enough light came in through the window above my head for me to read by. I was just reaching for a fresh cigarette, when I looked up and saw it on the foot of my bed. The edge of my hand was touching the golf club, and with a single motion I swept the club over and down, struck it a savage and accurate blow, and killed it. That was what I referred to before. Whatever kind of a man I am, I react as a man does. I think that any man, black, white or yellow, in China, Africa or Russia, would have done the same thing.

First I found that I was sweating all over, and then I knew I was going to be sick. I went outside to vomit, recalling that this hadn't happened to me since 1943, on my way to Europe on a tub of a Liberty Ship. Then I felt better and was able to go back into the shack and look at it. It was quite dead, but I had already made up my mind that I was not going to sleep alone in this shack.

I couldn't bear to touch it with my bare hands. With a piece of brown paper, I picked it up and dropped it into my fishing creel. That, I put into the trunk case of my car, along with what luggage I carried. Then I closed the door of the shack, got into my car and drove back to New York. I stopped once along the road, just before I reached the Thruway, to nap in the car for a little over an hour. It was almost dawn when I reached the city, and I had shaved, had a hot bath and changed my clothes before my wife awoke.

During breakfast, I explained that I was never much of a hand at the solitary business, and since she knew that, and since driving alone all night was by no means an extraordinary procedure for me, she didn't press me with any questions. I had two eggs, coffee and a cigarette. Then I went into my study, lit another cigarette, and contemplated my fishing creel, which sat upon my desk.

My wife looked in, saw the creel, remarked that it had too ripe a smell, and asked me to remove it to the basement.

"I'm going to dress," she said. The kids were still at camp. "I have a date with Ann for lunch—I had no idea you were coming back. Shall I break it?"

"No, please don't. I can find things to do that have to be done."

Then I sat and smoked some more, and finally I called the Museum, and asked who the curator of insects was. They told me his name was Bertram Lieberman, and I asked to talk to him. He had a pleasant voice. I told him that my name was Morgan, and that I was a writer, and he politely indicated that he had seen my name and read something that I had written. That is normal procedure when a writer introduces himself to a thoughtful person.

I asked Lieberman if I could see him, and he said that he had a busy morning ahead of him. Could it be tomorrow?

"I am afraid it has to be now," I said firmly.

"Oh? Some information you require."

"No. I have a specimen for you."

"Oh?" The "oh" was a cultivated, neutral interval. It asked and answered and said nothing. You have to develop that particular "oh."

"Yes. I think you will be interested."

"An insect?" he asked mildly.

"I think so."

"Oh? Large?"

"Quite large," I told him.

"Eleven o'clock? Can you be here then? Or the main floor, to the right, as you enter."

"I'll be there," I said.

"One thing—dead?"

"Yes, it's dead."

"Oh?" again. "I'll be happy to see you at eleven o'clock, Mr. Morgan."

My wife was dressed now. She opened the door to my study and said firmly, "Do get rid of that fishing creel. It smells."

"Yes, darling. I'll get rid of it."

"I should think you'd want to take a nap after driving all night."

"Funny, but I'm not sleepy," I said. "I think I'll drop around to the museum."

My wife said that was what she liked about me, that I never tired of places like museums, police courts and third-rate night clubs.

Anyway, aside from a racetrack, a museum is the most interesting and unexpected place in the world. It was unexpected to have two other men waiting for me, along with Mr. Lieberman, in his office. Lieberman was a skinny, sharp-faced man of about sixty. The government man, Fitzgerald, was small, dark-eyed, and wore gold-rimmed glasses. He was very alert, but he never told me what part of the government he represented. He just said "we," and it meant the government. Hopper, the third man, was comfortable-looking, pudgy, and genial. He was a United States senator with an interest in entomology, although before this morning I would have taken better than even money that such a thing not only wasn't, but could not be.

The room was large and square and plainly furnished, with shelves and cupboards on all walls.

We shook hands, and then Lieberman asked me, nodding at the creel, "Is that it?"

"That's it."

"May I?"

"Go ahead," I told him. "It's nothing that I want to stuff for the parlor. I'm making you a gift of it."

"Thank you, Mr. Morgan," he said, and then he opened the creel and looked inside. Then he straightened up, and the other two men looked at him inquiringly.

He nodded. "Yes."

The senator closed his eyes for a long moment. Fitzgerald took off his glasses and wiped them industriously. Lieberman spread a piece of plastic on his desk, and then lifted the thing out of my creel and laid it on the plastic. The two men didn't move. They just sat where they were and looked at it.

"What do you think it is, Mr. Morgan?" Lieberman asked me.

"I thought that was your department."

"Yes, of course. I only wanted your impression."

"An ant. That's my impression. It's the first time I saw an ant fourteen, fifteen inches long. I hope it's the last."

"An understandable wish," Lieberman nodded.

Fitzgerald said to me, "May I ask how you killed it, Mr. Morgan?"

"With an iron. A golf club, I mean. I was doing a little fishing with some friends up at St. Regis in the Adirondacks, and I brought the iron for my short shots. They're the worst part of my game, and when my friends left, I intended to stay on at our shack and do four or five hours of short putts. You see—"

"There's no need to explain," Hopper smiled, a trace of sadness on his face. "Some of our very best golfers have the same trouble."

"I was lying in bed, reading, and I saw it at the foot of my bed. I had the club—"

"I understand," Fitzgerald nodded.

"You avoid looking at it," Hopper said.

"It turns my stomach."

"Yes—yes, I suppose so."

Lieberman said, "Would you mind telling us why you killed it, Mr. Morgan."

"Why?"

"Yes—why?"

"I don't understand you," I said. "I don't know what you're driving at."

"Sit down, please, Mr. Morgan," Hopper nodded. "Try to relax. I'm sure this has been very trying."

"I still haven't slept. I want a chance to dream before I say how trying."

"We are not trying to upset you, Mr. Morgan," Lieberman said. "We do feel, however, that certain aspects of this are very important. That is why I am asking you why you killed it. You must have had a reason. Did it seem about to attack you?"

"No."

"Or make any sudden motion towards you?"

"No. It was just there."

"Then why?"

"This is to no purpose," Fitzgerald put in. "We know why he killed it."

"Do you?"

"The answer is very simple, Mr. Morgan. You killed it because you are a human being."

"Oh?"

"Yes. Do you understand?"

"No, I don't."

"Then why did you kill it?" Hopper put in.

"I was scared to death. I still am, to tell the truth."

Lieberman said, "You are an intelligent man, Mr. Morgan. Let me show you something." He then opened the doors of one of the wall cupboards, and there eight jars of formaldehyde and in each jar a specimen like mine—and in each case mutilated by the violence of its death. I said nothing. I just stared.

Lieberman closed the cupboard doors. "All in five days," he shrugged.

"A new race of ants," I whispered stupidly.

"No. They're not ants. Come here!" He motioned me

to the desk and the other two joined me. Lieberman took a set of dissecting instruments out of his drawer, used one to turn the thing over and then pointed to the underpart of what would be the thorax in an insect.

"That looks like part of him, doesn't it, Mr. Morgan?"

"Yes, it does."

Using two of the tools, he found a fissure and pried the bottom apart. It came open like the belly of a bomber; it was a pocket, a pouch, a receptacle that the thing wore, and in it were four beautiful little tools or instruments or weapons, each about an inch and a half long. They were beautiful the way any object of functional purpose and loving creation is beautiful—the way the creature itself would have been beautiful, had it not been an insect and myself a man. Using tweezers, Lieberman took each instrument off the brackets that held it, offering each to me. And I took each one, felt it, examined it, and then put it down.

I had to look at the ant now, and I realized that I had not truly looked at it before. We don't look carefully at a thing that is horrible or repugnant to us. You can't look at anything through a screen of hatred. But now the hatred and the fear was dilute, and as I looked, I realized it was not an ant although like an ant. It was nothing that I had ever dreamed of.

All three men were watching me, and suddenly I was on the defensive. "I didn't know! What do you expect when you see an insect that size?"

Leiberman nodded.

"What in the name of God is it?"

From the desk Lieberman produced a bottle and four small glasses. He poured and we drank it neat. I would not have expected him to keep good Scotch in his desk.

"We don't know," Hopper said. "We don't know what it is."

Lieberman pointed to the broken skull, from which

a white substance oozed. "Brain material—a great deal of it."

"It could be a very intelligent creature," Hopper nodded.

Lieberman said, "It is an insect in developmental structure. We know very little about intelligence in our insects. It's not the same as what we call intelligence. It's a collective phenomenon—as if you were to think of the component parts of our bodies. Each part is alive, but the intelligence is a result of the whole. If that same pattern were to extend to creatures like this one—"

I broke the silence. They were content to stand there and stare at it.

"Suppose it were?"

"What?"

"The kind of collective intelligence you were talking about."

"Oh? Well, I couldn't say. It would be something beyond our wildest dreams. To us—well, what we are to an ordinary ant."

"I don't believe that," I said shortly, and Fitzgerald, the government man, told me quietly, "Neither do we. We guess."

"If it's that intelligent, why didn't it use one of those weapons on me?"

"Would that be a mark of intelligence?" Hopper asked mildly.

"Perhaps none of these are weapons," Leiberman said.

"Don't you know? Didn't the others carry instruments?"

"They did," Fitzgerald said shortly.

"Why? What were they?"

"We don't know," Leiberman said.

"But you can find out. We have scientists, engineers —good God, this is an age of fantastic instruments. Have them taken apart!"

"We have."

"Then what have you found out?"

"Nothing."

"Do you mean to tell me," I said, "that you can find out nothing about these instruments—what they are, how they work, what their purpose is?"

"Exactly," Hopper nodded. "Nothing, Mr. Morgan. They are meaningless to the finest engineers and technicians in the United States. You know the old story—suppose you gave a radio to Aristotle? What would he do with it? Where should he find power? And what would he receive with no one to send? It is not that these instruments are complex. They are actually very simple. We simply have no idea of what they can or should do."

"But there must be a weapon of some kind."

"Why?" Lieberman demanded. "Look at yourself, Mr. Morgan—a cultured and intelligent man, yet you cannot conceive of a mentality that does not include weapons as a prime necessity. Yet a weapon is an unusual thing, Mr. Morgan. An instrument of murder. We don't think that way, because the weapon has become the symbol of the world we inhabit. Is that civilized, Mr. Morgan? Or is the weapon and civilization in the ultimate sense incompatible? Can you imagine a mentality to which the concept of murder is impossible—or let me say absent? We see everything through our own subjectivity. Why shouldn't some other—this creature, for example—see the process of mentation out of his subjectivity? So he approaches a creature of our world—and he is slain. Why? What explanation? Tell me, Mr. Morgan, what conceivable explanation could we offer a wholly rational creature for this—" pointing to the thing on his desk. "I am asking you the question most seriously. What explanation?"

"An accident?" I muttered.

"And the eight jars in my cupboard? Eight accidents?"

"I think, Dr. Leiberman," Fitzgerald said, "that you can go a little too far in that direction."

"Yes, you would think so. It's a part of your own background. Mine is as a scientist. As a scientist, I try to be rational when I can. The creation of a structure of good and evil, or what we call morality and ethics, is a function of intelligence—and unquestionably the ultimate evil may be the destruction of conscious intelligence. That is why, so long ago, we at least recognized the injunction 'thou shalt not kill!' even if we never gave more than lip service to it. But to a collective intelligence, such as this might be a part of, the concept of murder would be monstrous beyond the power of thought."

I sat down and lit a cigarette. My hands were trembling. Hopper apologized. "We have been rather rough with you, Mr. Morgan. But over the past days, eight other people have done just what you did. We are caught in the trap of being what we are."

"But tell me—where do these things come from?"

"It almost doesn't matter where they come from," Hopper said hopelessly. "Perhaps from another planet —perhaps from inside this one—or the moon or Mars. That doesn't matter. Fitzgerald thinks they come from a smaller planet, because their movements are apparently slow on earth. But Dr. Lieberman thinks that they move slowly because they have not discovered the need to move quickly. Meanwhile, they have the problem of murder and what to do with it. Heaven knows how many of them have died in other places— Africa, Asia, Europe."

"Then why don't you publicize this? Put a stop to it before it's too late!"

"We've thought of that," Fitzgerald nodded. "What then—panic, hysteria, charges that this is the result of the atom bomb? We can't change. We are what we are."

"They may go away," I said.

"Yes, they may," Lieberman nodded. "But if they

are without the curse of murder, they may also be without the curse of fear. They may be social in the highest sense. What does society do with a murderer?"

"There are societies that put him to death—and there are other societies that recognize his sickness and lock him away, where he can kill no more." Hopper said. "Of course, when a whole world is on trial, that's another matter. We have atom bombs now and other things, and are reaching out to the stars—"

"I'm inclined to think that they'll run," Fitzgerald put in. "They may just have that curse of fear, Doctor."

"They may," Lieberman admitted. "I hope so."

But the more I think of it the more it seems to me that fear and hatred are the two sides of the same coin. I keep trying to think back, to recreate the moment when I saw it standing at the foot of my bed in the fishing shack. I keep trying to drag out of my memory a clear picture of what it looked like, whether behind that chitinous face and the two gently waving antennae there was any evidence of fear and anger. But the clearer the memory becomes, the more I seem to recall a certain wonderful dignity and repose. Not fear and not anger.

And more and more, as I go about my work, I get the feeling of what Hopper called "a world on trial." I have no sense of anger myself. Like a criminal who can no longer live with himself, I am content to be judged.

FEAR HOUND

by KATHERINE MacLEAN

Although Katherine MacLean's socially oriented science fiction stories have been appearing since 1949, her total output has been modest but of high quality. She won a Nebula Award in 1971 for "The Missing Man," which is also the title of her best known novel (1975).

Stories of extrasensory perception are a staple theme in science fiction, but they are rarely handled with the skill and care exhibited in "Fear Hound."

HUNGER is not a bad thing. Some guys who knew Zen and jaine yogi had told me they could go without food thirty days. They showed me how. The only trouble is, when you skip meals, you shake. When I touched a building it felt like the world was trembling.

If I told the employment board that my student support money had run out, they'd give me an adult support pension and a ticket to leave New York and never come back. I wasn't planning on telling them.

Ahmed the Arab came along the sidewalk, going fast, his legs rangy and swinging. Ahmed used to be king of our block gang when we were smaller, and he used to ask me to help him sometimes. This year Ahmed had a job working for the Rescue Squad. Maybe he would let me help him; maybe he could swing a job for me.

I signaled him as he came close. "Ahmed."

He went on by, hurrying. "OK, George, come on."

I fell into stride beside him. "What's the rush?"

"Look at the clouds, man. Something's getting ready to happen. We've got to stop it."

I looked at the clouds. The way I felt was smeared all over the sky. Dangerous dark dirty clouds bulged down over the city, looking ready to burst and spill out fire and dirt. In high school Psychology-A they said that people usually match their mood. My mood was bad, I could see that, but I still did not know what the sky really looked like—dark, probably, but harmless.

"What is it?" I asked. "Is it smog?"

Ahmed stopped walking, and looked at my face. "No. It's fear."

He was right. Fear lay like the fog across the air. Fear was in the threatening clouds and in the darkness across the faces of the people. People went by under the heavy sky, hunched as if there were a cold rain falling. Buildings above us seemed to be swaying outward.

I shut my eyes, but the buildings seemed to sway out farther.

Last year when Ahmed had been training for the Rescue Squad he'd opened up a textbook and tried to explain something to me about the difference between inner reality and outer reality, and how mobs can panic when they all see the same idea. I opened my eyes and studied the people running at me, past me, and away from me as the crowds rushed by. Crowds always rush in New York. Did they all see the buildings as leaning and ready to fall? Were they afraid to mention it?

"Ahmed, you Rescue Squad fink," I said, "what would happen if we yelled Earthquake good and loud? Would they all panic?"

"Probably so." Ahmed was looking at me with interest, his lean face and black eyes intent. "How do you feel, George? You look sick."

"I feel lousy. Something wrong in my head. Dizzy." Talking made it worse. I braced my hand against a wall. The walls rocked, and I felt as if I were down flat while I was still standing up.

"What in creation is wrong with me?" I asked. "I can't get sick from skipping a meal or so, can I?" Mentioning food made my stomach feel strange and hollow and dry. I was thinking about death suddenly. "I'm not even hungry," I told Ahmed. "Am I sick?"

Ahmed, who had been king of our block gang when we were kids, was the one who knew the answers.

"Man, you've got good pickup." Ahmed studied my face. "Someone near here is in trouble and you're tuned in to it." He glanced at the sky east and west. "Which way is worst? We've got to find him fast."

I looked up Fifth Avenue. The giant glass office buildings loomed and glittered insecurely, showing clouds through in dark green, and reflecting clouds in gray as if dissolving into the sky. I looked along Forty-second Street to the giant arches of the transport center. I looked down Fifth Avenue, past the stone lions of the library, and then west to the neon signs and excitement. The darkness came at me with teeth, like a giant mouth. Hard to describe.

"Man, it's bad." I was shaken. "It's bad in every direction. It's the whole city!"

"It can't be," Ahmed said. "It's loud; we must be near where the victim is."

He put his wrist radio up to his mouth and pushed the signal button. "Statistics, please." A voice answered. "Statistics." Ahmed articulated carefully. "Priority call. Rescue Badge 54B. Give me today's trends in hospital admissions, all rises above sigma reciprocal 30. Point the center of any area with a sharp rise in"—he looked at me analytically—"dizziness, fatigue, and acute depression." He considered me further. "Run a check on general anxiety syndromes and hypochondria." He waited for the Statistics Department to collect data.

I wondered if I should be proud or ashamed or feeling sick.

He waited—lean, efficient, impatient, with black eyebrows and black intense eyes. He'd looked almost the same when he was ten and I was nine. His family were immigrants, speaking some un-American language, but they were the proud kind. Another person would burn with hate or love for girls, but Ahmed would burn about Ideas. His ideas about adventure made him king of our block gang. He'd lead us into strange adventures and grown-up no-trespassing places just to look at things, and when we were trapped he'd consult a little pack of cards, or some dice, and lead us out of trouble at high speed—like he had a map. He had an idea that the look and feel of a place told you its fate; a bad-luck place looked bad. When he consulted me, or asked me how a place looked to me, I'd feel proud.

He'd left us behind. We all dropped out in high school, but Ahmed the Arab got good marks, graduated and qualified for advanced training. All the members of our gang had taken their adult retirement pensions and left the city, except me and Ahmed the Arab—and I heard Ahmed was the best detector in the Rescue Squad.

The wrist radio whistled and he put it to his ear. The little voice crackled off figures and statistical terms. Ahmed looked around at the people passing, surprised, then looked at me more respectfully. "It's all over Manhattan. Women coming in with psychosomatic pregnancy. Pregnant women are coming in with nightmares. Men are coming in with imaginary ulcers and cancers. Lots of suicides and lots of hospital commitments for acute suicidal melancholy. You are right. The whole city is in trouble."

He started along Forty-second Street toward Sixth Avenue, walking fast. "Need more help. Try different techniques." A hanging sign announced, *Gypsy Tea Room, Oriental Teas, Exotic Pastries, Reading of Your Personality and Future.* Ahmed pushed through a swinging door and went up a moving escalator two steps at a time, with me right after him. We came out into the middle of a wide, low-ceiling restaurant, with little tables and spindly chairs.

Four old ladies were clustered around one table nibbling at cupcakes and talking. A businessman sat at a table near the window reading the *Wall Street Journal.* Two teener students sat leaning against the glass wall window looking down into Forty-second Street and its swirling crowds. A fat woman sat at a table in a corner, holding a magazine up before her face. She lowered it and looked at us over the top. The four old ladies stopped talking and the businessman folded his *Wall Street Journal* and put it aside as if Ahmed and I were messengers of bad news. They were all in a miserable, nervous mood like the one I was in—expecting the worst from a doomed world.

Ahmed threaded his way among the tables toward the corner table where the fat woman sat. She put her magazine aside on another table as we approached. Her face was round and pleasant, with smile creases all over it. She nodded and smiled at me and then did not smile at Ahmed at all, but instead stared straight back into his eyes as he sat down in front of her.

He leaned across the table. "All right, Bessie, you feel it, too. Have you located who it is?"

She spoke in a low, intense voice, as if afraid to speak loudly: "I felt it first thing I woke up this morning, Ahmed. I tried to trace it for the Rescue Squad, but she's feeling, not thinking. And it's echoing off too many people because they keep thinking up reasons why they feel so—" She paused and I knew what she was trying to describe. Trying to describe it made it worse.

She spoke in a lower voice and her round face was worried. "The bad dream feeling is hanging on, Ahmed. I wonder if I'm—"

She didn't want to talk about it, and Ahmed had his mouth open for a question, so I was sorry for her and butted in.

"What do you mean about people making echoes? How come all this crowd—" I waved my hand in a vague way, indicating the city and the people. The Rescue Squad was supposed to rescue lost people. The city was not lost.

Ahmed looked at me impatiently. "Adults don't like to use telepathy. They pretend they can't. But say a man falls down an elevator shaft and breaks a leg. No one finds him, and he can't reach a phone so he'll get desperate and pray and start using mind power. He'll try to send his thoughts as loud as he can. He doesn't know how loud he can send. But the dope doesn't broadcast his name and where he is, he just broadcasts: 'Help, I've got a broken leg!' They come limping into the emergency clinics and get X rays of good legs. The doctors tell them to go home. But they are picking up the thought, 'Help! I'm going to die unless I get help!' so they hang around the clinics and bother the doctors. They are scared. The Rescue Squad uses them as tracers. Whenever there is an abnormal wave of people applying for help in one district, we try to find the center of the wave and locate someone in real trouble."

The more he talked the better I felt. It untuned me from the bad mood of the day, and Rescue Squad work was beginning to sound like something I could do. I know how people feel just by standing close to them. Maybe the Rescue Squad would let me join if I showed them that I could detect people.

"Great," I said. "What about preventing murders? How do you do that?"

Ahmed took out his silver badge and looked at it. "I'll give you an example. Imagine an intelligent sensitive kid with a vivid imagination. He is being bullied by a stupid father. He doesn't say anything back; he just imagines what he will do to the big man when he grows up. Whenever the big man gets him mad the kid clenches his fists and smiles and puts everything he's got into a blast of mental energy, thinking of himself splitting the big man's skull with an ax. He thinks loud. A lot of people in the district have nothing much to do, nothing much to think about. They never plan or imagine much and they act on the few thoughts that come to them. Get it?"

"The dopes act out what he is thinking," I grinned.

Ahmed looked at my grin with a disgusted expression and turned back to the fat woman. "Bessie, we've got to locate this victim. What do the tea leaves say about where she is?"

"I haven't asked." Bessie reached over to the other table and picked up an empty cup. It had a few soggy tea leaves in the bottom. "I was hoping that you would find her." She heaved herself to her feet and waddled into the kitchen.

I was still standing. Ahmed looked at me with a disgusted expression. "Quit changing the subject. Do you want to help rescue someone or don't you?"

Bessie came back with a round pot of tea and a fresh cup on a tray. She put the tray on the table, and filled the cup, then poured half of the steaming tea back into the pot. I remembered that a way to get information from the group-mind is by seeing how people interpret peculiar shapes like ink blots and tea leaves, and I stood quietly, trying not to bother her.

She lowered herself slowly into her chair, swirled the tea in the cup, and looked in. We waited. She rocked the cup, looking; then shut her eyes and put the cup down. She sat still, eyes closed, the eyelids squeezed tight in wrinkles.

"What was it?" Ahmed asked in a low voice.

"Nothing, nothing, just a—" She stopped and choked. "Just a damned, lousy maggotty skull."

That had to be a worse sign than getting the ace of spades in a card cut. Death. I began to get that sick feeling again. Death for Bessie?

"I'm sorry," Ahmed said. "But push on, Bessie. Try another angle. We need the name and address."

"She was not thinking about her name and address," Bessie's eyes were still tightly shut.

Suddenly Ahmed spoke in a strange voice. I'd heard that voice years ago when he was head of our gang— when he hypnotized another kid. It was a deep smooth voice and it penetrated inside of you.

"You need help and no one has come to help you. What are you thinking?"

The question got inside my head. An answer opened up and I started to answer, but Bessie answered first. "When I don't think, just shut my eyes and hold still, I don't feel anything, everything goes far away. When the bad things begin to happen I can stay far away and refuse to come back." Bessie's voice was dreamy.

The same dark sleepy ideas had formed in my own head. She was saying them for me. Suddenly I was afraid that the darkness would swallow me. It was like a night cloud, or a pillow, floating deep down and inviting you to come and put your head on it, but it moved a little and turned and showed a flash of shark teeth, so you knew it was a shark waiting to eat anyone who came close.

Bessie's eyes snapped open and she straightened herself upright, her eyes so wide open that white showed around the rims. She was scared of sleeping. I was glad she had snapped out of it. She had been drifting down into the inviting dark toward that black monster.

"If you went in too deep, you could wake up dead," I said and put a hand on Ahmed's shoulder to warn him to slow down.

"I don't care which one of you speaks for her," he said, without turning around. "But you have to learn to separate your thoughts from hers. You're not thinking of dying—the victim is. She's in danger of death, somewhere." He leaned across the table to Bessie again. "Where is she?"

I tightened my grip on Ahmed's shoulder, but Bessie obediently picked up the teacup in fat fingers and looked in again. Her face was round and innocent, but I judged she was braver than I was.

I went around Bessie's side of the table to look into the teacup over her shoulder. A few tea leaves were at the bottom of the cup, drifting in an obscure pattern. She tapped the side of the cup delicately with a fat finger. The pattern shifted. The leaves made some sort of a picture, but I could not make out exactly what it was. It looked like it meant something, but I could not see it clearly.

Bessie spoke sympathetically. "You're thirsty, aren't you? There, there, Honeybunch. We'll find you. We haven't forgotten you. Just think where you are and we will—" Her voice died down to a low, fading mumble, like a windup doll running down. She put the cup down and put her head down into her spread hands.

I heard a whisper. "Tired of trying, tired of smiling. Let die. Let death be born. Death will come out to destroy the world, the worthless dry, rotten—"

Ahmed reached across and grasped her shoulders and shook them. "Bessie, snap out of it. That's not you. It's the *other* one."

Bessie lifted a changed face from her hands. The round smiling look was gone into sagging sorrowful folds like an old bloodhound. She mumbled, "It's true. Why wait for someone to help you and love you? We are born and die. No one can help that. No reason to hope. Hope hurts. Hope hurt *her*." It bothered me to hear Bessie talk. It was like she were dead. It was a corpse talking.

Bessie seemed to try to pull herself together and

focus on Ahmed to report, but one eye went off focus and she did not seem to see him.

She said, "Hope hurts. She hates hope. She tries to kill it. She felt my thinking and she thought my feelings of life and hope were hers. I was remembering how Harry always helped me, and she blasted in blackness and hate—" She put her face down in her hands again. "Ahmed, he's dead. She killed Harry's ghost in my heart. He won't ever come back anymore, even in dreams." Her face was dead, like a mask.

He reached over and shook her shoulder again. "Bessie, shame on you, snap out of it."

She straightened and glared. "It's true. All men are beasts. No one is going to help a woman. You want me to help you at your job and win you another medal for finding that girl, don't you? You don't care about her." Her face was darkening, changing to something worse, that reminded me of the black shapes of the clouds.

I had to pull her out of it, but I didn't know what to do.

Ahmed clattered the spoon against the teacup with a loud clash and spoke in a loud casual voice: "How's the restaurant business, Bessie? Are the new girls working out?"

She looked down at the teacup, surprised, and then looked vaguely around the restaurant. "Not many customers right now. It must be an off hour. The girls are in the kitchen." Her face began to pull back into its own shape, a pleasant restaurant-service mask, round and ready to smile. "Can I have the girls get you anything, Ahmed?"

She turned to me with a habit of kindness, and her words were less mechanical. "Would you like anything, young man? You look so energetic standing there! Most young people like our Turkish honey rolls." She still wasn't focused on me, didn't see me, really, but—I smiled back at her, glad to see her feeling better.

"No thank you, Ma'am," I said and glanced at Ahmed to see what he would want to do next.

"Bessie's honey rolls are famous," Ahmed said. "They are dripping with honey and have so much almond flavor they burn your mouth." He rose easily, looking lazy. "I guess I'll have a dozen to take along."

The fat woman sat blinking her eyes up at him. Her round face did not look sick and sagging anymore, just sort of rumpled and meaningless, like your own face looks in the mirror in the morning. "Turkish honey-and-almond rolls," she repeated. "One dozen." She rang a little bell in the middle of the table and rose.

"Wait for me, downstairs," Ahmed told me. He turned to Bessie.

"Remember the time a Shriners Convention came in and they all wanted lobster and palm reading at once? Where did you get all those hot lobsters?" They moved off together to the counter which displayed cookies and rolls. A pretty girl in a frilled apron trotted out of the kitchen and stood behind the counter.

Bessie laughed, starting with a nervous high-pitched giggle and ending up in a deep ho-ho sound like Santa Claus. "Do I remember? What a hassle! Imagine me on the phone trying to locate twenty palm readers in ten minutes! I certainly was grateful when you sent over those twenty young fellows and girls to read palms for my Shriners. I was really nervous until I saw they had their marks really listening, panting for the next word. I thought you must have gotten a circus tribe of gypsies from the cooler. *Ho-ho.* I didn't know you had sent over the whole police class in Suspect Personality Analysis."

I went out the door, down to the sidewalk. A few minutes later Ahmed came down the escalator two steps at a time and arrived at the sidewalk like a rocket. "Here, carry these." He thrust the paper bag of Turkish honey rolls at me. The warm, sweet smell was good. I took the bag and plunged my hand in.

"Just carry them. Don't eat any." Ahmed led the way down the subway stairs to the first underground walkway.

I pulled my hand out of the bag and followed. I was feeling so shaky I went down the stairs slowly one at a time instead of two at a time. When I got there Ahmed was looking at the signs that pointed in different directions, announcing what set of tracks led to each part of the city. For the first time I saw that he was uncertain and worried. He didn't know which way to go. It was a strange thought for me, that Ahmed did not know which way to go. It meant he had been running without knowing which way to run.

He was thinking aloud: "We know that the victim is female, adult, younger than Bessie, probably pregnant, and is trapped someplace where there is no food or water for her. She expected help from the people she loves, and was disappointed, and now is angry with the thought of love and hates the thought of people giving help."

I remembered Bessie's suddenly sick and flabby face, after the victim had struck out at Bessie's thought of giving help. *Angry* seemed to be the understatement of the year. I remembered the wild threatening sky, and I watched the people hurrying by, pale and anxious. Two chicks passed in bad shape. One was holding her stomach and muttering about Alka-Seltzer, and the other had red-rimmed eyes as if she had just been weeping. Can one person in trouble do that to a whole city full of people?

"Who is she, Ahmed?" I asked. "I mean, *what* is she anyhow?"

"I don't understand it myself," Ahmed said. Suddenly he attacked me again with his question, using that deep hypnotic voice to push me backward into the black whirlpools of the fear of death. *"If you were thirsty, very thirsty, and there was only one place in the city you could go to buy a thirst quencher where—"*

"I'm not thirsty." I tried to swallow, and my tongue felt swollen, my mouth seemed dry and filled with sand, and my throat was coated with dry gravel. The world tilted over sideways. I braced my feet to stand up. "I *am* thirsty. How did you do that? I want to go to the White Horse Tavern on Hudson Street and drink a gallon of ginger ale and a bottle of brown beer."

"You're my compass. Let's go there. I'll buy for you."

Ahmed ran down the Eighth Avenue subway stairs to the chair tracks. I followed, clutching the bag of sweet-smelling rolls as if it were a heavy suitcase full of rocks. The smell made me hungry and weak. I could still walk, but I was pretty sure that, if Ahmed pushed me deep into that black mood just once more, they'd have to send me back on a stretcher.

On the tracks we linked our chairs and Ahmed shifted the linked chairs from belt to belt until we were traveling at a good speed. The chairs moved along the tunnels, passing under bright store windows with beautiful mannequins dancing and displaying things to buy. I usually looked up when we got near the forest fire and waterfall three-dimensional pics, but today I did not look up. I sat with my elbows braced on my knees and my head hanging. Ahmed looked at me alertly, his black eyebrows furrowed and dark eyes scanning me up and down like I was a medical diagram.

"Man, I'd like to see the suicide statistics right now. One look at you and I know it's bad."

I had enough life left to be annoyed. "I have my own feelings, not just some chick's feelings. I've been sick all day. A virus or something."

"Damnit, will you never understand? We've got to rescue this girl because she's broadcasting. She's broadcasting feeling sick!"

I looked at the floor between my feet. "That's a lousy reason. Why can't you rescue her just because she's in trouble? Let her broadcast. High School Psych-A said that everybody broadcasts."

"Listen" Ahmed leaned forward ready to tell me an idea. His eyes began to glitter as the idea took him. "Maybe she broadcasts too loud. Statistics has been running data on trends and surges in popular action. They think that people who broadcast too loud might be causing some of the mass action."

"I don't get you, Ahmed."

"I mean like they get a big surge of people going to Coney Island on a cloudy day, and they don't have subway cars ready for it, and traffic ties up. They compare that day with other cloudy days, the same temperature and the same time of year other years, and try to figure out what caused it. Sometimes it's a factory vacation; but sometimes it's one man, given the day off, who goes to the beach, and an extra crowd of a thousand or so people from all over the city, people that don't know him, suddenly make excuses, clear schedules and go to the beach, sometimes arriving at almost the same time, jamming up the subways for an hour, and making it hard for the Traffic Flow Control people."

"Is it a club?" I was trying to make out what he meant, but I couldn't see what it had to do with anything.

"No," he said. "They didn't know each other. It's been checked. The Traffic Flow experts have to know what to expect. They started collecting names from the crowds. They found that most of the people in each surge are workers with an IQ below one hundred, but somehow doing all right with their lives. They seemed to be controlled by one man in the middle of the rush who had a reason to be going in that direction. The Statistics people call the man in the middle the *Archetype*. That's an old Greek word. The original that other people are copied from—one real man and a thousand echoes."

The idea of some people being echoes made me uneasy. It seemed insulting to anyone an echo. "They must be wrong," I said.

"Listen—" Ahmed leaned forward, his eyes brightening. "They think they are right—one man and a thousand echoes. They checked into the lives of the ones that seemed to be in the middle. The Archetypes are energetic ordinary people living average lives. When things go as usual for the Archetype, he acts normal and everybody controlled by him acts normal, get it?"

I didn't get it, and I didn't like it. "An average healthy person is a good joe. He wouldn't want to control anyone," I said, but I knew I was sugaring the picture. Humans can be bad. People love power over people. "Listen," I said, "some people like taking advice. Maybe it's like advice?"

Ahmed leaned back and pulled his chin. "It fits. Advice by ESP is what you mean. Maybe the Archetype doesn't know he is broadcasting. He does just what the average man wants to do. Solves the same problems—and does it better. He broadcasts loud, pleasant, simple thoughts and they are easy to listen to if you have the same kind of life and problems. Maybe more than half the population below an IQ of one hundred have learned to use telepathic pickup and let the Archetypes do their thinking for them."

Ahmed grew more excited, his eyes fixed on the picture he saw in his head. "Maybe the people who are letting Archetypes run their lives don't even know they are following anyone else's ideas. They just find these healthy, problem-solving thoughts going on in a corner of their mind. Notice how the average person believes that thinking means sitting quietly and looking far away, resting your chin in your hand like someone listening to distant music? Sometimes you say, 'When there's too much noise I *can't hear myself think*.' But when an intellectual, a real thinker is thinking—" He had been talking louder with more excitement as the subject got hold of him. He was leaning forward, his eyes glittering.

I laughed, interrupting. "When an intellectual is thinking he goes into high gear, leans forward, bugs his eyes at you and practically climbs the wall with each word, like you, Ahmed. Are you an Archetype?"

He shook his head. "Only for my kind of person. If an average kind of person started picking up my kind of thinking, it wouldn't solve his problems—so he would ignore it."

He quit talking because I was laughing so hard. Laughing drove away the ghosts of despair that were eating at my heart. "Your kind of person! Ho ho. Show me one. Ha ha. Ignore it? Hell, if a man found your thoughts in his head he'd go to a psychiatrist. He'd think he was going off his rails."

Ahead we saw the big "14" signs signaling Fourteenth Street. I shifted gears on the linked seats and we began to slide sideways from moving cables to slower cables, slowing and going uphill.

We stopped. On the slow strip coming along a girl was kneeling sideways in one of the seats. I thought she was tying a shoelace, but when I looked back I saw she was lying curled up, her knees under her chin, her tumb in her mouth. Regression. Retreat into infancy. Defeat.

Somehow it sent a shiver of fear through me. Defeat should not come so easily. Ahmed had leaped out of his chair and was halfway toward the stairs.

"Ahmed!" I shouted.

He looked back and saw the girl. The seat carried her slowly by in the low-speed lane.

He waved to me to follow him and bounded up the moving stairs. "Come on," he yelled back, "before it gets worse."

When I got up top I saw Ahmed disappearing into the White Horse Tavern. I ran down the block and went in after him, into the cool shadows and paneled wood—nothing seemed to move. My eyes adjusted slowly and I saw Ahmed with his elbows on the counter, sipping a beer, and discussing the weather with the bartender.

It was too much for me. The world was out of its mind in one way and Ahmed was out of his mind in a different way. I could not figure it out, and I was ready to knock Ahmed's block off.

I was thirsty, but there was no use trying to drink or eat anything around that nut. I put my elbows on the bar a long way from Ahmed and called over to the bartender. "A quart of bock to go." I tilted my head at Ahmed. "He'll pay for it."

I sounded normal enough, but the bartender jumped and moved fast. He plunked a bottle in a brown paper bag in front of me and rubbed the bar in front of me with wood polish.

"Nice weather," he said, and looked around his place with his shoulders hunched, looking over his shoulders. "I wish I was outside walking in the fresh air. Have you been here before?"

"Once," I said, picking up the bag. "I liked it." I remembered the people who had shown me the place. Jean Fitzpatrick—she had shown me some of her poetry at a party—and a nice guy, her husband. Mort Fitzpatrick had played a slide whistle in his own tunes when we were walking along over to the tavern, and some bearded friends of theirs walked with us and talked odd philosophy and strange shared trips. The girl told me that she and her husband had a house in the neighborhood, and invited me to a party there, which I turned down, and she asked me to drop in anytime.

I knew she meant the "anytime" invitation. They were villagers, Bohemians, the kind who collect art, and strange books, and farout people. Villagers always have the door open for people with strange stories and they always have a pot of coffee ready to share with you.

"Do Jean Fitzpatrick and Mort Fitzpatrick still live around here?" I asked the bartender.

"I see them around. They haven't been in recently." He began to wipe and polish the bar away from me, moving toward Ahmed. "For all I know they might have moved."

Ahmed sipped his beer and glanced at us sidelong, like a stranger.

I walked out into the gray day with a paper bag under my arm with its hard weight of bock beer inside. I could quit this crazy, sick-making business of being a detector. I could go look up somebody in the Village like Jean Fitzpatrick and tell how sick the day had been, and how I couldn't take it and had chickened out, until the story began to seem funny and the world became some place I could stand.

Ahmed caught up with me and put a hand on my arm. I stopped myself from spinning around to hit him and just stood—staring straight ahead.

"You angry?" he asked, walking around me to get a look at my face. "How do you feel?"

"Ahmed, my feelings are my own business. OK? There is a girl around here I want to look up. I want to make sure she is all right. OK? Don't let me hold you up on Rescue Squad business. Don't wait for me. OK?" I started walking again, but the pest was walking right behind me. I had spelled it out clear and loud that I didn't want company. I did not want to flatten him, because at other times he had been my friend.

"May I come along?" he asked politely. "Maybe I can help."

I shrugged, walking along toward the river. What difference did it make? I was tired and there was too much going on in New York City. Ahmed would go away soon on his business. The picture of talking to the girl was warm, dark, relaxing. We'd share coffee and tell each other crazy little jokes and let the world go forgotten.

The house of the Fitzpatricks was one of those little tilted houses left over from a hundred years ago when the city was a town, lovingly restored by hand labor and brightened under many coats of paint by groups of volunteer decorators. It shone with white paint and red doors and red shutters with windowboxes under each window growing green vines and weeds and wildflowers. The entire house was overhung by the gigantic girders of the Hudson River Drive with its hissing flow of traffic making a faint rumble through the air and shaking the ground underfoot.

I knocked on the bright red door. No one answered. I found an unused doorbutton at the side and pushed it. Chimes sounded, but nothing stirred inside.

Village places usually are lived in by guests. Day or night someone is there: broke artists, travelers, hitchhikers, stunned inefficient-looking refugees from the student or research worlds staving off a nervous breakdown by a vacation far away from pressure. It was considered legitimate to put your head inside and holler for attention if you couldn't raise anyone by knocking and ringing. I turned the knob to go in. It would not turn. It was locked.

I felt like they had locked the door when they saw me coming. The big dope, musclehead George is coming, lock the door. This was a bad day, but I couldn't go any farther. There was no place to go but here.

I stood shaking the knob dumbly, trying to turn it. It began to make a rattling noise like chains, and like an alarm clock in a hospital. The sound went through my blood and almost froze my hand. I thought something was behind the door, and I thought it was opening and a monster with a skull face was standing there waiting.

I turned my back to the door and carefully, silently went down the two steps to the sidewalk. I had gone so far off my rails that I thought I heard the door creaking open, and I thought I felt the cold wind of someone reaching out to grab me.

I did not look back, just strode away, walking along the same direction I had been going, pretending I had not meant to touch that door.

Ahmed trotted beside me, sidling to get a view of

my face, scuttling sideways and ahead of me like a big crab.

"What's the matter? What is it?"

"She's not— Nobody was—" It was a lie. Somebody or something was in that house. Ignore it, walk away faster.

"Where are we going now?" Ahmed asked.

"Straight into the river," I said and laughed. It sounded strange and hurt my chest like coughing. "The water is a mirage in the desert and you walk out on the dry sand looking for water to drown in. The sand is covered with all the lost dried things that sank out of sight. You die on the dry sand, crawling, looking for water. Nobody sees you. People sail overhead and see the reflection of the sky in the fake waves. Divers come and find your dried mummy on the bottom and make notes, wondering because they think there is water in the river. But it is all a lie."

I stopped. The giant docks were ahead, and between them the ancient, small wharfs. There was no use going in that direction, or in any direction. The world was shriveled and old, with thousands of years of dust settling on it—a mummy case. As I stood there the world grew smaller, closing in on me like a lid shutting me into a box. I was dead, lying down, yet standing upright on the sidewalk. I could not move.

"Ahmed," I said, hearing my voice from a great distance, "get me out of this. What's a friend for?"

He danced around me like some evil goblin. "Why can't you help yourself?"

"I can't move," I answered, being remarkably reasonable.

He circled me, looking at my face and the way I stood. He was moving with stops and starts, like a bug looking for a place to bite. I imagined myself shooting a spray can of insecticide at him.

Suddenly he used the *voice*, the clear deep hypnotic voice that penetrates into the dark private world where I live when I'm asleep and dreaming.

"Why can't you move?"

The gulf opened up beneath my feet. "Because I'd fall," I answered.

He used the voice again, and it penetrated to an interior world where the dreams lived and were real all the time. I was shriveled and weak, lying on dust and bits of old cloth. A foul and dusty smell was in my nostrils and I was looking down over an edge where the air came up from below. The air from below smelled better. I had been there a long time. Ahmed's voice reached me; it asked—

"How far would you fall?"

I measured the distance with my eye. I was tired and the effort to think was very hard. Drop ten or twelve feet to the landing, then tangle your feet in the ladder lying there and pitch down the next flight of steep stairs. . . . Death waited at the bottom.

"A long way," I answered. "I'm too heavy. Stairs are steep."

"You mouth is dry," he said.

I could feel the thirst like flames, drying up my throat, thickening my tongue as he asked the question, the jackpot question.

"Tell me, what is your name?"

I tried to answer with my right name, George Sanford. I heard a voice croak "Jean Dalais."

"Where do you live?" he asked in the penetrating voice that rang inside my skull and rang into the evil other world where I, or someone, was on the floor smelling dust for the duration of eternity.

"Downstairs," I heard myself answer.

"Where are you now?" he asked in the same penetrating voice.

"In hell," the voice answered from my head.

I struck out with careful aim to flatten him with the single blow. He was dangerous. I had to stop him, and leave him stopped. I struck carefully, with hatred. He fell backward and I started to run. I ran freely, one block, two blocks. My legs were my own, my body was my own, my mind was my own. I was George Sanford and I could move without fear of falling. No one was behind me. No one was in front of me. The sun shone through the clouds, the fresh wind blew along the empty sidewalks. I was alone. I had left that capsule world of dead horror standing behind me like an abandoned phone booth.

This time I knew what to do to stay out of it. Don't think back. Don't remember what Ahmed was trying to do. Don't bother about rescuing anyone. Take a walk along the edge of the piers in the foggy sunshine and think cheerful thoughts, or no thoughts at all.

I looked back and Ahmed was sitting on the sidewalk far back. I remembered that I was exceptionally strong and the coach had warned me to hold myself back when I hit. Even Ahmed? But he had been thinking, listening, off guard.

What had I said? *Jean Dalais*. Jean Fitzpatrick had showed me some of her poetry, and that had been the name signed to it. Was Jean Dalais really Jean Fitzpatrick? It was probably her name before she married Mort Fitzpatrick.

I had run by the white house with the red shutters. I looked back. It was only a half a block back. I went back, striding before fear could grip me again, and rattled the knob and pulled at the red door and looked at the lock.

Ahmed caught up with me.

"You know how to pick locks?" I asked him.

"It's too slow," he answered in a low voice. "Let's try the windows."

He was right. The first window we tried was only stuck by New York soot. With our hands black and grimy with soot we climbed into the kitchen. The kitchen was neat except for a dried-up salad in a bowl. The sink was dry, the air was stuffy.

It was good manners to yell announcement of our trespassing.

"Jean!" I called. I got back echoes and silence, and

something small falling off a shelf upstairs. The ghosts rose in my mind again and stood behind me, their claws outstretched. I looked over my shoulder and saw only the empty kitchen. My skin prickled. I was afraid of making a noise. Afraid death would hear me. Had to yell; afraid to yell. Had to move; afraid to move. Dying from cowardice. Someone else's thoughts, with the odor of illness, the burning of thirst, the energy of anger. I was shriveling up inside.

I braced a hand on the kitchen table. "Upstairs in the attic," I said. I knew what was wrong with me now. Jean Dalais was an Archetype. She was delirious and dreaming that she was I. Or I was really Jean Dalais suffering through another dream of rescue, and I was dreaming that strange people were downstairs in my kitchen looking for me. I, Jean, hated these hallucinations. I struck at the dream images of men with the true feeling of weakness and illness, with the memory of the time that had passed with no one helping me and the hatred of a world that trapped you and made hope a lie, trying to blast the lies into vanishing.

The George Sanford hallucination slid down to a sitting position on the floor of the kitchen. The bottle of bock in its paper bag hit the floor beside him, with a heavy clunk, sounding almost real. "You go look, Ahmed," said the George Sanford mouth.

The other figure in the dream bent over and placed a phone on the floor. It hit the linoleum with another clunk and a musical chiming sound that seemed to be heard upstairs. "Hallucinations getting more real. Can hear 'em now," muttered the Sanford self—or was it Jean Dalais who was thinking?

"When I yell, dial 0 and ask for the Rescue Squad to come over." Ahmed picked up the paper bag of bock. "OK, George?" He started looking through the kitchen drawers. "Great stuff, beer, nothing better for extreme dehydration. Has salt in it. Keeps the system from liquid shock."

He found the beer opener and slipped it into his hip pocket. "Liquid shock is from sudden changes in the water-versus-salt balance," he remarked, going up the stairs softly, two at a time. He went out of sight and I heard his footsteps, very soft and inquiring. Even Ahmed was afraid of stirring up ghosts.

What had Bessie said about the victim? "Hope hurts." She had tried to give the victim hope and the victim had struck her to the heart with a dagger of hatred and shared despair.

That was why I was sitting on the floor!

Danger George *don't think!* I shut my eyes and blanked my mind.

The dream of rescue and the man images were gone. I was Jean Dalais sinking down into the dark, a warm velvet darkness, no sensation, no thought, only distantly the pressure of the attic floor against my face.

A strange thump shook the floor and a scraping sound pulled at my curiosity. I began to wake again. It was a familiar sound, familiar from the other world and the other life, six days ago, an eternity ago, almost forgotten. The attic floor pushed against my face with a smell of dust. The thump and the scraping sound came again, metal against wood. I was curious. I opened dry, sand-filled eyes and raised my head, and the motion awakened my body to the hell of thirst and the ache of weakness.

I saw the two ends of the aluminum ladder sticking up through the attic trapdoor. The ladder was back now. It had fallen long ago, and now it was back, looking at me, expecting me to climb down it. I cursed the ladder with a mental bolt of hatred. What good is a ladder if you can't move? Long ago I had found that moving around brought on labor pains. Not good to have a baby here. Better to hold still.

I heard a voice. "She's here. George. Call the Rescue Squad." I hated the voice. Another imaginary voice in the long nightmare of imaginary rescues. Who was "George"? I was Jean Dalais.

George. Someone had called "George." Downstairs in the small imagined kitchen I imagined a small image of a man grope for a phone beside him on the floor. He dialed "0" clumsily. A female voice asked a question. The man image said "Rescue Squad," hesitantly.

The phone clicked and buzzed and then a deep voice said, "Rescue Squad."

In the attic I knew how a dream of the Rescue Squad should go. I had dreamed it before. I spoke through the small man-image. "My name is Jean Fitzpatrick. I am at 29 Washington Street. I am trapped in my attic without water. If you people weren't fools, you would have found me long ago. Hurry. I'm pregnant." She made the man-image drop the receiver. The dream of downstairs faded again as the man-image put his face in his hands.

My dry eyes were closed, the attic floor again pressed against my face. Near me was the creak of ladder rungs taking weight, and then the creaks of the attic floor, something heavy moving on it gently, then the rustle of clothing as somebody moved; the click of a bottle opener against a cap; the clink of the cap hitting the floor; the bubbling and hissing of a fizzing cool liquid. A hand lifted my head carefully and a cold bottle lip pushed against my mouth. I opened my mouth and the cool touch of liquid pressed within it and down the dry throat. I began to swallow.

George Sanford, me, took his hands away from his eyes and looked down at the phone. I was not lying down; I was not drinking; I was not thirsty. Had I dialed the Rescue Squad when Ahmed called me? A small mannequin of a man in Jean Fitzpatrick's mind had called and hung up, but the mannequin was me, George Sanford—six feet one and a half inches. I am no woman's puppet. The strength of telepathy is powered by emotion and need, and the woman upstairs had enough emotion and need, but no one could have done that to me if I did not want to help. No one.

A musical, two-toned note of a siren approaching, growing louder. It stopped before the door. Loud knocks came at the door. I was feeling all right but still dizzy and not ready to move.

"Come in," I croaked. They rattled the knob. I got up and let them in, then stood hanging onto the back of a chair.

Emergency squad orderlies in blue and white. "You sick?"

"Not me, the woman upstairs." I pointed and they rushed up the stairs, carrying their stretcher and medical kits.

There was no thirst or need driving her mind to intensity any more, but our minds were still connected somehow, for I felt the prick of a needle in one thigh, and then the last dizziness and fear dimmed and vanished, the world steadied out in a good upright position, the kitchen was not a dusty attic but only a clean empty kitchen and all the sunshine of the world was coming in the windows.

I took a deep breath and stretched, feeling the muscles strong and steady in my arms and legs. I went up to the second floor and steadied the ladder for the Rescue Squad men while they carried the unconscious body of a young woman down from the attic.

She was curly-haired with a dirt-and-tear streaked face and skinny arms and legs. She was bulging in the middle, as pregnant as a pumpkin.

I watched the blue and white Rescue truck drive away.

"Want to come and along and watch me make out my report?" Ahmed asked.

On the way out of the kitchen I looked around for the Turkish honey rolls, but the bag was gone. I must have dropped it somewhere.

We walked south a few blocks to the nearest police station, Ahmed settled down at a desk they weren't using to fill out his report, and I found a stack of comic magazines in the waiting room and chose the one with the best action on the cover. My hands shook a little because I was hungry, but I felt happy and important.

Ahmed filled out the top, wrote a few lines, and then started working the calculator on the desk. He stopped, stared off into space, glanced at me and started writing again, glancing at me every second. I wondered what he was writing about me. I wanted the Rescue Squad brass to read good things about me. I wanted the Rescue Squad brass to read good things about me so they would hire me for a job.

"I hunch good, don't I, Ahmed?"

"Yes." He filled something into a space, read the directions for the next question and began biting the end of his pen and staring at the ceiling.

"Would I make a good detector?" I asked.

"What kind of mark did you get in Analysis of Variance in high school?"

"I never took it. I flunked probability in algebra, in six B—"

"The Rescue Squad wants you to fill out reports that they can run into the statistics machines. Look"—I went over and he showed me a space where he filled out some numbers and a funny symbol like a fallen-down d—"can you read it, George?"

"What's it say?"

"It says probability .005. That means the odds were two hundred to one against you finding the White Horse Tavern just by accident, when it was the place the Fitzpatrick woman usually went to. I got the number by taking a rough count of the number of bars in the phone book. More than two hundred wrong bars, and there was only one bar you actually went to. Two hundred divided by one, or two hundred. If you had tried two bars before finding the right one your chance of being wrong would have been two hundred divided by two. That's one hundred. Your score for being right was your chance of being wrong, or the reciprocal of your chance of being right by luck. Your score is two hundred. Understand? Around here they think forty is a good score."

I stared at him, looking stupid. The school had tried relays of teachers and tutors on me for two terms before they gave up trying to teach me. It didn't seem to mean anything. It didn't seem to have anything to do with people. Without probability algebra and graphs I found out they weren't going to let me take Psychology B, History, Social Dynamics, Systems Analysis, Business Management, Programming or Social Work. They wouldn't even let me study to be a Traffic Flow cop. I could have taken Electronics Repair but I wanted to work with people, not TV sets, so I dropped out. I couldn't do school work, but the kind of thing the Rescue Squad wanted done, I could do.

"Ahmed, I'd be good in the Rescue Squad. I don't need statistics. Remember I told you you were pushing Bessie in too deep. I was right, wasn't I? And you were wrong. That shows I don't need training."

Ahmed looked sorry for me. "George, you don't get any score for that. Every soft-hearted slob is afraid when he sees someone going into a traumatic area in the subjective world. He always tries to make them stop. You would have said I was pushing her too deep anyhow, even if you were wrong."

"But I was right."

Ahmed half rose out of his chair, then made himself calm down.

He settled back, his lips pale and tight against his teeth. "It doesn't matter if you were right, unless you are right against odds. You get credit for picking the White Horse Tavern out of all the taverns you could have picked, and you get credit for picking the girl's house out of all the addresses you could have picked. I'm going to multiply the two figures by each other. It will run your score over eighty thousand probably. That's plenty of credit."

"But I only went to the tavern because I was thirsty.

You can't credit me with that. You made me thirsty somehow. And I went to the girl's house because I wanted to see her. Maybe she was pulling at me."

"I don't care what your reasons were! You went to the right place, didn't you? You found her, didn't you?" Ahmed stood up and shouted. "You're talking like a square. What do you think this is, 1950, or some time your grandmother was running a store? I don't care what your reasons are, nobody cares anymore what the reasons are. We only care about results, understand? We don't know why things happen, but if everyone makes out good reports about them, with clear statistics, we can run the reports into the machines, and the machines will tell us exactly what is happening, and we can work with that, because they're facts, and it's the real world. I know you can find people. Your reasons don't matter. Scientific theories about causes don't matter!"

He was red in the face and shouting, like I'd said something against his religion or something. "I wish we could get theories for some of it. But, if the statistics say that if something funny happens here and something else funny always happens over there, next, we don't have to know how the two connect; all we have to do is expect the second thing every time we see the first thing happen. See?"

I didn't know what he was talking about. My tutors had said things like that to me, but Ahmed felt miserable enough about it to shout. Ahmed was a friend.

"Ahmed," I said, "would I make a good detector?"

"You'd make a great detector, you dope!" He looked down at his report. "But you can't get into the Rescue Squad. The rules say that you've got to have brains in your head instead of rocks. I'll help you figure out someplace else you can get a job. Stick around. I'll loan you fifty bucks as soon as I finish this report. Go read something."

I felt lousy, but I stood there fighting it, because this was my last chance at a real job, and there was something right about what I was trying to do. The Rescue Squad needed me. Lost people were going to need me.

"Ahmed," I said, trying to make my meaning very clear to him. "I *should* be in your department. You gotta figure out a way to get me in."

It's hard watching a strong, confident guy go through a change. Generally Ahmed always knows what he is doing, he never wonders. He stared down at his report, holding his breath, he was thinking so hard. Then he got away from his desk and began to pace up and down. "What the hell is wrong with me? I must be going chicken. Desk work is softening me up." He grabbed up his report off the desk. "Come on, let's go buck the rules. Let's fight City Hall."

"We can't hire your friend." The head of the Rescue Squad shook his head. "He couldn't pass the tests. You said so yourself."

"The *rules* say that George has to pass the pen and paper tests." Ahmed leaned forward on the desk and tapped his hand down on the desk and tapped his hand down on the desk top, emphasizing words. "The rules are *trash* rules made up by trash bureaucrats so that nobody can get a job but people with picky little old-maid minds like them! Rules are something we use to deal with people we don't know and don't care about. We know George and we know we want him! How do we fake the tests?"

The chief held out one hand, palm down. "Slow down, Ahmed. I appreciate enthusiasm, but maybe we can get George in legitimately. I know he cut short an epidemic of hysteria and psychosomatics at the hospitals and saved the hospitals a lot of time and expense. I want him in the deparment if he can keep that up. But let's not go breaking up the system to get him in. We can use the system."

The chief opened the intercom switch and spoke into the humming box. "Get me Accounting, will you?"

The box answered after a short while and the chief spoke again. He was a big, square-built man, going slightly flabby. His skin was loose and slightly gray. "Jack, listen, we need the services of a certain expert. We can't hire him. He doesn't fit the height and weight regulations, or something like that. How do we pay him?"

The man at the other end spoke briefly in accounting technicalities: ". . . Contingencies, services, fees. Consultant. File separate services rendered, time and results, with statistics of probability rundown on departmental expenses saved by outside help and city expenses saved by the Rescue Squad action, et cetera, et cetera. Get it?"

"OK, thanks." He shut off the chatterbox and spoke to Ahmed. "We're in. Your friend is hired."

My feet were tired standing there. My hands were shaking slightly so I had stuffed them into my pockets, like a nonchalant pose. I was passing the time thinking of restaurants, all the good ones that served the biggest plates for the least money. "When do I get paid?" I asked.

"Next month," Ahmed said. "You get paid at the end of every month for the work you did on each separate case. Don't look so disappointed. You are a consultant expert now. You are on my expense account. I'm supposed to buy your meals and pay your transportation to the scene of the crime whenever I consult you."

"Consult me now," I said.

We had a great Italian meal at an old-fashioned Italian restaurant: lasagna, antipasto, French bread in thick, tough slices, lots of butter, four cups of hot black coffee and spumoni for dessert, rich and sweet. Everything tasted fresh and cooked just right, and they served big helpings. I stopped shaking after the second cup of coffee.

There was something funny about that restaurant.

Somebody was planning a murder, but I wasn't going to mention it to Ahmed until after dessert.

He'd probably want me to rescue somebody instead of eating.

POSITIVELY THE LAST PACT
WITH—THE DEVIL?
by J. O. JEPPSON

Marty Greenberg has done the headnotes for every story in this collection, except for this one and one other. I (Isaac Asimov) am undertaking the chore here. J. O. Jeppson (the J. stands for Janet) is a psychiatrist by vocation and a science fiction writer by lifelong determination. She has published two novels, *The Second Experiment* (1974) and *The Last Immortal* (1980), each one remarkable for scope and complexity. She has been rather slow at trying to penetrate the realm of the short story despite the insistence of her husband that she is even better in the short lengths. As evidence that he is right we offer the following, which will surely engage your sympathies for the poor devil (the character in the story, that is, not the husband). And since I've mentioned her husband, I just want to say she is married to a charming, talented, and devilishly handsome chap, for J. O. Jeppson is also Mrs. Isaac Asimov.

HEARKEN, oh Earthmen, to my sad story of disaster and outrage. Consider my woes, including the necessity of translating this into your miserably difficult language. Yes, weep for me, but don't let those damn human tears land on my hide—they chap.

I was once a happy being, content in my position as Computer Attendant on our planet, Uxslup the Beautiful, and determined to win the degree for which I had been working many years. The Computer is in the Building of Applied Science, a large and complex edifice in which the filing system gets overloaded, so that I am not entirely responsible for what happened.

It was certainly not my fault that although I had been studying Earth records for my doctorate, it was entirely by mistake that my name was included on the list of Uxsluppian Collectors and—horror of horrors—assigned to Earth. Furthermore, the relevant documents informing me of this new position went astray in the mails. I was not prepared.

Earth history was known to me not only because of my thesis—"Necessary Permutations of Medieval Social Norms Reflected in the Psychopathology of Fears of Adders and Serpents and Infernal Gate Inscriptions"—but also because your pushy little planet is a prime example of misguided intelligence in the dominant life form. There was, in addition, the mysterious disappearance of the previous Collector. However, I confess that we Uxsluppians, although so much more intelligent and sensible than Earthmen, tended to forget to notice what was going on in that obscure section of a remote spiral arm of an otherwise admirable galaxy.

I was just immersing myself in a deliciously hot bath when the unexpected summons came and I arrived in the living room of that infamous monster, Carson Boskov.

"You're dripping on my carpet," said Carson.

"But I. . . ."

"And I thought you'd be bigger."

I drew myself up to my full height, four feet in Earth measurements, and wished I had a towel. I surveyed the pentagram at my feet in distaste.

"I am an exceptionally tall Uxsluppian," I said as politely as possible from my central speaking aperture. My left horn twitched nervously, my hide puckered in the oxygen-rich air, and the fork in my tail itched.

Carson towered over me. "I can hardly understand you," he said in that typically heavy, oily Earthman voice. "Must you squeak?"

"Please be so kind as to inform me of how this happened," I said—plaintively, I admit.

"And you're bright red! Do you sweat sulfuric acid, because it seems to be eating my carpet . . ."

"I was in the bath," I said with dignity, "What do you want?"

"The usual," said Carson. "But first let me explain myself. I am a neurophysiologist, cyberneticist, extraordinary genius, winner of the Nobel prize for my work on computer analogues of the nervous system, and I've thought about devils for a long time. It occurred to me that perhaps the pentagram symbol was keyed into a telepathic computer somewhere in the galaxy that would respond to appropriate emotion-laden words. I have searched through libraries of the occult until I found what I thought were several verbal rituals in several languages. I tried them all, but being an unusually clear-headed, controlled, unimpassioned genius, I did not succeed in working up the required emotional fervency until tonight."

"And how did you manage tonight?" I asked, thinking mournfully of the charming female waiting for me at the Grand Kaludhat's party, which was why I'd been taking a bath.

"After I beat the one in the lab at chess today, I worked up an impassioned desire to have the best computer in the universe," said Carson, sitting down opposite the pentagram.

"Well, you can't have it since it belongs to Uxslup. Why not ask for your heart's desire?"

"That happens to be my heart's desire."

I scratched my tail. "I've always understood that humans had ordinary wishes—riches, power, long life, successful evasion of income tax—surely you could be satisfied with any of those? Intelligent beings on other planets are."

"Other planets?" Carson settled back in his comfortable chair, crossing his repulsively lanky legs while I continued to drip on the carpet.

"Since you have figured out that devils, as humans have always called us Uxsluppians, are not supernatural, you will readily understand that we need to keep our Central Computer growing. As top creature in the galaxy, we have always Collected suitable intelligent specimens from every parsec of space, even from this extremely unpleasant planet."

"Indeed," said Carson, "you've been around a lot lately. Things are a mess on Earth."

"Don't blame your troubles on us. No one has teleported to Earth for centuries, except for my unfortunate predecessor."

"What happened to him?"

"He had a terrible case of arthritis in his terminal tail joint—that's where we do a considerable amount of our logical thinking—and thought he would benefit from a vacation in a primitive environment. He actually asked to become Collector for Earth, but we've never heard from him."

Carson yawned, as I believe the expression is for that peculiar display of widening the speaking aperture to show the built-in chopping weapons. "What's your name?"

"Mef 27."

"Listen, Mef, how did Uxsluppians find Earth in the first place?"

"A typical story. Prehistoric members of the planet's most intelligent species start using tools, get to drawing pictures, using strong emotional expletives when the tools don't work or the pictures won't come out right, and before you know it they've invented oaths and the pentagram. So at times they're bound to tie into the telepathic network of our Computer. Fortunately, only Uxsluppians in high governmental positions—or scientific research, it being the same thing in our enlightened world—know the secret of using computers to focus psi powers and provide instantaneous teleportation anywhere. That way, we can control any rebellion within our Empire immediately."

"Then Earth is part of the Uxsluppian Empire?"

I shivered, possibly from the cold, but probably from premonition. "Certainly not. You are not civilized enough. Earth was used, before it got too dirty and crowded, primarily for tourist entertainment—fertility rites, black magic, witch hunts, and other fun and games."

A faint but ominously contemptuous smile flickered over Carson's bony face—give me handsome Uxsluppian blob any time—as he said, "But what about your habit of collecting souls?"

"Oh, that. Actually, we Collect brains, or rather the central intelligence agency of whatever nervous system we want to—why are you laughing?"

"Central intell—" Carson rose, chuckling, and strode over to a container of liquid to pour himself an evil-smelling drink. "Then what do you do with the Collected brains my red friend?"

"We hook them into our Computer, of course. While Uxsluppians are able to teleport onto any pentagram field to which the Computer focuses—even against their will, as you have witnessed—we are not telepathic and thus of no use in our Computer system."

Carson nodded thoughtfully and then sniffed suspiciously at me. "Chlorine? I thought it was supposed to be sulfur?"

I whitened in embarrassment. "Sulfur from the bath. Chlorine from, er, sweat—we do that when the atmosphere is too cold."

"Nervous, eh?" said Carson, maliciously penetrating my rationalization. He extracted a large piece of folded material from his pocket and threw it at me.

Gratefully—oh, the irony of it—I dried and draped myself, struggling to continue my narration. I had never read of such a wordy encounter with a human before. I'd always thought they simply made a deal, or got on their knees to pray.

"You see," I said, "while humans were in their medieval period, we switched our economy from one based on separate electromechanical computers of the antique type you now use to a unified micromolecular arrangement run on an electrochemical-neurophysiological basis. We Collected central intell—that is, brains, from all over the galaxy. On primitive planets like Earth, it was easier to do this by means of the pact-with-the-Devil routine. Signing a contract creates a psychological set in the brain that facilitates subsequent Collection and removal to the tank."

"Tank?"

"Yes, our beautiful tank of brains, all immortal, thanks to the artificial protoplasm we invented to protect and nourish the specimens. We haven't needed many new specimens for years—well, I mean—the economy hasn't permitted much scientific expansion."

"I know how that is," said Carson, reaching down to tap my right horn with a ball-point pen. I found out later that he always corrected manuscripts, wrote mathematical calculations, and did crossword puzzles with a pen.

"I suppose I ought to wish for a rich lode of uranium to be planted under my back yard," he said, meditatively stroking his ugly, protruding chin, "or perhaps a brief teleportation to the innards of Fort Knox, with enough longevity shots to have time and money to build my own computer . . ."

"Excellent," I said with relief, thinking I might be able to make it to the Grand Kaludhat's orgy after all. "You've shown that humans are capable of constructive thinking."

"But I've changed my mind," said Carson. "I will sell my brain to you for immediate placement in your Central Computer."

"My dear human! That's the punishment part of the pact, as I understand it. You shouldn't go against tradition. After all, the tank is called hell, just to please the human specimens."

"Take me to hell, Mef, immediately."

I sighed. "Very well. I didn't bring the official form with me, but I'll write it out on this paper from your desk." I reached for it, noting that at the top of the paper Carson's name was imprinted egocentrically—that ego I expected to have within our power soon.

"Here, Carson Boskov, Ph.D. Sign this."

"In blood?"

"Great Uc, no! It corrodes my fingers. I don't know how that legend got started. Use some other body fluid if you must. I believe your kidneys . . ."

"Certainly not."

"Spit?" I asked, conscious that the sweating of my hide was all too likely to produce a temporary ion deficiency and therefore a whopper of an Uxsluppian headache.

"Excuse the expression, Mef, but for hell's sake what do most of your victims use?"

"Ink."

Just short of an Uxsluppian year later, I was hard at work on my thesis, which had been turned down by my committee for the sixth time, when someone entered my room in the Building of Applied Science without knocking.

"It's been a most interesting and profitable experience," said Carson Boskov. "Thanks for Collecting me."

"You can't be here!" As I lept up in astonishment, my hooves tangled with my tail, and I discovered the floor to be exceedingly hard on my proximal tail joints. "You're only a brain in the tank," I shouted. "You have no body!"

This was unlikely, since there he was, flexing the muscles of his totally, repulsively nude body.

"Amazing what a properly run giant Computer can do with undifferentiated protoplasm when it puts its mind to it," he said.

I looked frantically around for the emergency alarm, never before used. I wished again that Uxsluppians were telepathic, and I was so unstrung I couldn't garner my psi forces for teleportation, always difficult without a pentagram.

"Don't work at trying to kill me," said Carson, "since there are several exact copies. I've made improvements in the original, equipping some bodies with special adaptive mechanisms for planets not ordinarily habitable by human beings, and all of us are telepathic, linking up with other telepaths throughout the galaxy. You Uxsluppians are out as top creature."

"I'll teleport for help!"

"We'll follow you. We can do it too, without pentagrams. We've gone to all the key planets of your Empire. We're running the galaxy now."

"But my dear Carson. . . ."

"The name is Dr. Boskov, Mef. If you're a good boy maybe you'll get that doctorate."

"I will not be led astray from the paths of virtue!"

"I said, do you want that degree, Mef?"

I was tempted, sorely tempted. "What must I do?"

"Just sign this contract for a place in my new business—Boskov's Bodies for Better Being."

"What's the catch?"

"If you'll read the fine print, you'll see that your new job as Computer Attendant is to make sure the tenants of the tank don't fudge up their linkages."

"But I already do that!"

"These will be new tenants, since the previous tank inhabitants have left. We'll use Uxsluppian brains—from high governmental positions, of course—and augment your species' teleporting power to do the heavy work of the galaxy—moving planets, even suns."

"You'll destroy galactic ecology!"

Carson grinned, a tail-chilling sight. "We may even rearrange the universe. Since we now live forever and the universe may ultimately rearrange itself to our disadvantage, we're going to control it. Uxsluppians will be performing a noble duty in the tank."

"Confined to hell!"

"Forever," said Carson remorselessly. "Sign here."

I succumbed to evil temptation. I signed. I had a terrible headache.

"By the way," said Carson, folding the pact, "I found out what happened to the Uxsluppian Collector who disappeared on Earth. It seems he teleported onto what he thought was a large, convenient homing diagram. It turned out to be the wet foundations of a huge five-sided structure we were building near Washington, D. C., U.S.A. Since you Uxsluppians can't move heavy weights unless several of you work together, and since he became part of the cement, he was trapped."

"And he's still there?"

"No, it seems he finally tunneled out, only to emerge in another building . . ."

"Not—not the white one . . ."

"You Uxsluppians have a lot to answer for. Get a move on, Mef."

I don't mean to complain, Earthmen, but please have pity. It's been two centuries now—and you untrustworthy sons of hell have not honored that last pact. I still don't have my Ph.D.!

REJOICE, REJOICE, WE HAVE NO CHOICE

by TERRY CARR

Terry Carr is one of the most important editors, both as a reprint anthologist and as a buyer/editor of original material, in the science fiction field. His Universe series of original anthologies has maintained an exceptionally high standard for many years, as have his "Best of the Year" books in science fiction and, more recently, in fantasy. He is also an infrequent but frequently superior writer—witness "Rejoice, Rejoice, We Have No Choice," a disaster story with a difference.

LIVING is a lot harder for Paul than for the rest of us, but there isn't much I can do about it. He makes things even harder than they have to be, and I don't know why. I can't read his mind: Paul is my father.

"Awful time for this to happen," he says, shading his eyes to scan the sky for weather. "Worst time of the year; we've got to get the crop in. I guess that sounds callous, Bennie, but it's just the way it is."

"I know," I say. I'm thinking that Paul is trying to cover up how he feels again. His brother is dying back at the house and Paul wants to worry about the harvest. Wants to.

"We can't look back," he tells me. "We've got to keep on living. Still got a lot of rebuilding to do." The sky is gray, a low cloud ceiling that promises neither rain nor sun. That's good, because if the rains start before we get the crop in we'll have to work around the clock till the fields are clear. We did that once, a few years ago when I was twelve.

Paul suddenly turns to me and looks searchingly into my eyes. Trying to read me—that's how people used to do it. He asks me, "Bennie, how do you feel about it?"

"You mean about Uncle Charles? I hope he gets well, but I guess he won't."

That's all I say, and after a bit Paul looks away from me. He hunches up his shoulders, shakes himself and looks at the sky again. It's a quiet day; I can hear the chickens cackling way back at the house.

"I guess what I mean," Paul says, "is do you ever think about when you'll have to work the farm by yourself, just you and Katie. It isn't rich land, you know; it won't give you anything extra. You think you'll be able to make a go?"

I say, "I'm not worrying about it. Anyway you'll be around for a long time yet."

He rubs his chin with the back of his hand. "I've got every intention," he says.

At night we sit around the kitchen table, Paul and me and Katie, my sister. We've all been working hard, Paul and me in the field and Katie taking care of Uncle Charles. Katie's thirteen and sort of mad at the world; she's had to take care of the house ever since Mom died two years ago.

"We got a lot done today," Paul says. "Got a jump on the weather. We could get the whole job done this week if Charlie wasn't sick. Ain't that much land that gives us any yield anyway."

"We could ask the Andersons," I suggest. They have a place just a mile away, and there are three kids in that family. *Lucy Anderson could take care of Uncle Charles,* Katie is thinking, *and I'd work in the field. I'd rather.*

"I don't like to ask neighbors for help," Paul says, blowing on his coffee. "Poor idea to get to where you need help; better to get used to making do by yourself."

"But they wouldn't mind," Katie says. "Remember when Lucy Anderson was here, she said if we needed any help they'd really be glad to come over. I mean, they know we've got sickness."

"I appreciate it," says Paul. "And it isn't that I'm ashamed to ask. But you kids have to get used to the idea you're alone in the world, you got to be able to do things for yourselves."

Katie avoids his eyes, pours a little more honey into her coffee. *Are we alone in the world?* she asks, amused.

Don't be smug, I tell her.

Next day there are rain clouds coming from the south, so we do ask the Andersons. Paul doesn't, he wouldn't, but I do. I wander out near their place in the morning so I can get in range, and I get in touch with Eddie Anderson. He's been milking, his mind wandering, so he's easy to reach.

Is your uncle bad? he wants to know.

He's dying, I tell Eddie. *They all are—you know. Uncle Charles just lasted longer than most of them.*

He used to be fat, that's why, Eddie giggles. He's only eight, and he thinks that's funny. He can't remember when everybody we knew was dying like Uncle Charles is now. I remember once going into town, and there was this sickly sweet smell.

When you come over, act like you're just dropping by, I tell him.

Eddie says, *Of course we will. You think I'm stupid?*

Eddie and Tony and Lucy come across fields and

fences after breakfast; they stop by and say they're going to the creek, going swimming.

"I wouldn't swim in that thing," Paul tells them. "How do you know what they poured into it? We had one summer here where all the fish died, the frogs too. Kids went swimming there, they came home with their eyes bloodshot and noses bleeding; that happened for months after. Funny things still happen there too, I don't care who says it's safe now." But they're not his kids, and he's only lecturing them, he can't give them orders. Anyway, Katie and I swim there sometimes, and he probably knows.

Tony says, "I feel a little funny about swimming there too, to tell the truth. Maybe you're right." Tony's about my age; he likes to act as the spokesman for the Anderson kids.

"Anyway it's clouding up," I say. "You'll have to walk all the way home in the rain."

"I don't care," Eddie says cheerfully, "I like to walk in the rain." (*Quit that,* Tony tells him.)

Lucy comes out of the kitchen with Katie, drying her hands on a towel. "Listen," she says, "I think I'll stay here today. You guys go swimming if you want, I'll visit with Katie."

Tony frowns at this. "Hey, you're gonna leave me stuck with just Eddie today? I didn't even want to go swimming in the first place."

Paul stands in the middle of our living room, his head swiveling from one to the other of us as we talk. No expression on his face; he's just waiting for us to come to the point.

Tony says, "Hey Bennie, come with us, that'll make three."

"No, we've got chores to do here," I say.

He looks surprised. "You didn't get your harvesting done? We saw the east fields all cleared slick as a whistle when we came through."

"We just have to finish the slope," I say. "There's

not much grows there anyway; we'll get it all finished today."

Paul nods. *I'm not asking for anything, he's watching that.*

Eddie says, "I wanted to go swimming today," and pouts. *Inside his head he's snickering; it's a game.*

Tony thinks a minute, then says, "How about this. Eddie and me can pitch in and help you here, and maybe we'll get done before dark that way. We could go swimming around sunset."

"I want to go swimming *now!*" Eddie cries.

Dammit, quit! Tony tells him.

Paul shifts his weight so that he's standing up more straight. He says, "You kids got no need to put yourselves out for us. We can get 'er done ourselves."

"But then Bennie can come swimming with us!" Tony says. "Anyway we don't mind the working, we got a bigger spread we work at home. Eddie's just being a brat, don't pay him no mind."

Eddie starts jumping up and down. "I'm *not* a brat, *you're* the brat!"

Tony ignores him. "All right then? Bennie? Mr. Oates? It's no trouble, truly. And Lucy's staying here today anyhow."

After a moment Paul smiles, widely and easily. "That'll be nice of you, Tony," he says in a voice he uses to talk to grownups, or to me. "Katie, you see there's a big dinner ready at noon, you hear?"

And Katie says, "Okay, we'll try," and grabs Lucy's hand to run into the pantry to see what we've got. I hear her thinking, *All that stupid talk, just to fool Paul.*

He's your Dad, I shoot after her, *you can take a little trouble for him.*

On the way to the tool shed Paul is quiet and distant. There's just the two of us, him and me, so I ask, "Are you worried about Uncle Charles?"

He shakes his head, "Charlie's as good as dead; no

use worrying about what you can't help. No, Bennie, and I'll tell you, I don't mind it when you kids get to thinking at each other around me, either. Only one thing—I wish when you talk you'd say the things you're thinking."

I don't know what to say to that, so we walk along in silence. Paul is my Dad, and I love him a lot right now.

Once I tried to tell Paul about reading minds; that was when I was real young and I hadn't quite accepted the idea that he couldn't do it. I thought he must be going along with the other grownups, all pretending they couldn't do it, for some grownup reason. Kids get ideas like that.

"It's just like regular talking, only even more," I told him. "You know, you just think loud."

Paul went right along with me. "Okay, I'm thinking loud right now," he said. "Can you hear me?"

I couldn't; nothing at all came to me from him. But I didn't believe he was trying, either. I thought he was just holding himself off from me, secret, closed up. I figured all the grownups did that—Mom, Uncle Charles, all the grownups I knew. Sometimes I'd try to eavesdrop on them, sort of sneak into their heads, but that never worked either.

"What are you thinking?" I asked sulkily, admitting defeat.

He grinned wide at me and gave me a hug. "I was thinking you're my son and I hope you live a good long life."

I was ashamed and embarrassed and about to cry all of a sudden. *I love you,* I thought at him, so loud I almost burst, but Paul just kept grinning and hugging me.

We're all coming back for dinner, sweating and itching even though the day's clouded over and cold, when I begin to get what Katie's thinking. Just snatches at first, but right away I know what's happened. . . . *clean him up, I guess . . . why do I always have to . . . at least it's over.*

I'm walking with Tony and I look at him to see if he's been hearing too. He probably can't pick up Katie as far away as I can, but Lucy must be thinking about the same thing, because he looks at me and says . . . well, he doesn't say anything really, he just looks at me inside and I know what he means.

I say, *It's all right; it'll be a relief.*

What about Paul? You ought to tell him, or Eddie'll blab it right out. The two of them are following right behind us, and if Tony can read his sister from here, so can Eddie.

I stop and pick up a clod of dirt, crumbling it in my fingers. I turn around and say, "Paul . . . Uncle Charles just died."

Paul stops dead still, looks at me uncertainly, then says, "Charlie died? Katie told you?"

I nod, looking him in the eye, trying for as much connection as I can get. I wish I could touch him inside his head the way I can the kids, but I can't.

"He died *five minutes ago*!" Eddie says triumphantly. "That's what Lucy says!"

Paul glances at Eddie, looks away, across the fields at nothing in particular. There's a wind coming up; it ruffles his hair, blows it in his eyes. Paul brushes it aside once, then ignores it. "Well," he says; but that's all. He resumes walking toward the house, passing Tony and me silently.

I run to catch up to him, and I walk beside him. Behind us Tony is telling his brother, *Just for once keep your mouth shut. Don't even think.*

I'm watching Paul, letting my head swing side to side like I'm not thinking of anything, but I'm looking at him every chance I get. He walks steadily and deliberately, eyes on the ground in front of him.

Finally he says, "It's gonna be a problem, Bennie. We ought to quit work for the day out of respect, but with the way it's clouded up and heading for us I just can't see it."

"Then let's all work the rest of the day," I say. "Katie and Lucy too. We can get it all in by dark for sure that way."

Paul thinks about that and says, "That's right, we could get it all done today; you're right, Bennie. We'll do it that way." There's relief in his voice, and I know without going into his mind and without him saying it in words that Paul wants the comfort of familiar work today.

"We don't have any crop to waste," Paul adds. "We've got to keep thinking about tomorrow." And with a stab of pain I suddenly wonder how much of a future Paul himself has. He's getting awfully skinny and wiry. We all are, there isn't enough food, but it's the grownups who die.

As long as I can remember, people have been dying. Grownups. It was like a plague when I was a kid, people suddenly getting weak and small and falling down in the road. The early ones went quick, maybe a day or two from the time it hit them till they were gone. They cried a lot and it used to scare me.

"Just be happy you're out in the country," Mom used to tell me. "Out here you won't catch it from people. If you only *knew* what's happening in the cities."

But it was happening here too. It was real bad in town, and folks had to go in to do business once in a while no matter what. So the farm people started dying too. I went to a lot of funerals when I was a kid.

Paul was usually the one in our family who went to town. "Don't worry about me none," he told everybody. "I'm too busy to do any dying." And it seemed like he was right too, except that Mom came down sick. She must have got it from him.

She got better for a while, but she never got real strong like she had been. And every now and then it would take her again and she'd be in bed for a week. Eventually the time came when she didn't get better.

Uncle Charles kept getting skinnier too, and sometimes he was sick. Paul looked awfully tired sometimes, but he only took to bed once. I skipped my chores that day and tried to help Uncle Charles take care of him, till Paul came around and saw what was happening. He said, "You get out of here, there's work to be done. All I got is a touch of flu."

And he did get out of bed the next day even though his eyes were still dark and he couldn't work more than an hour. But he sure made *us* work the whole day.

Meantime all the kids around were doing fine. I had chicken pox once, and mumps, and we had to get the doctor out to our place to take out Katie's appendix, but that was all. Tony Anderson said he had a cousin in Boise who died of the plague, but it turned out he'd been killed in a riot. Whatever the disease was, it never touched us kids. We used to talk about that, but not out loud, and now we don't talk about it at all, it just seems like it's the way life is.

Back at the house Katie is bustling around very self-importantly. She's got Uncle Charles dressed up in his Saturday-night suit, and she's propped him up on pillows so he looks like he's ready to receive visitors while he's laid up in bed with a bad back. Lucy's opened the windows to try to clear the deathbed smell of the room, and she even went out and picked a big bunch of gladiolas to put in a vase on the dresser.

We file into the house one by one, Paul first, then me, then Tony and finally Eddie. Paul holds up his hand as Katie comes running into the room excitedly, and he says, "We know about it, Katie, we heard."

She stops, disappointed. "Oh. . . . There wasn't anything we could do, Paul, honest. He just—"

"I know," Paul says. "Don't you worry about it."

"Anyway didn't we know it would happen?" she

asks. "I mean, we knew he wasn't going to get well this time."

"That's right," Paul says. He goes to the door of Uncle Charles's room and stands there looking in. Lucy comes out of the room, sliding quickly past Paul in the doorway like she feels she's been caught somewhere she didn't belong. Paul goes inside and closes the door behind him.

The rest of us, five kids, stand uneasily in the living room. Katie says, "Dinner ought to be just about ready," but nobody makes the first move toward the kitchen. Katie abruptly turns away and begins laying out dishes. "I *knew* he wasn't going to pull through," she says, and she's thinking, *All those months of bedpans and mess and waiting on him . . .*

"You couldn't of done nothing," Lucy says reassuringly.

"That's right," says Tony, "you did all you could."

Why do we bother so much about old people? Eddie wonders. *Sooner they die the better; they're weird.*

Tony says, *I told you to shut up, Pisspants,* and he's glaring at Eddie. Lucy looks shocked; she hurries into the dining room to help Katie put out forks and spoons.

Well, what good are they? Eddie wants to know. *Always talking about building everything back the way it used to be, and nothing was ever good anyway. Why don't we just admit it?* He looks from one to another of us belligerently. *Why don't we all quit talking out loud just for them? Who needs it?*

Shut up, Tony says.

But Eddie won't shut up. *What do we need to talk out for them for? Let them talk to each other, I'm tired of it.*

Lucy shudders and sits down suddenly at the table. She drops her head into her hands and begins to cry.

I say, *You do whatever you want to, Eddie. For me, I'm going to keep on talking out loud as long as they're still here.*

Eddie smirks at me. *How come you didn't say that out then?*

When Paul comes out of Uncle Charles's room his face is carefully put together, like he's just coming back from the bathroom. He sits down at the table, and the rest of us take our places too. Katie brings the stewpot and we fill our plates with carrots and beets and potatoes. The meat is a hawk that Paul shot; it's stringy.

"Let's get a lot of food in us," Paul says. "In case we don't get done in time for supper." So we all spoon out second helpings.

"Long as you're not using your mouths for talking, you might as well use 'em for eating," Paul says. I look quickly at him, but he keeps his attention on his plate.

Eddie sees my look and says, *He's just mad because he can't eat and talk at the same time too.*

Damn it Eddie, I'm gonna belt you one! Tony says.

No you won't, Eddie answers. *I'm just saying what's the difference between us. It's a survival thing.* He snickers.

Paul looks up and asks Eddie, "You finished eating, young man?"

"No sir," Eddie says, and he starts spooning stew into his mouth fast.

We do get all the work finished that afternoon, well before dark, but it's starting to rain so we don't go swimming. The Anderson kids go on home to tell their folks about Uncle Charles. Paul says we'll have the funeral in the morning.

Lying in bed that night, I stare at shapes in the dark and let my mind form them. It's a moonlit night and the light coming in my window makes ambiguous shapes of chair and dresser and closet door. I see them as tombstones, I see the old cemetery stretching much too far into the distance, I see a shadow like the sprawled body of a farmhand who once stopped to work our farm during the worst days of the plague. Clouds moving across the sky become fleets of combines reaping the land, as once they actually did here. My jacket hanging on a hook on the wall is a shambling, dying man who stopped at our gate to ask for food when I was five.

Go to sleep, you're scaring me with those horrible things, Katie says from the next room.

I can't help it.

Well, you didn't have to nurse Uncle Charles, I did. You've got no call to be scared in the dark.

I'm thinking about the funeral tomorrow, I say. *I don't like funerals.*

None of us do. But you know it isn't real.

It's real to Paul. There are two ways of looking at it, you know.

I can feel her turning over in the dark, pulling covers up to her chin. *You can't look at things two ways,* she says. *You have to pick your own way. Paul's wrong.*

What difference does that make? I ask.

The morning is gray and cold. Last night's rain wasn't heavy, and the earth is moist and fragrant as the eight of us stand around the fresh-dug grave: Paul, Katie and me, and the Andersons, parents and kids. Mr. Anderson is short and gnarled, the skin of his face as wrinkled as knuckles; I don't think he'll live much longer. His wife, Estelle, is a heavy-set woman in a faded black dress; she stands square and stolid and draws a bandana back and forth through her fingers.

The kids are subdued, even Eddie. Lucy is wearing a clean dress that's too big for her. Tony tries to catch my eye but I avoid him, and he respects my privacy with his mind.

"Ashes to ashes, dust to dust," Paul recites. He reads a funeral service that Mom wrote down years ago when so many people were dying that she was afraid soon there wouldn't be any preacher to do the ritual. She was soon right. Paul reads the service without emotion, his voice so matter-of-fact that I wonder how he can bear the pain he must be feeling.

Birds are singing not far away and the air is crisp. Uncle Charles's grave is on a slight ridge behind our house; Mom's grave marker is nearby, the wooden plaque now weathered to a dull gray. MARY ROGER OATES, it says, RETURNED TO THE LAND. Paul wrote that, carved it with his pocket knife. It doesn't mean the same thing to me that it does to him.

"We'll have a minute of silence," Paul says, and the eight of us stand unmoving on the little hill. A wind is coming up; it blows my jacket out behind me and I zip it up. Katie pulls a shawl around her shoulders, and she's thinking, *I hate this, I hate this, oh I hate it!*

Eddie says, *Yeah, it's stupid.* Katie glances at him, but she doesn't reply.

When the minute of silence is over Paul begins to shovel dirt into the grave; Mr. Anderson and I both join him. We work silently, the thunk and scrape of shovels mingling with the low drone of the wind. Estelle Anderson turns away, and I think she's crying.

Tony asks me, *Is tonight okay?*

I keep shoveling dirt down into the grave. *Tonight's best,* I say. *While the ground's still fresh.*

This whole thing is so stupid! Eddie says.

Be quiet! says someone. *Shut up, shut up, shut up, shut up!* I look up from the grave and see Lucy with her eyes shut tight. *Please, please be quiet,* she says.

Paul stays up late that night, drinking coffee and smoking cigarettes. He doesn't usually smoke. I lie in bed wide awake, listening to him move about. Katie has gone to sleep.

Eventually, sometime past midnight, Paul goes to his bed. It's beginning to rain again; the sound of the wind blowing against the side of the house has more body now. Paul has always said he liked that, so maybe it will lull him to sleep. I sit up in bed and listen for any sounds from outside other than the rain, but there's only an occasional creaking of wooden slats growing cold and wet.

In my mind a voice says, . . . *want to come too near unless it's all right. Bennie, can you hear us?*

I hear you, Tony. Come ahead, but no flashlights or anything like that.

No, of course not.

I go to the window to look for them, but they're coming around behind the house, Lucy, Tony and Eddie. Rain washes against the window and my feet are cold on the wooden floor. I get back in bed.

After a while I ask, *What are you doing?*

Digging, Tony says.

I'm sorry it had to rain tonight. I wish I could help.

You stay in the house, Tony says.

More silence, darkness, the cold creeping in through drafty walls. The rain outside isn't heavy, but it's steady. There's no sound from Paul's room.

How is it out there? I ask.

Cold and wet. It's heavy digging. We're about half-way down.

Boy, says Eddie, *did you have to dig this thing all the way to China?*

Tony says, *Eddie, you're a pain in the ass.*

He doesn't understand, Lucy says. *It's our land too—I mean we may all have to live off it together in a few years.*

I think about that for a while, lying under the covers in the cold darkness. When Paul dies . . . When Paul dies . . . But I can't even imagine it. Well, maybe Lucy and I will get married. Maybe Katie and Tony, too. Somehow that doesn't seem as important as what's to become of the land itself. The land, the land, that means living or starving.

We're down to the box, Tony says. *I think we can get it open without much trouble.*

Leave his clothes in the box, I say. *They wouldn't be good for anything. And be sure to cover over the grave again real good.*

Of course, of course.

I imagine them prying back the lid of the pine casket and lifting Uncle Charles's cold body out. I imagine that it's Paul's body instead, and a pain gnaws at my stomach. One day it *will* be Paul; I've got to get used to that. He's always told me to think of the future. One day it will be him.

Earlier tonight, while we sat alone together on the porch, Paul said to me, "Did you know Charlie was one of the first Americans sent to Vietnam? He was there two years before any peace marchers had ever heard of the place. Just did his job, and didn't get killed. Once he was on a plane that was hijacked to Cuba, too. He did a lot of things in his life."

"I liked him," I said.

"Hell, everybody liked Charlie. Wasn't a man I ever knew who didn't. Girls, too—he was a ladykiller in his day. He was a handsome man." Paul lit a cigarette, awkwardly cupping his hands around the wooden match to protect it from the wind. "It wasn't good, seeing how flabby and weak Charlie got these last few years. He wasn't that old; the plague wore him down."

The light from inside the house seemed to pick out lines of age in Paul's face, and I suddenly noticed that he didn't sit as straight as he used to. Paul's life was hard; he was wearing down too.

"But we've got to keep thinking about the future," I said to him.

"That's right," he said, "that's what I've always told you. We buried Charlie properly this morning, so let's make up our mind that's over with."

Okay, says Tony. *We're leaving to take him up to the slope. We'll use the flashlight and segment him there.*

Scatter him around where we put Mom, I say.

They go. They move away from me and soon I can't hear or see them even in my head. But I might as well be out there with them; the rain seems to soak my bones from the inside.

Still, there's a smell of freshness in the night air. *We'll get the slope fit for growing things again, wait and see,* I say into the dark.

AIR RAID

by JOHN VARLEY

John Varley is a young (born 1947) writer whose impact on the science fiction field in the late 1970s has been favorably compared to that of Robert A. Heinlein's in the early 1940s. His outstanding shorter work is collected in *The Persistence of Vision* (1978), the title story winning the Hugo and Nebula Awards in 1978/79. His *Ophiuchi Hotline* (1977) is an outstanding first novel, and *Titan* (1979) is an even better second one.

"Air Raid" is an excellent example of the powerful work that made his rise to fame so meteoric.

I WAS jerked awake by the silent alarm vibrating my skull. It won't shut down until you sit up, so I did. All around me in the darkened bunkroom the Snatch Team members were sleeping singly and in pairs. I yawned, scratched my ribs, and patted Gene's hairy flank. He turned over. So much for a romantic send-off.

Rubbing sleep from my eyes, I reached to the floor for my leg, strapped it on, and plugged it in. Then I was running down the rows of bunks toward Ops.

The situation board glowed in the gloom. Sun-Belt

201

Airlines Flight 128, Miami to New York, September 15, 1979. We'd been looking for that one for three years. I should have been happy, but who can afford it when you wake up?

Liza Boston muttered past me on the way to Prep. I muttered back, and followed. The lights came on around the mirrors, and I groped my way to one of them. Behind us, three more people staggered in. I sat down, plugged in, and at last I could lean back and close my eyes.

They didn't stay closed for long. Rush! I sat up straight as the sludge I use for blood was replaced with supercharged go-juice. I looked around me and got a series of idiot grins. There was Liza, and Pinky, and Dave. Against the far wall Cristabel was already turning slowly in front of the airbrush, getting a caucasian paint job. It looked like a good team.

I opened the drawer and started preliminary work on my face. It's a bigger job every time. Transfusion or no, I looked like death. The right ear was completely gone now. I could no longer close my lips; the gums were permanently bared. A week earlier, a finger had fallen off in my sleep. And what's it to you, bugger?

While I worked, one of the screens around the mirror glowed. A smiling young woman, blond, high brow, round face. Close enough. The crawl line read *Mary Katrina Sondegard, born Trenton, New Jersey, age in 1979: 25*. Baby, this is your lucky day.

The computer melted the skin away from her face to show me the bone structure, rotated it, gave me cross-sections. I studied the similarities with my own skull, noted the differences. Not bad, and better than some I'd been given.

I assembled a set of dentures that included the slight gap in the upper incisors. Putty filled out my cheeks. Contact lenses fell from the dispenser and I popped them in. Nose plugs widened my nostrils. No need for ears; they'd be covered by the wig. I pulled a blank plastiflesh mask over my face and had to pause while it melted in. It took only a minute to mold it to perfection. I smiled at myself. How nice to have lips.

The delivery slot clunked and dropped a blond wig and a pink outfit into my lap. The wig was hot from the styler. I put it on, then the pantyhose.

"Mandy? Did you get the profile on Sondergard?" I didn't look up; I recognized the voice.

"Roger."

"We've located her near the airport. We can slip you in before takeoff, so you'll be the joker."

I groaned, and looked up at the face on the screen. Elfreda Baltimore-Louisville, Director of Operational Teams: lifeless face and tiny slits for eyes. What can you do when all the muscles are dead?

"Okay." You take what you get.

She switched off, and I spent the next two minutes trying to get dressed while keeping my eyes on the screens. I memorized names and faces of crew members plus the few facts known about them. Then I hurried out and caught up with the others. Elapsed time from first alarm: twelve minutes and seven seconds. We'd better get moving.

"Goddam Sun-Belt," Cristabel groused, hitching at her bra.

"At least they got rid of the high heels," Dave pointed out. A year earlier we would have been teetering down the aisles on three-inch platforms. We all wore short pink shifts with blue and white stripes diagonally across the front and carried matching shoulder bags. I fussed trying to get the ridiculous pillbox cap pinned on.

We jogged into the dark Operations Control Room and lined up at the gate. Things were out of our hands now. Until the gate was ready, we could only wait.

I was first, a few feet away from the portal. I turned away from it; it gives me vertigo. I focused instead on the gnomes sitting at their consoles, bathed in yellow lights from their screens. None of them looked back at me. They don't like us much. I don't like them, either.

Withered, emaciated, all of them. Our fat legs and butts and breasts are a reproach to them, a reminder that Snatchers eat five times their ration to stay presentable for the masquerade. Meantime we continue to rot. One day I'll be sitting at a console. One day I'll be *built in* to a console, with all my guts on the outside and nothing left of my body but stink. The hell with them.

I buried my gun under a clutter of tissues and lipsticks in my purse. Elfred was looking at me.

"Where is she?" I asked.

"Motel room. She was alone from 10 P.M. to noon on flight day."

Departure time was 1:15. She cut it close and would be in a hurry. Good.

"Can you catch her in the bathroom? Best of all, in the tub?"

"We're working on it." She sketched a smile with a fingertip drawn over lifeless lips. She knew how I like to operate, but she was telling me I'd take what I got. It never hurts to ask. People are at their most defenseless stretched out and up to their necks in water.

"Go!" Elfreda shouted. I stepped through, and things started to go wrong.

I was faced the wrong way, stepping *out* of the bathroom door and facing the bedroom. I turned and spotted Mary Katrina Sondergard through the haze of the gate. There was no way I could reach her without stepping back through. I couldn't even shoot without hitting someone on the other side.

Sondergard was at the mirror, the worst possible place. Few people recognize themselves quickly, but she'd been looking right at herself. She saw me and her eyes widened. I stepped to the side, out of her sight.

"What the hell is . . . hey! Who the hell . . . ?" I noted the voice, which can be the trickiest thing to get right.

I figured she'd be more curious than afraid. My

guess was right. She came out of the bathroom, passing through the gate as if it wasn't there, which it wasn't, since it only has one side. She had a towel wrapped around her.

"Jesus Christ! What are you doing in my—?" Words fail you at a time like that. She knew she ought to say something, but what? *Excuse me, haven't I seen you in the mirror?*

I put on my best stew smile and held out my hand.

"Pardon the intrusion. I can explain everything. You see, I'm—" I hit her on the side of the head and she staggered and went down hard. Her towel fell to the floor. "—working my way through college." She started to get up, so I caught her under the chin with my artificial knee. She stayed down.

"Standard fuggin' *oil!*" I hissed, rubbing my injured knuckles. But there was no time. I knelt beside her, checked her pulse. She'd be okay, but I think I loosened some front teeth. I paused a moment. Lord, to look like that with no makeup, no prosthetics! She nearly broke my heart.

I grabbed her under the knees and wrestled her to the gate. She was a sack of limp noodles. Somebody reached through, grabbed her feet, and pulled. *So long, love! How would you like to go on a long voyage?*

I sat on her rented bed to get my breath. There were car keys and cigarettes in her purse, genuine tobacco, worth its weight in blood. I lit six of them, figuring I had five minutes of my very own. The room filled with sweet smoke. They don't make 'em like that anymore.

The Hertz sedan was in the motel parking lot. I got in and headed for the airport. I breathed deeply of the air, rich in hydrocarbons. I could see for hundreds of yards into the distance. The perspective nearly made me dizzy, but I live for those moments. There's no way to explain what it's like in the pre-meck world. The sun was a fierce yellow ball through the haze.

The other stews were boarding. Some of them knew Sondergard so I didn't say much, pleading a hangover.

That went over well, with a lot of knowing laughs and sly remarks. Evidently it wasn't out of character. We boarded the 707 and got ready for the goats to arrive.

It looked good. The four commandos on the other side were identical twins for the women I was working with. There was nothing to do but be a stewardess until departure time. I hoped there would be no more glitches. Inverting a gate for a joker run into a motel room was one thing, but in a 707 at 20,000 feet . . .

The plane was nearly full when the woman that Pinky would impersonate sealed the forward door. We taxied to the end of the runway, then we were airborne. I started taking orders for drinks in first.

The goats were the usual lot, for 1979. Fat and sassy, all of them, and as unaware of living in a paradise as a fish is of the sea. *What would you think, ladies and gents, of a trip to the future? No? I can't say I'm surprised. What if I told you this plane is going to—?*

My alarm beeped as we reached cruising altitude. I consulted the indicator under my Lady Bulova and glanced at one of the restroom doors. I felt a vibration pass through the plane. *Damn it, and so on.*

The gate was in there. I came out quickly, and motioned for Diana Gleason—Dave's pigeon—to come to the front.

"Take a look at this," I said, with a disgusted look. She started to enter the restroom, stopped when she saw the green glow. I planted a boot on her fanny and shoved. Perfect. Dave would have a chance to hear her voice before popping in. Though she'd be doing little but screaming when she got a look around . . .

Dave came through the gate, adjusting his silly little hat. Diana must have struggled.

"Be disgusted," I whispered.

"What a mess," he said as he came out of the restroom. It was a fair imitation of Diana's tone, though he'd missed the accent. It wouldn't matter much longer.

"What is it?" It was one of the stews from tourist.

We stepped aside so she could get a look, and Dave shoved her through. Pinky popped out very quickly.

"We're minus on minutes," Pinky said. "We lost five on the other side."

"Five?" Dave-Diana squeaked. I felt the same way. We had a hundred and three passengers to process.

"Yeah. They lost contact after you pushed my pigeon through. It took that long to realign."

You get used to that. Time runs at different rates on each side of the gate, though it's always sequential, past to future. Once we'd started the snatch with me entering Sondergard's room, there was no way to go back any earlier on either side. Here, in 1979, we had a rigid ninety-four minutes to get everything done. On the other side, the gate could never be maintained longer than three hours.

"When you left, how long was it since the alarm went in?"

"Twenty-eight minutes."

It didn't sound good. It would take at least two hours just customizing the wimps. Assuming there was no more slippage on '79-time, we might just make it. But there's *always* slippage. I shuddered, thinking about riding it in.

"No time for any more games, then," I said. "Pink, you go back to tourist and call both of the other girls up here. Tell 'em to come one at a time, and tell 'em we've got a problem. You know the bit."

"Biting back the tears. Got you." She hurried aft. In no time the first one showed up. Her friendly Sun-Belt Airlines smile was stamped on her face, but her stomach would be churning. *Oh God, this is it!*

I took her by the elbow and pulled her behind the curtains in front. She was breathing hard.

"Welcome to the twilight zone," I said, and put the gun to her head. She slumped, and I caught her. Pinky and Dave helped me shove her through the gate.

"Fug! The rotting thing's flickering."

Pinky was right. A very ominous sign. But the green glow stabilized as we watched, with who-knows-how-much slippage on the other side. Cristabel ducked through.

"We're plus thirty-three," she said. There was no sense talking about what we were all thinking: things were going badly.

"Back to tourist," I said. "Be brave, smile at everyone, but make it just a little bit too good, got it?"

"Check," Cristabel said.

We processed the other quickly, with no incident. Then there was no time to talk about anything. In eighty-nine minutes Flight 128 was going to be spread all over a mountain whether we were finished or not.

Dave went into the cockpit to keep the flight crew out of our hair. Me and Pinky were supposed to take care of first class, then back up Cristabel and Liza in tourist. We used the standard "coffee, tea, or milk" gambit, relying on our speed and their inertia.

I leaned over the first two seats on the left.

"Are you enjoying your flight?" Pop, pop. Two squeezes on the trigger, close to the heads and out of sight of the rest of the goats.

"Hi, folks. I'm Mandy. Fly me." Pop, pop.

Halfway to the galley, a few people were watching us curiously. But people don't make a fuss until they have a lot more to go on. One goat in the back row stood up, and I let him have it. By now there were only eight left awake. I abandoned the smile and squeezed off four quick shots. Pinky took care of the rest. We hurried through the curtains, just in time.

There was an uproar building in the back of tourist, with about sixty percent of the goats already processed. Cristabel glanced at me, and I nodded.

"Okay, folks," she bawled. "I want you to be quiet. Calm down and listen up. *You*, fathead, pipe *down* before I cram my foot up your ass sideways."

The shock of hearing her talk like that was enough to buy us a little time, anyway. We had formed a skirmish line across the width of the plane, guns out, steadied on seat backs, aimed at the milling, befuddled group of thirty goats.

The guns are enough to awe all but the most fool-hardy. In essence, a standard-issue stunner is just a plastic rod with two grids about six inches apart. There's not enough metal in it to set off a hijack alarm. And to people from the Stone Age to about 2190 it doesn't look any more like a weapon than a ball-point pen. So Equipment Section jazzes them up in a plastic shell to real Buck Rogers blasters, with a dozen knobs and lights that flash and a barrel like the snout of a hog. Hardly anyone ever walks into one.

"We are in great danger, and time is short. You must all do exactly as I tell you, and you will be safe."

You can't give them time to think, you have to rely on your status as the Voice of Authority. The situation is just *not* going to make sense to them, no matter how you explain it.

"Just a minute, I think you owe us—"

An airborne lawyer. I made a snap decision, thumbed the fireworks switch on my gun, and shot him.

The gun made a sound like a flying saucer with hemorrhoids, spit sparks and little jets of flame, and extended a green laser finger to his forehead. He dropped.

All pure kark, of course. But it sure is impressive.

And it's damn risky, too. I had to choose between a panic if the fathead got them to thinking, and a possible panic from the flash of the gun. But when a 20th gets to talking about his "rights" and what he is "owed," things can get out of hand. It's infectious.

It worked. There was a lot of shouting, people ducking behind seats, but no rush. We could have handled it, but we needed some of them conscious if we were ever going to finish the snatch.

"Get up. Get *up,* you *slugs!*" Cristabel yelled. "He's stunned, nothing worse. But I'll *kill* the next one who gets out of line. Now *get to your feet* and do what I tell you. *Children first! Hurry,* as fast as you can, to the front of the plane. Do what the stewardess tells you. Come on, kids, *move!*"

I ran back into first class just ahead of the kids, turned at the open restroom door, and got on my knees.

They were petrified. There were five of them—crying, some of them, which always chokes me up—looking left and right at dead people in the first class seats, stumbling, near panic.

"Come on kids," I called to them, giving my special smile. "Your parents will be along in just a minute. Everything's going to be all right, I promise you. Come on."

I got three of them through. The fourth balked. She was determined not to go through that door. She spread her legs and arms and I couldn't push her through. I will *not* hit a child, never. She raked her nails over my face. My wig came off, and she gaped at my bare head. I shoved her through.

Number five was sitting in the aisle, bawling. He was maybe seven. I ran back and picked him up, hugged him and kissed him, and tossed him through. God, I needed a rest, but I was needed in tourist.

"You, you, you, and you. Okay, you too. Help him, will you?" Pinky had a practiced eye for the ones that wouldn't be any use to anyone, even themselves. We herded them toward the front of the plane, then deployed ourselves along the left side where we could cover the workers. It didn't take long to prod them into action. We had them dragging the limp bodies forward as fast as they could go. Me and Cristabel were in tourist, with the others up front.

Adrenaline was being catabolized in my body now; the rush of action left me and I started to feel very tired. There's an unavoidable feeling of sympathy for the poor dumb goats that starts to get me about this stage of the game. Sure, they were better off, sure they were going to die if we didn't get them off the plane. But when they saw the other side they were going to have a hard time believing it.

The first ones were returning for a second load, stunned at what they'd just seen: dozens of people being put into a cubicle that was crowded when it was empty. One college student looked like he'd been hit in the stomach. He stopped by me and his eyes pleaded.

"Look, I want to *help* you people, just . . . what's going *on?* Is this some new kind of rescue? I mean, are we going to crash—"

I switched my gun to prod and brushed it across his cheek. He gasped, and fell back.

"Shut your fuggin' mouth and get moving, or I'll kill you." It would be hours before his jaw was in shape to ask any more stupid questions.

We cleared tourist and moved up. A couple of the work gang were pretty damn pooped by then. Muscles like horses, all of them, but they can hardly run up a flight of stairs. We let some of them go through, including a couple that were at least fifty years old. *Je*-zuz. Fifty! We got down to a core of four men and two women who seemed strong, and worked them until they nearly dropped. But we processed everyone in twenty-five minutes.

The portapak came through as we were stripping off our clothes. Cristabel knocked on the door to the cockpit and Dave came out, already naked. A bad sign.

"I had to cork'em," he said. "Bleeding captain just *had* to make his Grand March through the plane. I tried *everything.*"

Sometimes you have to do it. The plane was on autopilot, as it normally would be at this time. But if any of us did anything detrimental to the craft, changed the fixed course of events in any way, that would be it. All that work for nothing, and Flight 128 inaccessible to us for all Time. I don't know sludge about time theory, but I know the practical angles. We can do things in the past only at times and in places

where it won't make any difference. We have to cover
our tracks. There's flexibility; once a Snatcher left her
gun behind and it went in with the plane. Nobody
found it, or if they did, they didn't have the smoggiest
idea of what it was, so we were okay.

Flight 128 was mechanical failure. That's the best
kind; it means we don't have to keep the pilot unaware of the situation in the cabin right down to
ground level. We can cork him and fly the plane, since
there's nothing he could have done to save the flight
anyway. A pilot-error smash is almost impossible to
snatch. We mostly work midairs, bombs, and struc-
tural failures. If there's even one survivor, we can't
touch it. It would not fit the fabric of space-time,
which is immutable (though it can stretch a little),
and we'd all just fade away and appear back in the
ready-room.

My head was hurting. I wanted that portapak very
badly.

"Who has the most hours on a 707?" Pinky did, so I
sent her to the cabin, along with Dave, who could do
the pilot's voice for air traffic control. You have to
have a believable record in the flight recorder, too.
They trailed two long tubes from the portapak, and
the rest of us hooked in up close. We stood there, each
of us smoking a fistful of cigarettes, wanting to finish
them but hoping there wouldn't be time. The gate had
vanished as soon as we tossed our clothes and the
flight crew through.

But we didn't worry long. There's other nice things
about snatching, but nothing to compare with the
rush of plugging into a portapak. The wake-up transfusion is nothing but fresh blood, rich in oxygen and
sugars. What we were getting now was an insane
brew of concentrated adrenaline, supersaturated he-
moglobin, methedrine, white lightning, TNT, and
Kickapoo joyjuice. It was like a firecracker in your
heart; a boot in the box that rattled your sox.

"I'm growing hair on my chest," Cristabel said, solemnly. Everyone giggled.

"Would someone hand me my eyeballs?"

"The blue ones, or the red ones?"

"I think my ass just fell off."

We'd heard them all before, but we howled anyway. We were strong, *strong,* and for one golden moment we had no worries. Everything was hilarious. I could have torn sheet metal with my eyelashes.

But you get hyper on that mix. When the gate didn't show, and didn't show, and *didn't sweetjeez show* we all started milling. This bird wasn't going to fly all that much longer.

Then it did show, and we turned on. The first of the wimps came through, dressed in the clothes taken from a passenger it had been picked to resemble.

"Two thirty-five elapsed upside time," Cristabel announced.

"Jee-zuz."

It is a deadening routine. You grab the harness around the wimp's shoulders and drag it along the aisle, after consulting the seat number painted on its forehead. The paint would last three minutes. You seat it, strap it in, break open the harness and carry it back to toss through the gate as you grab the next one. You have to take it for granted they've done the work right on the other side: fillings in the teeth, fingerprints, the right match in height and weight and hair color. Most of those things don't matter much, especially on Flight 128 which was a crash-and-burn. There would be bits and pieces, and burned to a crisp at that. But you can't take chances. Those rescue workers are pretty thorough on the parts they *do* find; the dental work and fingerprints especially are important.

I hate wimps. I really hate 'em. Every time I grab the harness of one of them, if it's a child, I wonder if it's Alice. *Are you my kid, you vegetable, you slug, you slimy worm?* I joined the Snatchers right after the

brain bugs ate the life out of my baby's head. I couldn't
stand to think she was the last generation, that the
last humans there would ever be would live with
nothing in their heads, medically dead by standards
that prevailed even in 1979, with computers working
their muscles to keep them in tone. You grow up,
reach puberty still fertile—one in a thousand—rush to
get pregnant in your first heat. Then you find out
your mom or pop passed on a chronic disease bound
right into the genes, and none of your kids will be
immune. I *knew* about the paraleprosy; I grew up with
my toes rotting away. But this was too much. What do
you do?

Only one in ten of the wimps had a customized face.
It takes time and a lot of skill to build a new face that
will stand up to a doctor's autopsy. The rest came
premutilated. We've got millions of them; it's not hard
to find a good match in the body. Most of them would
stay breathing, too dumb to stop, until they went in
with the plane.

The plane jerked, hard. I glanced at my watch. Five
minutes to impact. We should have time. I was on my
last wimp. I could hear Dave frantically calling the
ground. A bomb came through the gate, and I tossed it
into the cockpit. Pinky turned on the pressure sensor
on the bomb and came running out, followed by Dave.
Liza was already through. I grabbed the limp dolls in
stewardess costume and tossed them to the floor. The
engine fell off and a piece of it came through the
cabin. We started to depressurize. The bomb blew
away part of the cockpit (the ground crash crew would
read it—we hoped—that part of the engine came
through and killed the crew: no more words from the
pilot on the flight recorder) and we turned, slowly, left
and down. I was lifted toward the hole in the side of
the plane, but I managed to hold onto a seat. Cristabel
wasn't so lucky. She was blown backwards.

We started to rise slightly, losing speed. Suddenly it
was uphill from where Cristabel was lying in the

aisle. Blood oozed from her temple. I glanced back; everyone was gone, and three pink-suited wimps were piled on the floor. The plane began to stall, to nose down, and my feet left the floor.

"Come on, Bel!" I screamed. That gate was only three feet away from me, but I began pulling myself along to where she floated. The plane bumped, and she hit the floor. Incredibly, it seemed to wake her up. She started to swim toward me, and I grabbed her hand as the floor came up to slam us again. We crawled as the plane went through its final death agony, and we came to the door. The gate was gone.

There wasn't anything to say. We were going in. It's hard enough to keep the gate in place on a plane that's moving in a straight line. When a bird gets to corkscrewing and coming apart, the math is fearsome. So I've been told.

I embraced Cristabel and held her bloodied head. She was groggy, but managed to smile and shrug. You take what you get. I hurried into the restroom and got both of us down on the floor. Back to the forward bulkhead, Cristabel between my legs, back to front. Just like in training. We pressed our feet against the other wall. I hugged her tightly and cried on her shoulder.

And it was there. A green glow to my left. I threw myself toward it, dragging Cristabel, keeping low as two wimps were thrown head-first through the gate above our heads. Hands grabbed and pulled us through. I clawed my way a good five yards along the floor. You can leave a leg on the other side and I didn't have one to spare.

I sat up as they were carrying Cristabel to Medical. I patted her arm as she went by on the stretcher, but she was passed out. I wouldn't have minded passing out myself.

For a while, you can't believe it all really happened. Sometimes it turns out it *didn't* happen. You come back and find out all the goats in the holding pen have softly and suddenly vanished away because the continuum won't tolerate the changes and paradoxes you've put into it. The people you've worked so hard to rescue are spread like tomato surprise all over some goddam hillside in Carolina and all you've got left is a bunch of ruined wimps and an exhausted Snatch Team. But not this time. I could see the goats milling around in the holding pen, naked and more bewildered than ever. And just starting to be *really* afraid.

Elfreda touched me as I passed her. She nodded, which meant well done in her limited repertoire of gestures. I shrugged, wondering if I cared, but the surplus adrenaline was still in my veins and I found myself grinning at her. I nodded back.

Gene was standing by the holding pen. I went to him, hugged him. I felt the juices start to flow. *Damn it, let's squander a little ration and have us a good time.*

Someone was beating on the sterile glass wall of the pen. She shouted, mouthing angry words at us. *Why? What have you done to us?* It was Mary Sondergard. She implored her bald, one-legged twin to make her understand. She thought she had problems. God, was she pretty. I hated her guts.

Gene pulled me away from the wall. My hands hurt, and I'd broken off all my fake nails without scratching the glass. She was sitting on the floor now, sobbing. I heard the voice of the briefing officer on the outside speaker.

". . . Centauri 3 is hospitable, with an Earthlike climate. By that, I mean *your* Earth, not what it has become. You'll see more of that later. The trip will take five years, shiptime. Upon landfall, you will be entitled to one horse, a plow, three axes, two hundred kilos of seed grain . . ."

I leaned against Gene's shoulder. At their lowest ebb, this very moment, they were so much better than us. I had maybe ten years, half of that as a basket case. They are our best, our very brightest hope. Everything is up to them.

". . . that no one will be forced to go. We wish to point out again, not for the last time, that you would all be dead without our intervention. There are things you should know, however. You cannot breathe our air. If you remain on Earth, you can never leave this building. We are not like you. We are the result of a genetic winnowing, a mutation process. We are the survivors, but our enemies have evolved along with us. They are winning. You, however, are immune to the diseases that afflict us . . ."

I winced and turned away.

". . . the other hand, if you emigrate you will be given a chance at a new life. It won't be easy, but as Americans you should be proud of your pioneer heritage. Your ancestors survived, and so will you. It can be a rewarding experience, and I urge you . . ."

Sure. Gene and I looked at each other and laughed. *Listen to this, folks. Five percent of you will suffer nervous breakdowns in the next few days and never leave. About the same number will commit suicide, here and on the way. When you get there, sixty to seventy percent will die in the first three years. You will die in childbirth, be eaten by animals, bury two out of three of your babies, starve slowly when the rains don't come. If you live, it will be to break your back behind a plow, sun-up to dusk. New Earth is Heaven, folks!*

God, how I wish I could go with them.

THE PI MAN

by ALFRED BESTER

Alfred Bester is the author of two of the most justly
famous novels in the history of science fiction, *The
Demolished Man* (1953) and *The Stars My Destina-
tion* (1956). His most recent novel is *The Computer
Connection* (1975). An urbane and witty man, Bester's
short stories were frequently written in the same
pyrotechnic style that characterized his novels, as in
"The Pi Man," one of his most brilliantly constructed
works.

HOW to say? How to write? When sometimes I can
be fluent, even polished, and then, *reculer pour nieux
sauter*, it takes hold of me. Push. Force. Compel. Sometimes

I

must

go

back

but

not

to

                    *   *   *

jump; no, not even to jump better. I have no control
over self, speech, love, fate. I must compensate. Always.

But I try anyway.

Quae nocent docent. Translation follows: Things that
injure, teach. I am injured and have hurt many. What
have we learned? However. I wake up the morning of
the biggest hurt of all wondering which house. Wealth,
you understand. Damme! Mews cottage in London,
villa in Rome, penthouse in New York, rancho in
California. I awake. I look. Ah! Layout is familiar.
Thus:

     Bedroom   Foyer

                            T

        Bath   e

        Bath   r

            Living Room   r

       Bedroom   a

        Kitchen   c

       Terrace   e

Oh-oh! I am in penthouse in New York; but that
bath-bath back-to-back. Pfui. All rhythm wrong. Balance off. Pattern painful. I telephone downstairs to
janitor-mans. At that moment I lose my English. (You
must understand I speak in all tongues. A goulash. I
am compelled. Why? Ah!)

"*Pronto. Ecco mi, Signore Storm.* No. Forced to *parlato
Italiano.* Wait. I call back in *cinque minuti.*"

Re infecta. Latin. The business being unfinished, I
shower body, teeth, hairs, shave face, dry everything

and try again. *Voilà!* The English, she come. Back to invention of A. G. Bell ("Mr. Watson, come here, I need you"). On telephone I speak to janitor. Nice chap. Gets a job of work done in two twos.

"Hallo? Abraham Storm here, again. Yes. Right. Chap in the penthouse. Mr. Lundgren, be my personal rabbi and get some workmen up here this morning. I want those two baths converted into one. Yes. I'll leave five thousand dollars on top of the refrigerator. Thanks, Mr. Lundgren."

Wanted to wear gray flannel this morning, but had to put on the sharkskin. Damnation! African nationalism has queer side-effects. Went to the back bedroom (see diagram) and unlocked the door which was installed by National Safe Co., Inc. I went in.

Everything broadcasting beautifully. Up and down the electromagnetic spectrum. Visual off from ultraviolet and jamming toward the infrared. Ultra shortwave screaming. Alpha, beta, and gamma radiation hearty. And the interruptors innn tt errrrr up ppp tttinggggg at random and comfortably. I am at peace. Christ Jesus! To know even a moment of peace!

I take subway to office in Wall Street. Chauffeur too dangerous; might become friendly. I don't dare have friends. Best of all, morning subway jam-packed, mass-packed; no patterns to adjust, no shiftings and compensatings required. Peace! I buy all morning papers; because of the patterns, you understand. Too many *Timeses* being read; I must read *Tribune* to balance pattern. Too many *Newses;* I read *Mirror.* Etc.

In subway car I catch a glimpse of an eye; narrow, bleak, gray-blue, the possession of an anonymous man who conveys the conviction that you've never seen him before and will never again. But I picked up that glance and it rang a bell in the back of my mind. He knew it. He saw the flash in my eye before I could conceal it. So I was being tailed again? But by whom? U.S.A.? U.S.S.R.? Matoids?

I blasted out of the subway at City Hall and gave them a false trail to the Woolworth Building, in case they were operating double-tails. The whole theory of the hunters and the hunted is not to avoid being spotted ... no one can escape that ... but to lay so many trails for them to follow that they become overextended. Then they're forced to abandon you. They have so many men for so many operations. It's a question of diminishing returns.

City Hall traffic was out of sync (as it always is) and I had to walk on the hot side of the street to compensate. Took elevator up to tenth floor of bldg. There I was suddenly seized by something from sss ome wwwhh ere. SS ommme tth inggg b addd. I began to cry, but no help. An elderly clerk emerge from office wearing alpaca coat, carry papers, gold spectacles.

"Not him," I plead with nowhere. "Nice mans. Not him. Please."

But I am force. Approach. Two blows; neck and gut. Down he go, writhing. I trample spectacles. Remove watch from pocket and smash. Shatter pens. Tear papers. Then I am permitted to get back into elevator and go downstairs again. It was 10:30. I was late. Damned inconvenient. Took taxi to 99 Wall Street. Tipped driver ten dollars. Sealed one thousand in envelope (secretly) and sent driver back to bldg to find and give to clerk.

Routine morning's work in office. Market jumpy; big board hectic; hell to balance and compensate, even though I know the patterns of money. I am behind by the sum of $109,872.43 by eleven-thirty; but, *a pas de géant* the patterns put me ahead $57,075.94 by half-past 12:00 noon, Daylight Saving Time, which my father used to call Woodrow Wilson time.

57075 makes nice pattern, but that 94¢. Pfui. Made the whole balance sheet look lopsided, ugly. Symmetry above all else. Only 24¢ in my pocket. Called secretary, borrowed 70¢ from her and threw sum total out window. Felt better as I watched it chime down to the street, but then I caught her looking at me with surprise and delight. Very bad. Very dangerous. Fired girl on the spot.

"But why, Mr. Storm? Why?" she asked, trying not to cry. Darling little thing. Freckled face and saucy, but not so saucy now.

"Because you're beginning to like me."

"What's the harm in that?"

"When I hired you I warned you not to like me."

"I thought you were kidding."

"I wasn't. Out you go. Beat it."

"But why?"

"I'm afraid I might start liking you."

"Is this a new kind of pass?" she asked.

"God forbid."

"Well, you don't have to fire me," she flared. "I hate you."

"Good. Then I can go to bed with you."

She turned crimson and opened her mouth to denounce me, the while her eyes twinkled at the corners. A darling girl. I could not endanger her. I put her into her hat and coat, gave her a year's salary for a bonus, and threw her out. *Punkt*. Made memo: Hire nothing but men, preferably married, misanthropic, and murderous. Men who could hate me.

So, lunch. Went to nicely balanced restaurant. Tables attached to floor. No moving them. All chairs filled by patrons. Nice pattern. No need for me to compensate and adjust. Ordered nicely patterned luncheon for self:

Martini   Martini

Martini

Croque M'sieu Roquefort

Salad

Coffee

*   *   *

But so much sugar being consumed in restaurant, I had to take my coffee black, which I dislike. However, still a nice pattern. Balanced.

X^2 + X + 41 = prime number. Excuse, please. Sometimes I'm in control and see what compensating must be done. Other times it's forced on me from God only knows where or why. Then I must do what I'm compelled to do, blindly, like speaking the gibberish I speak; sometimes hating it, like the clerk in the Woolworth Building. Anyway, the equation breaks down when x = 40.

The afternoon was quiet. For a moment I thought I might be forced to leave for Rome (Italy), but something adjusted without needing me. The A.S.P.C.A. finally caught up with me for beating my dog to death, but I'd contributed $10,000 to their Shelter. Got off with a shaking of heads. I penciled mustaches on posters, rescued a drowning kitten, saved a woman from a mugging and had my head shaved. Normal day.

In the evening to the ballet to relax with all the beautiful patterns, balanced, peaceful, soothing. Then I take deep breath, quash my nausea, and force myself to go to *Le Bitnique,* the beatnik joint. I hate *Le Bitnique,* but I need a woman and I must go where I hate. That freckled girl I fire . . . so slender and full of delicious mischief, and making eyes at me. *So, poisson d'avril,* I advance myself to *Le Bitnique.*

Chaos. Blackness. Sounds and smells a cacophony. One twenty-five-watt bulb in ceiling. One maladroit pianist play Progressive. Against L. wall sit beatnik boys, wearing berets, black glasses, and pubic beards, playing chess. Against R. wall is bar and beatnik girls with brown paper bags under arms containing toilet articles. They are shuffling and maneuvering for a pad for the night.

Those beatnik girls! All skinny . . . exciting to me tonight because too many American men dream about overstuffed women, and I must compensate. (In England I like overstuff because England like women skinny.)

All wear tight slack, loose sweater, Brigitte Bardot hair, Italian make-up . . . black eye, white lip . . . and when they walk they make with the gait that flipped that Herrick cat three centuries ago when he split and wrote:

> *Next, when I lift mine eyes and see*
> *That brave vibration each way free;*
> *Oh how that glittering taketh me!*

I pick one who glitter. I talk. She insult. I insult back and buy drinks. She drink and insult.[2] I hope she is lesbian and insult.[3] She snarl and hate, but helpless. No pad for tonight. The pathetic brown paper bag under her arm. I quell sympathy and hate back. She does not bathe. Her thinking patterns are jangles. Safe. No harm can come to her. I take her home to seduce by mutual contempt. And in living room (see diagram) sits slender little freckly-face secretary, recently fired, now waiting for me.

```
              !
              I
            now
           write
          part of
      s           P
      t           a
      o           r
      r           i
      y    in     s
      Capital of France
```

Address: 49 bis Avenue Hoche. Paris, 8ème, France.

Forced to go there by what happened in Singapore, you understand. It needed extreme compensation and adjustment. Almost, for a moment, I thought I would have to attack the conductor of the *Opéra Comique*, but fate was kind and let me off with nothing worse than indecent exposure under the *Petite Carousel*. And I was able to found a scholarship at the Sorbonne before I was taken away.

Anyway, she sat there, my little one, in my penthouse now with one (1) bathroom, and $1,997.00 change on top of the refrigerator. Ugh! Throw $6.00 out window and am soothed by lovely 1991 remaining. She sat there, wearing a basic black cocktail dress with tight skirt, sheer black stockings, black opera pumps. The freckly skin gleamed reddish rose from embarrassment. Also red for danger. Her saucy face was very tight from the daring thing she thought she was doing. Damme! I like that.

I also like the nice even curve of the legs, and the bosom. Balanced, you understand? * * Like so; but not too thrusting. Tactful. Also her cleavage. Like so; and just as rosy as her face, despite desperate powdering to make her skin milky. That powder; a nuisance. I go to kitchen and rub burnt cork on shirt-front to compensate.

"Oh-so," I say. "Me-fella be ve'y happy ask why you-fella chop-chop invade along my apa'tment. Excep' mus' now speak pidgin-English. Ve'y much embarrass along me. Excuse please,until change come."

"I bribed Mr. Lundgren," she blurted. "I told him you needed important papers from your office."

"Entschuldigen Sie, bitte. Meine pidgin haben sich geaendert. Sprachen Sie Deutsch?"

"No."

"Dann warte ich."

The beatnik turned on her heel and bounced out, her brave vibration each way free. I caught up with her in front of the elevator, put 101 (perfect pattern) into her hand and said good night in Spanish. She hated me. I did a naughty thing to her * * (no excuse) and returned to the apartment when my American-English returned to me.

"What's she got?" the Freckle ask.

"What's your name?" I indict.

"My God! I've been working in your office for three months. You don't know my name? You really don't?"

"No, and I don't want to know it now."

"I'm Lizzie Chalmers."

"Go away, Lizzie Chalmers."

"So that's why you always called me 'Miss.' Why did you shave your head?"

"Trouble in Vienna."

"It's chic," she said judgmatically, "but I don't know. You remind me of a movie star I loathe. What do you mean, trouble in Vienna?"

"None of your business. What are you doing here? What do you want from me?"

"You," she said, blushing fiery.

"Will you, for God's sake, go away!"

"What did she have that I don't?" Lizzie Chalmers demanded. Then her face crinkled. "Don't? Is that right? What. Did. She. Have. That. I. Do. Not. Yes, right. I'm going to Bennington. They're strong on aggression, but weak on grammar."

"What do you mean, you're going to Bennington?"

"Why, it's a college. I thought everybody knew."

"But *going?*"

"I'm in my junior year. They drive you out with whips to acquire practical experience in your field."

"What's your field?"

"It used to be economics. Now it's you. How old are you?"

"One hundred and nine thousand eight hundred and seventy-two."

"Oh, come on! Forty?"

"Thirty."

"No! Really?" She nodded contentedly. "That makes ten years difference between us. Just right."

"Are you in love with me, Lizzie?"

"Well, I'm trying to get something going."

"Does it have to be me?"

"I know it sounds like a notion." She lowered her

eyes. "And I suppose women are always throwing themselves at you."

"Not always."

"What are you, blasé, or something? I mean . . . I know I'm not staggering, but I'm not exactly repulsive."

"You're lovely."

"Then why don't you touch me?"

"I'm trying to protect you."

"I can protect myself when the time comes."

"The time is now, Lizzie."

"The least you could do is offend me the way you did that girl in front of the elevator."

"You snooped?"

"Sure I snooped. You didn't expect me to sit here on my hands, did you? I've got my man to take care of."

"*Your* man?"

"It happens," she said in a low voice. "I never believed it, but it happens. You fall in and out of love, and each time you think it's for real and forever. And then you meet somebody and it isn't a question of love any more. You just know he's your man, and you're stuck. I'm stuck."

She raised her eyes and looked at me . . . violet eyes, full of youth and determination and tenderness, and yet older than twenty years . . . much older. And I knew how lonely I was, never daring to love, always compelled to live with those I hated. I could fall into those violet eyes and never come up.

"I'm going to shock you," I said. I looked at the clock. 1:30 A.M. A quiet time. Please God the American tongue would stay with me a while longer. I took off my jacket and shirt and showed her my back, cross-hatched with scars. Lizzie gasped.

"Self-inflicted," I told her. "Because I permitted myself to like a man and become friendly with him. This is the price I paid, and I was lucky. Now wait here."

I went into the master bedroom where my heart's

shame was embalmed in a silver case hidden in the right-hand drawer of my desk. I brought it to the living room. Lizzie watched me with great eyes.

"Five years ago a girl fell in love with me," I told her. "A girl like you. I was lonely then, as always. Instead of protecting her from myself, I indulged myself. Now I want to show you the price *she* paid. You'll loathe me for this but I must show you . . ."

A flash caught my eye. Lights in a building down the street going on. I leaped to the window and stared. The lights in the building three down from me went off . . . five seconds eclipse . . . then on. It happened to the building two down, and then to the one next door. The girl came to my side and took my arm. She trembled slightly.

"What is it?" she asked. "What's the matter?"

"Wait," I said.

The lights in my apartment went out for five seconds and then came on again.

"They've located me," I told her.

"They? Located?"

"They've spotted my broadcasts by d/f."

"What's d/f?"

"Direction-finder. Then they turned off the current in each building in the neighborhood for five seconds . . . building by building . . . until the broadcast stopped. Now they know I'm in this house, but they don't know which apartment." I put on my shirt and jacket. "Good night, Lizzie. I wish I could kiss you."

She clamped her arms around my neck and gave me a smacking kiss; all warmth, all velvet, all giving. I tried to push her away.

"You're a spy," she said. "I'll go to the chair with you."

"I wish to Heaven I were a spy," I said. "Goodbye, my dearest love. Remember me."

Soyez ferme. A great mistake letting that slip. It happen, I think, because my American slip, too. Suddenly talk jumble again. As I run out, the little devil kick off opera pumps and rip slit in cocktail skirt up to thigh so she can run. She is alongside me going down the fire stairs to the garage in basement. I hit her to stop, and swear at her. She hit back and swear worse, all the time laughing and crying. I love her for it. Damnation! She is doomed.

We get into car, Aston-Martin, but with left-hand drive, and speed west on Fifty-third Street, east on Fifty-fourth Street, and north on First Avenue. I am making for Fifty-ninth Street bridge to get off Manhattan island. I own plane in Babylon, Long Island, which is always ready for this sort of awkwardness.

"*J'y suis, J'y reste* is not my motto," I tell Elizabeth Chalmers, whose French is as uncertain as her grammar . . . an endearing weakness. "Once they trapped me in London at post office. I received mail at General Delivery. They sent me a blank letter in a red envelope, and that's how they followed me to 139 Piccadilly, London W.1. Telephone Mayfair 7211. Red for danger. Is your skin red all over?"

"It's not red!" she said indignantly.

"I mean rosy."

"Only where the freckles merge," she said. "What is all this escape? Why do you talk so funny, and act so peculiar? Are you sure you're not a spy?"

"Only positive."

"Are you a being from another world who came on an Unidentified Flying Object?"

"Would that horrify you?"

"Yes, if it meant we couldn't make love."

"What about conquering earth?"

"I'm only interested in conquering you."

"I am not and have never been a being from another world who came on an Unidentified Flying Object."

"Then what are you?"

"A compensator."

"What's that?"

"Do you know dictionary of Mister Funk & Wagnalls?

Edited by Frank H. Vizetelly, Litt.D., LL.D.? I quote:
One who or that which compensates, as a device for
neutralizing the influence of local attraction upon a
compass-needle or an automatic apparatus for equal-
izing the pressure of gas in the—Damn!"

Litt.D. Frank H. Vizetelly does not use that bad
word. Is my own because roadblock now faces me on
Fifty-ninth Street bridge. Should have anticipated.
Should have felt patterns, but too swept up with this
darling girl. Probably there are roadblocks on all
bridges and tunnels leading out of this $24.00 island.
Could drive off bridge but might harm my angelic
Elizabeth Chalmers which would make me a *brute
figura* as well as sadden me beyond redemption. So.
Stop car. Surrender.

"Kammerade," I pronounce, and ask: "Who you? Ku
Klux Klan?"

Hard-faced mans say no.

"White Supremacists of the World, Inc.?"

No agains. I feel better. Always nasty when captured by lunatic fringes looking for figureheads.

"U.S.S.R.?"

He stare, then speak. "Special Agent Krimms from
the FBI," and show his badge. I enthuse and embrace
him in gratitude. FBI is salvation. He recoil and wonder if I am fairy. I don't care. I kiss Elizabeth Chalmers
and she open mouth under mine to mutter: "Admit
nothing; deny everything. I've got a lawyer."

Brilliant lights in the office in Foley Square. The
chairs are placed just so; the shadows arranged just
so. I have been through this so often before. The anonymous man with the bleak eyes from the subway this
morning is questioning me. His name is S. I. Dolan.
We exchange a glance. His says: I goofed this morning.
Mine says: So did I. We respect each other, and then
the grilling starts.

"Your name is Abraham Mason Storm?"

"The nickname is 'Base.' "

"Born December 25?"

"I was a Christmas baby."

"1929?"

"I was a Depression baby."

"You seem pretty jaunty."

"Gallows humor, S. I. Dolan. Despair. I know you'll never convict me of anything, and I'm desperate."

"Very funny."

"Very tragic. I want to be convicted ... but it's hopeless."

"Hometown San Francisco?"

"Yes."

"Grand High School. Two years at Berkeley. Four years in the Navy. Finished at Berkeley. Majored in statistics."

"Yes. Hundred percent American boy."

"Present occupation, financier?"

"Yes."

"Offices in New York, Rome, Paris, London?"

"Also Rio."

"Known assets from bank deposits, stock and bond holdings, three million dollars?"

"No, no, no!" I was agonized. "Three million, three hundred and thirty-three thousand, three hundred and thirty-three dollars and thirty-three cents."

"Three million dollars," Dolan insisted. "In round numbers."

"There are no round numbers; there are only patterns."

"Storm, what the hell are you up to?"

"Convict me," I pleaded. "I want to go to the chair and get this over with."

"What are you talking about?"

"You ask and I'll explain."

"What are you broadcasting from your apartment?"

"Which apartment? I broadcast from all of them."

"In New York. We can't break the code."

"There is no code; only randomness."

"Only what?"

"Only peace, Dolan."

"Peace!"

"I've been through this so often before. In Geneva, Berlin, London, Rio. Will you let me explain it my own way, and for God's sake trap me if you can?"

"Go ahead."

I took a breath. It's always so difficult. You have to do it with metaphor. But it was 3:00 A.M. and my American would hold for a while. "Do you like to dance?"

"What the hell . . . ?"

"Be patient. I'm explaining. Do you like to dance?"

"Yes."

"What's the pleasure of dancing? It's a man and woman making rhythms together . . . patterns. Balancing, anticipating, following, leading, cooperating. Yes?"

"So?"

"And parades. Do you like parades? Masses of men and women cooperating to make patterns. Why is war a time of joy for a country, although nobody admits it? Because it's an entire people cooperating, balancing and sacrificing to make a big pattern. Yes?"

"Now wait a minute, Storm . . ."

"Just listen, Dolan. I'm sensitive to patterns . . . more then dancing or parades or war; far more. More than the 2/4 pattern of day and night, or the 4/4 pattern of the seasons . . . far, far more. I'm sensitive to the patterns of the whole spectrum of the universe . . . sight and sound, gamma rays, groupings of peoples, acts of hostility and benign charity, cruelties and kindnesses, the music of the spheres . . . and I'm forced to compensate. Always."

"Compensate?"

"Yes. If a child falls and hurts itself, the mother kisses it. Agreed? That's compensation. It restores a pattern. If a man beats a horse, you beat him. Yes? Pattern again. If a begger wrings too much sympathy from you, you want to kick him, don't you? More compensation. The husband unfaithful to the wife is never more kind to her. All wives know that pattern, and dread it. What is sportsmanship but a compensating pattern to offset the embarrassment of winning or losing? Do not the murderer and murderee seek each other to fulfill their patterns?

"Multiply that by infinity and you have me. I have to kiss and kick. I'm driven. Compelled. I don't know how to name my compulsion. They call Extra Sensory Perception Psi. What do you call Extra Pattern Perception? Pi?"

"Pie? What pie?"

"Sixteenth letter of the Greek alphabet. It designates the relation of the circumference of a circle to its diameter. 3.14159 +. The series goes on endlessly. It is transcendental and can never be resolved into a finite pattern; and it's agony to me ... like pi in printing, which means jumbled and confused type, without order or pattern."

"What the hell are you talking about?"

"I'm talking about patterns; order in the universe. I'm compelled to keep it and restore it. Sometimes I'm compelled to do wonderful and generous things; other times I'm forced to do insane things ... talk garbage languages, go to strange places, perform abominable acts ... because patterns which I can't perceive demand adjustment."

"What abominable acts?"

"You can pry and I can confess, but it won't do any good. The patterns won't permit me to be convicted. They won't let me end. People refuse to testify. Facts will not give evidence. What is done becomes undone. Harm is transformed into good."

"Storm, I swear you're crazy."

"Maybe, but you won't be able to get me committed to an asylum. It's been tried before. I even tried committing myself. It didn't work."

"What about those broadcasts?"

"We're flooded with wave emissions, quanta, particles, and I'm sensitive to them, too; but they're too garbled to shape into patterns. They have to be neutralized. So I broadcast an anti-pattern to jam them and get a little peace."

"Are you claiming to be a superman?"

"No. Never. I'm just the man *Simple Simon* met."

"Don't clown."

"I'm not clowning. Don't you remember the jingle? *Simple Simon met a pieman, going to the fair . . . ?* For Pee-eye-ee-man, read Pee-eye-man. I'm the Pi Man."

Dolan scowled. At last he said: "My full name is Simon Ignatius Dolan."

"I'm sorry. I didn't know. Nothing personal implied."

He glared at me, then threw my dossier down. He sighed and slumped into a chair. That made the pattern wrong and I had to shift. He cocked an eye at me.

"Pi Man," I explained.

"All right," he said. "We can't hold you."

"They all try," I said, "but they never can."

"Who try?"

"Governments, thinking I'm in espionage; police, wanting to know why I'm involved with so many people in such cockeyed ways; politicos in exile hoping I'll finance a counterrevolution; fanatics, dreaming I'm their rich messiah; lunatic fringes; religious sects; flat-worlders; Forteans . . . They all track me down, hoping they can use me. Nobody can. I'm part of something much bigger. I think maybe we all are, only I'm the first to be aware of it."

"Off the record, what's this about abominable acts?"

I took a breath. "That's why I can't have friends. Or a girl. Sometimes things get so bad somewhere that I have to make frightful sacrifices to restore the pattern. I must destroy something I love. I—There was a dog I loved. A Labrador retriever . . . I don't like to think about him. I had a girl once. She loved me. And I—And a guy in the navy with me. He—I don't want to talk about it."

"Chicken, all of a sudden?"

"No, damn you; I'm accursed! Because some of the patterns I must adjust to are out-world rhythms ... like nothing you ever felt on earth. 29/51 ... 108/303 ... tempi like that. What are you staring at? You don't think that can be terrifying? Beat a 7/5 tempo for me."

"I don't know music."

"This has nothing to do with music. Try to beat five with one hand and seven with the other, and make them come out even. Then you'll understand the complexity and terror of those strange patterns that are coming to me. From where? I don't know. It's an unknown universe, too big to comprehend; but I have to beat the tempi of its patterns and make them come out even ... with my actions, reactions, emotions, senses, while those giant pressures   push

               and reverse me
                      back
                 and turn me
          forth   inside
       and   out
back ..."

"The other arm now," Elizabeth said firmly. "Lift."

I am on my bed, me. Thinking upheaved again. Half (½) into pajamas; other half (½) being wrestled by freckly girl. I lift. She yank. Pajama now on, and it's my turn to blush. They raise me prudish in San Francisco.

"Om mani padme hum," I said. "Translation follows: Oh, the jewel in the lotus. Meaning you. What happened?"

"You passed out," she said. "Keeled over. Mr. Dolan had to let you go. Mr. Lundgren helped carry you into the apartment. How much should I give him?"

"Cinque lire. No. Parla Italiano, gentile Signorina?"

"Mr. Dolan told me what you told him. Is that your patterns again?"

"Si." I nod and wait. After stopovers in Greece and Portugal, American-English finally returns to me. "Why

don't you get the hell out of here while the getting's good, Lizzie Chalmers?"

"I'm still stuck," she said. "Get into bed . . . and make room for me."

"No."

"Yes. You can marry me later."

"Where's the silver case?"

"Down the incinerator."

"Do you know what was in it?"

"I know what was in it."

"And you're still here?"

"It was monstrous, what you did. Monstrous!" The saucy little face was streaked with mascara. She had been crying. "Where is she now?"

"I don't know. The checks go out every quarter to a number account in Switzerland. I don't want to know. How much can the heart endure?"

"I think I'm going to find out," she said. She put out the lights. In the darkness came the sound of rustling clothes. Never before have I heard the music of one I love undressing for me . . . for me. I make one last attempt to save this beloved.

"I love you," I said, "and you know what that means. When the patterns demand a sacrifice, I may be even crueler to you, more monstrous. . . ."

"No," she said. "You never were in love before. Love creates patterns, too." She kissed me. Her lips were parched, her skin was icy. She was afraid, but her heart beat hot and strong. "Nothing can hurt us now. Believe me."

"I don't know what to believe any more. We're part of a universe that's big beyond knowledge. What if it turns out to be too gigantic for love?"

"All right," she said composedly. "We won't be dogs in the manger. If love is a little thing and has to end, then let it end. Let all the little things like love and honor and mercy and laughter end . . . if there's something bigger beyond."

"But what can be bigger? What can be beyond?"

"If we're too small to survive, how can we know?"

She crept close to me, the tips of her body like frost. And so we huddled together, breast to breast, warming ourselves with our love, frightened creatures in a wonderous world beyond knowing . . . fearful, and yet an tic ccip ppat inggg.

PROTOTAPH

by KEITH LAUMER

Keith Laumer is a former State Department Foreign
Service officer whose tales of Jamie Retief, interstellar
diplomat and troubleshooter, were among the most
popular stories of the 1960s and early 1970s. A
prolific writer, he is also a good one—for evidence,
consult such books as *Worlds of the Imperium* (1962),
The Other Side of Time (1965), *A Plague of Demons*
(1965), and *The Best of Keith Laumer* (1976).

"Prototaph" is a powerful short-short about a man
with a lot to worry about.

I WAS already sweating bullets when I got to the
Manhattan Life Concourse; then I had to get behind
an old dame that spent a good half hour in the Policy
Vending Booth, looking at little pieces of paper and
punching the keys like they were fifty-credit bet le-
vers at the National Lottery.

When I got in, I was almost scared to code my order
into the Vendor; but I was scareder not to. I still thought
maybe what happened over at Prudential and Gibraltar
was some kind of fluke, even though I knew all the
companies worked out of the Federal Actuarial Table
Extrapolator; and Fate never makes a mistake.

But this had to be a mistake.

I punched the keys for a hundred thousand C's of Straight Life; nothing fancy, just a normal workingman's coverage. Then I shoved my ID in the slot and waited. I could feel sweat come out on my scalp and run down by my ear while I waited. I could hear the humming sound all around me like some kind of bees bottled up back of the big gray panel; then the strip popped out of the slot, and I knew what it said before I looked at it:

UNINSURABLE.

I got the door open and shoved some guy out of my way and it was like I couldn't breathe. I mean, think about it: Twenty-one years old, out in the city to take my chances all alone, with no policy behind me. It was like the sidewalk under your feet turned to cracked ice, and no shore in sight.

A big expensive-looking bird in executive coveralls came out of a door across the lobby; I guess I yelled. Everybody was looking at me. When I grabbed his arm, he got that mad look and started to reach for his lapel button—the kind that goes with a Million Cee Top Crust policy.

"You got to listen," I told him. "I tried to buy my insurance—and all I got was this!" I shoved the paper in his face. "Look at me," I told him. "I'm healthy, I'm single, I finished Class Five Subtek school yesterday, I'm employed! What do you mean, uninsurable?"

"Take your hands off me," he said in a kind of choky voice. He was looking at the paper, though. He took it and gave me a look like he was memorizing my face for picking out of a line-up later.

"Your ID." He held out his hand and I gave it to him. He looked at it and frowned an important-looking frown.

"Hm-m-m. Seems in order. Possibly some, er . . ." He pushed his mouth in and out and changed his mind about saying it; he knew as well as I did that the big actuarial computer doesn't make mistakes. "Come along." He turned his back and headed for the lift bank.

"What have I got, some kind of incurable disease or something?" I was asking them; they just looked at me and goggled their eyes. More of them kept coming in, whispering together; then they'd hurry away and here would come a new bunch. And none of them told me anything.

"The old crock in front of me, she was ninety if she was a day!" I told them. "She got her policy! Why not me?"

They didn't pay any attention. Nobody cared about me; how I felt. I got up and went over to the first guy that had brought me up here.

"Look," I said. I was trying to sound reasonable. "What I mean is, even a guy dying in the hospital can get a policy for *some* premium. It's the law; everybody's got a right to be insured. And—"

"I know the laws governing the issuance of policies by this company," the man barked at me. He was sweating, too. He got out a big tissue and patted himself with it. He looked at a short fat man with a stack of papers in his hand.

"I don't care what kind of analysis you ran," he told him. "Run another one. Go all the way back to Primary if you have to, but get to the bottom of this! I want to know why this"—he gave me a look—"this individual is unique in the annals of actuarial history!"

"But, Mr. Tablish—I even coded in a trial run based on a one hundred percent premium, with the same result: No settlement of such a claim is possible—"

"I'm not interested in details; just get me results! The computer has available to it every fact in the known universe; see that it divulges the reasoning behind this . . . this anomaly!"

The fat man went away. They took me to another room and a doctor ran me through the biggest med

machine I ever saw. When he finished I heard him tell
the big man I was as sound as a Manhattan Term
Policy.

That made me feel a little better—but not much.

Then the fat man came back, and his face was a
funny white color—like some raw bread I saw once on
a field trip through Westside Rationing. He said something to the others, and they all started to talk at
once, and some of them were yelling now. But do you
think any of them told me anything? I had to wait
another hour, and then a tall man with white hair
came in and everybody got quiet and he looked at the
papers and they all got their heads together and
muttered; and then they looked at me, and I felt my
heart pounding up under my ribs and I was feeling
sick then, med machine or no med machine.

Then they told me.

. That was two days ago. They got me in this room
now, a fancy room up high in some building. They're
guys around to do whatever I want—servants, I guess
you'd call 'em. They gave me new clothes, and the
food—West Rat never put out anything like this. No
liquor, though—and no smokes. And when I said I
wanted to go out, all I got was a lot of talk. They treat
me—careful. Not like they like me, you know, but like
I was a bomb about to go off. It's a funny feeling. I
guess I got more power than anybody that ever
lived—more power than you can even get your mind
around the thought of. But a lot of good it does me.
There's only one way I can use it—and when I think
about that, I get that sick feeling again.

And meanwhile, I can't even go for a walk in the
park.

The president was here just now. He came in, looking
just like the Tri-D, only older, and he came over and
looked at me kind of like I looked at him. I guess it
figures: There's only one of each of us.

"Are you certain there's not some . . . some error,

George?" he said to the wrinkly-faced man that walked just behind him.

"The Actuarial Computer is the highest achievement of a thousand years of science, Mr. President," he said in a deep voice like the mud on the bottom of the ocean. "Our society is based on the concept of its infallibility within the physical laws of the Universe. Its circuits are capable of analyses and perceptions that range into realms of knowledge as far beyond human awareness as is ours beyond that of a protozoan. An error? No, Mr. President."

He nodded. "I see." That's all he said. Then he left.

Now I'm just sitting here. I don't know what to do next—what to say. There's a lot to this—and in a way, there's nothing. I got to think about it, dope it out. There's got to be something I can do—but what?

The machine didn't say much. They took me down to the sub-vault where the big voice panel is located and where the primary data goes in, and let me hear for myself. It didn't give any explanations; it just told me.

Funny; in a way it was like something I've always known, but when you hear Fate come right out and say it, it's different.

When I die, the world ends.

BLACK CHARLIE

by GORDON R. DICKSON

Best known for his "Dorsai" novels that form part of
what he calls his "Childe Cycle," Gordie Dickson
has been quietly building a most impressive body of
work in science fiction for more than thirty years.
His forty published sf works include such notable
novels as *The Alien Way* (1965), *Sleepwalker's
World* (1971), and *Masters of Everon* (1979), as
well as the excellent fantasy *The Dragon and the
George* (1976). His remarkable story on the theme
of leadership, "Call Him Lord," won a Nebula Award
in 1966.

"Black Charlie" is about what it means to be
human and the way human beings sometimes treat
each other, themes that have been at the center of
his work since he began writing.

YOU ask me, what is art? You expect me to have a
logical answer at my fingertips because I have been a
buyer for museums and galleries long enough to acquire a plentiful crop of gray hairs. It's not that simple.

Well, what is art? For forty years I've examined,
felt, admired, and loved many things fashioned as
hopeful vessels for that bright spirit we call art—and
I'm unable to answer the question directly. The layman
answers easily—beauty. But art is not necessarily beautiful. Sometimes it is ugly. Sometimes it is crude.
Sometimes it is incomplete.

I have fallen back, as many men have in the business of making like decisions, on *feel* for the judgment of art. You know this business of *feel*. Let us say that you pick up something—a piece of statuary or, better, a fragment of stone, etched and colored by some ancient man of prehistoric times. You look at it. At first it is nothing, a half-developed reproduction of some wild animal, not even as good as a grade-school child could accomplish today.

But then, holding it, your imagination suddenly reaches through rock and time, back to the man himself, half squatted before the stone wall of his cave—and you see there not the dusty thing you hold in your hand—but what the man himself saw in the hour of its creation. You look beyond the physical reproduction to the magnificent accomplishment of his imagination.

This, then, may be called art—no matter what strange guise it appears in—this magic which bridges all gaps between the artist and yourself. To it, no distance, nor any difference, is too great. Let me give you an example from my own experience.

Some years back, when I was touring the newer worlds as a buyer for one of our well-known art institutions, I received a communication from a man named Cary Longan, asking me, if possible, to visit a planet named Elman's World and examine some statuary he had for sale.

Messages rarely came directly to me. They were usually referred to me by the institution I was representing at the time. Since, however, the world in question was close, being of the same solar system as the planet I was then visiting, I spacegraphed my answer that I would come. After cleaning up what remained of my business where I was, I took an interworld ship and, within a couple of days, landed on Elman's World.

It appeared to be a very raw, very new planet in-

deed. The port we landed at was, I learned, one of the
only two suitable for deepspace vessels. And the city
surrounding it was scarcely more than a village. Mr.
Longan did not meet me at the port, so I took a cab
directly to the hotel where I had made a reservation.

That evening, in my rooms, the annunciator rang,
then spoke, giving me a name. I opened the door to
admit a tall, brown-faced man with uncut, dark hair
and troubled, green-brown eyes.

"Mr. Longan?" I asked.

"Mr. Jones?" he countered. He shifted the unvar-
nished wooden box he was carrying to his left hand and
put out his right to shake mine. I closed the door
behind him and led him to a chair.

He put the box down, without opening it, on a small
coffee table between us. It was then that I noticed his
rough, bush-country clothes, breeches, and tunic of
drab plastic. Also an embarrassed air about him, like
that of a man unused to city dealings. An odd sort of
person to be offering art for sale.

"Your spacegram," I told him, "was not very explic-
it. The institution I represent—"

"I've got it here," he said, putting his hand on the
box.

I looked at it in astonishment. It was no more than
half a meter square by twenty centimeters deep.

"There?" I said. I looked back at him, with the beginnings of a suspicion forming in my mind. I suppose I
should I have been more wary when the message had
come direct, instead of through Earth. But you know
how it is—something of a feather in your cap when
you bring in an unexpected item. "Tell me, Mr. Longan," I said, "where does this statuary come from?"

He looked at me a little defiantly. "A friend of mine
made them," he said.

"A friend?" I repeated—and I must admit I was
growing somewhat annoyed. It makes a man feel like
a fool to be taken in that way. "May I ask whether

this friend of yours has ever sold any of his work before?"

"Well, no . . ." Longan hedged. He was obviously suffering—but so was I, when I thought of my own wasted time.

"I see," I said, getting to my feet. "You've brought me on a very expensive side trip merely to show me the work of some amateur. Goodbye, Mr. Longan. And please take your box with you when you leave!"

"You've never seen anything like this before!" He was looking up at me with desperation.

"No doubt," I said.

"Look. I'll show you . . ." He fumbled, his fingers nervous on the hasp. "Since you've come all this way, you can at least look."

Because there seemed no way of getting him out of there, short of having the hotel manager eject him forcibly, I sat down with bad grace. "What's your friend's name?" I demanded.

Longan's fingers hesitated on the hasp. "Black Charlie," he replied, not looking up at me.

I stared. "I beg your pardon. Black—Charles Black?"

He looked up quite defiantly, met my eye, and shook his head. "Just Black Charlie," he said with sudden calmness. "Just the way it sounds. Black Charlie." He continued unfastening the box.

I watched rather dubiously as he finally managed to loosen the clumsy, handmade wooden bolt that secured the hasp. He was about to raise the lid, then apparently changed his mind. He turned the box around and pushed it across the coffee table.

The wood was hard and uneven under my fingers. I lifted the lid. There were five small partitions, each containing a rock of fine-grained gray sandstone of different but thoroughly incomprehensible shape.

I stared at them—then looked back at Longan to see if this weren't some sort of elaborate joke. But the tall man's eyes were severely serious. Slowly, I began to take out the stones and line them up on the table.

* * *

I studied them one by one, trying to make some sense out of their forms. But there was nothing there, absolutely nothing. One vaguely resembled a regular-sided pyramid. Another gave a foggy impression of a crouching figure. The best that could be said of the rest was that they bore a somewhat disconcerting resemblance to the kind of stones people pick up for paperweights. Yet they all had obviously been worked on. There were noticeable chisel marks on each one. And, in addition, they had been polished as well as such soft, grainy rock could be.

I looked up at Longan. His eyes were tense with waiting. I was completely puzzled about his discovery —or what he felt was a discovery. I tried to be fair about his acceptance of this as art. It was obviously nothing more than loyalty to a friend, a friend no doubt as unaware of what constituted art as himself. I made my tone as kind as I could.

"What did your friend expect me to do with these, Mr. Longan?" I asked gently.

"Aren't you buying things for that museum place on Earth?" he said.

I nodded. I picked up the piece that resembled a crouching animal figure and turned it over in my fingers. It was an awkward situation. "Mr. Longan," I said. "I have been in this business many years—"

"I know," he interrupted. "I read about you in the newsfax when you landed on the next world. That's why I wrote you."

"I see," I said. "Well, I've been in it a long time, as I say, and I think I can safely boast that I know something about art. If there is art in these carvings your friend has made, I should be able to recognize it. And I do not."

He stared at me, shock in his greenish-brown eyes.

"You're . . ." he said, finally. "You don't mean that. You're sore because I brought you out here this way."

"I'm sorry," I said. "I'm *not* sore and I *do* mean it.

These things are not merely not good—there is nothing of value in them. Nothing! Someone has deluded your friend into thinking that he has talent. You'll be doing him a favor if you tell him the truth."

He stared at me for a long moment, as if waiting for me to say something to soften the verdict. Then, suddenly, he rose from the chair and crossed the room in three long strides, staring tensely out the window. His callused hands clenched and unclenched spasmodically.

I gave him a little time to wrestle it out with himself. Then I started putting the pieces of stone back into their sections of the box.

"I'm sorry," I told him.

He wheeled about and came back to me, leaning down from his lanky height to look in my face. "Are you?" he said. "*Are* you?"

"Believe me," I said sincerely, "I am." And I was.

"Then will you do something for me?" The words came in a rush. "Will you come and tell Charlie what you've told me? Will *you* break the news to him?"

"I . . ." I meant to protest, to beg off, but with his tortured eyes six inches from mine, the words would not come. "All right," I said.

The breath he had been holding came out in one long sigh. "Thanks," he said. "We'll go out tomorrow. You don't know what this means. Thanks."

I had ample time to regret my decision, both that night and the following morning, when Longan roused me at an early hour, furnished me with a set of bush clothes like his own, including high, impervious boots, and whisked me off in an old air-ground combination flyer that was loaded down with all kinds of bush-dweller's equipment. But a promise is a promise—and I reconciled myself to keeping mine.

We flew south along a high chain of mountains until we came to a coastal area and what appeared to be the swamp delta of some monster river. Here, we began to descend—much to my distaste. I have little affection for hot, muggy climates and could not conceive of anyone wanting to live under such conditions.

We set down lightly in a little open stretch of water—and Longan taxied the flyer across to the nearest bank, a tussocky mass of high brown weeds and soft mud. By myself, I would not have trusted the soggy ground to refrain from drawing me down like quicksand—but Longan stepped out onto the bank confidently enough, and I followed. The mud yielded, little pools of water springing up around my boot soles. A hot rank smell of decaying vegetation came to my nose. Under a thin but uniform blanket of cloud, the sky looked white and sick.

"This way," said Longan, and led off to the right.

I followed him along a little trail and into a small, swampy clearing with dome-shaped huts of woven branches, plastered with mud, scattered about it. And, for the first time, it struck me that Black Charlie might be something other than an expatriate Earthman—might, indeed, be a native of this planet, though I had heard of no other humanlike race on other worlds before. My head spinning, I followed Longan to the entrance of one of the huts and halted as he whistled.

I don't remember now what I expected to see. Something vaguely humanoid, no doubt. But what came through the entrance in response to Longan's whistle was more like a large otter with flat, muscular grasping pads on the end of its four limbs, instead of feet. It was black with glossy, dampish hair all over it. About four feet in length, I judged, with no visible tail and a long, snaky neck. The creature must have weighed one hundred to, perhaps, one hundred and fifty pounds. The head on its long neck was also long and narrow, like the head of a well-bred collie—covered with the same black hair, with bright, intelligent eyes and a long mouth.

"This is Black Charlie," said Longan.

The creature stared at me, and I returned his gaze. Abruptly, I was conscious of the absurdity of the situation. It would have been difficult for any ordinary person to think of this being as a sculptor. To add to this a necessity, an obligation, to convince it that it was *not* a sculptor—mind you, I could not be expected to know a word of its language—was to pile Pelion upon Ossa in a madman's farce. I swung on Longan.

"Look here," I began with quite natural heat, "how do you expect me to tell—"

"He understands you," interrupted Longan.

"Speech?" I said incredulously. "Real human speech?"

"No," Longan shook his head. "But he understands actions." He turned from me abruptly and plunged into the weeds surrounding the clearing. He returned immediately with two objects that looked like gigantic puffballs and handed one to me.

"Sit on this," he said, doing so himself. I obeyed.

Black Charlie—I could think of nothing else to call him—came closer, and we sat down together. Charlie was half squatting on ebony haunches. All this time, I had been carrying the wooden box that contained his sculptures, and now that we were seated, his bright eyes swung inquisitively toward it.

"All right," said Longan, "give it to me."

I passed him the box, and it drew Black Charlie's eyes like a magnet. Longan took it under one arm and pointed toward the lake with the other—to where we had landed the flyer. Then his arm rose in the air in a slow, impressive circle and pointed northward, from the direction we had come.

Black Charlie whistled suddenly. It was an odd note, like the cry of a loon—a far, sad sound.

Longan struck himself on the chest, holding the box with one hand. Then he struck the box and pointed to

me. He looked at Black Charlie, looked back at me—
then put the box into my numb hands.

"Look them over and hand them back," he said, his
voice tight. Against my will, I looked at Charlie.

His eyes met mine. Strange, liquid, black, inhuman
eyes, like two tiny pools of pitch. I had to tear my own
gaze away.

Torn between my feeling of foolishness and a real
sympathy for the waiting creature, I awkwardly opened
the box and I lifted the stones from their compartments. One by one, I turned them in my hand and put
them back. I closed the box and returned it to Longan,
shaking my head, not knowing if Charlie would understand that.

For a long moment, Longan merely sat facing me,
holding the box. Then, slowly, he turned and set it,
still open, in front of Charlie.

Charlie did not react at first. His head, on its long
neck, dropped over the open compartments as if he
was sniffing them. Then, surprisingly, his lips wrinkled back, revealing long, chisel-shaped teeth. Dainti-
ly, he reached into the box with these and lifted out
the stones, one by one. He held them in his forepads,
turning them this way and that, as if searching for
the defects of each. Finally, he lifted one—it was the
stone that faintly resembled a crouching beast. He
lifted it to his mouth—and, with his gleaming teeth,
made slight alterations in its surface. Then he brought
it to me.

Helplessly I took it in my hands and examined it.
The changes he had made in no way altered it toward
something recognizable. I was forced to hand it back,
with another headshake, and a poignant pause fell
between us.

I had been desperately turning over in my mind
some way to explain, through the medium of panto-
mime, the reasons for my refusal. Now something
occurred to me. I turned to Longan.

"Can he get me a piece of unworked stone?" I asked.

Longan turned to Charlie and made motions as if he were breaking something off and handing it to me. For a moment, Charlie sat still, as if considering this. Then he went into his hut, returning a moment later with a chunk of rock the size of my hand.

I had a small pocket knife, and the rock was soft. I held the rock out toward Longan and looked from him to it. Using my pocket knife, I whittled a rough, lumpy caricature of Longan seated on the puffball. When I was finished, I put the two side by side, the hacked piece of stone insignificant on the ground beside the living man.

Black Charlie looked at it. Then he came up to me—and, peering up into my face, cried softly, once. Moving so abruptly that it startled me, he turned smoothly, picked up in his teeth the piece of stone I had carved. Soon he disappeared back into his hut.

Longan stood up stiffly, like a man who has held one position too long. "That's it," he said. "Let's go."

We made our way to the combination and took off once more, headed back toward the city and the spaceship that would carry me away from this irrational world. As the mountains commenced to rise, far beneath us, I stole a glance at Longan, sitting beside me at the controls of the combination. His face was set in an expression of stolid unhappiness.

The question came from my lips before I had time to debate internally whether it was wise or not to ask it.

"Tell me, Mr. Longan," I said, "has—er—Black Charlie some special claim on your friendship?"

The tall man looked at me with something close to amazement.

"Claim!" he said. Then, after a short pause, during which he seemed to search my features to see if I was joking, "He saved my life."

"Oh," I said. "I see."

"You do, do you?" he countered. "Suppose I told you

it was just after I'd finished killing his mate. They mate for life, you know."

"No, I didn't know," I answered feebly.

"I forget people don't know," he said in a subdued voice. I said nothing, hoping that, if I did not disturb him, he would say more. After a while he spoke. "This planet's not much good."

"I noticed," I answered. "I didn't see much in the way of plants and factories. And your sister world—the one I came from—is much more populated and built up."

"There's not much here," he said. "No minerals to speak of. Climate's bad, except on the plateaus. Soil's not much good." He paused. It seemed to take effort to say what came next. "Used to have a novelty trade in furs, though."

"Furs?" I echoed.

"Off Charlie's people," he went on, fiddling with the combination's controls. "Trappers and hunters used to be after them, at first, before they knew. I was one of them."

"You!" I said.

"Me!" His voice was flat. "I was doing fine, too, until I trapped Charlie's mate. Up till then, I'd been getting them out by themselves. They did a lot of traveling in those swamps. But, this time, I was close to the village. I'd just clubbed her on the head when the whole tribe jumped me." His voice trailed off, then strengthened. "They kept me under guard for a couple of months.

"I learned a lot in that time. I learned they were intelligent. I learned it was Black Charlie who kept them from killing me right off. Seems he took the point of view that I was a reasonable being and, if he could just talk things over with me, we could get together and end the war." Longan laughed, a little bitterly. "They called it a war, Charlie's people did." He stopped talking.

I waited. And when he remained quiet, I prompted him. "What happened?" I asked.

"They let me go, finally," he said. "And I went to bat for them. Clear up to the Commissioner sent from Earth. I got them recognized as people instead of animals. I put an end to the hunting and trapping."

He stopped again. We were still flying through the upper air of Elman's World, the sun breaking through the clouds at last, revealing the ground below like a huge green relief map.

"I see," I said, finally.

Longan looked at me stonily.

We flew back to the city.

I left Elman's World the next day, fully believing that I had heard and seen the last of both Longan and Black Charlie. Several years later, at home in New York, I was visited by a member of the government's Foreign Service. He was a slight, dark man, and he didn't beat about the bush.

"You don't know me," he said. I looked at his card—*Antonio Walters*. "I was Deputy Colonial Representative on Elman's World at the time you were there."

I looked up at him, surprised. I had forgotten Elman's World by that time.

"Were you?" I asked, feeling a little foolish, unable to think of anything better to say. I turned his card over several times, staring at it, as a person will do when at a loss. "What can I do for you, Mr. Walters?"

"We've been requested by the local government on Elman's World to locate you, Mr. Jones," he answered. "Cary Longan is dying—"

"Dying!" I said.

"Lung fungus, unfortunately," said Walters. "You catch it in the swamps. He wants to see you before the end—and, since we're very grateful to him out there for the work he's been doing all these years for the natives, a place has been kept for you on a government courier ship leaving for Elman's World right away—if you're willing to go."

"Why, I . . ." I hesitated. In common decency, I could not refuse. "I'll have to notify my employers."

"Of course," he said.

Luckily, the arrangements I had to make consisted of a few business calls and packing my bags. I was, as a matter of fact, between trips at the time. As an experienced traveler, I could always get under way with a minimum of fuss. Walters and I drove out to Government Port in northern New Jersey and, from there on, the authorities took over.

Less than a week later, I stood by Longan's bedside in the hospital of the same city I had visited years before. The man was now nothing more than a barely living skeleton, the hard vitality all but gone from him, hardly able to speak a few words at a time. I bent over to catch the whispered syllables from his wasted lips.

"Black Charlie . . ." he whispered.

"Black Charlie," I repeated. "Yes, what about him?"

"He's done something new," whispered Longan. "That carving of yours started him off, copying things. His tribe don't like it."

"They don't?" I said.

"They," whispered Longan, "don't understand. It's not normal, the way they see it. They're afraid—"

"You mean they're superstitious about what he carves?" I asked.

"Something like that. Listen—he's an artist . . ."

I winced internally at the last word, but held my tongue for the sake of the dying man.

". . . an artist. But they'll kill him for it, now that I'm gone. You can save him, though."

"Me?" I said.

"You!" The man's voice was like a wind rustling through dry leaves. "If you go out—take this last thing from him—act pleased . . . then they'll be scared to touch him. But hurry. Every day is that much closer . . ."

His strength failed him. He closed his eyes, and his straining throat muscles relaxed to a little hiss of air that puffed between his lips. The nurse hurried me from his room.

The local government helped me. I was surprised, and not a little touched, to see how many people knew Longan. How many of them admired his attempts to pay back the natives by helping them in any way he could. They located Charlie's tribe on a map for me and sent me out with a pilot who knew the country.

We landed on the same patch of slime. I went alone toward the clearing. With the brown weeds still walling it about, the locale showed no natural change, but Black Charlie's hut appeared broken and deserted. I whistled and waited. I called. And, finally, I got down on my hands and knees and crawled inside. But there was nothing there save a pile of loose rock and a mass of dried weeds. Feeling cramped and uncomfortable, for ı am not used to such gymnastics, I backed out to find myself surrounded by a crowd.

It looked as if all the other inhabitants of the village had come out of their huts and congregated before Charlie's. They seemed agitated, milling about, occasionally whistling at each other on that one low, plaintive note which was the only sound I had ever heard Charlie make. Eventually, the excitement seemed to fade, the group fell back, and one individual came forward alone. He looked up into my face for a brief moment, then turned and glided swiftly on his pads toward the edge of the clearing.

I followed. There seemed nothing else to do. And, at that time, it did not occur to me to be afraid.

My guide led me deep into the weed patch, then abruptly disappeared. I looked around surprised and undecided, half inclined to turn about and retrace my steps by the trail of crushed weeds I had left in my floundering advance. Then a low whistle sounded close by. I went forward and found Charlie.

· He lay on his side in a little circular open area of crushed weeds. He was too weak to do more than raise his head and look at me, for the whole surface of his body was crisscrossed and marked with the slashings of shallow wounds, from which dark blood seeped slowly and stained the reeds in which he lay. In Charlie's mouth I had seen the long chisel-teeth of his kind, and I knew what had made those wounds. A gust of rage went through me, and I stooped to pick him up in my arms.

He came up easily, for the bones of his kind are cartilaginous, and their flesh is far lighter than our human flesh. Holding him, I turned and made my way back to the clearing.

The others were waiting for me as we came out into the open. I glared at them—and then the rage inside me went out like a blown candle. For there was nothing there to hate. *They* had not hated Charlie. They had merely feared him—and their only crime was ignorance.

They moved back from me, and I carried Charlie to the door of his own hut. There I laid him down. The chest and arms of my jacket were soaked from his dark body fluid, and I saw that his blood was not clotting as our own does.

Clumsily, I took off my shirt and, tearing it into strips, made a poor attempt to bind up the torn flesh. But the blood came through in spite of my first aid. Charlie, lifting his head, with a great effort, from the ground, picked feebly at the bandages with his teeth, so that I gave up and removed them.

I sat down beside him then, feeling sick and helpless. In spite of Longan's care and dying effort, in spite of all the scientific developments of my own human race, I had come too late. Numbly, I sat and looked down at him and wondered why I could not have come one day earlier.

From this half stupor of self-accusation I was roused by Charlie's attempts to crawl back into his hut. My first reaction was to restrain him. But, from somewhere, he seemed to have dredged up a remnant of his waning strength—and he persisted. Seeing this, I changed my mind and, instead of hindering, helped. He dragged himself through the entrance, his strength visibly waning.

I did not expect to see him emerge. I believed some ancient instinct had called him, that he would die then and there. But, a few moments later, I heard a sound as of stones rattling from within—and, in a few seconds, he began to back out. Halfway through the entrance, his strength finally failed him. He lay still for a minute, then whistled weakly.

I went to him and pulled him out the rest of the way. He turned his head toward me, holding in his mouth what I first took to be a ball of dried mud.

I took it from him and began to scrape the mud off with my fingernails. Almost immediately, the grain and surface of the sandstone he used for his carvings began to emerge—and my hands started to shake so hard that, for a moment, I had to put the stone down while I got myself under control. For the first time, the true importance to Charlie of these things he had chewed and bitten into shape got home to me.

In that moment, I swore that whatever bizarre form this last and greatest work of his might possess, I would make certain that it was accorded a place in some respectable museum as a true work of art. After all, it had been conceived in honesty and executed in the love that took no count of labor, provided the end was achieved.

And then, the rest of the mud came free in my hands. I saw what it was, and I could have cried and laughed at the same time. For, of all the shapes he could have chosen to work in stone, he had picked the one that no critic would have selected as the choice of an artist of his race. For he had chosen no plant or animal, no structure or natural shape out of his environment, to express the hungry longing of his spirit. None of these had he chosen—instead, with painful clumsiness, he had fashioned an image from the soft and grainy rock—a statue of a standing man.

And I knew what man it was.

Charlie lifted his head from the stained ground and looked toward the lake where my flyer waited. I am not an intuitive man—but, for once, I was able to understand the meaning of a look. He wanted me to leave while he was still alive. He wanted to see me go, carrying the thing he had fashioned. I got to my feet, holding it, and stumbled off. At the edge of the clearing, I looked back. He still watched. And the rest of his people still hung back from him. I did not think they would bother him now.

And so I came home.

But there is one thing more to tell. For a long time, after I returned from Elman's World, I did not look at the crude statuette. I did not want to, for I knew that seeing it would only confirm what I had known from the start, that all the longing and desires in the world cannot create art where there is no talent, no true visualization. But at the end of one year I was cleaning up all the little details of my office. And, because I believe in system and order—and also because I was ashamed of myself for having put it off so long—I took the statuette from a bottom drawer of my desk, unwrapped it, and set it on the desk's polished surface.

I was alone in my office at the time, at the end of a day, when the afternoon sun, striking red through the tall window beside my desk, touched everything between the walls with a clear, amber light. I ran my fingers over the grainy sandstone and held it up to look at it.

And then—for the first time—I saw it, saw through the stone to the image beyond, saw what Black Charlie had seen, with Black Charlie's eyes, when he looked at Longan. I saw men as Black Charlie's kind saw men—and I saw what the worlds of men meant to Black Charlie. And, above all, overriding all, I saw art as Black Charlie saw it, through his bright alien eyes—saw the beauty he had sought at the price of his life, and had half found.

But, most of all, I saw that this crude statuette was *art*.

One more word. Amid the mud and weeds of the swamp, I had held the carving in my hands and promised myself that this work would one day stand on display. Following that moment of true insight in my office, I did my best to place it with the institution I represented, then with others who knew me as a reputable buyer.

But I could find no takers. No one, although they trusted me individually, was willing to exhibit such a poor-looking piece of work on the strength of a history that I, alone, could vouch for. There are people, close to any institution, who are only too ready to cry, "Hoax!" For several years, I tried without success.

Eventually, I gave up on the true story and sold the statuette, along with a number of other odd pieces, to a dealer of minor reputation, representing it as an object whose history I did not know.

Curiously, the statuette has justified my belief in what is art, by finding a niche for itself. I traced it from the dealer, after a time, and ran it to Earth quite recently. There is a highly respectable art gallery on this planet which has an extensive display of primitive figures of early American Indian origin.

And Black Charlie's statuette is among them. I will not tell which or where it is.

WITH MORNING COMES MISTFALL

by GEORGE R. R. MARTIN

George "Railroad" Martin won a Hugo Award for "A Song for Lya," the title story of his first story collection (1976), and he has been a strong contender for other awards since his first appearance in the field in 1971. His other books include an excellent first novel, *Dying of the Light* (1977), and a second story collection, *Songs of Stars and Shadows* (1977).

There is a strong sense of the cosmic and the mysteries of the universe in his work, beautifully portrayed in this haunting story.

I WAS early to breakfast that morning, the first day after landing. But Sanders was already out on the dining balcony when I got there. He was standing alone by the edge, looking out over the mountains and the mists.

I walked up behind him and muttered hello. He didn't bother to reply. "It's beautiful, isn't it?" he said, without turning.

And it was.

Only a few feet below balcony level the mists rolled, sending ghostly breakers to crash against the stones

of Sanders' castle. A thick white blanket extended
from horizon to horizon, cloaking everything. We could
see the summit of the Red Ghost, off to the north; a
barbed dagger of scarlet rock jabbing into the sky. But
that was all. The other mountains were still below
mist level.

But we were above the mists. Sanders had built his
hotel atop the tallest mountain in the chain. We were
floating alone in a swirling white ocean, on a flying
castle amid a sea of clouds.

Castle Cloud, in fact. That was what Sanders had
named the place. It was easy to see why.

"Is it always like this?" I asked Sanders, after drinking it all in for a while.

"Every mistfall," he replied, turning toward me with
a wistful smile. He was a fat man, with a jovial red
face. Not the sort who should smile wistfully. But he
did.

He gestured toward the east, where Wraithworld's
sun rising above the mists made a crimson-and-orange
spectacle of the dawn sky.

"The sun," he said. "As it rises, the heat drives the
mists back into the valleys, forces them to surrender
the mountains they've conquered during the night.
The mists sink, and one by one the peaks come into
view. By noon the whole range is visible for miles and
miles. There's nothing like it on Earth, or anywhere
else."

He smiled again, and led me over to one of the
tables scattered around the balcony. "And then, at
sunset, it's all reversed. You must watch mistrise tonight," he said.

We sat down, and a sleek robowaiter came rolling
out to serve us as the chairs registered our presence.
Sanders ignored it. "It's war, you know," he continued. "Eternal war between the sun and the mists. And
the mists have the better of it. They have the valleys,
and the plains, and the seacoasts. The sun has only a
few mountaintops. And them only by day."

He turned to the robowaiter and ordered coffee for both of us, to keep us occupied until the others arrived. It would be fresh-brewed, of course. Sanders didn't tolerate instants or synthetics on his planet.

"You like it here," I said, while we waited for the coffee.

Sanders laughed. "What's not to like? Castle Cloud has everything. Good food, entertainment, gambling, and all the other comforts of home. Plus this planet. I've got the best of both worlds, don't I?"

"I suppose so. But most people don't think in those terms. Nobody comes to Wraithworld for the gambling, or the food."

Sanders nodded. "But we do get some hunters. Out after rockcats and plains devils. And once in a while someone will come to look at the ruins."

"Maybe," I said. "But those are your exceptions. Not your rule. Most of your guests are here for one reason."

"Sure," he admitted, grinning. "The wraiths."

"The wraiths," I echoed. "You've got beauty here, and hunting and fishing and mountaineering. But none of that brings the tourists here. It's the wraiths they come for."

The coffee arrived then, two big steaming mugs accompanied by a pitcher of thick cream. It was very strong, and very hot, and very good. After weeks of spaceship synthetic, it was an awakening.

Sanders sipped at his coffee with care, his eyes studying me over the mug. He set it down thoughtfully. "And it's the wraiths you've come for, too," he said.

I shrugged. "Of course. My readers aren't interested in scenery, no matter how spectacular. Dubowski and his men are here to find wraiths, and I'm here to cover the search."

Sanders was about to answer, but he never got the chance. A sharp, precise voice cut in suddenly. "If there are any wraiths to find," the voice said.

We turned to face the balcony entrance. Dr. Charles

Dubowski, head of the Wraithworld Research Team, was standing in the doorway, squinting in the light. He had managed to shake the gaggle of research assistants who usually trailed him everywhere.

Dubowski paused for a second, then walked over to our table, pulled out a chair, and sat down. The robowaiter came rolling out again.

Sanders eyed the thin scientist with unconcealed distaste. "What makes you think the wraiths aren't there, Doctor?" he asked.

Dubowski shrugged, and smiled lightly. "I just don't feel there's enough evidence," he said. "But don't worry. I never let my feelings interfere with my work. I want the truth as much as anyone. So I'll run an impartial expedition. If your wraiths *are* out there, I'll find them."

"Or they'll find you," Sanders said. He looked grave. "And that might not be too pleasant."

Dubowski laughed. "Oh, come now, Sanders. Just because you live in a castle doesn't mean you have to be so melodramatic."

"Don't laugh, Doctor. The wraiths have killed people before, you know."

"No proof of that," said Dubowski. "No proof at all. Just as there's no proof of the wraiths themselves. But that's why we're here. To find proof. Or disproof. But come, I'm famished." He turned to our robowaiter, who had been standing by and humming impatiently.

Dubowski and I ordered rockcat steaks, with a basket of hot, freshly baked biscuits. Sanders took advantage of the Earth supplies our ship had brought in last night, and got a massive slab of ham with a half-dozen eggs.

Rockcat has a flavor that Earth meat hasn't had in centuries. I loved it, although Dubowski left much of his steak uneaten. He was too busy talking to eat.

"You shouldn't dismiss the wraiths so lightly," Sanders said after the robowaiter had stalked off with our orders. "There is evidence. Plenty of it. Twenty-two deaths since this planet was discovered. And eyewitness accounts of wraiths by the dozens."

"True," Dubowski said. "But I wouldn't call that real evidence. Deaths? Yes. Most are simple disappearances, however. Probably people who fell off a mountain, or got eaten by a rockcat, or something. It's impossible to find the bodies in the mists. More people vanish every day on Earth, and nothing is thought of it. But here, every time someone disappears, people claim the wraiths got him. No, I'm sorry. It's not enough."

"Bodies have been found, Doctor," Sanders said quietly. "Slain horribly. And not by falls or rockcats, either."

It was my turn to cut in. "Only four bodies have been recovered that I know of," I said. "And I've backgrounded myself pretty thoroughly on the wraiths."

Sanders frowned. "All right," he admitted. "But what about those four cases? Pretty convincing evidence, if you ask me."

The food showed up about then, but Sanders continued as we ate. "The first sighting, for example. That's never been explained satisfactorily. The Gregor Expedition."

I nodded. Dave Gregor had captained the ship that had discovered Wraithworld, nearly seventy-five years earlier. He had probed through the mists with his sensors, and set his ship down on the seacoast plains. Then he sent teams out to explore.

There were two men in each team, both well armed. But in one case, only a single man came back, and he was in hysteria. He and his partner had gotten separated in the mists, and suddenly he heard a blood-curdling scream. When he found his friend, he was quite dead. And something was standing over the body.

The survivor described the killer as manlike, eight feet tall, and somehow insubstantial. He claimed that when he fired at it, the blaster bolt went right through it. Then the creature had wavered, and vanished in the mists.

Gregor sent other teams out to search for the thing. They recovered the body, but that was all. Without special instruments, it was difficult to find the same place twice in the mists. Let alone something like the creature that had been described.

So the story was never confirmed. But nonetheless, it caused a sensation when Gregor returned to Earth. Another ship was sent to conduct a more thorough search. It found nothing. But one of its search teams disappeared without a trace.

And the legend of the mist wraiths was born, and began to grow. Other ships came to Wraithworld, and a trickle of colonists came and went, and Paul Sanders landed one day and erected the Castle Cloud so the public might safely visit the mysterious planet of the wraiths.

And there were other deaths, and other disappearances, and many people claimed to catch brief glimpses of wraiths prowling through the mists. And then someone found the ruins. Just tumbled stone blocks, now. But once, structures of some sort. The homes of the wraiths, people said.

There was evidence, I thought. And some of it was hard to deny. But Dubowski was shaking his head vigorously.

"The Gregor affair proves nothing," he said. "You know as well as I this planet has never been explored thoroughly. Especially the plains area, where Gregor's ship put down. It was probably some sort of animal that killed that man. A rare animal of some sort native to that area."

"What about the testimony of his partner?" Sanders asked.

"Hysteria, pure and simple."

"The other sightings? There have been an awful lot of them. And the witnesses weren't always hysterical."

"Proves nothing," Dubowski said, shaking his head. "Back on Earth, plenty of people still claim to have seen ghosts and flying saucers. And here, with those damned mists, mistakes and hallucinations are naturally even easier."

He jabbed at Sanders with the knife he was using to butter a biscuit. "It's these mists that foul up everything. The wraith myth would have died long ago without the mists. Up to now, no one has had the equipment or the money to conduct a really thorough investigation. But we do. And we will. We'll get the truth once and for all."

Sanders grinned. "If you don't get yourself killed first. The wraiths may not like being investigated."

"I don't understand you, Sanders," Dubowski said. "If you're so afraid of the wraiths and so convinced that they're down there prowling about, why have you lived here so long?"

"Castle Cloud was built with safeguards," Sanders said. "The brochure we send prospective guests describes them. No one is in danger here. For one thing, the wraiths won't come out of the mists. And we're in sunlight most of the day. But it's a different story down in the valleys."

"That's superstitious nonsense. If I had to guess, I'd say these mist wraiths of yours were nothing but transplanted Earth ghosts. Phantoms of someone's imagination. But I won't guess—I'll wait until the results are in. Then we'll see. If they are real, they won't be able to hide from us."

Sanders looked over at me. "What about you? Do you agree with him?"

"I'm a journalist," I said carefully. "I'm just here to cover what happens. The wraiths are famous, and my readers are interested. So I've got no opinions. Or none that I'd care to broadcast, anyway."

Sanders lapsed into a disgruntled silence, and attacked his ham and eggs with a renewed vigor. Dubowski took over for him, and steered the conversation over to the details of the investigation he was planning. The rest of the meal was a montage of eager talk about wraith traps, and search plans, and robo-probes, and sensors. I listened carefully and took mental notes for a column on the subject.

Sanders listened carefully, too. But you could tell from his face that he was far from pleased by what he heard.

Nothing much else happened that day. Dubowski spent his time at the space field, built on a small plateau below the castle, and supervised the unloading of his equipment. I wrote a colunn on his plans for the expedition, and beamed it back to Earth. Sanders tended to his other guests, and did whatever else a hotel manager does, I guess.

I went out to the balcony again at sunset, to watch the mists rise.

It was war, as Sanders had said. At mistfall, I had seen the sun victorious in the first of the daily battles. But now the conflict was renewed. The mists began to creep back to the heights as the temperature fell. Wispy gray-white tendrils stole up silently from the valleys, and curled around the jagged mountain peaks like ghostly fingers. Then the fingers began to grow thicker and stronger, and after a while they pulled the mists up after them.

One by one the stark, wind-carved summits were swallowed up for another night. The Red Ghost, the giant to the north, was the last mountain to vanish in the lapping white ocean. And then the mists began to pour in over the balcony ledge, and close around Castle Cloud itself.

I went back inside. Sanders was standing there, just inside the doors. He had been watching me.

"You were right," I said. "It was beautiful."

He nodded. "You know, I don't think Dubowski has bothered to look yet," he said.

"Busy, I guess."

Sanders sighed. "Too damn busy. C'mon. I'll buy you a drink."

The hotel bar was quiet and dark, with the kind of mood that promotes good talk and serious drinking. The more I saw of Sanders' castle, the more I liked the man. Our tastes were in remarkable accord.

We found a table in the darkest and most secluded part of the room, and ordered drinks from a stock that included liquors from a dozen worlds. And we talked.

"You don't seem very happy to have Dubowski here," I said after the drinks came. "Why not? He's filling up your hotel."

Sanders looked up from his drink, and smiled. "True. It is the slow season. But I don't like what he's trying to do."

"So you try to scare him away?"

Sanders' smile vanished. "Was I that transparent?"

I nodded.

He sighed. "Didn't think it would work," he said. He sipped thoughtfully at his drink. "But I had to try something."

"Why?"

"Because. Because he's going to destroy this world, if I let him. By the time he and his kind get through, there won't be a mystery left in the universe."

"He's just trying to find some answers. Do the wraiths exist? What about the ruins? Who built them? Didn't you ever want to know those things, Sanders?"

He drained his drink, looked around, and caught the waiter's eye to order another. No robowaiters in here. Only human help. Sanders was particular about atmosphere.

"Of course," he said when he had his drink. "Everyone's wondered about those questions. That's why people come here to Wraithworld, to Castle Cloud. Each guy who touches down here is secretly hoping he'll have an adventure with the wraiths, and find out all the answers personally.

"So he doesn't. So he slaps on a blaster and wanders

around the mist forests for a few days, or a few weeks, and finds nothing. So what? He can come back and search again. The dream is still there, and the romance, and the mystery.

"And who knows? Maybe one trip he glimpses a wraith drifting through the mists. Or something he thinks is a wraith. And then he'll go home happy, because he's been part of a legend. He's touched a little bit of creation that hasn't had all the awe and the wonder ripped from it yet by Dubowski's sort."

He fell silent, and stared morosely into his drink. Finally, after a long pause, he continued. "Dubowski! Bah! He makes me boil. He comes here with his ship full of lackeys and his million-credit grant and all his gadgets, to hunt for wraiths. Oh, he'll get them all right. That's what frightens me. Either he'll prove they don't exist, or he'll find them, and they'll turn out to be some kind of submen or animals or something."

He emptied his glass again, savagely. "And that will ruin it. Ruin it, you hear? He'll answer all the questions with his gadgets, and there'll be nothing left for anyone else. It isn't fair."

I sat there and sipped quietly at my drink and said nothing. Sanders ordered another. A foul thought was running around in my head. Finally I had to say it aloud.

"If Dubowski answers all the questions," I said, "then there will be no reason to come here any more. And you'll be put out of business. Are you sure that's not why you're so worried?"

Sanders glared at me, and I thought he was going to hit me for a second. But he didn't. "I thought you were different. You looked at mistfall, and understood. I thought you did, anyway. But I guess I was wrong." He jerked his head toward the door. "Get out of here," he said.

I rose. "All right," I said. "I'm sorry, Sanders. But it's my job to ask nasty questions like that."

He ignored me, and I left the table. When I reached the door, I turned and looked back across the room. Sanders was staring into his drink again, and talking loudly to himself.

"Answers," he said. He made it sound obscene. "Answers. Always they have to have answers. But the questions are so much finer. Why can't they leave them alone?"

I left him alone then. Alone with his drinks.

The next few weeks were hectic ones, for the expedition and for me. Dubowski went about things thoroughly, you had to give him that. He had planned his assault on Wraithworld with meticulous precision.

Mapping came first. Thanks to the mists, what maps there were of Wraithworld were very crude by modern standards. So Dubowski sent out a whole fleet of roboprobes, to skim above the mists and steal their secrets with sophisticated sensory devices. From the information that came pouring in, a detailed topography of the region was pieced together.

That done, Dubowski and his assistants then used the maps to carefully plot every recorded wraith sighting since the Gregor Expedition. Considerable data on the sightings had beem compiled and analyzed long before we left Earth, of course. Heavy use of the matchless collection on wraiths in the Castle Cloud library filled in the gaps that remained. As expected, sightings were most common in the valleys around the hotel, the only permanent human habitation on the planet.

When the plotting was completed, Dubowski set out his wraith traps, scattering most of them in the areas where wraiths had been reported most frequently. He also put a few in distant, outlying regions, however, including the seacoast plain where Gregor's ship had made the initial contact.

The traps weren't really traps, of course. They were squat duralloy pillars, packed with most every type of sensing and recording equipment known to Earth science. To the traps, the mists were all but nonexistent. If some unfortunate wraith wandered into survey range, there would be no way it could avoid detection.

Meanwhile, the mapping roboprobes were pulled in to be overhauled and reprogrammed, and then sent out again. With the topography known in detail, the probes could be sent through the mists on low-level patrols without fear of banging into a concealed mountain. The sensing equipment carried by the probes was not the equal of that in the wraith traps, of course. But the probes had a much greater range, and could cover thousands of square miles each day.

Finally, when the wraith traps were deployed and the roboprobes were in the air, Dubowski and his men took to the mist forests themselves. Each carried a heavy backpack of sensors and detection devices. The human search teams had more mobility than the wraith traps, and more sophisticated equipment than the probes. They covered a different area each day, in painstaking detail.

I went along on a few of those trips, with a backpack of my own. It made for some interesting copy, even though we never found anything. And while on search, I fell in love with the mist forests.

The tourist literature likes to call them "the ghastly mist forests of haunted Wraithworld." But they're not ghastly. Not really. There's a strange sort of beauty there, for those who can appreciate it.

The trees are thin and very tall, with white bark and pale gray leaves. But the forests are not without color. There's a parasite, a hanging moss of some sort, that's very common, and it drips from the overhanging branches in cascades of dark green and scarlet. And there are rocks, and vines, and low bushes choked with misshapen purplish fruits.

But there's no sun, or course. The mists hide everything. They swirl and slide around you as you walk, caressing you with unseen hands, clutching at your feet.

Once in a while, the mists play games with you. Most of the time you walk through a thick fog, unable to see more than a few feet in any direction, your own shoes lost in the mist carpet below. Sometimes, though, the fog closes in suddenly. And then you can't see at all. I blundered into more than one tree when that happened.

At other times, though, the mists—for no apparent reason—will roll back suddenly, and leave you standing alone in a clear pocket within a cloud. That's when you can see the forest in all its grotesque beauty. It's a brief, breathtaking glimpse of never-never land. Moments like that are few and short-lived. But they stay with you.

They stay with you.

In those early weeks, I didn't have much time for walking in the forests, except when I joined a search team to get the feel of it. Mostly I was busy writing. I did a series on the history of the planet, highlighted by the stories of the most famous sightings. I did feature profiles on some of the more colorful members of the expedition. I did a piece on Sanders, and the problems he encountered and overcame in building Castle Cloud. I did science pieces on the little known about the planet's ecology. I did mood pieces about the forests and the mountains. I did speculative-thought pieces about the ruins. I wrote about rockcat hunting, and mountain climbing, and the huge and dangerous swamp lizards native to some offshore islands.

And, of course, I wrote about Dubowski and his search. On that I wrote reams.

Finally, however, the search began to settle down into dull routine, and I began to exhaust the myriad other topics Wraithworld offered. My output began to decline. I started to have time on my hands.

That's when I really began to enjoy Wraithworld. I began to take daily walks through the forests, rang-ing wider each day. I visited the ruins, and flew half a continent away to see the swamp lizards firsthand instead of by holo. I befriended a group of hunters passing through, and shot myself a rockcat. I accompanied some other hunters to the western seacoast, and nearly got myself killed by a plains devil.

And I began to talk to Sanders again.

Through all this, Sanders had pretty well ignored me and Dubowski and everyone else connected with the wraith research. He spoke to us grudgingly if at all, greeted us curtly, and spent all his free time with his other guests.

At first, after the way he had talked in the bar that night, I worried about what he might do. I had visions of him murdering someone out in the mists, and trying to make it look like a wraith killing. Or maybe just sabotaging the wraith traps. But I was sure he would try something to scare off Dubowski; or otherwise undermine the expedition.

Comes of watching too much holovision, I guess. Sanders did nothing of the sort. He merely sulked, glared at us in the castle corridors, and gave us less than full cooperation at all times.

After a while, though, he began to warm up again. Not toward Dubowski and his men. Just toward me.

I guess that was because of my walks in the forests. Dubowski never went out into the mists unless he had to. And then he went out reluctantly, and came back quickly. His men followed their chief's example. I was the only joker in the deck. But then, I wasn't really part of the same deck.

Sanders noticed, of course. He didn't miss much of what went on in his castle. And he began to speak to me again. Civilly. One day, finally, he even invited me for drinks again.

It was about two months into the expedition. Winter was coming to Wraithworld and Castle Cloud, and the air was getting cold and crisp. Dubowski and I were out on the dining balcony, lingering over coffee after another superb meal. Sanders sat at a nearby table, talking to some tourists.

I forget what Dubowski and I were discussing. Whatever it was, Dubowski interrupted me with a shiver at one point. "It's getting cold out here," he complained. "Why don't we move inside?" Dubowski never liked the dining balcony very much.

I sort of frowned. "It's not that bad," I said. "Besides, it's nearly sunset. One of the best parts of the day."

Dubowski shivered again, and stood up. "Suit yourself," he said. "But I'm going in. I don't feel like catching a cold just so you can watch another mistfall."

He started to walk off. But he hadn't taken three steps before Sanders was up out of his seat, howling like a wounded rockcat.

"Mistfall," he bellowed. *"Mistfall!"* He launched into a long, incoherent string of obscenities. I had never seen Sanders so angry, not even when he threw me out of the bar that first night. He stood there, literally trembling with rage, his face flushed, his fat fists clenching and unclenching at his sides.

I got up in a hurry, and got between them. Dubowski turned to me, looking baffled and scared. "Wha—" he started.

"Get inside," I interrupted. "Get up to your room. Get to the lounge. Get somewhere. Get anywhere. But get out of here before he kills you."

"But—but—what's wrong? What happened? I don't—"

"Mistfall is in the morning," I told him. "At night, at sunset, it's mistrise. Now *go.*"

"That's *all?* Why should that get him so—so—"

"GO!"

Dubowski shook his head, as if to say he still didn't understand what was going on. But he went.

I turned to Sanders. "Calm down," I said. "Calm down."

He stopped trembling, but his eyes threw blaster

bolts at Dubowski's back. "Mistfall," he muttered. "Two months that bastard has been here, and he doesn't know the difference between mistfall and mistrise."

"He's never bothered to watch either one," I said. "Things like that don't interest him. That's his loss, though. No reason for you to get upset about it."

He looked at me, frowning. Finally he nodded. "Yeah," he said. "Maybe you're right." He sighed. "But *mistfall!* Hell." There was a short silence, then, "I need a drink. Join me?"

I nodded.

We wound up in the same dark corner as the first night, at what must have been Sanders' favorite table. He put away three drinks before I had finished my first. Big drinks. Everything in Castle Cloud was big.

There were no arguments this time. We talked about mistfall, and the forests, and the ruins. We talked about the wraiths, and Sanders lovingly told me the stories of the great sightings. I knew them all already, of course. But not the way Sanders told them.

At one point, I mentioned that I'd been born in Bradbury when my parents were spending a short vacation on Mars. Sanders' eyes lit up at that, and he spent the next hour or so regaling me with Earthman jokes. I'd heard them all before, too. But I was getting more than a little drunk, and somehow they all seemed hilarious.

After that night, I spent more time with Sanders than with anyone else in the hotel. I thought I knew Wraithworld pretty well by that time. But that was an empty conceit, and Sanders proved it. He showed me hidden spots in the forests that have haunted me ever since. He took me to island swamps, where the trees are of a very different sort and sway horribly without a wind. We flew to the far north, to another mountain range where the peaks are higher and sheathed in ice, and to a southern plateau where the mists pour eternally over the edge in a ghostly imitation of a waterfall.

I continued to write about Dubowski and his wraith hunt, of course. But there was little new to write about, so most of my time was spent with Sanders. I didn't worry too much about my output. My Wraith-world series had gotten excellent play on Earth and most of the colony worlds, so I thought I had it made.

Not so.

I'd been on Wraithworld just a little over three months when my syndicate beamed me. A few systems away, a civil war had broken out on a planet called New Refuge. They wanted me to cover it. No news was coming out of Wraithworld anyway, they said, since Dubowski's expedition still had over a year to run.

Much as I liked Wraithworld, I jumped at the chance. My stories had been getting a little stale, and I was running out of ideas, and the New Refuge thing sounded like it could be very big.

So I said goodbye to Sanders and Dubowski and Castle Cloud, and took a last walk through the mist forests, and booked passage on the next ship through.

The New Refuge civil war was a firecracker. I spent less than a month on the planet, but it was a dreary month. The place had been colonized by religious fanatics, but the original cult had schismed, and both sides accused the other of heresy. It was all very dingy. The planet itself had all the charm of a Martian suburb.

I moved on as quickly as I could, hopping from planet to planet, from story to story. In six months, I had worked myself back to Earth. Elections were coming up, so I got slapped onto a political beat. That was fine by me. It was a lively campaign, and there was a ton of good stories to be mined.

But throughout it all, I kept myself up on the little news that came out of Wraithworld. And finally, as I'd expected, Dubowski announced a press conference. As the syndicate's resident wraith, I got myself assigned to cover, and headed out on the fastest starship I could find.

I got there a week before the conference, ahead of everyone else. I had beamed Sanders before taking ship, and he met me at the spaceport. We adjourned to the dining balcony, and had our drinks served out there.

"Well?" I asked him, after we had traded amenities. "You know what Dubowski's going to announce?"

Sanders looked very glum. "I can guess," he said. "He called in all his damn gadgets a month ago, and he's been cross-checking findings on a computer. We've had a couple of wraith sightings since you left. Dubowski moved in hours after each sighting, and went over the area with a fine-tooth comb. Nothing. That's what he's going to announce, I think. Nothing."

I nodded. "Is that so bad, though? Gregor found nothing."

"Not the same," Sanders said. "Gregor didn't look the way Dubowski has. People will believe him, whatever he says."

I wasn't so sure of that, and was about to say so, when Dubowski arrived. Someone must have told him I was there. He came striding out on the balcony, smiling, spied me, and came over to sit down.

Sanders glared at him, and studied his drink. Dubowski trained all of his attention on me. He seemed very pleased with himself. He asked what I'd been doing since I left, and I told him, and he said that was nice.

Finally I got to ask him about the results. "No comment," he said. "That's what I've called the press conference for."

"C'mon," I said. "I covered you for months when everybody else was ignoring the expedition. You can give me some kind of beat. What have you got?"

He hesitated. "Well, O.K.," he said doubtfully. "But don't release it yet. You can beam it out a few hours ahead of the conference. That should be enough time for a beat."

I nodded agreement. "What do you have?"

"The wraiths," he said. "I have the wraiths, bagged neatly. They don't exist. I've got enough evidence to prove it beyond a shadow of a doubt." He smiled broadly.

"Just because you didn't find anything?" I started. "Maybe they were avoiding you. If they're sentient, they might be smart enough. Or maybe they're beyond the ability of your sensors to detect."

"Come now," Dubowski said. "You don't believe that. Our wraith traps had every kind of sensor we could come up with. If the wraiths existed, they would have registered on something. But they didn't. We had the traps planted in the areas where three of Sanders' so-called sightings took place. Nothing. Absolutely nothing. Conclusive proof that those people were seeing things. Sightings, indeed."

"What about the deaths, the vanishings?" I asked. "What about the Gregor Expedition and the other classic cases?"

His smile spread. "Couldn't disprove all the deaths, of course. But our probes and our searches turned up four skeletons." He ticked them off on his fingers. "Two were killed by a rockslide, and one had rockcat claw marks on the bones."

"The fourth?"

"Murder," he said. "The body was buried in a shallow grave, clearly by human hands. A flood of some sort had exposed it. It was down in the records as a disappearance. I'm sure all the other bodies could be found, if we searched long enough. And we'd find that all died perfectly normal deaths."

Sanders raised his eyes from his drink. They were bitter eyes. "Gregor," he said stubbornly. "Gregor and the other classics."

Dubowski's smile became a smirk. "Ah, yes. We searched that area quite thoroughly. My theory was right. We found a tribe of apes nearby. Big brutes. Like giant baboons, with dirty white fur. Not a very successful species, either. We found only one small tribe, and they were dying out. But clearly, that was what Gregor's man sighted. And exaggerated all out of proportion."

There was silence. Then Sanders spoke, but his voice was beaten. "Just one question," he said softly. "Why?"

That brought Dubowski up short, and his smile faded. "You never have understood, have you, Sanders?" he said. "It was for truth. To free this planet from ignorance and superstition."

"Free Wraithworld?" Sanders said. "Was it enslaved?"

"Yes," Dubowski answered. "Enslaved by foolish myth. By fear. Now this planet will be free, and open. We can find out the truth behind those ruins now, without murky legends about half-human wraiths to fog the facts. We can open this planet for colonization. People won't be afraid to come here, and live, and farm. We've conquered the fear."

"A colony world? Here?" Sanders looked amused. "Are you going to bring big fans to blow away the mists, or what? Colonists have come before. And left. The soil's all wrong. You can't farm here, with all these mountains. At least not on a commercial scale. There's no way you can make a profit growing things on Wraithworld.

"Besides, there are hundreds of colony worlds crying for people. Did you need another so badly? Must Wraithworld become yet another Earth?"

Sanders shook his head sadly, drained his drink, and continued. "You're the one who doesn't understand, Doctor. Don't kid yourself. You haven't freed Wraithworld. You've destroyed it. You've stolen its wraiths, and left an empty planet."

Dubowski shook his head. "I think you're wrong. They'll find plenty of good, profitable ways to exploit this planet. But even if you were correct, well, it's just too bad. Knowledge is what man is all about. People like you have tried to hold back progress since the beginning of time. But they failed, and you failed. Man needs to know."

"Maybe," Sanders said. "But is that the *only* thing man needs? I don't think so. I think he also needs mystery, and poetry, and romance. I think he needs a few unanswered questions, to make him brood and wonder."

Dubowski stood up abruptly, and frowned. "This conversation is as pointless as your philosophy, Sanders. There's no room in my universe for unanswered questions."

"Then you live in a very drab universe, Doctor."

"And you, Sanders, live in the stink of your own ignorance. Find some new superstitions if you must. But don't try to foist them off on me with your tales and legends. I've got no time for wraiths." He looked at me. "I'll see you at the press conference," he said. Then he turned and walked briskly from the balcony.

Sanders watched him depart in silence, then swiveled in his chair to look out over the mountains. "The mists are rising," he said.

Sanders was wrong about the colony, too, as it turned out. They did establish one, although it wasn't much to boast of. Some vineyards, some factories, and a few thousand people; all belonging to no more than a couple of big companies.

Commercial farming did turn out to be unprofitable, you see. With one exception—a native grape, a fat gray thing the size of a lemon. So Wraithworld has only one export, a smoky white wine with a mellow, lingering flavor.

They call it mistwine, of course. I've grown fond of it over the years. The taste reminds me of mistfall somehow, and makes me dream. But that's probably me, not the wine. Most people don't care for it much.

Still, in a very minor way, it's a profitable item. So

Wraithworld is still a regular stop on the spacelanes. For freighters, at least.

The tourists are long gone, though. Sanders was right about that. Scenery they can get closer to home, and cheaper. The wraiths were why they came.

Sanders is long gone, too. He was too stubborn and too impractical to buy in on the mistwine operations when he had the chance. So he stayed behind his ramparts at Castle Cloud until the last. I don't know what happened to him afterwards, when the hotel finally went out of business.

The castle itself is still there. I saw it a few years ago, when I stopped for a day en route to a story on New Refuge. It's already crumbling, though. Too expensive to maintain. In a few years, you won't be able to tell it from those other, older ruins.

Otherwise the planet hasn't changed much. The mists still rise at sunset, and fall at dawn. The Red Ghost is still stark and beautiful in the early morning light. The forests are still there, and the rockcats still prowl.

Only the wraiths are missing.

Only the wraiths.

END AS A WORLD

by FLOYD L. WALLACE

F. L. Wallace is one of the shamefully neglected writers of the 1950s. He was apparently lost in the flood of talent publishing in *Galaxy Science Fiction* during that decade, but he was the equal of most of them with stories like "Accidental Flight," "Mezzerow Loves Company," "Tangle Hold," "Big Ancestor," and "Student Body," among others. He has never had a collection, an honor that he deserves and that is long overdue.

"End as a World" is a richly imaginative story concerned with an important chicken-and-egg question.

EVERY paper said so in all the languages there were, I guess. I kept reading them, but didn't know what to believe. I know what I wanted to think, but that's different from actually knowing.

There was the usual news just after Labor Day. The Dodgers were winning or losing, I forget which, and UCLA was strong and was going to beat everybody they met that fall. An H-bomb had been tested in the Pacific, blowing another island off the map, just as if we had islands to spare. Ordinarily this was important, but now it wasn't. They put stuff like this in the

back pages and hardly anybody reads it. There was
only one thing on the front pages and it was all people
talked about. All I talked about, anyway.

It began long before. I don't know how long because
they didn't print that. But it began and there it was,
right upon us that day. It was Saturday. Big things
always seem to happen on Saturdays. I ate breakfast
and got out early. I had the usual things to do, mowing the lawn, for instance. I didn't do it, nor anything
else, and nobody said anything. There wasn't any use
in mowing the lawn on a day like that.

I went out, remembering not to slam the door. It
wasn't much, but it showed thoughtfulness. I went
past the church and looked at the sign that was set
diagonally at the corner so that it could be read from
both streets. There it was in big letters, quoting from
the papers: THIS IS THE DAY THE WORLD ENDS!
Some smart reporter had thought it up and it seemed
so true that that was the only way it was ever said.
Me? I didn't know.

It was a bright day. People were out walking or just
standing and looking at the sky. It was too early to
look up. I went on. Paul Eberhard was sitting on the
lawn when I came along. He tossed me the football
and I caught it and tried to spin it on my finger. It
didn't spin. It fell and flopped out with crazy bounces
into the street. The milk truck stopped, while I got it
out of the way. I tossed the football back to Paul. He
put his hands on it and sat there.

"What'll we do?" he said.

I made a motion with my hands. "We can throw the
ball around," I said.

"Naw," he said. "Maybe you've got some comic books."

"You've seen them all," I said. "You got some?"

"I gave them to Howie," he said, thoughtfully
screwing the point of the ball into the center of a
dandelion. "He said he was going to get some new
ones, though. Let's go see." He got up and tossed the
ball toward the porch. It hit the railing and bounced

back into the bushes. That's where he usually kept it.

"Paul," called his mother as we started out.

"Yeah?"

"Don't go far. I've got some things I want you to do."

"What?" he said patiently.

"Hauling trash out of the basement. Helping me move some of the potted plants around in front."

"Sure," he said. "I'll be back."

We went past another church on the way to Howie's. The sign was the same there. THIS IS THE DAY THE WORLD ENDS! They never said more than that. They wanted it to hang in our minds, something we couldn't quite touch but we knew was there.

Paul jerked his head at the sign. "What do you think of it?"

"I don't know." I broke off a twig as we passed a tree. "What about you?"

"We got it coming." He looked at the sky.

"Yeah, but will we get it?"

He didn't answer that. "I wonder if it will be bright?"

"It is now."

"It might cloud over."

"It won't matter. It'll split the sky." That was one thing sure. Clouds or anything weren't going to stand in the way.

We went on and found Howie. Howie is a Negro, smaller than we are and twice as fast. He can throw a football farther and straighter than anyone else on the team. We pal around quite a bit, especially in the football season.

He came out of the house like he was walking on whipped cream. I didn't let that fool me. More than once I've tried to tackle him during a practice game. Howie was carrying a model of a rocket ship, CO_2-powered. It didn't work. We said Hi all around and then he suggested a game of keepaway. We'd left the football at Paul's and we couldn't, so we walked over to the park.

We sat down and began talking about it. "I'm wondering if it will really come," said Paul. We all squinted up.

"Where'll the President watch it from?" I said. "He should have a good view from the White House."

"No better than us right here," said Howie.

"What about Australia? Will they see it there?" I said.

"They'll see it all over."

"Africa, too? And what about the Eskimos?"

"It doesn't matter whether they actually see it or not. It will come to everyone at the same time."

I didn't see how it could, but I didn't feel like an argument. That's what they were saying on TV and you can't talk back to that.

"Everybody," said Howie. "Not just in this town, but all over. Wherever there are people. Even where they're not."

"You read that," said Paul.

"Sure," said Howie. "You lent me the comic books. It's even in them."

We didn't say much after that. I kept thinking of the man who made the H-bomb. I bet he felt silly and spiteful, blowing up an island. Somebody might have wanted to live on it if he'd just left it there. He must have felt mean and low when something really big like this came along.

We talked on for a while, but we'd talked it out long ago. There was really nothing new we could say. Every so often we'd look up at the sky, but it wasn't going to come until it got here.

Finally we drifted apart. There wasn't anything left to do. We walked home with Howie and then I went with Paul, leaving him to come back to my house. I looked at the lawn and without thinking about it got busy and mowed it. I surprised myself.

It was hot, or it seemed to me it was. I went in to eat. Ma came by and shut off the sound of TV. I could still see the picture in the other room. The announcer was making faces, but, of course, I didn't hear what he said. He looked pretty funny, I thought. I thought we were all probably pretty funny, moving our mouths and blinking our eyes and waving our hands. Only nothing real was coming out. Not yet, anyway.

"Sit still," said Ma. "It will happen without your help. It's going to be all right."

"Think so?" I said. She would have told me anything to keep me quiet. She gets nervous when I fidget.

"I think so," she said, giving me my allowance. It was early for that. Usually I didn't get it until after supper. "Why don't you run uptown and watch it from there?"

"Maybe I will," I said, dabbling my hands in the water at the sink. "Are you going to go?"

"Of course I'm not. Why should I get into that mob? I can watch it just as well from here."

Sure she could. But it was not the same. Everybody I knew was going to be there. I changed shirts before I left. I took a rag and wiped the dust from my shoes. I wasn't trying to be fussy or dressed up or anything. I just thought I should do it.

There was shade and sun on the streets and a few big clouds in the sky.

A car slowed up and stopped beside me. The window rolled down and Jack Goodwin leaned toward me. "Going uptown?"

"Yeah."

"Want a lift?"

"Sure." Actually I didn't. I'd rather have walked, looking around as I went.

Jack Goodwin grinned as I got in. He's got gray hair, where he has hair. The rest is bald. He looked me over. "I don't see any comets on your shoulders," he said gravely.

"I never had any," I said. Some people seem to think everyone under seventeen is a kid.

"You'll be needing them," he said.

"Maybe," I said. I ought to have walked.

I never knew how slow a day could pass. I suppose I should have slept late and kept busy doing something. This was worse than putting on a uniform and waiting until gametime. At least there was a coach on the field to tell you what to do as you ran through the drill.

Jack Goodwin stopped at a light. I had a notion to get out. But I didn't. Goodwin grinned again as the light changed and we started up. "I don't blame you for being edgy," he said. "It's the suspense. If we only had some way of knowing for sure, radio maybe."

"There's no radio," I said. "The calculations have been checked."

"Sure, but maybe there's something we forgot. Or don't know. All sorts of things can go wrong."

He must have talked on and on, but I didn't listen. Howie and me and Paul had gone over everything he was saying.

"Thanks," I said as he stopped and I got out.

"Don't mention it," he said. He nearly scraped the rear fender of the car as he drove off. It was a new car, too. He wasn't so bad. Maybe he was just worried.

I wandered to the newsstand and looked at magazines and pocketbooks. Old lady Simpson didn't ask me if I was going to buy and didn't chase me away. She was busy arguing with some customers. Even so it was the first time she didn't pay attention to me when I came in. I had a good chance to look at things I never buy. There was nothing in them I wanted to see. I was thirsty. I had a Coke and was still thirsty. I asked for a glass of water, drank half of it and went out.

Down the street there was a TV set in a store window. I watched it. They were showing a street in India, people looking up. They flashed all around, to Italy, China, Brazil. Except for their clothes, it wasn't much different from here. They were all looking up.

I did the same. For the first time I noticed there was a slight overcast. Big billowing clouds had passed, but this was worse. I hoped it would clear away in time. Not that it really mattered.

It was more crowded than usual for Saturday, but at the same time it was quiet. People were shopping, but they weren't really buying much or else they bought it faster. Nobody wanted to miss it. They all seemed to have one eye on their lists and another on the clock.

Howie and Paul came up the street and we nodded and said something. A few other boys from the school passed by and we stopped. We gathered together. It was getting closer—and the space between the minutes was growing longer and longer.

I looked at Paul's watch. He said it was on the minute. I decided there was time to go in and get a candy bar. All of a sudden I was hungry. I didn't know where it came from. I'd had to stuff down lunch not long ago. And now I was hungry.

I went to a store and had to fight my way in. People were coming out. Not just customers, but the clerks and owner, too. There was a big television screen inside, but nobody wanted to see it on that. They wanted to be outside where it would happen to them. Not just see it, have it happen. The store was empty. Not closed—empty.

I turned and rushed out to join the others. I couldn't miss it. There were still minutes to go, but suppose there *had* been a miscalculation. I knew what that would mean, but even so I had to be there. I would almost die, too.

Now we were all looking up—all over the world people were, I suppose. It was quiet. You could hear them breathing.

And then it came, a flash across the sky, a silver streak, the biggest vapor trail there ever was. It went from this side to that side in no time. It split the sky and was gone before the shock blast hit us. Nobody said anything. We stood there and shivered and straightened up after the rumbling sound passed.

But there was the vapor trail that stretched farther than anyone could see. It would go around the world at least once before it came to an end somewhere in the desert. I saw my science teacher—he was trying to smile, but couldn't. And then there was the pharmacist who had wanted to be a research chemist, but wasn't good enough.

In front of me, old Fred Butler, who drives the bus to Orange Point and King City, cracked his knuckles. "He did it," he whispered. "All the way to Mars and back. Safe and right on schedule." He jumped up in the air and kept jumping up. He hadn't been that high off the ground in several years. He never would be again unless he took an elevator. And I knew he hated elevators.

Factory whistles started blowing. They sounded louder than Gabriel. I wondered if he heard them. I grabbed hold of the nearest person and started hugging. I didn't know it was the snooty girl from the next block until she hugged back and began kissing me. We yelled louder than the factory whistles. We had a right.

It was just like the papers said: This was the day the world ended—

And the Universe began.

THE MATHENAUTS

by NORMAN KAGAN

Norman Kagan holds an M.F.A. and a Ph.D. (in mathematics) from Columbia University, is a writer-producer whose television program *The Science Report* is avidly watched in some *one hundred* countries around the globe, and is the author of *The War Film,* one of the best critical studies of that genre. He was also a most promising young science fiction writer in the mid-1960s who produced only a handful of stories, all of them memorable: "Four Brands of Impossible" (*The Magazine of Fantasy and Science Fiction,* September 1964); "Laugh Along with Franz" (*Galaxy,* December 1965); and this stunning tale (*Worlds of If,* July 1964).

Science fiction will be well served if he chooses to pass this way again.

IT happened on my fifth trip into the spaces, and the first ever made under the private-enterprise acts. It took a long time to get the P.E.A. through Congress for mathenautics, but the precedents went all the way back to the Telstar satellite a hundred years ago, and most of the concepts are in books anyone can buy, though not so readily understand. Besides, it didn't matter if BC-flight was made public or not. All mathenauts are crazy. Everybody knows that.

Take our crew. Johnny Pearl took a pin along whenever he went baby-sitting for the grad students at

Berkeley, and three months later the mothers invariably found out they were pregnant again. And Pearl was our physicist.

Then there was Goldwasser. Ed Goldwasser always sits in those pan-on-a-post cigarette holders when we're in New York, and if you ask him, he grumbles; "Well, its an ash tray, ain't it?" A punster and a pataphysicist. I would never have chosen him to go, except that he and I got the idea together.

Ted Anderson was our metamathematician. He's about half a nanosecond behind Ephraim Cohen (the co-inventor of BC-flight) and has about six nervous breakdowns a month trying to pass him. But he's got the best practical knowledge of the BC-drive outside Princeton—if practical knowledge means anything with respect to a pure mathematical abstraction.

And me—topologist. A topologist is a man who can't tell a doughnut from a cup of coffee. (I'll explain that some other time.) Seriously, I specialize in some of the more abstruse properties of geometric structures. "Did Galois discover that theorem before or after he died?" is a sample of my conversation.

Sure, mathenauts are mathenuts. But as we found out, not quite mathenutty enough.

The ship, the *Albrecht Dold,* was a twelve-googol scout that Ed Goldwasser and I'd picked up cheap from the N.Y.U. Courant Institute. She wasn't the Princeton I.A.S. *Von-Neumann,* with googolplex coils and a chapter of the D.A.R., and she wasn't one of those new toys you've been seeing for a rich man and his grandmother. Her coils were DNA molecules, and the psychosomatics were straight from the Brill Institute at Harvard. A sweet ship. For psychic ecology we'd gotten a bunch of kids from the Bronx College of the New York City University, commonsense types— business majors, engineers, pre-meds. But kids.

I was looking over Ephraim Cohen's latest paper, *Nymphomaniac Nested Complexes with Rossian Irrevelancies* (old Ice Cream Cohen loves sexy titles), when the trouble started. We'd abstracted, and Goldwasser and Pearl had signaled me from the lab that they were ready for the first tests. I made the *Dold* invariant, and shoved off through one of the passages that linked the isomorphomechanism and the lab. (We kept the ship in free fall for convenience.) I was about halfway along the tube when the immy failed and the walls began to close in.

I spread my legs and braked against the walls of the tube, believing with all my might. On second thought I let the walls sink in and braked with my palms. It would've been no trick to hold the walls for a while. Without the immy my own imagination would hold them, this far from the B.C.N.Y. kids. But that might've brought more trouble—I'd probably made some silly mistake, and the kids, who might not notice a simple contraction or shear, would crack up under some weirdomorphism. And if we lost the kids . . .

So anyway I just dug my feet in against the mirage and tried to slow up, on a surface that no one'd bothered to think any friction into. Of course, if you've read some of the popular accounts of math-sailing, you'd think I'd just duck back through a hole in the fiftieth dimension to the immy. But it doesn't work out that way. A ship in BC-flight is a very precarious structure in a philosophical sense. That's why we carry a psychic ecology, and that's why Brill conditioning takes six years, plus, with a Ph.D. in pure math, to absorb. Anyway, a mathenaut should never forget his postulates, or he'll find himself floating in 27-space, with nary a notion to be named.

Then the walls really did vanish—NO!—and I found myself at the junction of two passages. The other had a grabline. I caught it and rebounded, then swarmed back along the tube. After ten seconds I was climbing down into a funnel. I caught my breath, swallowed some Dramamine, and burst into the control room.

The heart of the ship was pulsing and throbbing. For a moment I thought I was back in Hawaii with my aqualung, an invader in a shifting, shimmering world of sea fronds and barracuda. But it was no immy, no immy—a rubber room without the notion of distance that we take for granted (technically, a room with topological properties but no metric ones). Instrument racks and chairs and books shrank and ballooned and twisted, and floor and ceiling vibrated with my breath.

It was horrible.

Ted Anderson was hanging in front of the immy, the isomorphomechanism, but he was in no shape to do anything. In fact, he was in no shape at all. His body was pulsing and shaking, so his hands were too big or too small to manipulate the controls, or his eyes shrank or blossomed. Poor Ted's nerves had gone again.

I shoved against the wall and bulleted toward him, a fish in a weaving, shifting undersea landscape, concentrating desperately on my body and the old structure of the room. (This is why physical training is so important.) For an instant I was choking and screaming in a hairy blackness, a nightmare inside-out total inversion; then I was back in the control room, and had shoved Ted away from the instruments, cursing when nothing happened, then bracing against the wall panels and shoving again. He drifted away.

The immy was all right. The twiddles circuits between the B.C.N.Y. kids and the rest of the *Dold* had been cut out. I set up an orthonormal system and punched the immy.

Across the shuddering, shifting room Ted tried to speak, but found it too difficult. Great Gauss, he was lucky his aorta hadn't contracted to a straw and given him a coronary! I clamped down on my own circulatory system viciously, while he struggled to speak. Finally he kicked off and came tumbling toward me, mouthing and flailing his notebook.

I hit the circuit. The room shifted about and for an instant Ted Anderson hung, ghostly, amid the isomorphomechanism's one-to-ones. Then he disappeared.

The invention of BC-flight was the culmination of a century of work in algebraic topology and experimental psychology. For thousands of years men had speculated as to the nature of the world. For the past five hundred, physics and the physical sciences had held sway. Then Thomas Brill and Ephraim Cohen peeled away another layer of the reality union, and the space-sciences came into being.

If you insist on an analogy—well, a scientist touches and probes the real universe, and abstracts an idealization into his head. Mathenautics allows him to grab himself by the scruff of the neck and pull himself up into the idealization. See—I *told* you.

Okay, we'll try it slowly. Science assumes the universe to be ordered, and investigates the nature of the ordering. In the "hard" sciences, mathematics is the basis of the ordering the scientist puts on nature. By the twentieth century, a large portion of the physical processes and materials in the universe were found to submit to such an ordering (e.g.: analytic mechanics and the motions of the planets). Some scientists were even applying mathematical structures to aggregates of living things, and to living processes.

Cohen and Brill asked (in ways far apart), "If order and organization seem to be a natural part of the universe, why can't we remove these qualities from coarse matter and space, and study them separately?" The answer was BC-flight.

Through certain purely mathematical "mechanisms" and special psychological training, selected scientists (the term "mathenaut" came later, slang from the faddy "astronautics") could be shifted into the abstract.

The first mathenautical ships were crewed with young scientists and mathematicians who'd received Tom Brill's treatments and Ephraim Cohen's skull-cracking sessions on the BC-field. The ships went into BC-flight and vanished.

By the theory, the ships didn't *go* anywhere. But the effect was somehow real. Just as a materialist might *see* organic machines instead of people, so the mathenauts saw the raw mathematical structure of space—Riemann space, Hausdorf space, vector space —without matter. A crowd of people existed as an immensely complicated *something* in vector space. The study of these *somethings* was yielding immense amounts of knowledge. Pataphysics, patasociology, patapsychology were wild, baffling new fields of knowledge.

But the math universes were strange, alien. How could you learn to live in Flatland? The wildcat minds of the first crews were too creative. They became disoriented. Hence the immies and their power supplies—SayCows, DaughtAmRevs, the B.C.N.Y. kids— fatheads, stuffed shirts, personality types that clung to common sense where there was none, and preserved (locally) a ship's psychic ecology. Inside the BC-field, normalcy. Outside, raw imagination.

Johnny, Ted, Goldy and I had chosen vector spaces with certain topological properties to test Goldy's commercial concept. Outside the BC-field there was dimension but no distance, structure but no shape. Inside—

"By Riemann's tensors!" Pearl cried.

He was at the iris of one of the tubes. A moment later Ed Goldwasser joined him. "What happened to Ted?"

"I—I don't know. No—yes, I do!"

I released the controls I had on my body, and stopped thinking about the room. The immy was working again. "He was doing something with the controls when the twiddles circuit failed. When I got them working again and the room snapped back into shape, he happened to be where the immy had been. The commonsense circuits rejected him."

"So where did he go?" asked Pearl.

"I don't know."

I was sweating. I was thinking of all the things that could've happened when we lost the isomorphomechanism. Some subconscious twitch and you're rotated

half a dozen dimensions out of phase, so you're floating in the raw stuff of thought, with maybe a hair-
thin line around you to tell you where the ship has
been. Or the ship takes the notion to shrink pea-size,
so you're squeezed through all the tubes and compartments and smashed to jelly when we orthonormal-
ize. Galois! We'd been lucky.

The last thought gave me a notion. "Could we have
shrunk so we're inside his body? Or he grown so we're
floating in his liver?"

"No," said Goldy. "Topology is preserved. But I
don't—or, hell—I really don't know. If he grew so big
he was outside the psychic ecology, he might just have
faded away." The big pataphysicist wrinkled up his
face inside his beard. "*Alice* should be required reading for mathenauts," he muttered. "The real trouble is
no one has ever been outside and been back to tell
about it. The animal experiments and the *Norbert
Wiener* and Wilbur on the *Paul R. Halmos*. They just
disappeared."

"You know," I said, "You can map the volume of a
sphere into the whole universe using the ratio $IR:R$
equals $R:OR$, where IR and OR are the inside and
outside distances for the points. Maybe that's what
happened to Ted. Maybe he's just outside the ship,
filling all space with his metamath and his acne?"

"Down boy," said Goldwasser. "I've got a simpler
suggestion. Let's check over the ship, compartment by
compartment. Maybe he's in it somewhere, unconscious."

But he wasn't on the ship.

We went over it twice, every tube, every compartment. (In reality, a mathenautic ship looks like a
radio, ripped out of its case and flying through the
air.) We ended up in the ecology section, a big
Broadway-line subway car that roared and rattled in
the middle of darkness in the middle of nothing. The
B.C.N.Y. kids were all there—Freddi Urbont clucking
happily away to her boyfriend, chubby and smily and

an education major; Byron and Burbitt, electronics engineers, ecstatic over the latest copy of *C-Quantum;* Stephen Seidmann, a number-theory major, quietly proving that since Harvard is the best school in the world, and B.C.N.Y. is better than Harvard, that B.C.N.Y. is the best school in the world; two citizens with nose jobs and names I'd forgotten, engaged in a filthy discussion of glands and organs and meat. The walls were firm, the straw seats scratchy and uncomfortable. The projectors showed we were just entering the 72nd Street stop. How real, how comforting! I slid the door open to rejoin Johnny and Ed. The subway riders saw me slip into free fall, and glimpsed the emptiness of vector space.

Hell broke loose!

The far side of the car bulged inward, the glass smashing and the metal groaning. The CUNYs had no compensation training!

Freddi Urbont burst into tears. Byron and Burbitt yelled as a bubble in the floor swallowed them. The wall next to the nose jobs sprouted a dozen phallic symbols, while the seat bubbled with breasts. The walls began to melt. Seidmann began to yell about the special status of N. Y. City University Honors Program students.

Pearl acted with a speed and a surety I'd never have imagined. He shoved me out of the way and launched himself furiously at the other end of the car, now in free fall. There he pivoted, smiled horribly and at the top of his lungs began singing "The Purple and the Black."

Goldy and I had enough presence of mind to join him. Concentrating desperately on the shape and form of the car, we blasted the air with our devotion to Sheppard Hall, our love of Convent Avenue and our eternal devotion to Lewisohn Stadium. Somehow it saved us. The room rumbled and twisted and reformed, and soon the eight of us were back in the tired old subway car that brough its daily catch of Beavers to 139th Street.

The equilibrium was still precarious. I heard Goldwasser telling the nose jobs his terrible monologue about the "Volvo I want to buy. I can be the first to break the door membranes, and when I get my hands on that big, fat steering wheel, ohh!, it'll be a week before I climb out of it!"

Pearl was cooing to Urbont how wonderful she was as the valedictorian at her junior high, how great the teaching profession was, and how useful, and how interesting.

As for me: "Well, I guess you're right, Steve. I should have gone to B.C.N.Y. instead of Berkeley."

"That's right, Jimmy. After all, B.C.N.Y. has some of the best number-theory people in the world. And some of the greatest educators, too. Like Dean Cashew who started the Privileged Student Program. It sure is wonderful."

"I guess you're right, Steve."

"I'm right, all right. At schools like Berkeley, you're just another student, but at B.C.N.Y. you can be a P.S., and get all the good professors and small classes and high grades."

"You're right, Steve."

"I'm right, all right. Listen, we have people that've quit Cornell and Harvard and M.I.T. Of course, they don't do much but run home after school and sit in their houses, but their parents all say how much happier they are—like back in high school . . ."

When the scrap paper and the gum wrappers were up to our knees and there were four false panhandlers in the car, Johnny called a halt. The little psychist smiled and nodded as he walked the three of us carefully out the door.

"Standard technique," he murmured to no one in particular. "Doing *something* immediately rather than the best thing a while later. Their morale was shot, so I—" He trailed off.

"Are they really that sensitive?" Goldwasser asked. "I thought their training was better than that."

"You act like they were components in an electronics rig," said Pearl jerkily. "You know that Premedial Sensory Perception, the ability to perceive the dull routine that normal people ignore, is a very delicate talent!"

Pearl was well launched. "In the dark ages such people were called dullards and subnormals. Only now, in our enlightened age, do we realize their true ability to know things outside the ordinary senses—a talent vital for BC-flight."

The tedium and meaninglessness of life which we rationalize away—

"A ship is more mind than matter, and if you upset that mind—"

He paled suddenly. "I, I think I'd better stay with them," he said. He flung open the door and went back into the coach. Goldwasser and I looked at each other. Pearl was a trained mathenaut, but his specialty was people, not paramath.

"Let's check the lab," I muttered.

Neither of us spoke as we moved toward the lab—slap a wall, pull yourself forward, twist round some instrumentation—the "reaction swim" of a man in free fall. The walls began to quiver again, and I could see Goldy clamp down on his body and memories of this part of the ship. We were nearing the limits of the BC-field. The lab itself, and the experimental apparatus, stuck out into vector space.

"Let's make our tests and go home," I told Goldy.

Neither of us mentioned Ted as we entered the lab.

Remember this was a commercial project. We weren't patasociologists studying abstract groups, or superpurists looking for the first point. We wanted money.

Goldy thought he had a moneymaking scheme for us, but Goldy hasn't been normal since he took Polykarp Kusch's "Kusch of Death" at Columbia, "Electrodimensions and Magnespace." He was going to build four-dimensional molecules.

Go back to Flatland. Imagine a hollow paper pyramid on the surface of that two-dimensional world. To a Flatlander, it is a triangle. Flop down the sides—four triangles. Now put a molecule in each face—one molecule, four molecules. And recall that you have infinite dimensions available. Think of the storage possibilities alone. All the books of the world in a viewer, all the food in the world in your pack. A television the size of a piece of paper; circuits looped through dim-19. Loop an entire industrial plant through hyperspace, and get one the size and shape of a billboard. Shove raw materials in one side—pull finished products out the other!

But how do you make 4-dim molecules? Goldy thought he had a way, and Ted Anderson had checked over the math and pronounced it workable. The notion rested in the middle of the lab: a queer, half-understood machine of mind and matter called a Grahm-Schmidt generator.

"Jeez, Ed! This lab looks like your old room back in Diego Borough."

"Yeah," said Goldwasser. "Johnny said it would be a good idea. Orientation against *that*."

That was the outside of the lab, raw topological space, without energy or matter or time. It was the shape and color of what you see in the back of your head.

I looked away.

Goldwasser's room was a duplicate of his old home —the metal desk, the electronics rigs, the immense bookshelves, half filled with physics and half with religious works. I picked up a copy of Stace's *Time and Eternity* and thumbed through it, then put it down, embarrassed.

"Good reading for a place like this." Goldwasser smiled.

He sat down at the desk and began to check out his

"instruments" from the locked drawer where he'd kept them. Once he reached across the desk and turned on a tape of Gene Gerard's *Excelsior!* The flat midwestern voice murmured in the background.

"First, I need some hands," said Ed.

Out in the nothingness two pairs of lines met at right angles. For an instant, all space was filled with them, jammed together every which way. Then it just settled down to two.

The lab was in darkness. Goldwasser's big form crouched over the controls. He wore his engineer's boots and his hair long, and a beard as well. He might have been some medieval monk, or primitive witchdoctor. He touched a knob and set a widget, and checked in his copy of *Birkhoff and MacLane.*

"Now," he said, and played with his instruments. Two new vectors rose out of the intersections. "Crossproducts. Now I've a right- and a left-handed system."

All the while Gene Gerard was mumbling in the background: 'Ah, now, my pretty,' snarled the Count. 'Come to my bedchamber, or I'll leave you to Igor's mercies.' The misshapen dwarf cackled and rubbed his paws. 'Decide, decide!' cried the Count. His voice was a scream. 'Decide, my dear. SEX—ELSE, IGOR!'

"Augh," said Goldwasser, and shut it off. "Now," he said, "I've got some plasma in the next compartment."

"Holy Halmos," I whispered.

Ted Anderson stood beside the generator. He smiled, and went into topological convulsions. I looked away, and presently he came back into shape. "Hard getting used to real space again," he whispered. He looked thinner and paler than ever.

"I haven't got long," he said, "so here it is. You know I was working on Ephraim's theories, looking for a flaw. There isn't any flaw."

"Ted, you're rotating," I cautioned.

He steadied, and continued, "There's no flaw. But the theory is wrong. It's backwards. *This is the real universe,*" he said, and gestured. Beyond the lab topological space remained as always, a blank, the color of the back of your head through your own eyes.

"Now listen to me, Goldy and Johnny and Kidder." I saw that Pearl was standing in the iris of the tube. "What is the nature of intelligence? I guess it's the power to abstract, to conceptualize. I don't know what to say beyond that—I don't know what it is. But I know where it came from! Here! In the math spaces—they're alive with thought, flashing with mind!

"When the twiddles circuits failed, I cracked. I fell apart, lost faith in it all. For I had just found what I thought was a basic error in theory. I died, I vanished . . .

"But I didn't. I'm a metamathematician. An operational philosopher, you might say. I may have gone mad—but I think I passed a threshold of knowledge. I understand . . .

"They're out there. The things we thought we'd invented ourselves. The concepts and the notions and the pure structures—if you could see them . . ."

He looked around the room, desperately. Pearl was rigid against the iris of the tube. Goldy looked at Ted for a moment, then his head darted from side to side. His hands whitened on the controls.

"Jimmy," Ted said.

I didn't know. I moved toward him, across the lab to the edge of topological space, and beyond the psychic ecology. No time, no space, no matter. But how can I say it? How many people can stay awake over a book of modern algebra, and how many of those can understand?

—I saw a set bubbling and whirling, then take purpose and structure to itself and become a group, generate a second-unity element, mount itself and become a group, generate a second unity element, mount itself and become a field, ringed by rings. Near it, a mature field, shot through with ideals, threw off a splitting field in a passion of growth, and became complex.

—I saw the life of the matrices; the young ones sporting, adding and multiplying by a constant, the mature ones mating by composition: male and female make male, female and male make female—sex through anticommunitivity! I saw them grow old, meeting false identities and loosing rows and columns into nullity.

—I saw a race of vectors, losing their universe to a newer race of tensors that conquered and humbled them.

—I watched the tyranny of the Well Ordering Principle, as a free set was lashed and whipped into structure. I saw a partially ordered set, free and happy broken before the Axiom of Zemelo.

—I saw the point sets, with their cliques and clubs, infinite numbers of sycophants clustering round a Bolzano-Weirstrauss aristocrat—the great compact medieval coverings of infinity with denumerable shires—the conflicts as closed sets created open ones, and the other way round.

—I saw the rigid castes of a society of transformations, orthogonal royalty, inner product gentry, degenerates—where intercomposition set the caste of the lower on the product.

—I saw the proud old cyclic groups, father and son and grandson, generating the generations, rebel and blacksheep and hero, following each other endlessly. Close by were the permutation groups, frolicking in a way that seemed like the way you sometimes repeat a sentence endlessly, stressing a different word each time.

There was much I saw that I did not understand, for mathematics is a deep, and even a mathenaut must choose his wedge of specialty. But that world of abstractions flamed with a beauty and meaning that chilled the works and worlds of men, so I wept in futility.

Presently we found ourselves back in the lab. I sat beside Ted Anderson and leaned on him, and I did not speak for fear my voice would break.

Anderson talked to Johnny and Ed.

"There was a—a race, here, that grew prideful. It knew the Riemann space, and the vector space, the algebras and the topologies, and yet it was unfulfilled. In some way—oddly like this craft," he murmured, gesturing—"they wove the worlds together, creating the real universe you knew in your youth.

"Yet still it was unsatisfied. Somehow the race yearned so for newness that it surpassed itself, conceiving matter and energy and entropy and creating them.

"And there were laws and properties for these: inertia, speed, potential, quantumization. Perhaps life was an accident. It was not noticed for a long time, and proceeded apace. For the proud race had come to know itself, and saw that the new concepts were . . . flawed." Anderson smiled faintly, and turned to Ed.

"Goldy, remember when we had Berkowitz for algebra?" he asked. "Remember what he said the first day?"

Goldwasser smiled. "Any math majors?"

"Hmm, that's good."

"Any physics majors?

"Physics majors! You guys are just super engineers!

"Any chemistry majors?

"Chemistry major! You'd be better off as a cook!"

Ted finished, "And so on, down to the, ahem, baloney majors."

"He was number-happy," said Ed, smiling.

"No. He was right, in a way." Ted continued. "The race had found its new notions were crudities, simple copies of algebras and geometries past. What it thought was vigor was really sloth and decay.

"It knew how to add and multiply, but it had forgotten what a field was, and what communitivity was. If entropy and time wreaked harm on matter, they did worse by this race. It wasn't interested in expeditions through the fiber bundles; rather it wanted to count apples.

"There was conflict and argument, but it was too late to turn back. The race had already degenerated too far to turn back. Then life was discovered.

"The majority of the race took matter for a bride. It's esthetic and creative powers ruined, it wallowed in passion and pain. Only remnants of reason remained.

"For the rest, return to abstraction was impossible. Time, entropy, had robbed them of their knowledge, their heritage. Yet they still hoped and expended themselves to leave, well, call it a 'seed' of sorts."

"Mathematics?" cried Pearl.

"It explains some things," mused Goldwasser softly. "Why abstract mathematics, developed in the mind, turns out fifty years or a century later to accurately describe the physical universe. Tensor calculus and relativity, for example. If you look at it this way, the math was there first."

"Yes, yes, yes. Mathematicians talked about their subject as an art form. One system is more 'elegant' than another if its logical structure is more austere. But Occam's Razor, the law of simplest hypothesis, isn't logical.

"Many of the great mathematicians did their greatest work as children and youths before they were dissipated by the sensual world. In a trivial sense, scientists and mathematicians most of all are described as 'unworldly' . . ."

Anderson bobbled his head in the old familiar way. "You have almost returned," he said quietly. "This ship is really a heuristic device, an aid to perception. You are on the threshold. You have come all the way back."

The metamathematician took his notebook, and seemed to set all his will upon it. "See Ephraim gets this," he murmured. "He, you, I . . . the oneness—"

Abruptly he disappeared. The notebook fell to the floor.

I took it up. Neither Ed nor Johnny Pearl met my eyes. We may have sat and stood there for several hours, numbed, silent. Presently the two began setting up the isomorphomechanism for realization. I joined them.

The National Mathenautics and Hyperspace Administration had jurisdiction over civilian flights then, even as it does today. Ted was pretty important, it seemed. Our preliminary debriefing won us a maximum-security session with their research chief.

Perhaps, as I'd thought passionately for an instant, I'd have done better to smash the immy, rupture the psychic ecology, let the eggshell be shattered at last. But that's not the way of it. For all of our progress, some rules of scientific investigation don't change. Our first duty was to report back. Better heads than ours would decide what to do next.

They did. Ephraim Cohen didn't say anything after he heard us out and looked at Ted's notebook. Old Ice Cream sat there, a big teddy-bear-shaped genius with thick black hair and a dumb smile, and grinned at us. It was in Institute code.

The B.C.N.Y kids hadn't seen anything, of course. So nobody talked.

Johnny Pearl married a girl named Judy Shatz and they had fifteen kids. I guess that showed Johnny's views on the matter of matter.

Ed Goldwasser got religion. Zen-Judaism is pretty orthodox these days, yet somehow he found it suited him. But he didn't forget what happened back out in space. His book, *The Cosmic Mind,* came out last month, and it's a good summation of Ted's ideas, with a minimum of spiritual overtones.

Myself. Well, a mathematician, especially a topologist, is useless after thirty, the way progress is going along these days. But *Dim-Dustries* is a commercial enterprise, and I guess I'm good for twenty years more as a businessman.

Goldwasser's Grahm-Schmidt generator worked, but that was just the beginning. Dimensional extension's made Earth a paradise, with housing hidden in the probabilities and automated industries tucked away in the dimensions.

The biggest boon was something no one anticipated. A space of infinite dimensions solves all the basic problems of modern computer-circuit design. Now all components can be linked with short electron paths, no matter how big and complex the device.

There have been any number of other benefits. The space hospitals, for example, where topological surgery can cure the most terrible wounds—and topological psychiatry the most baffling syndromes. (Four years of math is required for pre-meds these days.) Patapsychology and patasociology finally made some progress, so that political and economic woes have declined—thanks, too, to the spaces, which have drained off a good deal of poor Earth's overpopulation. There are even spaces resorts, or so I'm told—I don't get away much.

I've struck it lucky. Fantastically so.

The Private Enterprise Acts had just been passed, you'll recall, and I had decided I didn't want to go spacing again. With the training required for the subject, I guess I was the only qualified man who had a peddler's pack, too. Jaffee, one of my friends down at Securities and Exchange, went so far as to say that *Dim-Dustries* was a hyperspherical trust (math is required for pre-laws too). But I placated him and I got some of my mathemateers to realign the Street on a moebius strip, so he had to side with me.

Me, I'll stick to the Earth. The "real" planet is a garden spot now, and the girls are very lovely.

Ted Anderson was recorded lost in topological space. He wasn't the first, and he was far from the last. Twiddles circuits have burned out, Naught-Ams-Revs have gone mad, and no doubt there have been some believers who have sought out the Great Race.

HOW CAN WE SINK WHEN
WE CAN FLY?

by ALEXEI PANSHIN

A noted critic (*Heinlein in Dimension*, 1968; *SF In Dimension*, 1976) as well as an author, Alexei Panshin won the Nebula Award of the Science Fiction Writers of America in 1968 for *Rite of Passage*. A graduate of sf fandom, he was at one time one of its best-known figures and was awarded a Hugo in 1967 for fan writing. Other notable sf works include *The Thurb Revolution* (1968) and the excellent story collection *Farewell to Yesterday's Tomorrow*. His work has appeared much too infrequently in recent years.

This beautiful novelette was one of the best stories of 1971.

In the final analysis civilization can be saved only if we are willing to change our ways of life. We have to invent utopias not necessarily to make them reality but to help us formulate worthwhile human goals.

—René Dubos

ENDINGS of stories come easy. It is the beginnings, when anything is still possible, that come hard.

To think yourself into somewhere strange and someone new, and then to live it, takes the nerve of a revolutionary or a bride. If writers had that kind of nerve, they wouldn't be writers. They would be starting revolutions and getting married, like everyone else. As it is, we tend to cultivate our gardens and mull a lot.

When the beginnings come harder than usual and

when the only news that penetrates the Pennsylvania outback is of lost causes and rumors of lost causes, I give a call to Rob to grab whoever he can find between Springfield, Massachusetts, and here, and come on down for the weekend. The people around here are good people, but all they know is what they hear on the evening news. And they can't talk shop. Rob talks good shop, and he has a completely unique set of rumors. His news is no better, but it isn't the common line.

It does him good to come, too. Springfield is no place to live. In a sense I feel responsible for Rob. Springfield was founded by William Pynchon, who was an ancestor of mine. He wrote a book in Greek called *The Meritorious Price of Our Redemption,* which was burned on Boston Common in 1650 as religiously unsound, and he went back to England. He stayed long enough to found Springfield and a branch of my mother's family, and make me responsible for Rob.

If I ever meet Thomas Pynchon, who wrote *V.,* I intend to ask him how he feels about Springfield, Mass. In the meantime Rob has some leeway with me, which he takes advantage of on occasion.

I was expecting Rob and Leigh, but when we picked them up on Friday morning at the lunch-counter bus stop across the river in New Jersey, they had a kid with them. Leigh is in her thirties, good silent strong plain people. She writes Westerns. Rob had collected her in New York. Where he'd gotten the kid I didn't know.

"This is Juanito," Rob said.

The kid was blond as Maytime, dressed in worn blue jeans and a serape. He was wishing for a beard. I didn't know him, but he looked like a member of the tribe.

"I'm Alex and this is Cory," I said, and he nodded. Then the five of us headed for our 1951 Plymouth, our slow beast.

"I'm just as glad to get out of here," Rob said, looking

back as we headed onto the bridge to Pennsylvania. "It reminds me of Springfield."

It is a depressing battered little town. A good place to leave behind.

Cory said, "And you know, there are people who commute to work in New York from here every day. Two hours each way."

"It's a long way to come for flaking paint and tumbledown houses," Rob said, "But I suppose if that's the way you like to live . . ."

He turned to look at the brighter prospect of the Pennsylvania hills. "Well," he said, "let's get going. Bring on your sheep and geese and cats."

I said, "There are a couple of ducks now, and Gemma had three kittens."

The only part of the livestock that belongs to us is two of the cats. There are two stray tomcats on the place and some independent bullfrogs. The sheep and their lambs are the farmer's. The rest belongs to our landlady up in the big house.

Leigh said, "How old are the kittens?"

Cory turned and said over the seat back, "They haven't even got their eyes open."

Across the Delaware in Pennsylvania we passed a broad field full of dead auto bodies rusting into the land, crossed the shortest covered bridge in the county, and headed up into the hills.

"Well," said Rob. "How badly are you stuck?"

"Stuck," I said. "I'm doing a story based on an idea by Isaac Asimov for an anthology of new stories."

"You're a hack," said Rob. "You work for money."

"Right," I said. "I work to live, and live to work. No, my problem is that I want to respect Asimov's idea without following it to the letter. I guess the problem is that I can't see any way to get from our now to his future. When I listen to the news, I wonder about any future at all. So I sit in front of the typewriter, but I don't write. I'll find the story, I'll see the way, but right now I'm still trying to find my beginning."

"Don't brood about it," said Leigh. "Sit down and write it the simplest way." Kind advice, because in spite of what Leigh may sometimes say about her own work, that's not the way she writes.

"Seen any movies lately?" Rob asked. Not an idle question.

"None," I said. The movies they've been bringing around here haven't been the ones I'm planning to catch. Not Anthony Quinn and Ingrid Bergman in a love story for the ages. Besides, I couldn't take the chance of getting that far from the typewriter. Not with the birth of a story imminent.

"Hey, you had a sale?" Automatic question.

"My first this year, and just in time, too. We need the money. They're supposed to pay at the end of the month, and today is already the tenth."

"What about letters?" Rob asked. "Have you really been answering your mail?"

"Letters? I'm busy. All my times goes to writing— that is, not writing."

"Travel? Have you been anyplace recently?"

The size of a mental block can be fairly estimated by the writer's list of austerities. It is less a matter of income than an inability to put anything ahead of writing—that is, not writing. If a writer does nothing whatsoever but sit very very still and pretend to think, you know he is up the creek without a paddle.

Cory answered that one. "Not since Christmas," she said.

"Fine," said Rob, like any doctor in possession of a juicy symptom. "Are you able to read?"

"I never stop reading," I said. "I've never been that petrified."

"Name a good novel you read recently."

"Does it have to be good?"

"Name a novel," Rob said. "It doesn't have to be good."

"All right," I said. "I'm not reading fiction. *Creative Mythology,* the fourth volume of *The Masks of God.*"

"Is that as heavy as it sounds?"

Cory said, "I lost momentum half through it."

"That one is for inspiration," I said. "Then *Personal Knowledge,* by Polanyi. That's food for thought. And *Heroes and Heretics: A Social History of Dissent.* That's for the times. I pick one or the other up in the morning, read a paragraph or a page, and then I think about the Asimov story."

"Oh, you lucky writers," Leigh said. "Your time is your own."

Rob finally let me off the hook. "Let me see what Asimov wrote when we get to your place. Maybe we can talk it out."

A deer suddenly flashed onto the road ahead of us, showed tail, and bounded off through the wooded hillside. Only Cory and I in the front and Juanito in the back got a good look. Leigh caught just a glimpse, and Rob missed it entirely. I try to bring people by the scenic route, but they have to be prepared to look at things fast. Rob never bothers.

"Nice," said Leigh.

"We sat at sunset over on Geigel Hill Road the other week and watched a whole herd—twelve or more, and even more down in the draw—cross the road and stream up the long open hillside," I said. "And when our landlady's daughter was here for Easter from England, she said there was a herd in the woods on the State Park land just behind the farm."

"Just behind the farm?" Leigh said. "How far would it be?"

Cory said, "Not far. A ten-minute walk. We could go up this afternoon and look."

Rob said, "Not me. I've been up for thirty hours. I need sack time."

"I'll go," said Juanito.

This Pennsylvania countryside offers you just about anything you want. We've been here the better part of a year and still discover surprises within five miles, and even within one, or within three hundred yards:

wild onion, wild strawberries, poison ivy. In the space
of a mile on a single road you can find high-speed
intersection, three-hundred-year-old farmstead, random
suburbia, crossroad community, and woodlands in any
order and combination you like, strung across little
valleys, hidden in hollows, up and over hills. There
are even pockets of industry.

"What is that?" Juanito asked.

It's part of the scenery, but you have to be particularly quick to see it. If you could see more of it,
perhaps it would have been closed down sooner.

I stopped our old Plymouth tank and backed up the
hill to the curve. In early April, with the trees still
bare or only barely budding, you can see it from one
vantage on the road. Tinny prefab buildings and the
half a dozen chemical lagoons perched overlooking the
creek, with blue and yellow gullies staining the hillside.

"Every time it rains there's overflow," I said. "That's
the Revere Chemicals dump. It was put in in 1965,
and the State Health people said at the time that it
was going to do this, and it took them five years to
close it down. Now it just sits there and leaks. The
manager is trying to start a new operation in the next
township."

"I hope the deer doesn't drink from that stream,"
Leigh said.

"He has to take his chances the same as the rest of
us," Rob said. Growing up in Springfield has left Rob
with more than a little sourness.

When we got to the farm, I stopped the car at the
head of the long gravel drive. "Somebody hop out and
check the mailbox," I said.

Rob made no move. I said, "Rob, it's your side."

"I've been up for thirty hours," he said.

Juanito said, "I'll look."

He dropped the door on the big white mailbox with
the blue-and-red hex sign matching the white hexes

on the barn. I could see that it was empty—and the mail truck not in sight yet.

Juanito hesitated in order to let a semi pass, the wind by-blow whipping his hair and his serape, and then he came back to the car. He had a nonreturnable beer bottle in his hand, one of the little squat ones. It had been on the roadside long enough for the label to wash free, but then it has been a wet spring.

"What about this?" he said.

I was irritated. I had expected the mail to be there when we got back from the run to Frenchtown.

"Oh, throw it back!" I said. "Unless you mean to pick up all the trash along the frontage. Start with the chrome and the broken headlights up at the second phone pole."

The kid looked slightly bewildered at my vehemence. I was immediately sorry.

I switched the engine off, set the brake, and hopped out. "I'll tell you what," I said. "We'll strike a blow."

I walked to the back of the car and opened up the humpback trunk. Then I said, "Throw your bottle in there," and the kid did.

I stepped down into the front field and picked up the black and raddled truck-tire carcass I'd been meaning to police up ever since it was abandoned there. I lugged it up the grade and slung it into the trunk.

"There," I said.

The geese set up their automatic clank and clatter when we drove into the yard. Pheobe is the goose, Alexander the gander. Alexander is the main squawk of the barnyard, Phoebe just the harmony, but when they trudge around the farm, it is Phoebe who leads and Alexander who walks behind attempting to look impressive.

Fang skirted the geese and came skittering past us, tail briefly raised in acknowledgement, a miniature panther in penguin clothes. We followed her into the house for lunch.

The house was once a carriage house. The original

beams, marked with the holes and gouges of the gear used to raise and lower carriages, cross the twelve-foot ceiling of the living room, and a glass chandelier hangs from the lowest beam. The kitchen behind and the bedrooms upstairs in the original building and the library and study in the addition are cut to less heroic proportion. It's a tidy small house with an overwhelming living room. It has all the charms of Frank Lloyd Wright without the dim constricted little hallways Wright insisted on designing.

During lunch Cory took me aside and said, "We're going to need more bacon and a dozen eggs."

"I'll go to the Elephant this afternoon," I said.

"Get a couple of half gallons of milk, too." Then she said, "Who is this boy, Alexei? He keeps looking around, but he doesn't say much."

I said, "He seems within the normal range of Rob's friends."

"Well, Rob's strange."

"True. I don't suppose I'd want to put this Juanito to a vote of the neighbors.

Then Cory said, "Alexei, what are we going to do about the taxes if the money doesn't come?"

I said, "We know it's coming. If worse comes to worst, I'll mail our check and we can deposit Henry's check as soon as it comes. Don't brood."

I don't worry about the money except when I absolutely have to. I juggle without thinking, and the money usually comes from somewhere when it has to be found. If I worried about money, I'd be too busy to stare at my typewriter.

After lunch, Rob said, "All right. Let me have a look at that Asimov idea before I collapse."

Cory and Leigh and Juanito went walking back toward the State Park land to look for the deer herd. Two lambs clowning in the plowed lands went ducking urgently under the wire fencing looking for mama at the passage of the people.

Rob and I went back inside the house and into the

study. It's a small room. The people before us used it for a nursery. Now it holds our desks, two small armchairs, three small bookcases of reference books, including our prize, the eleventh-edition *Britannica* we bought for $50 in Doylestown, and a catbox in the closet to keep us humble.

I scooped Wolf, our lesser cat, out of my easy chair. She's a tortoiseshell, pine needles and shadow, with an orange nose and a wide black greasepaint mustache. She keeps me company when I write. At five months, she is still small enough to curl up to sleep in my typing-paper box like a mouse tucked up for winter inside a Swiss cheese. I sat down with her on my lap.

Rob said, "How's that collaboration with Cory coming?"

Cory and I have a contract for a fantasy novel in four books.

I said, "Cory has just been reading the novel I did at eighteen to give herself encouragement. She found it very encouraging."

"It's pretty bad?"

"I don't remember it too well, fortunately. Cory says it's about an incredibly narrow and suspicious young man whose only distinguishing feature is that he wants a way to leave."

"That's all?"

"That's all. I made the story up as I went along. I remember that much."

That wasn't all, but that's the way I talk to Rob. I remember there was a galactic empire in the story that did nasty things, and my hero wanted a way to leave it. If I were writing the story now, I suppose he'd try to change it.

"Hmm," said Rob. He wrote a novel at eighteen, too, making it up as he went along. The difference is that his was published and mine wasn't, so he has more to regret. "Let me see what Asimov has to say."

I searched through the clutter on the right-hand corner of my desk. While I was searching, Rob looked through the books on the opposite corner. He came up with *Personal Knowledge* by Michael Polanyi and began to thumb it.

"You weren't kidding about this, were you?" he said. "What do you get out of all this?" It's a crabbed book in small type with heavy footnotes.

"I don't generally recommend it," I said. "It's epistemology. The nature and limits of knowledge."

"What have you gotten out of it?"

"The power of mind to shape the world. The need for responsible belief," I said. "Not that the idea is new. One of my ancestors . . ."

"I know. One of your ancestors founded Springfield." Rob isn't too sure whether I'm lying in whole or in part about William Pynchon. We do work at misleading each other. I like to tell the truth so that it comes out sounding like a lie for the pure artistic beauty of doing it, and I don't know how much to make of the stories Rob tells me.

"I was about to say, one of my ancestors was the brother of Hosea Ballou, who found the Universalists. 'The Father of American Universalism.' "

"What's that?"

"They amalgamated with the Unitarians. They're all Unitarian Universalists now. And another ancestor was a cousin of Sam Adams. The point is, they were men of conscience."

"For whatever that means."

"For whatever that means." I handed him the Asimov proposal. "Here, read. This is the relevant part."

Rob read it several times. It said:

The Child as Young God. In this one we picture the society as possessing few children. If the average life expectancy has reached five hundred years, let us suppose, then the percentage of children should be, say, one-twentieth what it is now. In such a society biologic parenthood gives a person immense social prestige but no special rights in the child one has created. All children are children of society in general, with everyone anxious to share in the rights of mothering and fathering. The child is the Golden Boy/Girl of the neighborhood, and there is considerable distress if one of these children approaches adulthood without another child being born to take its place. This story can be poignant and young, for I see it told from the viewpoint of a child who is approaching adulthood and who doesn't want to lose the Goldenness of his position and is perhaps jealous of another child on the way: sibling rivalry on a grand scale.

I stroked Wolf while Rob read. Wolf was purring but not lying quietly. She batted at my hand. I picked up a pipe cleaner and wrapped it into a coil around my little finger and dropped it on the floor. Wolf pushed off my lap, seized the little woolly spring in her jaws, growled fiercely, and ran out of the study. When she isn't batting them under the bookcases in the library and then fishing them out again, she loves to run from room to room with a pipe cleaner in her mouth, growling all the while. She's very fierce.

Rob finished reading, looked up, and said, "It's like something you've done, isn't it?"

"What's that?"

"Rite of Passage."

Rite of Passage was my first novel. It's about a girl, a bright superchild on the verge of adulthood in a low-population future society. Otherwise it's not much the same.

"Hmm. I guess I see what you mean, but I don't think the similarity has to be close enough to be any problem. The thought of repeating myself is not what's hanging me up. What do you think of the proposal?"

"Well," said Rob, "when did you say the story is supposed to take place?"

I flipped to the front page of the proposal to check. "The next century. The only date mentioned is 2025. After 2025, I guess."

"Fifty years from now? Where do all the five-hundred-year-olds come from?"

I waved that aside. "I'm willing to make it one

hundred or one hundred and fifty plus great expectations."

"These people would have to be alive now," Rob said.

"True," I said. "It's something to think about."

It was a good point, just the sort of thing I wanted Rob to come up with. It raised possibilities.

"Are there any restrictions on what you write?"

"Fifteen thousand words and no nasty language."

"What about nasty ideas?"

"Nothing said about that, but I don't suppose they are worried. Everybody knows I never had a nasty idea in my life."

"Oh, yes. Um-hmm," said Rob. "Look, I know this is a radical suggestion, but what's wrong with writing the idea as it stands? There is a story there."

"I know," I said. "I thought of writing it for a long time, but then when I tried I just couldn't do it. That's where I got hung up. I like the opening phrase. I like it—'the child as young god.' That's provocative. It speaks to me. But what a distance to come for nothing. Sibling rivalry? Sibling rivalry? Why write it as science fiction? Why write it at all?"

"What's the matter, Alex?" Rob said. "Are you yearning for relevance again?"

It's a point of philosophical contention between us. Rob believes that all a story has to do is be entertaining.

I said, "Just read this." And I picked the *Whole Earth Catalog* off Cory's desk. I showed him their statement of purpose:

We *are* as gods and might as well get good at it. So far, remotely done power and glory—as via government, big business, formal education, church—has succeeded to the point where gross defects obscure actual gains. In response to this dilemma and to these gains a realm of intimate personal power is developing—power of the individual to conduct his own education, find his own inspiration, shape his own environment, and share his adventure with whoever is interested. Tools that aid this process are sought and promoted by the *Whole Earth Catalog*.

"I'd like to speak to that," I said. "I don't have any final solutions. In fifteen thousand words I'm not going to lay out a viable and functioning and uncriticizable utopia, but for God's sake, Rob, shouldn't I at least try to say something relevant? As it is, I don't think the chances are overwhelming that any of us are going to be alive in twenty years, let alone five hundred."

"I know. You've said that before."

"Not in print. If the society has solved the problems Asimov says—and we're going to have to—that's what I ought to write about, isn't it? At the price of being relevant and not just entertaining. There is a story in the Asimov proposal that I want to write. Somewhere. And it isn't about a kid who doesn't want to grow up. I just have to find it."

Rob said, "How do you propose to do it?"

"Sit and stare at the typewriter until it comes to me, I guess. Or putter in the garden."

"Do you really have a garden?"

"Of course," I said. "Tom Disch tells me that a half hour in the garden every days keeps the soul pure." Tom's another writer. We tend to pass basic tips like this around our little circles. "I'm going to try it and see what good it does me."

"You do that," said Rob. "And good luck. But I've got to hit the sack now. I'm about to drop off."

I turned off my desk lamp. As I got up, I said, "By the way, just who is this kid, Juanito?"

Rob said, "He's no kid. He's your age."

I wouldn't have thought it. I'm pushing thirty. I said, "Who is he?"

"Who is he?" Rob grinned. He grins like that when he is about to say something that's more entertaining than relevant. "He's Juanito the Watcher. He's your test of relevance. He's watching and assessing. If you're okay, that's cool. But if you aren't right, he'll split without a word. Take your chances."

"Thanks a lot, friend," I said.

Rob went upstairs to flake out, and I walked down to the road to see if the mail had come. It had. My check hadn't. Junk mail.

I sorted the mail as I walked up the long gravel drive to the farm, and I stopped off at the main house to leave Mrs. S. her share of the bills and fliers. I collected ducklings and a spade and set to work on the garden.

I was unhappy about the check not coming, so I lit into the work with a vengeance, turning sod and earth. The ducklings, twice their Easter-morning size but still clothed in yellow down, went *reep-a-cheep* and *peep-a-deep* around my heels and gobbled happily when I turned up worms for their benefit. They knew there was someone looking out for their welfare. I was wishing I knew as much.

Spring this year was wet and late, and the only thing in bloom was the weeping willow in the back yard, with its trailing yellow catkins. The trees spread over the running hills to the next farm were still winter sticks. The day was cool enough for a light jacket in spite of the work, and the sky was partly overcast. Gardening was an act of faith that the seasons would change and warmth and flower come. Gardening is an act of faith. I'm a pessimist, but still I garden.

It's much like the times.

Our society is imperfect. That's what we say, and we shrug and let it go at that. Societies change in their own good time, and there isn't much that individuals can do to cause change or direct it. Most people don't try. They have a living to make, and whatever energies are left over they know how to put to good use. They leave politics to politicians.

But let's be honest. Our society is not just imperfect. Our society is an unhappy shambles. And leaving politics to politicians is proving to be as dangerous a business as leaving science to scientists, war to generals, and profits to profiteers.

I read. I watch. I listen. And I judge by my own experience.

The best of us are miserable. We all take drugs—alcohol, tobacco, and pills by the handful. We do work in order to live and live in order to work—an endless unsatisfying round. The jobs are no pleasure. Employers shunt us from one plastic paradise to another. One quarter of the country moves each year. No roots, no stability.

We live our lives in public, with less and less opportunity to know each other. To know anybody.

Farmers can't make a living farming. Small businessmen can't make a living any more, either. Combines and monoliths take them over or push them out. And because nobody questions the ways of a monolith and stays or rises in one, the most ruthless monoliths survive, run by the narrowest and hungriest and most self-satisfied among us.

The results: rivers that stink of sewage, industrial waste, and dead fish. City air that's the equivalent of smoking two packs of cigarettes a day. Countryside turned to rubble. Chemical lagoons left to stain hillsides with their overflow. Fields of rusting auto bodies.

And all the while, the population is growing. Progress. New consumers. But when I was born, in 1940, there were 140 million people in this country, and now there are more than 200 million, half of them born since 1940. Our institutions are less and less able to cope with the growth. Not enough houses. Not enough schools. Not enough doctors or teachers or jobs. Not enough room at the beach. Not enough beaches.

Not enough food. The world is beginning to starve, and for all the talk of Green Revolutions, we no longer have surplus food. We are importing lamb from Australia and beef from Argentina now. How soon before we all start pulling our belts a notch tighter?

And our country acts like one more self-righteous monolith. Policing the world in the name of one ideal or another. In practice, supporting dictators, suppressing people who want fresh air to breathe as much as any of us, with just as much right. In practice, taking, taking, taking, with both hands. Our country has 6 percent of the world's population. We consume 50 percent of the world's production. How long will we be allowed to continue? Who will we kill to continue?

And as unhappiness rises, crime rises. Women march. Blacks burn their slums and arm themselves. Kids confront. And nobody is sure of his safety. I'm not sure of mine.

All of us are police, or demonstrators, or caught in between. And there is more of the same to come.

Our society may be worse than a shambles. Certainly, in spite of the inventions, the science, the progress, the magic at our command, our problems are not growing less. Each year is more chaotic than the one before. Marches. Demonstrations. Riots. Assassinations. Crime. Frustration. Malaise. General inability to cope.

We are in a hell of a mess. And nobody has any solutions.

Head-beatings and suppression are not solutions. Barricades are no solution. Bloody revolutions merely exchange one set of power brokers for another.

But the problems we have are real and immediate. Those who are hungry, unskilled, jobless, homeless, or simply chronically unhappy, cannot be told to shut up. The 100 million of us who are young cannot be told to go away. The 100 million of us who are old cannot be ignored. The 20 million of us who are black cannot be killed, deported, or subjugated longer at any cost short of our total ruin as human beings. And so far we have no solutions. Merely the same old knee-jerk reactions of confrontation and suppression.

There may in fact be no solutions.

We may be on the one-way trip to total destruction.

These may be the last years of the human race, or the last bearable ones that any of us will know.

In times like these, gardening is an act of faith. That the seasons will change and warmth and flower come. But it is the best thing I know to do. We do garden.

So I worked and thought—and thought about my story. And how we might get from this now of ours to a brighter future. I'd like to believe in one.

And so I worked. As wet as the spring had been, the ground I was turning was muddy, and I was up to my knees in it. And down on my knees. And up to my elbows. Finding worms for the ducklings when I could. Some of the mud—or its cousin—appears on the fourth page of this manuscript. If our printer is worth his salt, I trust it will appear in true and faithful reproduction when you read this. When and wherever you read this, a touch of garden.

After a time, Alexander the gander came waddling over to investigate us, me and the ducklings. There is truth to the adage "cross as a goose." There is also truth to the adage "loose as a goose," but that is of no moment. Alexander lowers his head, opens his beak, and hisses like an angry iguana. He and I have struck a truce. When he acts like an iguana, I act like an iguana back, and I am bigger than he is, so Alexander walks away.

The ducklings don't have my advantages, and Alexander began to run them around in circles. They peeped and ran, peeped and ran. Alexander was doing them no harm, but he was upsetting them mightily. They were too upset to eat worms, and that is upset.

After a few minutes of this I put down my spade and grabbed an armful of disgruntled goose. I held Alexander upside down and began to stroke his belly feathers. Stroke. Stroke. Stroke. After a moment he became less angry. He ceased to hiss. His eyes glazed and he began to tick, every few seconds a wave passing through like the wake behind a canoe. At last I set him back on his feet and Alexander walked dazedly away. He seemed bewildered, not at all certain of what had happened to him. He shook his little head and then reared back and flapped his wings as though he were stretching for the morning. At last he found a place in the middle of the gravel drive and stood there like a sentinel, muttering to himself in goose talk.

It's what I call Upgraded Protective Reaction. I'd like to try it on our so-called leaders.

A sudden stampede of lambs back under the fence announced the return of Cory, Leigh, and Juanito from their walk to the State Park.

"Hello, love," I said. "Did you see anything?"

Cory smiled widely. "We set up the whole herd down by Three Mile Run. They bounded across the valley, and then one last one like an afterthought trying to catch up."

"Oh, fine," I said in appreciation.

Leigh nodded, smiling too. She doesn't talk a lot. She isn't verbal. I am, so we talk some, just as Rob and I talk. But when she and Rob talk, she gestures and he nods, and then he gestures and she nods. She found a worm in my well-turned mud and held it at a dangle for the smaller duckling, who gobbled it down.

Cory said, "We're going to have a look at Gemma's kittens."

"Good," I said. "I think I've put in my half hour here. I'll come along."

"Have you gone to the Elephant yet?"

"Oh," I said. "It slipped my mind. I checked on the mail, though. The mail came."

"What?"

"Nothing good," I said. "Juanito, want to go to the Elephant with me?"

He really didn't look my age. But then I don't look my age, either.

"All right," he said.

Cory and Leigh walked off toward the main house to have their look at the kittens. The ducklings hesi-

tated and then went pell-melling after them wagging
their beam ends faster than a boxer puppy.

"Now's our chance," I said.

But when Juanito and I got to the car, I remembered
the truck tire.

"Just a minute," I said, and took it out of the truck.
"Let me put this away while I think of it. Grab your
bottle."

He fished the beer bottle from behind the spare tire
where it had rolled. Then he followed me as I hefted
the tire and carried it through the machine shop and
into the tractor shed. I dumped the tire by the great
heavy trash cans.

"Bottle there," I said, pointing to a can, and Juanito
set it on top of the trash like a careful crown.

"What's going to happen to it?" he asked.

"When the ground dries, the farmer will take it all
down and dump it in the woods." Out of sight, out of
mind.

"Oh," he said.

We lumbered off to the Elephant in the old Plymouth.
It was once a hotel, a wayside inn. Now it's a cross-
roads store and bar. We shop there when we need
something in a hurry. It's a mile down the road. Everything else is five miles or more. Mostly more.

Juanito said, "Do you drive alone much?"

"Not much," I said. "Cory can't drive yet, so we go
shopping together about twice a week." I'm conscious
of the trips to Doylestown and Quakertown because
they so often cut into my writing.

"Whereabouts you from, Juanito?" I asked.

"Nowhere in particular these days," he said. "I pretty
much keep on the move. I stay for a while, and then I
move on to the next place."

"Always an outside agitator?" I asked, maneuvering
to avoid a dead possum in the road. Possums like to
take evening walks down the center of the highway.

"Something like that, I guess," he said.

"I couldn't do it," I said. "I hitched across the country when I was eighteen, but I couldn't take the uncertainty of always being on the move. I couldn't work without roots and routine."

On our right as we drove up the winding hill to the Elephant was a decaying set of grandstands.

"What is that?" asked Juanito.

"The Vargo Dragway," I said. "On a Sunday afternoon you could hear them winding up and gearing down all the way back at the farm. They finally got it shut down last year. It took five years. It always seems to take them five years."

I swung into the gravel parking lot beside the bar. They kept the bacon, eggs, and milk in the refrigerator behind the bar, so we went inside there rather than around to the store. There were two men drinking, but there was no one behind the bar, so we waited. Behind the bar are pictures and an old sign that says, "Elephant Hotel—1848," around the silhouette of an elephant.

One of the drinkers looked us over. A wrinkled pinchface in working clothes.

He said in a loud voice to no one in particular, "Hippies! I don't like 'em. Dirty hippies. Ruining the country. We don't want 'em moving in around here. Bums."

The man sitting at the other end of the bar seemed acutely uncomfortable and looked away from him. I leaned back against the pool table. This sort of thing doesn't happen to me often enough that I know what to do about it.

The drinker kept up the comments. At last I took two steps toward him and said something inane like, "Look, do you want everybody to dress and think like you?" It was inane because he and I were dressed much the same.

He threw his hands up in front of his face and said anxiously, "Get away from me! Get away from me!"

So I stopped and shut up and moved back to the pool table. And he returned to his comments to no one.

"Creeps! Making trouble."

From the doorway to the store, Mrs. Lokay said, "Mr. Pinchen," and I turned, grateful for the interruption. She hasn't got my name straight and she knows nothing of William Pynchon or *The Meritorious Price of Our Redemption,* but at times when I've come in for the Sunday *New York Times* and found no change in my jeans, they've put me down in the book on trust.

We followed her into the store. She said, "Don't mind him. He's mad about his stepson. He shouldn't talk to you that way. Thank you for not making trouble. We'll talk to him."

I shrugged and said, "That's all right," because I didn't know what else to say. I was calm, but I was upset.

Juanito and I waited in the store while Mrs. Lokay went back into the bar for our order. I carried the sack all the way around the building rather than walk back through and set him off again.

I don't really like trouble much, and I'll go out of my way to avoid violence. I clutched the wheel tightly. Instead of driving directly home, I turned off into East Rockhill where the farm country plays out and the woods take over. I set my jaw and drove and thought about all the things I might have said.

I could have said, "That's all right, buddy. I've got a license to look like this. They call it the Constitution."

I could have said, "Have you seen Lyndon Johnson's hair hanging over his collar lately?"

I could have said, "What's the matter? Can't you tell a simple country boy when you see one?"

But I hadn't.

Juanito said, "What you ought to do is get a big plastic sack with a zipper and rig it up. You have two controls. One for warm saline solution, the other for your air line. Spend the night in that. It's very calming."

I said, "It sounds like what I've read about Barry Goldwater falling asleep on the bottom of his swimming pool. Never mind, I have something as good."

I stopped the car, pulling it off to the side of the road. On that side were woods. On the other were fountains, fieldstone walkways, planting, dogwoods, and two scaled-down pyramids, one six feet tall, the other twenty.

"What's this place?" Juanito asked.

"It's the Rosicrucian Meditation Garden," I said, and got out of the car.

The signs say it is open from 8:30 every morning. I've never seen anyone else walking there, but no one has ever come out to ask me to prove that I was meditating.

After I walked around for a time and looked at the tadpoles swimming in the pool around the smaller pyramid—just like the Great Pyramid in Egypt—I got a grip on myself. Thank the Rosicrucians.

As we drove back to the farm, we passed the rock quarry. "Rock quarry," I said in answer to Juanito's question. They don't call it East Rockhill for nothing.

"It won't always be that ugly," I said. "When they have the dam in, all this will be under water. Until the valley silts up, all we'll have to worry about is an invasion and speedboats."

They don't have lakes in this part of Pennsylvania, so they propose to make them.

"I know about that," Juanito said. "Cory mentioned it."

The lake will run through the State Park land. Where the deer herd is now. I don't relish the trade. Ah, but progress.

After dinner, after dark, we all gathered in the living room. Cory collected me from the study where I was taking ten minutes after dinner to stare at my typewriter.

"Are you getting anywhere?" she asked.

I shook my head. "Nothing written. Great and fleeting ideas only."

"Alexei, what are we going to do about the money?"

I said, "Henry said he mailed the check. We just have to trust it to come."

I opened my desk drawer and took out the checkbook with the undernourished balance. I wrote a check out to Internal Revenue for $371.92—more than we had to our name.

"Here," I said. "Put this in the envelope with the return. We'll mail it when the check comes from Henry or on the fifteenth, whichever comes sooner."

Cory tucked the check under the flap of the envelope, but left it unsealed. She set it on top of the phonograph speaker by the front door.

When we came into the living room, Rob said, "Oh, hey. I almost forgot. I brought something for you."

He fished in his bag while I waited. I like presents, even if I don't lie awake on Christmas Eve in anticipation anymore. He came up with a paperback and handed it to me. It was *The Tales of Hoffman,* portions of the transcript of the Chicago Eight trial.

"Thank you," I said. "I'll read it tomorrow."

It was just the book for Rob to give me. His idea of the most pressing urgency in this country is court reform. Which is needed, as anybody who has been through the agonies of waiting in jails and courtrooms can attest. I'm more bothered by the debasement of thought and language starting with calling the War Department the Department of Defense and proceeding down the line from there. One thumbing of the book told me Rob and I had a common meeting ground.

Rob said, "What about your story?"

I said, "I'll read the book in the bathtub."

"Are you going to spend the day in the bathtub?"

"If I have to."

We turned off the lights except for the chandelier, dim and yellow, and Cory brought out a candle and set it to pulsing in its wine-colored glass. Four of us sat on the floor around the candle, and Leigh sat in the easy chair. The light from the chandelier played

off the dark veneer and outlined the carriage beams.
The candlelight made the rug glow like autumn.

We talked of one thing and another, and I played
records. Great Speckled Bird. Crosby, Stills, Nash and
Young. The new Baez. Rob pulled out *Highway 61
Revisited,* and I got into it as I never had before.

Wolf and Fang went freaking in the candlelight,
chasing each other round and round the room. I put
on Quicksilver Messenger Service, the first album,
and when "The Fool" reached its peak, Wolf went
dashing in and out of the room, ending on the deep
window ledge with the last bent note.

And sitting there into the night, we speculated.

Rob, sitting tailor-fashion, said, the conversation
having carried him there in some drifting fashion, "Is
there really a Mafia?"

"I don't know," I said. "You're closer to it than I
am."

"I'm in daily contact with people who think there
is," he said thoughtfully. "They think they belong. I
could get myself killed. But what I'm asking is, is
there *really* a Mafia? Or are there only a lot of people
pretending?"

It's a good question. Is there really such a thing as
the United States, or just a lot of people pretending?

I said, "Is there really a Revolution?"

Last summer, just before Cory and I left Cambridge
to move down here, in fact the day before we moved, I
got a call from William James Heckman. Bill had
been my roommate my senior year in prep school, and
I hadn't heard from him since the day we graduated.
He and I had never been friends and never seen much
of interest in each other. But I told him sure, come on
over.

I was curious. In the spring, eleven years after we
graduated, they'd gotten around to throwing a tenth
reunion of my class. I'd had a book to finish and had
to miss it, and been sorry. I'd been an outsider at
Mount Hermon, and I was curious to know what had

become of all the Golden People. I like to know the ending to stories, and eleven years later is a good place to put a period to high school. Bill hadn't been Golden People, either, but under the circumstances I was willing to let him serve as a substitute for the reunion.

Bill had changed. Fair enough—I've changed, too. His hair was starting to thin. He wore a mustache with droopy ends, sideburns, and a candystripe shirt.

We traded neutralities and ate chips and dip. He was in Cambridge to visit his former wife. He was studying theater at Cornell. He'd taken a course from Joanna Russ, a writer friend of mine, and mentioned that he had known me, and she had given him my address.

We spoke about relevance. He said that he wanted to do more than just entertain, too.

Then, in the hallway as he was leaving, he said suddenly and with more than a little pride, "I'm really a revolutionary. I'm working for the Revolution."

"So am I," I said. As he disappeared around the curve in the hallway, I called, with a certain sense of joy, "So are we all."

Is there really a Revolution, or are there just a lot of people pretending? What will happen when enough people pretend hard enough, long enough?

The five of us and the two cats gathered around our candle late on a spring night. If there really is a Revolution, are we its leaders? What if we pretended to be long enough, hard enough?

And I wondered in how many other rooms people were gathered around a flame thinking the same things, dreaming the same dreams. There have to be new ways, there have to be better ways, and we all know it.

Later that night, when we were in bed, Cory said, "Did you find out anything about Juanito? I asked Leigh while you were gone and Rob was sleeping, but she didn't know anything. He was with Rob when Rob showed up."

I said, "All I got from Rob was a put-on." And I told her about it. We laughed and we fell asleep.

But when we got up in the morning, Juanito was gone.

Rob was still sleeping on the couch. Leigh was asleep in the second bedroom. And Juanito was gone.

I went outside to look for him. There was a full-grown ewe nibbling on the rosebush by the barn, and I waved my arms and stampeded her back under the wire, kneeling and humping to get through and leaving wool behind. But no Juanito.

There was a trash can by the front door that I hadn't left there. It was full of beer cans, soft-drink cans, rusty oil tins riddled by shot, beer bottles, plastic ice-cream dishes and spoons, cigarette butts, cigarette packs, a partly decayed magazine, and plastic, glass, and chrome from the last auto accident.

I hauled the trash can away, thinking. Cory was standing by the front door when I came back.

"I've got my story," I said. "I've got my story."

"At last," she said.

2

At the age of thirty Little John was still a child, with a child's impatience to be grown. More than anything—more than the long study and the slow ripening that his Guide assured him were the true road to his desires, as indeed they were, in part—he wished to be finished now, matured now, set free from the eternal lessons of the past now. He was a child, one of the chosen few, favored, petted, and loved just for living. On the one hand, he accepted it as his proper due; on the other, he found it a humiliation. It meant he was still only one of the Chosen, only a boy, and he wished to be a grown-up god like everyone else.

It was not that he lacked talent for it. People even more ordinary than he had made Someone of themselves. He simply hadn't yet gotten the idea. Chosen, but not yet called.

He conceived progress in his lessons to be his road to grace. It was what Samantha had taught him to believe, and believing it, he was impatient to gulp down one lesson and be on to the next. He had been led to believe that sheer accumulation was sufficient in itself, and he had closets full of notes. He had also been taught not to believe everything he was told and to think for himself, but this information was lost somewhere on note cards in one of his closets.

Impatient though he was, he tried to conceal his impatience from Samantha. He was awed by his Guide. He was awed by her age, by her reputation, by her impenetrability, and by the sheer living distance between the two of them, her and him. At the same time he accepted as right and proper that someone like her should be his Guide, for, after all, he was one of the Chosen.

Samantha encouraged his awe. Awe, like impatience, was a mark of his greenness, a measure of the distance he had to travel to reach the insight that lessons are to be applied, not merely amassed—that one thing in all the world that she could not tell him but could only leave him to discover for himself in his own time. Behind her impenetrable expression, however, she sighed at his awe, shook her head at his pride in advancement, and smiled at his wriggling impatience. And then tried his patience all the harder.

When he returned from his trip to 1381, she gave him a week to think about the experience before they began to discuss it.

"I could live in 1381 and be a god," Little John said. "It wouldn't be easy, but I saw enough. It takes endurance. That's the chief thing."

They talked about it for a month, day after day. The problems of being a peasant in those times, and still a god, relating as a god should to his fellow men. The problems of overcoming ignorance. And all the while, Little John visibly eager to be done and on to the next trip.

At last she sent him on one. She sent him back to 1381 for another look from a new perspective. It is, after all, one problem to be a powerless peasant courting godhood, and quite another, as Buddha knew, to be a noble aiming for the same end. Little John didn't really see that. All he recognized was 1381 come 'round again when he felt he ought to be off to a new time and new problems of godhood. As though godliness could be measured in trips and not in what was made of them.

So he said again, "I could live in 1381 and be a god. Endurance. That's the main thing. Isn't it?"

She told him to think it over. So they talked about it for another month. And in time he finally said something about the psychological difficulty of shedding power when power is held to be a birthright.

He said, "You could give your money and property to the Church. That's a way."

"Is it a godly way?"

"Well, it could be," he said. "They thought it could."

"Do you think so?"

"I met a very decent Franciscan."

"Organized godliness?"

So they talked further about the times and how it might have been possible to live well in them when your fellow wolves were ready to stay wolves until they died and ready to die to stay wolves. And Little John saw that it was indeed a very different problem than being the godly victim of wolves.

He felt that the last juice had been squeezed from the trip and was ready for the next long before Samantha was ready to send him. And when that trip was back to 1381 again for a stay in a monastery, he felt—well, not cheated, but distinctly disappointed.

And he took nothing away from the experience, except for the usual stack of notes.

And after a week of discussion his impatience finally got the better of him.

He said, "Keats died at twenty-five. Masaccio died at twenty-seven, and so did Henry Gwyn-Jeffreys Moseley." He had memorized a long series of people like that, from Emily Brontë to Mikhail Yurievich Lermontov. "I'm nearly thirty. I want to do what I have to do and be done, and be out in the world."

He didn't understand the point. If you are going to do, you do. Those who wait for freedom are never free.

And Samantha, who had a reputation for tartness, said, "Yes, and Christopher Marlowe died at twenty-nine and still wrote all of Shakespeare. Do you think forty or fifty years are too many to spend in preparation for a life as long as you have ahead of you?"

"Oh, no," he said. "Oh, no." But in his heart he did. "It's just that I'm tired of 1381. It's easy to be a god then. It's too easy. I want something harder. Send me to 1970. I'm ready. Really I am."

1970 had a reputation. If you could be a god then, you could be a god anytime. Little John looked on it as a final examination of sorts, and he wanted nothing more than to go.

"Do you believe you're ready to handle 1970?" Samantha asked.

"Oh, yes," he said. "Please."

He was sitting cross-legged before her. They were on the hilltop circle standing high above the community buildings and the flowering fields. The outdoor theater was here, and convocation when decisions had to be made. It was a good place to watch sunset and moonrise. His walks with Samantha often brought them here.

He was more than a little apprehensive at making his request, and he watched Samantha's face closely as she considered, anxious for the least sign of the nature of her answer, impatient for the first clue.

And, as usual, her face was composed and gave him no hint.

Little John waited so long and her face was so still that he was half afraid she would fall asleep. He tried to make a still center of himself no less than three times before she spoke, and each time fell victim to wonder and lost the thread. He managed silence and reasonable stillness, and that was all.

At last, she said, "This is not a matter of haste. I think we've spoken enough for today. Walk, meditate, consider your lessons."

"And then?"

"Why, come tomorrow to my chambers at the regular time." And she gave him the sign of dismissal.

So he rose, and gathered his notes, and went down the hill, leaving Samantha still sitting. He turned for a look where the stony path made a corner, and she was still sitting, looking over the valley.

Shelley Anne Fenstermacher, the other Chosen, who was ten years old and half his size and used him as a signpost as he had used Hope Saltonstall when he was younger, was waiting for him. She emptied her bucket of garbage into the hog trough, climbed down from the fence, and came running.

"Did you ask? Did you ask? What did she say?"

"She said I was to walk and meditate," said Little John.

"What do you think it means?"

"I don't know."

He went into his room and got his latest notes from the closet. He didn't know what Samantha had in mind, but if it made the slightest difference, he meant to follow her advice. He always followed her advice to the best of his understanding.

"Can I come?" Shelley asked when he came outside.

"Not today," he said. "Today I'd better walk alone."

"Oh," she said.

"I'm sorry."

So he walked in the woods and meditated and read

his note cards, anxious to stuff the least and last of it into his head. If it made a difference, if she quizzed him, he meant to be ready. He had every word she had said to him down on paper. Ask him anything, he'd show he was ready.

And the next day when he and Samantha met, he was ready, that is, ready for anything except what he received, which was nothing. Samantha acted as though he had never spoken. She took up the discussion where he had broken it the day before, and they walked and they talked as usual and she never said a word about his request.

And Little John, afraid to speak, said never a word, either. He did wriggle a lot, though.

At the end of the two hours, however, she said, "A fruitful session, was it not?"

And dumbly, he nodded. And then he said, "Please ma'am, have you made a decision?"

"Yes," she said. "I brought you something." She reached into her pants pocket and brought out an embroidered pouch. "It's a present. Take this grass up on Roundtop tonight, and when the moon is two full hands above the horizon, smoke it and meditate."

That night he sat up on Roundtop on his favorite log. He watched the sun set and he watched the moon rise. And he measured with his hands. When the moon was two full hands above the horizon, he filled his pipe and smoked. And he thought, and his thoughts filled the night to its conclusion. They were good thoughts, but they were all of 1970 and of graduation to godhood. It was good grass.

In gratitude he brought Samantha the best apple he could pick. He searched the whole orchard before he made a choice.

His teacher was pleased with the apple. "Thank you, Little John," she said. She ate it as they walked and wrapped up the core for the pigs.

"What conclusions did you come to last night?" she asked.

His thoughts had been ineffable, so what he said was, "Novalis died at twenty-eight."

"So he did," Samantha said.

They walked on in silence. They walked in silence for two hours. For someone her age Samantha was a brisk and sturdy walker. They circled Roundtop. The day was heavy and hot. There was a skyhawk wheeling high overhead, drifting on the current, and Little John envied it. He wanted to fly free, too.

When they reached home, walking up the lane between the ripe fields, Samantha finally spoke. "Spend the night in Mother," she said. "Then see me tomorrow."

"Without Tempus?" he asked.

"Yes, without Tempus."

"But I've never done that."

She said, "We had Mother before we had Tempus. Try it and see."

"Yes, ma'am," he said.

He had kept Shelley Anne apprised of his progress. When she sought him out after dinner, sitting on the porch in the warm and quiet of the evening, he told her what Samantha wished him to do.

"Really?" she said. "I never heard of that. Does she expect you to change your mind?"

"I don't know," he said. "But I have to do it if she wants me to."

While they were talking, Lenny came out on the porch. "Hi, children," he said. "Are you going to the convo tonight?"

Shelly Anne said she was. Little John said he was busy and had other plans. When Lenny left, Shelley Anne went with him, and Little John was left alone in the evening. He could see the fire up on Roundtop and hear the voices.

At last he went inside and set up Mother, just as though he were going on a trip, but without the drug. He checked the air line. He checked the solution line. And he set the alarm to rouse himself.

He undressed himself and kicked his clothes into the corner. It was something he'd been known to do since he had decided that it wasn't necessarily ungodlike. He picked them up himself sometime; and as long as he did that eventually he figured it was all right.

Then he unzipped Mother and climbed inside. It was overcool on his bare skin until he got used to it, like settling down on a cold toilet seat. He fitted the mouthpiece of the air line into place. He didn't close the bag until he was breathing comfortably.

As the warm saline solution rose in the bag, he cleared his mind. He basked and floated. He had never used Mother except on official trips and had never thought to wonder why it was called Mother. Now he leaned back, drifted and dreamed in Mother's warm arms, and she was very good to him.

Strange undirected dreams flitted through his mind. Pleasant dreams. He saw Shelley Anne Fenstermacher as an old woman, and she nodded, smiled and said, "Hi," just like she always did. He saw Samantha as a ten-year-old with a doll in her arms. He saw his old friends in the monastery in 1381, making their cordials and happily sampling them. And he wheeled through the blue skies along with his friend the skyhawk, coasting on the summer breeze high above the temperate world.

And then he passed beyond dreams.

In the morning, the cool, calm morning, he sat in the slanting sunlight listening to the song of a mockingbird shift and vary, and tried to pick it out with his eye in the leaf-cloaked branches of a walnut tree. At last Samantha came out to join him. He thought he could see the ten-year-old in her, even without the doll.

She said, "How did the night pass?"

Though his skin was prunish, he didn't think to mention it. "Well," he said. "I never spent a night like that before." But already he planned to again. "It was very soothing."

"Ah, was it?" And then, without further preamble, she said, "Do you still want to travel to 1970?"

"Yes, ma'am," he said. "I'm ready for it. I'll show you I am. What else do you want me to do first?"

"Nothing. If you still want to go, if you're still determined to go, I'll send you."

Little John nearly jumped up and gave her a hug, but awe restrained him. If Samantha had been asked, perhaps she would have had him retain that much awe.

So Little John got his trip to 1970, his chance to graduate. Mother was readied again, not for general wandering, but for a directed dream. Samantha calculated the mix of Tempus herself.

She said, "This won't be like any other time you've been."

"Oh, I know that," he said.

"Do you? I almost remember it myself, and it wasn't like now."

"I can handle it."

"Let us hope," she said. "I'm going to see that you are in good hands. Nothing too serious should happen to you."

"Please," he said. "Don't make it too easy."

"Say that again after you've returned. I'm going to give you a mnemonic. If you want to abort the trip and come back before the full period, then concentrate on the mnemonic. Do you understand?"

"I understand," he said.

She checked him out on all points, once, twice, and then again before she was satisfied. Then, at last, he climbed inside Mother and drank the draft she handed him.

"Have a good trip," she said.

"Oh, I will, ma'am. Don't worry about that," Little John said as the sack filled and he drifted away from her, back in time, back in his mind. "I expect to have a *good* time."

That's what he said. Nothing hard about being a god in 1970. They had had all the materials, and by now he had had experience in godhood. He was ready.

But he came back early. And he didn't have a *good* time.

In fact, he was heartsick, subdued, drained. He wouldn't speak to Shelley Anne Fenstermacher. And without prompting by Samantha or anyone he disappeared into the woods to be by himself, and he didn't come back for two days.

He spent the whole time thinking, trying to make sense of what he had seen, and he wasn't able to do it. He missed two whole sessions with Samantha. And when he did turn up at last, he didn't apologize for being missing.

"You were right," he said simply. "I wasn't ready. Send me back to 1381 again. Please."

"Perhaps," Samantha said.

"I don't understand. I don't understand. I knew things weren't right then, but I didn't think they would be like that. Taxes was what they cared about. They didn't even see what was going on. Not really. And it was just before the Revolution. Are things always that bad before they change?"

"Yes," she said. "Always. The only difference this time is the way things changed. And you didn't see the worst of it. Not by half, Little John."

"I didn't?" he said in surprise. "I thought it must be."

She was too kind to laugh. "No."

"But it was so awful. So ruthless. So destructive."

Samantha said, "Those people weren't so bad. As it happens, they were my parents."

"Oh, I'm sorry, ma'am," he said.

"And your grandparents weren't so different. And they did learn better. That's the important thing to remember. If you take away nothing else, remember that. If they hadn't changed, none of us would be here now."

He cried out, "But they had so much power. They all had the power of gods, and they used it so badly."

Little John may have been stupid, abysmally stupid, he may have been green, and he may have had more years ahead of him than little Shelley Anne Fenstermacher before he was fit to be let out in the world, but there were some things he was able to recognize. Some things are writ plain.

3

Endings of stories come easy. It is the beginnings, when anything is still possible, that come hard.

Start now.

THE RED QUEEN'S RACE

by ISAAC ASIMOV

This is the other story which Marty wouldn't write
the headnote for. He felt my modesty was such that
my greatness couldn't be adequately handled by a
mere outsider. And he's right, too. I (Isaac Asimov)
am so certain that my utter majesty is adequately
recognized by the world generally that I won't say a
word about it. On to other things. As an oddity,
"The Red Queen's Race" was the first story I wrote
after obtaining my Ph.D., so it was the first story
written by "the Good Doctor." Secondly, it was one
of the very few stories which I wrote in the first
person. Finally, I once innocently said that I had
never written a tough-guy detective story, and someone else said, "Oh, no? Then how about 'The Red
Queen's Race'?" I at once went back to it and
reread it to see if I had written such a story without
realizing it. Have I?—I leave it to you.

HERE'S a puzzle for you, if you like. Is it a crime to
translate a chemistry textbook into Greek?

Or let's put it another way. If one of the country's
largest atomic power plants is completely ruined in an
unauthorized experiment, is an admitted accessory to
that act a criminal?

These problems only developed with time, of course.
We started with the atomic power plant—drained. I
really mean *drained*. I don't know exactly how large
the fissionable power source was—but in two flashing
microseconds, it had all fissioned.

347

No explosion. No undue gamma ray density. It was merely that every moving part of the entire structure was fused. The entire main building was mildly hot. The atmosphere for two miles in every direction was gently warm. Just a dead, useless building which later on took a hundred million dollars to replace.

It happened about three in the morning, and they found Elmer Tywood alone in the central source chamber. The findings of twenty-four close-packed hours can be summarized quickly.

1. Elmer Tywood—Ph.D., Sc.D., Fellow of This and Honorary That, one-time youthful participant of the original Manhattan Project, and now full Professor of Nuclear Physics—was no interloper. He had a Class-A Pass—Unlimited. But no record could be found as to his purpose in being there just then. A table on casters contained equipment which had not been made on any recorded requisition. It, too, was a single fused mass—not quite too hot to touch.

2. Elmer Tywood was dead. He lay next to the table; his face congested, nearly black. No radiation effect. No external force of any sort. The doctor said apoplexy.

3. In Elmer Tywood's office safe were found two puzzling items: i.e. twenty foolscap sheets of apparent mathematics, and a bound folio in a foreign language which turned out to be Greek, the subject matter, on translation, turning out to be chemistry.

The secrecy which poured over the whole mess was something so terrific as to make everything that touched it *dead*. It's the only word that can describe it. Twenty-seven men and women, all told, including the Secretary of Defense, the Secretary of Science, and two or three others so top-notch that they were completely unknown to the public entered the power plant during the period of investigation. Any man who had been in the plant that night, the physicist who had identified Tywood, the doctor who had examined him, were retired into virtual home arrest.

No newspaper ever got the story. No inside dopester got it. A few members of Congress got part of it.

And naturally so! Anyone or any group or any country that could suck all the available energy out of the equivalent of perhaps fifty to a hundred pounds of plutonium without exploding it had America's industry and America's defense so snugly in the palm of the hand that the light and life of one hundred sixty million people could be turned off between yawns.

Was it Tywood? Or Tywood and others? Or just others, through Tywood?

And my job? I was decoy; or front man, if you like. Someone has to hang around the university and ask questions about Tywood. After all, he was missing. It could be amnesia, a hold-up, a kidnapping, a killing, a runaway, insanity, accident—I could busy myself with that for five years and collect black looks, and maybe divert attention. To be sure, it didn't work out that way.

But don't think I was in on the whole case at the start. I wasn't one of the twenty-seven men I mentioned a while back, though my boss was. But I knew a little—enough to get started.

Professor John Keyser was also in Physics. I didn't get to him right away. There was a good deal of routine to cover first in as conscientious a way as I could. Quite meaningless. Quite necessary. But I was in Keyser's office now.

Professors' offices are distinctive. Nobody dusts them except some tired cleaning woman who hobbles in and out at eight in the morning, and the professor never notices dust anyway. Lots of books without much arrangement. The ones close to the desk are used a lot—lectures are copied out of them. The ones out of reach are wherever a student put them back after borrowing them. Then there are professional journals that look cheap and are darned expensive, which are waiting about and which may someday be read. And plenty of paper on the desk; some of it scribbled on.

Keyser was an elderly man—one of Tywood's generation. His nose was big and rather red, and he smoked a pipe. He had that easygoing and nonpredatory look in his eyes that goes with an academic job—either because that kind of job attracts that kind of man or because that kind of job makes that kind of man.

I said: "What kind of work is Professor Tywood doing?"

"Research physics."

Answers like that bounce off me. Some years ago they used to get me mad. Now, I just said: "We know that, professor. It's the details I'm after."

And he twinkled at me tolerantly: "Surely the details can't help much unless you're a research physicist yourself. Does it matter—under the circumstances?"

"Maybe not. But he's gone. If anything's happened to him in the way of"—I gestured, and deliberately clinched—"foul play, his work may have something to do with it—unless he's rich and the motive is money."

Keyser chuckled dryly: "College professors are never rich. The commodity we peddle is but lightly considered, seeing how large the supply is."

I ignored that, too, because I know my looks are against me. Actually, I finished college with a "very good" translated into Latin so that the college president could understand it, and never played in a football game in my life. But I look rather the reverse.

I said: "Then we're left with his work to consider."

"You mean spies? International intrigue?"

"Why not? It's happened before! After all, he's a nuclear physicist, isn't he?"

"He is. But so are others. So am I."

"Ah, but perhaps he knows something you don't."

There was a stiffening to the jaw. When caught off-guard, professors can act just like people. He said, stiffly: "As I recall offhand, Tywood has published papers on the effect of liquid viscosity on the wings of the Rayleigh line, on higher-orbit field equation, and on spin-orbit coupling of two nucleons, but his main work is on quadrupole moments. I am quite competent in these matters."

"Is he working on quadrupole moments now?" I tried not to bat an eye, and I think I succeeded.

"Yes—in a way." He almost sneered, "He may be getting to the experimental stage finally. He's spent most of his life, it seems, working out the mathematical consequences of a special theory of his own."

"Like this," and I tossed a sheet of foolscap at him.

That sheet was one of those in the safe in Tywood's office. The chances, of course, were that the bundle meant nothing, if only because it was a professor's safe. That is, things are sometimes put in at the spur of the moment because the logical drawer was filled with unmarked exam papers. And, of course, nothing is ever taken out. We had found in that safe dusty little vials of yellowish crystals with scarcely legible labels, some mimeographed booklets dating back to World War II and marked "Restricted," a copy of an old college yearbook, and some correspondence concerning a possible position as Director of Research for American Electric, dated ten years back, and, of course, chemistry in Greek.

The foolscap was there, too. It was rolled up like a college diploma with a rubber band about it and had no label or descriptive title. Some twenty sheets were covered with ink marks, meticulous and small—

I had one sheet of that foolscap. I don't think any one man in the world had more than one sheet. And I'm sure that no man in the world but one knew that the loss of his particular sheet and of his particular life would be as nearly simultaneous as the government could make it.

So I tossed the sheet at Keyser, as if it were something I'd found blowing about the campus.

He stared at it and then looked at the back side, which was blank. His eyes moved down from the top to the bottom, then jumped back to the top.

"I don't know what this is about," he said, and the words seemed sour to his own taste.

I didn't say anything. Just folded the paper and shoved it back into the inside jacket pocket.

Keyser added petulantly: "It's a fallacy you laymen have that scientists can look at an equation and say, 'Ah, yes—' and go on to write a book about it. Mathematics has no existence of its own. It is merely an arbitrary code devised to describe physical observations or philosophical concepts. Every man can adapt it to his own particular needs. For instance, no one can look at a symbol and be sure of what it means. So far, science has used every letter in the alphabet, large, small and italic, each symbolizing many different things. They have used bold-faced letters, Gothic-type letters, Greek letters, both capital and small, subscripts, superscripts, asterisks, even Hebrew letters. Different scientists use different symbols for the same concept and the same symbol for different concepts. So if you show a disconnected page like this to any man, without information as to the subject being investigated or the particular symbology used, he could absolutely not make sense out of it."

I interrupted: "But you said he was working on quadrupole moments. Does that make this sensible?" and I tapped the spot on my chest where the foolscap had been slowly scorching a hole in my jacket for two days.

"I can't tell. I saw none of the standard relationships that I'd expect to be involved. At least I recognized none. But I obviously can't commit myself."

There was a short silence, then he said: "I'll tell you. Why don't you check with his students?"

I lifted my eyebrows: "You mean in his classes?"

He seemed annoyed: "No, for Heaven's sake. His research students! His doctoral candidates! They've been working with him. They'll know the details of that work better than I, or anyone in the faculty, could possibly know it."

"It's an idea," I said, casually. It was, too. I don't know why, but I wouldn't have thought of it myself. I guess it's because it's only natural to think that any professor knows more than any student.

Keyser latched onto a lapel as I rose to leave. "And, besides," he said, "I think you're on the wrong track. This is in confidence, you understand, and I wouldn't say it except for the unusual circumstances, but Tywood is not thought of too highly in the profession. Oh, he's an adequate teacher, I'll admit, but his research papers have never commanded respect. There has always been a tendency towards vague theorizing, unsupported by experimental evidence. That paper of yours is probably more of it. No one could possible want to . . . er, kidnap him because of it."

"Is that so? I see. Any ideas, yourself, as to why he's gone, or where he's gone?"

"Nothing concrete," he said pursing his lips, "but everyone knows he is a sick man. He had a stroke two years ago that kept him out of classes for a semester. He never did get well. His left side was paralyzed for a while and he still limps. Another stroke would kill him. It could come any time."

"You think he's dead, then?"

"It's not impossible."

"But where's the body, then?"

"Well, really— That is *your* job, I think."

It was, and I left.

I interviewed each one of Tywood's four research students in a volume of chaos called a research laboratory. These student research laboratories usually have two hopefuls working therein, said two constituting a floating population, since every year or so they are alternately replaced.

Consequently, the laboratory has its equipment stacked in tiers. On the laboratory benches is the equipment immediately being used, and in three or four of the handiest drawers are replacements or supplements which are likely to be used. In the farther drawers, in the shelves reaching up to the ceiling, in odd corners, are fading remnants of the past student generations—oddments never used and never discarded. It is claimed, in fact, that no research student ever knew all the contents of his laboratory.

All four of Tywood's students were worried. But three were worried mainly by their own status. That is, by the possible effect the absence of Tywood might have on the status of their "problem." I dismissed those three—who all have their degrees now, I hope—and called back the fourth.

He had the most haggard look of all, and had been least communicative—which I considered a hopeful sign.

He now sat stiffly in the straight-backed chair at the right of the desk, while I leaned back in a creaky old swivel-chair and pushed my hat off my forehead. His name was Edwin Howe and *he* did get his degree later on, I know that for sure, because he's a big wheel in the Department of Science now.

I said: "You do the same work the other boys do, I suppose?"

"It's all nuclear work in a way."

"But it's not all exactly the same?"

He shook his head slowly. "We take different angles. You have to have something clear-cut, you know, or you won't be able to publish. We've got to get our degrees."

He said it exactly the way you or I might say, "We've got to make a living." At that, maybe it's the same thing for them.

I said: "All right. What's *your* angle?"

He said: "I do the math. I mean, with Professor Tywood."

"What kind of math?"

And he smiled a little, getting the same sort of atmosphere about him that I had noticed in Professor Keyser's case that morning. A sort of "Do-you-really-think-I-can-explain-all-my-profound-thoughts-to-stupid-little-you?" sort of atmosphere.

All he said aloud, however, was: "That would be rather complicated to explain."

"I'll help you," I said. "Is that anything like it?" And I tossed the foolscap sheet at him.

He didn't give it any once-over. He just snatched it up and let out a thin wail: "Where'd you get this?"

"From Tywood's safe."

"Do you have the rest of it, too?"

"It's safe," I hedged.

He relaxed a little—just a little: "You didn't show it to anybody, did you?"

"I showed it to Professor Keyser."

Howe made an impolite sound with his lower lip and front teeth. *"That* jackass. What did he say?"

I turned the palms of my hands upward and Howe laughed. Then he said, in an offhand manner: "Well, that's the sort of stuff I do."

"And what's it all about? Put it so I can understand it."

There was a distinct hesitation. He said: "Now look. This is confidential stuff. Even Pop's other students don't know anything about it. I don't even think I know *all* about it. This isn't just a degree I'm after, you know. It's Pop Tywood's Nobel Prize, and it's going to be an Assistant Professorship for me at Cal Tech. This has got to be published before it's talked about."

And I shook my head slowly and made my words very soft: "No, son. You have it twisted. You'll have to talk about it before it's published, because Tywood's gone and maybe he's dead and maybe he isn't. And if he's dead, maybe he's murdered. And when the department has a suspicion of murder, everybody talks. Now it will look bad for you, kid, if you try to keep some secrets."

It worked. I knew it would, because everyone reads murder mysteries and knows all the clichés. He jumped out of his chair and rattled the words off as if he had a script in front of him.

"Surely," he said, "you can't suspect *me* of . . . of anything like that. Why . . . why, my career—"

I shoved him back into his chair with the beginnings of a sweat on his forehead. I went into the next line: "I don't suspect anybody of anything *yet*. And you won't be in any trouble, if you talk, chum."

He was ready to talk. "Now this is all in strict confidence."

Poor guy. He didn't know the meaning of the word "strict." He was never out of eyeshot of an operator from that moment till the government decided to bury the whole case with the one final comment of "?" Quote. Unquote. (I'm not kidding. To this day, the case is neither opened nor closed. It's just "?")

He said, dubiously, "You know what time travel is, I suppose?"

Sure I knew what time travel was. My oldest kid is twelve and he listens to the afternoon video programs till he swells up visibly with the junk he absorbs at the ears and eyes.

"What about time travel?" I said.

"In a sense, we can do it. Actually, it's only what you might call micro-temporal-translation—"

I almost lost my temper. In fact, I think I did. It seemed obvious that the squirt was trying to diddle me; and without subtlety. I'm used to having people think I look dumb; but not *that* dumb.

I said through the back of my throat: "Are you going to tell me that Tywood is out somewhere in time—like Ace Rogers, the Lone Time Ranger?" (That was Junior's favorite program—Ace Rogers was stopping Genghis Khan single-handed that week.)

But he looked as disgusted as I must have. "No," he yelled. "I don't know where Pop is. If you'd *listen* to me—I said micro-temporal-translation. Now this isn't a video show and it isn't magic; this happens to be science. For instance, you know about matter-energy equivalence, I suppose."

I nodded sourly. Everyone knows about that since Hiroshima in the last war but one.

"All right, then," he went on, "that's good for a start. Now if you take a known mass of matter and apply temporal translation to it—you know, send it back in time—you are, in effect, creating matter at the point in time to which you are sending it. To do that, you must use an amount of energy equivalent to the amount of matter you have created. In other words, to send a gram—or, say, an ounce—of anything back in time, you have to disintegrate an ounce of matter completely, to furnish the energy required."

"Hm-m-m," I said, "that's to create the ounce of matter in the past. But aren't you destroying an ounce of matter by removing it from the present? Doesn't that *create* the equivalent amount of energy?"

And he looked just about as annoyed as a fellow sitting on a bumblebee that wasn't quite dead. Apparently laymen are never supposed to question scientists.

He said: "I was trying to simplify it so you would understand it. Actually, it's more complicated. It would be very nice if we could use the energy of disappearance to cause it to disappear but that would be working in a circle, believe me. The requirements of entropy would forbid it. To put it more rigorously, the energy is required to overcome temporal inertia and it just works out so that the energy in ergs required to send back a mass, in grams, is equal to that mass times the square of the speed of light in centimeters per second. Which just happens to be the Einstein Mass-Energy Equivalence Equation. I can give you the mathematics, you know."

"I know," I waxed some of that misplaced eagerness back. "But was all this worked out experimentally? Or is it just on paper?"

Obviously, the thing was to keep him talking.

He had that queer light in his eye that every research student gets, I am told, when he is asked to discuss his problem. He'll discuss it with anyone, even a "dumb flatfoot"—which was convenient at the moment.

"You see," he said like a man slipping you the inside dope on a shady business deal, "what started the whole thing was this neutrino business. They've been trying to find that neutrino since the late thirties and they haven't succeeded. It's a subatomic particle which has no charge and has a mass much less than even an electron. Naturally, it's next to impossible to spot, and it hasn't been spotted yet. But they keep looking because without assuming that a neutrino exists, the energetics of some nuclear reactions can't be balanced. So Pop Tywood got the idea about twenty years ago that some energy was disappearing, in the form of matter, back into time. We got working on that—or he did—and I'm the first student he's ever had tackle it along with him.

"Obviously, we had to work with tiny amounts of material and . . . well, it was just a stroke of genius on Pop's part to think of using traces of artificial radioactive isotopes. You could work with just a few micrograms of it, you know, by following its activity with counters. The variation of activity with time should follow a very definite and simple law which has never been altered by any laboratory condition known.

"Well, we'd send a speck back fifteen minutes, say, and fifteen minutes before we did that—everything was arranged automatically, you see—the count jumped to nearly double what it should be, fell off normally, and then dropped sharply at the moment it was sent back below where it would have been normally. The material overlapped itself in time, you see, and for fifteen minutes we counted the doubled material—"

I interrupted: "You mean you had the same atoms existing in two places at the same time."

"Yes," he said, with mild surprise, "why not? That's

why we use so much energy—the equivalent of creating those atoms." And then he rushed on, "Now I'll tell you what my particular job is. If you send back the material fifteen minutes, it is apparently sent back to the same spot relative to the Earth despite the fact that in fifteen minutes, the Earth moved sixteen thousand miles around the Sun, and the Sun itself moves more thousand miles and so on. But there are certain tiny discrepancies which I've analyzed and which turn out to be due, possibly to two causes.

"First, there is a frictional effect—if you can use such a term—so that matter does drift a little with respect to the Earth, depending on how far back in time it is sent, and on the nature of material. Then, too, some of the discrepancy can only be explained by the assumption that passage through time itself takes time."

"How's that?" I said.

"What I mean is that some of the radioactivity is evenly spread throughout the time of translation as if the material tested had been reacting during backward passage through time by a constant amount. My figures show that—well, if you were to be moved backward in time, you would age one day for every hundred years. Or, to put it another way, if you could watch a time dial which recorded the time outside a 'time-machine,' your watch would move forward twenty-four hours while the time dial moved back a hundred years. That's a universal constant, I think, because the speed of light is a universal constant. Anyway, that's my work."

After a few minutes, in which I chewed all this, I asked: "Where did you get the energy needed for your experiments?"

"They ran out a special line from the power plant. Pop's a big shot there, and swung the deal."

"Hm-m-m. What was the heaviest amount of material you sent into the past?"

"Oh"—he sent his eyes upwards—"I think we shot

back one hundredth of a milligram once. That's ten micrograms."

"Ever try sending anything into the future?"

"That won't work," he put in quickly. "Impossible. You can't change signs like that because the energy required becomes more than infinite. It's a one-way proposition."

I looked hard at my fingernails: "How much material could you send back in time if you fissioned about . . . oh, say, one hundred pounds of plutonium?" Things, I thought were becoming, if anything too obvious.

The answer came quickly: "In plutonium fission," he said, "not more than one or two percent of the mass is converted into energy. Therefore, one hundred pounds of plutonium when completely used up would send a pound or two back into time."

"Is that all? But could you handle all that energy? I mean a hundred pounds of plutonium can make quite an explosion."

"All relative," he said, a bit pompously. "If you took all that energy and let it loose a little at a time, you could handle it. If you released it all at once, but used it just as fast as you released it, you could still handle it. In sending back material through time, energy can be used much faster than it can possibly be released even through fission. Theoretically, anyway."

"But how do you get rid of it?"

"It's spread through time, naturally. Of course, the minimum time through which material could be transferred would, therefore, depend on the mass of the material. Otherwise, you're liable to have the energy density with time too high."

"All right, kid," I said. "I'm calling up headquarters, and they'll send a man here to take you home. You'll stay there awhile."

"But— What for?"

"It won't be for long."

It wasn't—and it was made up to him afterwards.

I spent the evening at Headquarters. We had a

library there—a very special kind of library. The very morning after the explosion two or three operators had drifted quietly into the chemistry and physics libraries of the University. Experts in their way. They located every article Tywood had ever published in any scientific journal and had snapped each page. Nothing was disturbed otherwise.

Other men went through magazine files and through book lists. It ended with a room at Headquarters that represented a complete Tywoodana. Nor was there a definite purpose in doing this. It merely represented part of the thoroughness with which a problem of this sort is met.

I went through that library. Not the scientific papers. I knew there'd be nothing there that I wanted. But he had written a series of articles for a magazine twenty years back, and I read those. And I grabbed at every piece of private correspondence they had available.

After that I just sat and thought—and got scared.

I got to bed about four in the morning and had nightmares.

But I was in the Boss' private office at nine in the morning just the same.

He's a big man, the Boss, with iron-gray hair slicked down tight. He doesn't smoke, but he keeps a box of cigars on his desk and when he doesn't want to say anything for a few seconds, he picks one up, rolls it about a little, smells it, then sticks it right into the middle of his mouth and lights it in a very careful way. By that time, he either has something to say or doesn't have to say anything at all. Then he puts the cigar down and lets it burn to death.

He used up a box in about three weeks, and every Christmas, half his gift-wraps held boxes of cigars.

He wasn't reaching for any cigars now, though. He just folded his big fists together on the desk and looked up at me from under a creased forehead. "What's boiling?"

I told him. Slowly, because micro-temporal-translation doesn't sit well with anybody, especially when you call it time travel, which I did. It's a sign of how serious things were that he only asked me once if I were crazy.

Then I was finished and we stared at each other.

He said: "And you think he tried to send something back in time—something weighing a pound or two—and blew an entire plant doing it?"

"It fits in," I said.

I let him go for a while. He was thinking and I wanted him to keep on thinking. I wanted him, if possible, to think of the same thing I was thinking, so that I wouldn't have to tell him—

Because I hated to *have* to tell him—

Because it was nuts, for one thing. And too horrible, for another.

So I kept quiet and he kept on thinking and every once in a while some of his thoughts came to the surface.

After a while, he said: "Assuming the student, Howe, to have told the truth—and you'd better check his notebooks, by the way, which I hope you've impounded—"

"The entire wing of that floor is out of bounds, sir. Edwards has the notebooks."

He went on: "All right. Assuming he told us all the truth he knows, why did Tywood jump from less than a milligram to a pound?"

His eyes came down and they were hard: "Now you're concentrating on the time-travel angle. To you, I gather, that is the crucial point, with the energy involved as incidental—purely incidental."

"Yes, sir," I said grimly. "I think exactly that."

"Have you considered that you might be wrong? That you might have matters inverted?"

"I don't quite get that."

"Well, look. You say you've read up on Tywood. All right. He was one of that bunch of scientists after

World War II that fought the atom bomb; wanted a world state—you know about that, don't you?"

I nodded.

"He had a guilt complex," the Boss said with energy. "He'd helped work out the bomb, and he couldn't sleep nights thinking of what he'd done. He lived with that fear for years. And even though the bomb wasn't used in World War III, can you imagine what every day of uncertainty must have meant to him? Can you imagine the shriveling horror in his soul as he waited for others to make the decision at every crucial moment till the final Compromise of 'Sixty-five?

"We have a complete psychiatric analysis of Tywood and several others just like him, taken during the last war. Did you know that?"

"No, sir."

"It's true. We let up after 'sixty-five, of course, because with the establishment of world control of atomic power, the scrapping of the atomic bomb stockpile in all countries, and the establishment of research liaison among the various spheres of influence on the planet, most of the ethical conflict in the scientific mind was removed.

"But the findings at the time were serious. In 1964, Tywood had a morbid subconscious hatred for the very concept of atomic power. He began to make mistakes, serious ones. Eventually, we were forced to take him off research of any kind. And several others as well, even though things were pretty bad at the time. We had just lost India, if you remember."

Considering that I was in India at the time, I remembered. But I still wasn't seeing his point.

"Now what," he continued, "if dregs of that attitude remained buried in Tywood to the very end? Don't you see that this time travel is a double-edged sword? Why throw a pound of anything into the past, anyway? For the sake of proving a point? He had proved his case just as much when he sent back a fraction of a milligram. That was good enough for the Nobel Prize, I suppose.

"But there was *one* thing he could do with a pound of matter that he couldn't do with a milligram, and that was *to drain a power plant*. So that was what he must have been after. He had discovered a way of consuming inconceivable quantities of energy. By sending back eighty pounds of dirt, he could remove all the existing plutonium in the world. End atomic power for an indefinite period."

I was completely unimpressed, but I tried not to make that too plain. I just said: "Do you think he could possibly have thought he could get away with it more than once?"

"This is all based on the fact that he wasn't a normal man. How do I know what he could imagine he could do? Besides, there may be men behind him— with less science and more brains—who are quite ready to continue onwards from this point."

"Have any of these men been found yet? Any evidence of such men?"

A little wait, and his hand reached for the cigar box. He stared at the cigar and turned it end for end. Just a little wait more. I was patient.

Then he put it down decisively without lighting it.

"No," he said.

He looked at me, and clear through me, and said: "Then you still don't go for that?"

I shrugged, "Well—It doesn't sound right."

"Do you have a notion of your own?"

"Yes. But I can't bring myself to talk about it. If I'm wrong, I'm the wrongest man that ever was; but if I'm right, I'm the rightest."

"I'll listen," he said, and he put his hand under the desk.

That was the pay-off. The room was armored, soundproof, and radiation-proof to anything short of a nuclear explosion. And with that little signal showing on his secretary's desk, the President of the United States couldn't have interrupted us.

I leaned back and said: "Chief, do you happen to remember how you met your wife? Was it a little thing?"

He must have thought it a *non sequitur*. What else could he have thought? But he was giving me my head now; having his own reasons, I suppose.

He just smiled and said: "I sneezed and she turned around. It was at a street corner."

"What made you be on that street corner just then? What made her be? Do you remember just why you sneezed? Where you caught the cold? Or where the speck of dust came from? Imagine how many factors had to intersect in just the right place at just the right time for you to meet your wife."

"I suppose we would have met some other time, if not then?"

"But you can't *know* that. How do you know whom you *didn't* meet, because once when you might have turned around, you didn't; because once when you might have been late, you weren't. Your life forks at every instant, and you go down one of the forks, almost at random, and so does everyone else. Start twenty years ago, and the forks diverge further and further with time.

"You sneezed, and met a girl, and not another. As a consequence, you made certain decisions, and so did the girl, and so did the girl you didn't meet, and the man who did meet her, and the people you all met thereafter. And your family, her family, their family—and your children.

"Because you sneezed twenty years ago, five people, or fifty, or five hundred, might be dead now who would have been alive or might be alive, who would have been dead. Move it two hundred years ago; two thousand years ago, and a sneeze—even by someone no history ever heard of—might have meant that no one now alive would have been alive."

The Boss rubbed the back of his head: "Widening ripples. I read a story once—"

"So did I. It's not a new idea—but I want you to think about it for a while, because I want to read to you from an article by Professor Elmer Tywood in a magazine twenty years old. It was just before the last war."

I had copies of the film in my pocket and the white wall made a beautiful screen, which was what it was meant to do. The boss made a motion to turn about, but I waved him back.

"No, sir," I said. "I want to read this to you. And I want you to listen to it."

He leaned back.

"The article," I went on, is entitled: 'Man's First Great Failure!' Remember, this was just before the war, when the bitter disappointment at the final failure of the United Nations was at its height. What I will read are some excerpts from the first part of the article. It goes like this:

" '. . . That Man, with his technical perfection has failed to solve the great sociological problems of today is only the second immense tragedy that has come to the race. The first, and perhaps the greater, was that once these same great sociological problems *were* solved; and yet these solutions were not permanent because the technical perfection we have today did not then exist.

" 'It was a case of having bread without butter, or butter without bread. Never both together. . . .

" 'Consider the Hellenic world from which our philosophy, our mathematics, our ethics, our art, our literature—our entire culture, in fact—stem. . . . In the days of Pericles, Greece, like our own world, in microcosm, was a surprisingly modern potpourri of conflicting ideologies and ways of life. But then Rome came, adopting the culture, but bestowing, and enforcing, peace. To be sure, the *Pax Romana* lasted only two hundred years, but no like period has existed since. . . .

" 'War was abolished. Nationalism did not exist. The Roman citizen was Empire-wide. Paul of Tarsus and Flavius Josephus were Roman citizens. Spaniards, North Africans, Illyrians assumed the purple. Slavery existed, but it was an indiscriminate slavery, imposed as a punishment, incurred as the price of economic failure, brought on by the fortunes of war. No man was a *natural* slave, because of the color of his skin, or the place of his birth.

" 'Religious toleration was complete. If an exception was made early in the case of the Christians, it was because they refused to accept the principle of toleration; because they insisted that only they themselves knew the truth—a principle abhorrent to the civilized Roman. . . .

" 'With all of Western culture under a single *polis*, with the cancer of religious and national particularism and exclusivism absent; with a high civilization in existence—why could not Man hold his gains?

" 'It was because technologically, ancient Hellenism remained backward. It was because without a machine civilization, the price of leisure—and hence civilization and culture—for the few, was slavery for the many. Because the civilization could not find the means to bring comfort and ease to *all* the population.

" 'Therefore, the depressed classes turned to the other world, and to religions which spurned the material benefits of this world—so that science was made impossible in any true sense for over a millennium. And further, as the initial impetus of Hellenism waned, the Empire lacked the technological powers to beat back the barbarians. In fact, it was not till after 1500 A.D. that war became sufficiently a function of the industrial resources of a nation to enable the settled people to defeat invading tribesmen and nomads with ease. . . .

" 'Imagine then, if somehow the ancient Greeks had learned just a hint of modern chemistry and physics. Imagine if the growth of the Empire had been accompanied by the growth of science, technology and industry. Imagine an Empire in which machinery replaced slaves; in which all men had a decent share of the world's goods; in which the legion became the armored column, against which no barbarians could stand. Imagine an Empire which would therefore spread all over the world, *without* religious or national prejudices.

" 'An Empire of all men—all brothers—eventually all free. . . .

" 'If history could be changed. If that first great failure could have been prevented—' "

And I stopped at that point.

"Well?" said the Boss.

"Well," I said, "I think it isn't difficult to connect all that with the fact that Tywood blew an entire power plant in his anxiety to send something back to the past, while in his office safe we found sections of a chemistry textbook translated into Greek."

His face changed, while he considered.

Then, he said heavily: "But nothing's happened."

"I know. But then I've been told by Tywood's student that it takes a day to move back a century in time. Assuming that ancient Greece was the target area, we have twenty centuries, hence twenty days."

"But can it be stopped?"

"*I* wouldn't know. Tywood might, but he's dead."

The enormity of it all hit me at once, deeper than it had the night before—

All humanity was virtually under sentence of death. And while that was merely horrible abstraction, the fact that reduced it to a thoroughly unbearable reality, was that I was, too. And my wife, and my kid.

Further, it was a death without precedence. A ceasing to exist, and no more. The passing of a breath. The vanishing of a dream. The drift into eternal non-space and non-time of a shadow. I would not be dead at all, in fact. I would merely never have been born.

Or would I? Would I exist—my individuality—my

ego—my soul, if you like? Another life? Other circumstances?

I thought none of that in words, then. But if a cold knot in the stomach could ever speak under the circumstances it would sound like that I think.

The Boss moved in on my thoughts—hard.

"Then we have about two and a half weeks. No time to lose. Come on."

I grinned with one side of my mouth: "What do we do? Chase the book?"

"No," he replied coldly, "but there are two courses of action we must follow. First, you may be wrong—altogether. All of this circumstantial reasoning may still represent a false lead, perhaps deliberately thrown before us, to cover up the real truth. That must be checked.

"Secondly, you may be right—but there may be some way of stopping the book: other than chasing it in a time machine, I mean. If so, we must find out how."

"I would just like to say, sir, if this is a false lead, only a madman would consider it a believable one. So suppose I'm right, and suppose there's no way of stopping it?"

"Then, young fellow, I'm going to keep pretty busy for two and a half weeks, and I'd advise you to do the same. The time will pass more quickly that way."

Of course he was right.

"Where do we start?" I asked.

"The first thing we need is a list of all men and women on the government payroll under Tywood."

"Why?"

"Reasoning. Your specialty, you know. Tywood doesn't know Greek, I think we can assume with fair safety, so someone else must have done the translating. It isn't likely that anyone would do a job like that for nothing, and it isn't likely that Tywood would pay out of his personal funds—not on a professor's salary."

"He might," I pointed out, "have been interested in more secrecy than a government payroll affords."

"Why? Where was the danger? Is it a crime to translate a chemistry textbook into Greek? Who would ever deduce from that a plot such as you've described?"

It took us half an hour to turn up the name of Mycroft James Boulder, listed as "Consultant," and to find out that he was mentioned in the University Catalogue as Assistant Professor of Philosophy and to check by telephone that among his many accomplishments was a thorough knowledge of Attic Greek.

Which was a coincidence—because with the Boss reaching for his hat, the interoffice teletype clicked away and it turned out that Mycroft James Boulder was in the anteroom, at the end of a two-hour continuing insistence that he see the Boss.

The Boss put his hat back and opened his office door.

Professor Mycroft James Boulder was a gray man. His hair was gray and his eyes were gray. His suit was gray, too.

But most of all, his expression was gray; gray with a tension that seemed to twist at the lines in his thin face.

Boulder said, softly: "I've been trying for three days to get a hearing, sir, with a responsible man. I can get no higher than yourself."

"I may be high enough," said the Boss. "What's on your mind?"

"It is quite important that I be granted an interview with Professor Tywood."

"Do you know where he is?"

"I am quite certain that he is in government custody."

"Why?"

"Because I know that he was planning an experiment which would entail the breaking of security regulations. Events since, as nearly as I can make them out, flow naturally from the supposition that security regulations have indeed been broken. I can presume then that the experiment has at least been attempted. I must discover whether it has been successfully concluded."

"Professor Boulder," said the Boss, "I believe you can read Greek."

"Yes, I can"—coolly.

"And have translated chemical texts for Professor Tywood on government money."

"Yes—as a legally employed consultant."

"Yet such translation, under the circumstances, constitutes a crime, since it makes you an accessory to Tywood's crime."

"You can establish a connection?"

"Can't you? Or haven't you heard of Tywood's notions on time travel, or ... what do you call it ... micro-temporal-translation?"

"Ah?" and Boulder smiled a little. "He's told you, then."

"No he hasn't," said the Boss, harshly. "Professor Tywood is dead."

"What?" Then, "I don't believe you."

"He died of apoplexy. Look at this."

He had one of the photographs taken that first night in his wall safe. Tywood's face was distorted but recognizable—sprawled and dead.

Boulder's breath went in and out as if the gears were clogged. He stared at the picture for three full minutes by the electric clock on the wall. "Where is this place?" he asked.

"The Atomic Power Plant."

"Had he finished his experiment?"

The Boss shrugged: "There's no way of telling. He was dead when we found him."

Boulder's lips were pinched and colorless. "That must be determined somehow. A commission of scientists must be established, and if necessary the experiment must be repeated—"

But the Boss just looked at him, and reached for a cigar. I've never seen him take longer—and when he put it down, curled in its unused smoke, he said: "Tywood wrote an article for a magazine, twenty years ago—"

"Oh," and the professor's lips twisted, "is *that* what gave you your clue. You may ignore that. The man is only a physical scientist and knows nothing of either history or sociology. A schoolboy's dreams and nothing more."

"Then you don't think sending your translation back will inaugurate a Golden Age, do you?"

"Of course not. Do you think you can graft the developments of two thousand years of slow labor onto a child society not ready for it? Do you think a great invention or a great scientific principle is born full-grown in the mind of a genius divorced from his cultural *milieu?* Newton's enunciation of the Law of Gravity was delayed for twenty years because the then-current figure for the Earth's diameter was wrong by ten percent. Archimedes almost discovered calculus, but failed because Arabic numerals, invented by some nameless Hindu or group of Hindus, were unknown to him.

"For that matter, the mere existence of a slave society in ancient Greece and Rome meant that machines could scarcely attract much attention—slaves being so much cheaper and more adaptable. And men of true intellect could scarcely be expected to spend their energies on devices intended for manual labor. Even Archimedes, the greatest engineer of antiquity, refused to publish any of his practical inventions—only mathematic abstractions. And when a young man asked Plato of what use geometry was, he was forthwith expelled from the Academy as a man with a mean, unphilosophic soul.

"Science does not plunge forward—it inches along in the directions permitted by the greater forces that mold society and which are in turn molded by society. And no great man advances but on the shoulders of the society that surrounds him—"

The Boss interrupted him at that point. "Suppose you tell us what your part in Tywood's work was, then. We'll take your word for it that history cannot be changed."

"Oh it can, but not purposefully. You see, when Tywood first requested my services in the matter of translating certain textbook passages into Greek, I agreed for the money involved. But he wanted the translation on parchment; he insisted on the use of ancient Greek terminology—the language of Plato, to use his words—regardless of how I had to twist the literal significance of passages, and he wanted it handwritten in rolls.

"I was curious. I, too, found his magazine article. It was difficult for me to jump to the obvious conclusion, since the achievements of modern science transcend the imaginings of philosophy in so many ways. But I learned the truth eventually, and it was at once obvious that Tywood's theory of changing history was infantile. There are twenty million variables for every instant of time, and no system of mathematics—no mathematic psychohistory, to coin a phrase—has yet been developed to handle that ocean of varying functions.

"In short, any variation of events two thousand years ago would change all subsequent history but in *no predictable way*."

The Boss suggested, with a false quietness: "Like the pebble that starts the avalanche, right?"

"Exactly. You have some understanding of the situation, I see. I thought deeply for weeks before I proceeded, and then I realized how I must act—*must* act."

There was a low roar. The Boss stood up and his chair went over backward. He swung around his desk, and he had a hand on Boulder's throat. I was stepping out to stop him, but he waved me back—

He was only tightening the necktie a little. Boulder could still breathe. He had gone very white, and for all the time that the Boss talked, he restricted himself to just that—breathing.

And the Boss said: "Sure, I can see how you decided you must act. I know that some of you brain-sick philosophers think the world needs fixing. You want to throw the dice again and see what turns up. Maybe you don't even care if you're alive in the new setup—or that no one can possibly know what you've done. But you're going to create just the same. You're going to give God another chance, so to speak.

"Maybe I just want to live—but the world could be worse. In twenty million different ways, it could be worse. A fellow named Wilder once wrote a play called *The Skin of Our Teeth.* Maybe you've read it. Its thesis was that Mankind survived by just that skin of their teeth. No, I'm not going to give you a speech about the Ice Age nearly wiping us out. I don't know enough. I'm not even going to talk about the Greeks winning at Marathon; the Arabs being defeated at Tours; the Mongols turning back at the last minute without even being defeated—because I'm no historian.

"But take the Twentieth Century. The Germans were stopped at the Marne twice in World War I. Dunkirk happened in World War II, and somehow the Germans were stopped at Moscow and Stalingrad. We could have used the atom bomb in the last war and we didn't, and just when it looked as if both sides would have to, the Great Compromise happened—just because General Bruce was delayed in taking off from the Ceylon airfield long enough to receive the message directly. One after the other, just like that, all through history—lucky breaks. For every 'if' that didn't come true, that would have made wonder-men of all of us, if it had, there were twenty 'ifs' that didn't come true, that would have broght disaster to all of us, if they had.

"You're gambling on that one-in-twenty chance—gambling every life on Earth. And you've succeeded, too, because Tywood *did* send that text back."

He ground out that last sentence, and opened his fist, so that Boulder could fall out and back into his chair.

And Boulder laughed.

"You fool," he gasped, bitterly. "How close you can be and yet how widely you can miss the mark. Tywood *did* send his book back then? You are sure of that?"

"No chemical textbook in Greek was found on the scene," said the Boss, grimly, "and millions of calories of energy had disappeared. Which doesn't change the fact, however, that we have two and a half weeks in which to—make things interesting for you."

"Oh, nonsense. No foolish dramatics, please. Just listen to me, and try to understand. There were Greek philosophers once, named Leucippus and Democritus, who evolved an atomic theory. All matter, they said, was composed of atoms. Varieties of atoms were distinct and changeless and by their different combinations with each other formed the various substances found in nature. That theory was not the result of experiment or observation. It came into being, somehow, full-grown.

"The didactic Roman poet Lucretius, in his *De Rerum Natura,*—'On the Nature of Things'—elaborated on that theory and throughout manages to sound startlingly modern.

"In Hellenistic times, Hero built a steam engine and weapons of war became almost mechanized. The period has been referred to as an abortive mechanical age, which came to nothing because, somehow, it neither grew out of nor fitted into its social and economic *milieu*. Alexandrian science was a queer and rather inexplicable phenomenon.

"Then one might mention the old Roman legend about the books of the Sibyl that contained mysterious information direct from the gods—

"In other words, gentlemen, while you are right that any change in the course of past events, however trifling, would have incalculable consequences, and while I also believe that you are right in supposing that any random change is much more likely to be for the worse than for the better, I must point out that you are nevertheless wrong in your final conclusions.

"*Because* THIS *is the world in which the Greek chemistry text* WAS *sent back.*

"This has been a Red Queen's race, if you remember your *Through the Looking Glass*. In the Red Queen's country, one had to run as fast as one could merely to stay in the same place. And so it was in this case! Tywood may have thought he was creating a new world, but it was *I* who prepared the translations, and I took care that only such passages as would account for the queer scraps of knowledge the ancients apparently got from nowhere would be included.

"And my only intention, for all my racing, was to stay in the same place."

Three weeks passed; three months; three years. Nothing happened. When nothing happens, you have no proof. We gave up trying to explain, and we ended, the Boss and I, by doubting it ourselves.

The case never ended. Boulder could not be considered a criminal without being considered a world savior as well, and vice versa. He was ignored. And in the end, the case was neither solved, nor closed out; merely put in a file all by itself, under the designation "?" and buried in the deepest vault in Washington.

The Boss is in Washington now; a big wheel. And I'm Regional Head of the Bureau.

Boulder is still assistant professor, though. Promotions are slow at the University.

AFTERWORD: SPEAKING FROM THE CENTER

by BARRY N. MALZBERG

This is the second opening for this essay. The first, a discarded draft which now reposes on grey carpeting somewhere to the near left, went like this:

"First person, the protagonist (or involved principal) as narrator, should be the ideal form for science fiction—since it would impart an effect of naturalness and immediacy to the alien landscape, inner and outer, which is the premise of the form—but oddly it is not; although exceptional stories written in the first person, many of which are in this book, grace the category, the main thrust of science fiction through its fifty-four years as a discrete subgenre of American literature has been carried in the more conventional third person which—"

Which what? This might play in the provinces but it will not play in this book. For the fact is that the discarded opening is a false premise; a great deal of important work, perhaps even a disproportionate amount, has been done in American science fiction in the first person. Isaac Asimov notes in his introduction that he has almost never worked in the form; "The Red Queen's Race" (his best story of the forties, for my money, just as *The Dead Past*—a novella—was his best of the fifties) is his only published exhibit in the form, but Isaac is the exception and an inordinate number of examples-in-proof abound of which I would cite only a few and in somewhat random order: Robert Heinlein's last three novels have been first-person, Theodore Sturgeon's *Baby Is Three* (the brilliant novella centering *More than Human*) is first-person, Tom Sherred's "E for Effort," surely the finest story to appear in 1947, was first-person. So is Robert Silverberg's *Dying Inside* (1972) and *Shadrach in the Furnace*, my own *Beyond Apollo* (1972) Arthur C. Clarke's Hugo Award–winning "The Star," Lester del Rey's "Helen O'Loy," Mark Clifton's "What Have I Done?," Thomas M. Disch's novel *Camp Concentration* (1967), Samuel R. Delany's famous short story "Aye and Gomorrah" . . .

It is an imposing list. Proportionate to the body of first-rate work in the genre, science fiction has probably employed the first person more successfully than the American literary novel or any branch of American commercial fiction. With all due respect to Isaac Asimov—who is one of the five living writers who center this form—he is the exception; his reluctance to use or struggle with the first-person format are atypical, and this afterword cannot deplore underutilization but only celebrate plenitude . . . and venture, cautiously, into personal terrain.

I have written a great deal in the first person. The bibliographers are welcome to take a look at this, I cannot, but at a fast estimate close to fifty percent of my twenty-five science fiction novels and approximately two hundred short stories have been written in that fashion. First person has always come easily to me; my first published science fiction story ("We're Coming Through the Windows," 1967) used it (in epistolary format), and *Beyond Apollo*, my best-known if not best novel, is written in alternate first- and third-person by its schizoid protagonist. *Tactics of Conquest* (the novel which was inflated madly from the short story "Closed Sicilian") and *The Men Inside* are first-person; so is *Revelations* and my own favorite novel, *Underlay*. I like the form; as a failed playwright (Schubert Foundation Fellow, Syracuse University 1964/5, you could look it up) I enjoy the way it can burrow into a protagonist, get inside him, adapt his voice, work against authorial weaknesses or pomposity.

First person has another valuable function, at least to a writer like myself, and I am about, for any would-be novelists in the gallery, to reveal for the first time ever a Trade Secret: first person enables a writer to disguise gaps in research, knowledge, experience, or apprehension *because he can build his own limitations into the voice of the character and make them an essential part of that persona.* Never knowing a hell of a lot about hard technology, the actual appearance of the surface of Mercury, or the intricacies of the three-stage rocket, I used over and over again characters who were either similarly unfamiliar with the material or who once having been familiar were losing control, going over the edge, and their ignorance thus became—witness *Beyond Apollo*—a metaphor for their psychic breakdown and that of their culture. First person is a technique surely created for old maneuverers like your faithful undersigned: applied skillfully it can convert weaknesses to strengths. Don't blame me, folks, the captain was the one going insane. *I* may

know a hydraulic valve from a hole in the ground but
the captain has gone over the edge; he can barely
segregate the hawks from the handsaws. All a narrative device: take it up with the captain. (I feel safe in
disclosing my trade secret now; it is many years since
my period of peak efficiency, in the first place, and in
the second, too many people have Caught On. I think
my own major contribution to science fiction may have
been to teach a flock of new writers that you can write
science fiction not only without technological knowledge
but without even deference to it . . . one can wallow in
one's own ignorance. Several critics have raised this
point about my own work, and they may even be
right. Still, it is better to wallow in ignorance than to
shadow-box with knowledge, as the bishop said to the
widow.)

First person—to continue this technical discussion a
little—has certain built-in traps, to be sure. The voice
can become too idiosyncratic; circling in upon itself, it
can lose account of extrinsic circumstance or relationships (Ring Lardner, a magnificent writer, was *not*
magnificent all of the time, and many of his first-
person stories show this weakness). Characterization,
particularly of the narrator, cannot be trusted because
of the idiosyncratic voice; physical description of the
narrator—barring the Mirror Device and similar
scams—is impossible. And the fact that the narrator
is himself alive to tell the tale makes the use of the
first person almost impossible in a suspense format
where the very life of the narrator is suggested to
hang in balance. Furthermore, unless one is using a
diary format (such as in *Camp Concentration* or the
famous Daniel Keyes *Flowers for Algernon*), which is
a tricky technique for all but the most sophisticated of
us, true characteriological *change* is impossible to de-
pict in the first person; the narrator is fully developed
at the outset of the story as the result of the events of
the story; he cannot be perceived to be changing during the narrative span itself, and since change is one

of the key aspects of fiction the first-person writer is stripping himself of advantage at the outset.

(It is this absence of change which so many reviewers through the years have pointed out is the one flaw in the Pohl/Kornbluth *Space Merchants*—the narrator has presumably matured as the result of the events of the story, yet the callow fool who narrates the opening half *must* have that voice or there is no credible conflict-and-development.)

Still. There are two more masterpieces or near-masterpieces for the roster: *The Space Merchants* and *Flowers for Algernon*. No, science fiction has had no paucity of important material in the form. And as technology becomes more confusing, misunderstandings more complex, the failure of resolution more characteristic of the last years of this century, the first person is likely to remain a central facet of the genre, if not to literally overtake third person for those works written at the divining, at the cutting edge.

I hope to play some small part in those works and years which lie ahead, and I point out to readers faithful and unfaithful alike my sullen and stolid consistence and discipline: *this* afterword is itself in the first person. Even though, more and more, ah doctor!, my own life seems to be lived in the third.

NEW FROM FAWCETT CREST

**From planet Earth
you will be able to
communicate with other worlds—
Just read—
SCIENCE FICTION**

THE GODS THEMSELVES by Isaac Asimov	23756	$1.95
BLACK HOLES edited by Jerry Pournelle	23962	$2.25
THE NAKED SUN by Isaac Asimov	24243	$1 95
BALLROOM OF THE SKIES by John D. MacDonald	14143	$1.75
DAUGHTER OF IS by Michael Davidson	04285	$1.75
EARTH ABIDES by George Stewart	23252	$1.95
THE JARGOON PARD by Andre Norton	23615	$1.95
STAR RANGERS by Andre Norton	24076	$1.95
THE SEVEN DEADLY SINS OF SCIENCE FICTION	24349	$2.50
Edited by: Isaac Asimov, Charles G. Waugh, and Martin H. Greenberg		

Buy them at your local bookstore or use this handy coupon for ordering.

This offer expires 1 September 81   8102

CLASSIC BESTSELLERS
from FAWCETT BOOKS

THE GHOST WRITER by Philip Roth	24322	$2.75
IBERIA by James A. Michener	23804	$3.50
THE ICE AGE by Margaret Drabble	04300	$2.25
ALL QUIET ON THE WESTERN FRONT by Erich Maria Remarque	23808	$2.50
TO KILL A MOCKINGBIRD by Harper Lee	08376	$2.50
SHOW BOAT by Edna Ferber	23191	$1.95
THEM by Joyce Carol Oates	23944	$2.50
THE SLAVE by Isaac Bashevis Singer	24188	$2.50
THE FLOUNDER by Gunter Grass	24180	$2.95
THE CHOSEN by Chaim Potok	24200	$2.25
THE SOURCE by James A. Michener	23859	$2.95

Buy them at your local bookstore or use this handy coupon for ordering.

This offer expires 1 September 81

8105